The Lore Hunter: Brown Mountain

Clifton Wilcox

Fredericksburg, Virginia

Print ISBN: 978-1-969770-31-9

EBook ISBN: 978-1-969770-23-4

Published by Windward Publishing LLC., Fredericksburg, Virginia.

Wilcox, Clifton

The Lore Hunter: Brown Mountain

Windward Publishing, LLC

2026

They say the mountain keeps its secrets.
That isn't true.
It keeps the people.

Books by Clifton Wilcox

Non-Fiction

Scape Goat: Targeted for Blame
Groupthink: An Impediment to Success
Bias: The Unconscious Deceiver
Witch-hunt: The Assignment of Blame
The Fall of the Kingdom of Northumbria
Witch-hunt: The Class of Cultures
Road to War: The Quest for a New World Order
Envy: A Deeper Shade of Green
The Rise of the Nazi SS
The Horrible Void Between the Trenches

Fiction

Cool's Last Stand
Where Despair Comes to Play
The Monuments Must Bleed
Keeper of the Fallen Ages
I, Monster
Harvest of Eyes
The Case Against Jasper
Crimson Plume: The Song of Corvus
Framed in Love
Echoes of the Forgotten
Blacktop Harvest
The Plagiarist Game
The Black Forest Protocol
Outcome without Appeal
Deliberation

Table of Contents

Prologue

The Mountain That Remembers

The fog rolled across the ridge like something alive.

Ryan Dalton had heard his entire life about the shadow of Brown Mountain, and he was about to learn that the mountain kept its own hours. Tourists came for the famous lights that sometimes floated in the darkness—blue, white, sometimes blood-orange—dancing silently over the forest valleys. Scientists argued about gases and reflections. Locals had different explanations. Ryan, now separated from his friends, had never cared much for the stories.

Until tonight.

His flashlight blinked once and died as he climbed the narrow trail. The batteries had been new. He checked them again, anyway, tapping the plastic casing as the fog thickened around the trees. The forest had gone quiet—too quiet for late autumn. No wind. No insects. No noise from his friends. No distant highway noise from the valley below. Just the slow drip of condensation from what leaves remained. Ryan had hunted and camped his whole life. He knew the difference between quiet and wrong.

Then the lights appeared.

At first it was just one—hovering low above the trees like a lantern held by an invisible hand. It pulsed softly, bluish-white, illuminating the fog in a dim halo. Ryan froze, his breath clouding in front of him. Another light flickered into existence beside it. Then a third. They drifted silently over the treetops, weaving together like curious animals circling a stranger. He reached slowly for the camera hanging from his neck. The moment his fingers touched the shutter, every light turned toward him at once.

And something moved in the fog behind them.

It wasn't a shape exactly. More like the darkness itself had decided to stand up. Ryan felt the sudden and unmistakable sensation of being watched—not by something wandering through the woods, but by something that had always been there, waiting beneath the mountain. Waiting beneath the stories.

By morning, the trail would be empty.

Ryan Dalton would be gone without a trace. His flashlight would be found on the ground beside the path, its batteries drained to nothing. His camera would remain intact—except for a single photograph burned into the memory card.

A photograph that no one could explain.

And hundreds of miles away, a folklore professor named Adrian Cross would soon receive a visitor with a message.

"You study legends. Come see what made this one."

Chapter 1

The Search Begins

Eli Foster had worked enough searches in Pisgah to know the first lie people told themselves.

It was that the woods were empty.

In daylight, the trails felt familiar, even friendly. The Blue Ridge gave you overlooks and switchbacks and rhododendron tunnels you could photograph and later remember as a pleasant inconvenience. At night, the same terrain took on a different purpose. The slopes didn't guide you; they funneled you. Hollows swallowed sound. Ridges carried it too far, scattering it into places you couldn't see. And the forest, when it wanted to, could make a person feel watched without offering any proof.

They'd been briefed at the ranger station just after nine, under fluorescent lights that made everyone's faces look pale and slightly angry.

Missing hiker. Off-trail. Last confirmed sighting at the ridge line near a popular overlook that drew leaf-peepers even in October. A college kid with friends from out of state, the kind who packed snacks and cheap ponchos and assumed the mountains would behave like a park.

Name: Ryan Dalton. Age: twenty-one. Wearing a gray hoodie under a light jacket, jeans, running shoes that were fine for a campus sidewalk and a bad idea on wet mountain rock. He had a flashlight, allegedly. The friends weren't sure. They were sure about the other thing.

"He saw something," one of them kept saying. "Like, lights. Over there."

Mercer had been in the room for the briefing, standing near the wall with his hands in his pockets, listening more than talking. He wasn't Eli's supervisor, not directly, but he had the kind of quiet authority that settled over a group the moment he spoke. When someone said lights, Mercer's eyes had shifted toward the darkened window like he expected to see something staring back.

Eli had done enough of these to keep his questions simple.

"When did he leave the trail?"

"Maybe eight-thirty?" the kid's friend said. "We were messing around, taking pictures. It got dark fast and we got seperated. Then those lights showed up across the valley. Ryan said it looked like someone signaling."

"Someone in trouble?" Eli asked.

"Or, I don't know," the friend said, frustrated, exhausted. "We could see Ryan ahead of us. It looked close. Like it was right there."

Eli knew the ridge lines. He knew how distance lied out here. How a point of light could look like it hovered just beyond the tree line when it was actually miles away. But the friend's certainty didn't come from logic. It came from the heat of having watched someone walk away and not return.

Mercer had asked one question, soft enough it barely carried.

"Did Ryan say anything else? Before he went?"

The friend's face had tightened like he was embarrassed to answer.

"He said… he said it was like it was waiting. Like it wanted him to come look."

That had earned a shift in the room. Some of the volunteers had glanced at each other. One older man, local, not a ranger, had made a sound in his throat that was almost a laugh. Not because it was funny. Because it was familiar.

"People always follow the lights," he'd said, and it had landed wrong. Not a warning. Not sympathy. Just a plain statement, like gravity.

Eli had ignored it then. There wasn't room for superstition in procedure. You made a grid. You set teams. You checked radio channels. You logged timestamps. You sent boots into the dark and hoped the terrain didn't make a liar out of you.

Alvarez had been assigned to Eli's team ten minutes later, young enough that the newness still sat on him like a stiff jacket. Good ranger, fast learner, but he carried nerves the way some men carried caffeine: as fuel, as habit.

"You good?" Eli had asked him while they packed.

Alvarez nodded too quickly. "Yeah. I'm good."

He'd watched the volunteers gather at the back of the station, headlamps bobbing, jackets zipped, gloved hands adjusting straps. They were locals and weekend hikers and one man who said he'd hunted these slopes since he was a kid. Their confidence made Eli uneasy. Confidence got people hurt when it was built on pride instead of preparation.

By ten, they were on the trail.

The air had turned sharp, the kind of cold that didn't bite so much as press itself into your lungs and stay there. Fog rolled in low bands, not thick yet, but enough that the trees beyond their beams seemed to begin and end abruptly, like scenery in a play. Leaves underfoot were slick and quiet, dampened by the night. Every so often a branch snapped somewhere downslope, not close enough to be a person, but close enough to make everyone's heads turn.

Eli kept his voice low out of habit.

“Call out every five,” he said. “Short. Simple. Don’t wander your lane. If you see anything, you radio before you move.”

Alvarez held his flashlight too tight, the beam jittering whenever he tried to scan ahead. Eli wanted to tell him to steady it, but he didn’t. The jitter wasn’t the problem. The problem was what the light revealed when it didn’t shake.

Nothing.

No eyeshine. No flicker of movement. No distant rustle that resolved into an animal shifting through brush. The usual small noises, the background life that filled the woods at night, had thinned out until the forest felt staged.

Too quiet.

Eli tried to inventory the silence the way he inventoried everything else. Wind: minimal. Birds: none. Insects: quiet. A creek: far off, but muffled. Even their own breathing sounded loud in the narrow corridor of headlamp light.

“Radio check,” Eli said into the handset as they climbed.

“Team Two, loud and clear,” came a voice, faint but present.

He tried Team Three.

"Team Three, copy," came a reply, then a hiss of static that swallowed the last syllables.

The static wasn't unusual. The terrain did that. Rock and ridge and dense canopy. Still, it put Eli on edge. Static felt like isolation. Like being cut loose.

They reached a point where the trail narrowed along the ridge. To their left the slope dropped away sharply, a dark ravine filling with fog. To their right, the mountain rose in a steady wall of trunks and stone. Their beams made the path look like a pale ribbon pinned between two kinds of darkness.

Eli stopped and listened again.

Nothing answered.

Not even the old, constant sound of the woods shifting.

Alvarez slowed behind him. "Sir?"

Eli held up a hand. "Wait."

He didn't like it. The mountain had moods, and this one felt like held breath.

He keyed the radio again. "Search Team Two, report."

Static answered, thick and immediate, the kind that sounded like someone had poured gravel into the speaker.

Eli frowned. He lifted the radio higher, turned his head slightly, as if posture could coax signal out of rock.

"Team Two, this is Ranger Foster. Repeat."

Nothing but a thin hiss.

He tried Team Three. "Team Three, check in."

More static, then a faint pop, then silence. Not even the courtesy of interference. Just absence.

Eli lowered the radio and glanced back down the trail. The line of headlamps behind them had spaced out, each person maintaining their lane, their little circle of light. Their boots made almost no sound. The fog thickened in the ravine, glowing faintly where their beams skimmed it, like spilled milk catching moonlight.

He didn't want to think about Ryan Dalton out here alone.

A kid in jeans and running shoes, chasing what he thought was a signal. The human brain loved patterns. Loved invitations. Loved to decide that a thing meant for you was, in fact, meant for you.

"Alvarez," Eli said quietly. "You remember the kid's friends said he had a headlamp?"

"Yeah."

"If you see a light, don't assume it's him. You call it in."

Alvarez swallowed. "You think he could still be moving?"

"I think people do stupid things when they're scared," Eli said. "Or when they think they're not scared. Same outcome."

Alvarez nodded, but his eyes had started scanning beyond the path, as if he expected something to step into their beam.

They walked another fifty yards. The trail bent slightly, offering a partial view across the valley. In daylight, Eli knew, you could see the opposite ridge in layers: tree line, rock face, a clearing where tourists stood. At night, the ridge was a darker shape against a darker sky.

Eli paused again. He hated pausing. Pausing meant waiting and waiting made room for imagination. But his instincts had been honed by years of not ignoring the wrong feeling.

The woods were too quiet.

Alvarez had stopped walking.

Eli turned. "What is it?"

Alvarez didn't answer at first. His face had gone still in a way Eli recognized: the moment your eyes locked onto something your mind didn't immediately categorize.

"Did you see that?" Alvarez whispered.

Eli followed the direction of his pointing hand, out across the valley.

At first, he saw only fog and black trees and the faint scatter of stars above. Then, through the haze, something pale appeared, small and steady.

A white point of light, hovering where no light should be.

Eli felt his stomach tighten, not because he believed in mountain stories, but because he knew the difference between expected problems and unexpected ones. A turned ankle was expected. Hypothermia was expected. Panic was expected.

A light that held still above the trees on the far ridge, as if it had chosen its position, was not.

Alvarez's voice came out thin. "Headlamp?"

Eli didn't answer. He raised the radio slowly, as if a sudden movement might startle the night.

The point of light drifted sideways, smooth as a thought.

Eli keyed the handset. "All teams, report status. Do you have visual on any light sources off trail?"

Only static replied.

And somewhere in that hollow quiet, the mountain seemed to listen.

Eli kept his eyes on the light across the valley until his vision started to play tricks, until he couldn't tell if it was moving or if the fog was.

He forced himself to look away.

Searches failed when you stared at the wrong thing.

"Alvarez," he said quietly. "Eyes on the trail. We're not here to chase a glow."

Alvarez didn't argue, but his shoulders stayed high, tense. His flashlight beam kept slipping off the path and into the trees as if he expected the missing hiker to step out and apologize.

Eli clicked his radio again, changing his angle, raising it over his head.

"Command, this is Foster. Radio check."

Nothing. Static, then a thin, distant hiss that didn't resolve into voice.

He lowered the handset and listened. Far down the ridge the other volunteers' footfalls had slowed. You could feel a group's confidence leak away in small, physical ways: people compressing closer to one another, beams overlapping, voices quieting like the forest had issued an order.

Eli didn't like what that did to decision-making.

He stepped to the edge of the path and swept his light downward, searching for the simplest clues.

Broken branches. Scraped leaves. Anything that suggested a person had passed through in a hurry.

The ridge here was narrow enough that one wrong step could send you sliding into the ravine. The fog pooled thickly below, swallowing the slope in a gray smear. It looked soft. Eli knew better. Under fog there was rock and deadfall and angles sharp enough to break a man in one clean mistake.

A missing hiker wasn't a story. It was physics.

"Ryan Dalton," Eli said aloud, not as a call but as a reminder to himself. Twenty-one, gray hoodie, running shoes.

He'd seen the kid's photograph at the station, lifted from a social media page. A face that hadn't learned to look guarded yet. Smile tilted slightly as if someone had told a joke just before the picture was taken. The kind of kid who still believed the world would answer him if he asked loudly enough.

The friend's words replayed in Eli's mind: It wanted him to come look.

Eli didn't believe in wanting lights. But he believed in the effect of that sentence. Belief changed posture. Belief changed risk.

He motioned Alvarez closer, keeping his voice low.

"We're approaching the point-of-last-known," he said. "The overlook area should be another quarter mile. His friends were somewhere near there."

Alvarez nodded. "And the light… that's the thing they saw?"

"Could be." Eli didn't add the rest, because he didn't want to feed it. Could be the same. Could be different. Could be nothing. Could be something that didn't care about their categories.

They moved forward carefully. The trail leveled out for a stretch, then widened where a spur led to a small rocky outcropping used as an informal lookout. Eli recognized it by the way the trees thinned. You could see more sky, which made the darkness feel bigger instead of safer.

He stopped at the junction and crouched, angling his beam across the ground.

Footprints. Several sets, overlapping. Most were clear boot treads, deep lugs, the kind you wanted on wet mountain soil. A few were sneaker prints, shallower, with a repeating pattern that could have been any athletic shoe sold in a mall.

Eli's stomach tightened.

He pointed. "There."

Alvarez bent down. "Those could be from earlier hikers."

"They could," Eli agreed, because you never married a theory too early. But then he traced a gloved finger alongside one sneaker print. It cut through the leaf layer sharply, fresher than the rest. Leaves had been pushed aside, not settled back over it. The edges were still crisp.

"Look at the heel drag," Eli said. "And the spacing. He was moving quick."

Alvarez swallowed. "Running?"

"Or slipping." Eli stood and swept his light farther off the trail, beyond the spur. "If he left the path, it would be from right around here. This is where people get tempted. They see an open view and think the mountain is less dense than it is."

He stepped a few feet into the trees, careful not to trample what he might need to read. The ground here fell away gradually, then more steeply. Ferns and laurel made the slope look plush, but Eli knew how it hid holes and slick stone.

He found the first sign about ten yards in: a snapped twig at shoulder height, still pale where the bark had torn.

Then another, lower, where someone had shoved through.

Eli's beam caught a thin scrape on the trunk of a young maple, fresh enough that the inner wood looked raw.

Alvarez leaned close. “Could be an animal.”

“Animals don’t usually break branches at shoulder height and keep going downhill in a straight line,” Eli said.

He keyed the radio again out of habit more than hope.

“Team Two, possible track off trail at the overlook spur. Foster investigating.”

Static answered, thicker now, like the mountain had moved closer to the frequency.

Eli lowered the handset. “They’re not hearing us.”

Alvarez’s voice went tight. “How can all the radios go out at once?”

Eli didn’t have a good answer that didn’t sound like folklore, and he wasn’t going to hand that to the night.

“Terrain,” he said. “Rock. Angle. We keep moving.”

They followed the signs downhill, slow and deliberate. Eli moved like he was trying to avoid waking the forest. Alvarez stayed close behind him, his beam overlapping Eli’s, turning the ground bright enough to see every wet leaf shine.

Ten more yards and Eli spotted something that didn’t belong to the woods: a small rectangle of reflective plastic caught in a branch.

He reached up and plucked it free.

A keycard. The kind you used to access a dorm building or a campus gym. It had a university logo on it and a young man's name printed beneath a grainy photo.

Ryan Dalton.

Alvarez exhaled like the sound had been trapped in him. "That's him."

Eli stared at the card for a second too long. Finding an item should have been reassuring. It meant you were on the right track. But it also meant Ryan had been here, and now he wasn't. It meant a simple human truth: somewhere on this mountain, in this cold, a kid had moved through the dark and left pieces of his life behind like breadcrumbs he hadn't intended to drop.

Eli clipped the card into a plastic evidence sleeve from his pack. "Mark the spot," he said.

Alvarez pulled a strip of orange tape from his pocket and tied it around a branch, hands shaking just enough to make the knot sloppy.

Eli scanned the ground again. The sneaker prints continued, then veered slightly left, toward a deeper thickening of laurel. The slope steepened there, and beyond it the ravine dropped hard.

"Ryan," Eli called, just once, not shouting. He kept his tone calm, professional, the way you spoke to someone you needed not to panic. "This is Ranger Foster. If you can hear me, call back."

His voice felt wrong in the silence. Too loud, too human.

No answer came. Not even the echo you sometimes got off the rocks.

Alvarez shifted. "Maybe he's unconscious."

"Maybe," Eli said, though the word felt thin.

He moved forward another few steps and stopped abruptly. His light had caught a patch of fabric snagged on a thorny branch, gray cloth stretched and torn.

He reached out, careful. The hoodie material was damp and cold. He could see the way it had been pulled, not brushed. As if someone had yanked free and kept going.

Alvarez's voice cracked slightly. "That's his hoodie."

Eli didn't say yes. He didn't say no. He studied the surrounding brush and the direction of the tear. The snag angle suggested Ryan had moved downslope fast, not climbing. Not returning. Not reconsidering.

Eli's mind filled in the picture: Ryan sees lights, believes they are close, leaves the trail to get a better look, pushes through laurel, slips, scrambles, keeps going. A rational sequence driven by one irrational assumption: that the thing ahead of him would stay where it was.

Eli looked back up toward the trail. Their headlamps were no longer visible through the trees. The fog had thickened, and the forest swallowed distance.

Isolation crept in, not as fear but as math. Two rangers off-trail. Radios failing. Unknown terrain. A missing hiker leaving a trail of dropped identifiers like he'd been shedding himself.

Eli took a slow breath and did what procedure demanded even when the mountain didn't cooperate. He pulled out his GPS unit, marked their location, and then reached for his whistle.

He hesitated.

He remembered the older volunteer's tone at the station. People always follow the lights.

He thought of the way the valley light had moved sideways, smooth as intention. He thought of the radio going dead all at once, as if something had decided they didn't need to speak to one another.

Eli lowered the whistle back into his pocket without using it.

"Stay close," he told Alvarez. "No sudden sounds. We keep searching, but we don't rush."

Alvarez stared at him. "No whistle? Isn't that standard?"

"Standard assumes the mountain is honest," Eli said, then immediately regretted the wording. It sounded too much like a story.

Before Alvarez could ask what he meant, a faint glow appeared through the trees ahead of them.

Not a reflection. Not a beam.

A pale, steady light, hovering low among the laurel.

Alvarez froze.

Eli felt the muscles in his spine tighten as his body recognized the same wrongness it had recognized across the valley, only now it was closer. Close enough that it lit the edges of wet leaves without casting a normal shadow.

He lifted his flashlight and aimed it directly at the glow, trying to force it into a shape he understood.

The light didn't brighten like something being illuminated.

It held its own.

It drifted a few inches to the left, as if adjusting its view.

Alvarez whispered, barely audible. "Is that… Ryan's headlamp?"

Eli didn't answer. He watched the light hover there, patient and steady, and felt a sudden, irrational certainty settle over him.

This was not something they had found.

This was something that had noticed them.

The glow hovered just beyond the reach of Eli's flashlight beam, as if it existed in its own separate pocket of brightness.

He kept the light trained on it anyway, forcing himself into the habit of procedure. Identify. Assess. Approach only if safe. But nothing about this felt like the kind of problem the handbook had been written for.

"Ryan?" Eli called again, softer this time, as though volume might be taken as aggression. "If that's you, say something."

No voice answered.

The orb drifted a few inches higher, clearing the laurel leaves. It wasn't a beam. There was no cone of illumination, no hot spot, no wobble. It lit the edges of the brush around it with an even, cold clarity. The wet leaves looked lacquered.

Alvarez's breathing had gone shallow. Eli could hear it, too loud in the quiet.

"Don't move toward it," Eli said, keeping his own voice level. "Stay where you are."

"I'm not," Alvarez whispered, but his feet had shifted without him seeming to notice.

The light held still.

It felt, absurdly, like a pause in a conversation. Like waiting for the next response.

Eli glanced down at the ground, searching for the simplest explanation. A dropped lantern. A headlamp caught in a branch. Something reflective. Anything physical he could point at and name. But there was nothing beneath it except slick leaves and shadow.

The orb slid sideways, slipping between two branches with the smoothness of something that didn't have to push through.

Alvarez flinched. "It moved."

"I saw it."

The orb drifted a little farther downslope, and Eli's first instinct was the same instinct he'd seen in the missing hiker's friends: It's going away. If we don't follow, we'll lose it. The thought came with a burst of urgency that didn't feel like his own.

He let it pass without obeying it.

"Alvarez," he said, "look at me."

Alvarez tore his gaze from the glow. His eyes were wide, pupils stretched, and Eli saw the exact moment embarrassment tried to mask fear.

"You're going to want to follow it," Eli said. "You're going to feel like it's leading you to him. That's not logic. That's bait."

Alvarez swallowed. "Bait from what?"

Eli didn't answer because any answer would sound like a campfire story, and he couldn't afford to give the story more room.

The orb continued drifting downslope. Not fast. Not fleeing. Just moving with a measured patience, like it knew they'd watch.

Eli took a step backward, deliberately, crunching leaves under his boot to break the trance of silence. "We go back up to the trail," he said. "We mark this location. We get more people down here in daylight."

Alvarez's head turned, reluctant, toward the slope above them. The trees swallowed their route. Fog hung between trunks like a curtain. For a moment Eli couldn't tell which direction was up. The mountain had a way of making everything feel like it angled toward deeper trouble.

The orb stopped.

Eli froze. Alvarez froze.

The light held steady for three heartbeats.

Then it moved toward them.

Not quickly. Not with the darting zip of an insect. It approached in a straight, unwavering line, and Eli's skin prickled as the distance closed. Ten yards. Eight. Six.

Alvarez whispered, "It's coming closer."

"I see it," Eli said, and hated how thin his own voice sounded.

The orb paused again, now close enough that Eli could see it wasn't perfectly round. The edge shimmered, slightly uneven, like heat haze, but the light itself was cold. It didn't throw normal shadows. Leaves around it seemed to brighten without any directionality, as if the air had become luminous.

Eli's flashlight beam struck it and did nothing.

The orb did not flare. It did not reflect. It simply remained, as if the two light sources were separate languages that did not translate.

Eli's hand tightened on the radio. He raised it again, more out of instinct than hope. "Command, this is Foster. We have a… we have an unknown light source off trail near the overlook spur. Requesting status from all teams."

Static, immediate and heavy.

Then, beneath the static, something else. A faint voice, broken and far away, as though coming through a tunnel.

"…hello? Anyone copy?"

Eli's shoulders went rigid. He keyed the handset hard enough that his thumb hurt. "Say again. Identify."

The voice crackled, half-swallowed. "Team Two… I see it."

Eli's throat went dry. "See what? The light?"

A pause, then a breathy, disoriented sound. "Yeah. It's… it's right—"

The transmission cut, replaced by a hiss that rose and fell like wind through a pipe.

Alvarez stared at the radio. "That was one of ours."

"It wasn't Team Two," Eli said automatically, though he wasn't sure. Their designation meant nothing if the channels had scrambled. The important thing was that someone else was out there, seeing what they were seeing, and the mountain had chosen that moment to let a voice through.

The orb inches from them brightened, subtly, as if responding to the burst of sound.

Eli's mind returned to the keycard and the torn hoodie. Ryan Dalton had come this way. The evidence said so. The orb was here now, present and attentive. And the one clear instruction in Eli's training screamed in his head: Do not let the situation make you stupid.

He forced his legs to move. Another step backward. Slow. No sudden movements.

Alvarez mirrored him, shaky but obeying.

The orb followed.

Not at the same speed. It lagged just enough to keep the distance constant, like a handler walking a dog that didn't need a leash. Eli hated the thought as soon as it formed, because it made the thing feel too intelligent, too purposeful.

They retreated up the slope, angling toward where Eli believed the trail to be. Laurel grabbed at their pants. Wet branches slapped at their sleeves. Eli kept his light on the ground to avoid tripping, but his peripheral vision stayed pinned to the glow.

It kept pace. Always just ahead and to the side, never blocking their route, never leaving.

"Stop looking at it," Eli said through his teeth.

"I can't," Alvarez whispered.

"Yes, you can," Eli snapped, sharper than he meant. "You're going to. Or you're going to walk right into a hole because you're staring at a damn glow."

Alvarez blinked hard and forced his gaze down. His foot caught on a root anyway, and he stumbled. Leaves slid under him, slick as grease. Eli grabbed his arm and hauled him upright.

The orb brightened again at the sudden movement. It drifted closer, almost shoulder-level now, and Eli felt a coldness brush his cheek, not wind, but something like damp cellar air.

His stomach rolled.

Alvarez made a strangled sound, then clamped his mouth shut as if afraid of making noise.

Eli pushed him forward. “Move,” he said. “Keep moving.”

Up ahead through the trees, a second glow appeared.

Then a third.

They winked into existence one after another along the slope, spaced as if placed. Eli’s heart hammered harder with each new point of light. The quiet seemed to deepen around them, as though the forest had shifted from listening to watching.

Alvarez whispered, “There’s more.”

Eli didn’t answer, because there was no answer that helped.

The lights drifted in loose arcs between trunks, slow and steady. They were not random. Eli saw it in the way they adjusted when Alvarez’s boots slid, the way one dipped when Eli raised his radio again, as if sound and motion were currents they could ride.

Eli fought for the trail. He needed open ground. He needed lines of sight. He needed other people.

A branch snapped somewhere upslope.

Eli swung his flashlight toward the sound, expecting to catch a volunteer's headlamp, a reflective strip, anything reassuringly human.

What he caught was another light, already there, hovering between two trees like a pale eye.

And in the gap beyond it, further across the ravine, more lights had appeared on the opposite ridge. Dozens, scattered through fog like slow-moving fireflies, only far brighter and too steady.

The valley seemed to fill with them.

Alvarez's voice went thin. "That ain't Ryan."

"No," Eli said, and the admission tasted like surrender.

The radio hissed again. Another voice, fainter than before. "I'm following it."

Eli's blood ran cold.

He keyed the handset. "Negative," he said, forcing authority into each syllable. "Do not pursue the light. Stay on the trail. Repeat, do not pursue."

Static swallowed him.

Then a fragment of reply slipped through, like a dying ember. "It's… it's leading—"

Cut.

Eli looked at Alvarez. Alvarez looked back, and in that glance Eli saw the same thought in both of them: Someone else was off-trail. Someone else had chosen the glow over the map in their head. Someone else was about to become another missing name in a folder.

"We have to get back," Alvarez said, voice breaking. "We have to tell Mercer."

"We're going," Eli said.

The nearest orb stopped abruptly, hovering at about chest height in front of them, blocking their line of travel the way a person might step into your path.

Eli halted.

Alvarez halted so hard he nearly collided with Eli's back.

The light held still, and for one insane moment Eli felt the pressure of being evaluated. Not by eyes. By attention. A sensation like standing under a spotlight when you couldn't see the audience.

Eli forced himself to breathe. He lifted his flashlight again, useless, and then lowered it. He didn't know why the gesture felt right, only that it did.

The orb drifted sideways, opening a gap.

Eli took it. He pulled Alvarez with him, moving through the gap without looking directly at the light again.

They climbed, slipping and scrambling. The fog thickened, turning the world into a narrow tunnel of headlamp and breath.

Behind them, the lights followed.

Then, from somewhere deep in the trees below, a scream tore through the hollow quiet.

It was short, raw, and immediately cut off as if someone had closed a door on it.

Alvarez made a sound of horror.

Eli's grip tightened on his arm. "Keep moving," he said, though his own legs felt like they'd forgotten how.

The radio in Mercer's team would be silent too. Eli understood that now. Whatever this was, it didn't just live on the mountain. It controlled the mountain's ability to let them speak to each other.

The lights drifted through the fog behind them, patient and steady, as though they had all the time in the world.

And Eli Foster, who had spent his career believing the woods were dangerous only in the ways you could measure, realized with a sick certainty that something on Brown Mountain had learned a simple human rule:

If you want someone to come to you, all you have to do is look like you're waiting.

Chapter 2

The Story Beneath the Story

Dr. Adrian Cross knew the moment the laughter started that he had lost the room.

Not entirely. Not in the way a bad professor loses a class. They were still listening, still looking at him, still taking notes in the dutiful, half-automated way undergraduates did when they sensed a slide might contain something that would later be on an exam.

But the laughter meant they had decided, somewhere in the space between his first sentence and the last one, that what he taught was an elective kind of truth. A decorative truth. A truth you could wear like a vintage jacket and then hang up when you went back to real life.

The Folklore Department occupied the oldest building on Great Lakes State University's campus, a gray limestone structure that had been constructed when the school was still a normal college and not a sprawling institution with corporate donors and a sports complex. The lecture hall smelled faintly of chalk dust and radiator heat. The desks were bolted down in tidy ranks as if knowledge required containment. High windows let in a cold, watery light that made October feel like it was already halfway into November.

Adrian stood at the front with a piece of chalk between his fingers and watched his students settle.

Twenty of them today, maybe twenty-two. A few had coffee. One had a blanket wrapped around her shoulders like she expected the building itself to be haunted by drafts. On the back row, a boy in a sweatshirt with the university logo leaned back so far his chair threatened to give up on him.

Adrian had seen this posture before. He called it the campfire lean. The body language of someone waiting to be entertained.

He wrote one word on the board.

Folklore.

Then he turned and faced them.

"Let's start with a simple question," he said. "What do you think folklore is?"

Hands rose with cautious optimism. People always had opinions about the thing they assumed was made of opinions.

"A myth," a student offered.

"A fairy tale," another said.

"Old stories," someone else said, a little dismissive, like the age of a story automatically made it less credible.

Adrian nodded as if each answer had value. He was patient by nature or at least practiced in patience. Folklore required it.

"And what," he asked, "do you think folklore is for?"

That got fewer hands.

A student near the front, hair pulled into a tight bun, said, "Entertainment?"

A ripple of agreement moved through the room. Someone snorted softly.

Adrian capped the chalk against the board, leaving a small white click.

"That's the answer I hear most often," he said. "And it's the answer that keeps folklore trapped in a costume closet. Fun. Decorative. A thing you take out for Halloween."

He paused, letting the room quiet itself.

"Folklore is not the opposite of truth," Adrian said. "It is what communities remember after history forgets."

He wrote three more words beneath the first.

Story. Tradition. Survival.

He underlined survival hard enough that the chalk squealed.

"Every legend persists because it does something," he continued. "It warns. It explains. It binds. It gives structure to fear. Sometimes it hides information inside a form people will repeat without realizing what they're carrying."

The campfire lean in the back row shifted slightly forward, curiosity beginning to win over cynicism.

A hand rose near the middle. A young woman with clear eyes and a skeptical mouth. Adrian had seen her in office hours once. She wanted everything to be measurable.

"So, you think folklore is real?" she asked.

Adrian smiled faintly. He liked that question because it forced people to reveal what they meant by real.

"I think the wrong question is whether folklore is real," he said. "Because that assumes folklore is making a claim you can test like a chemical reaction."

A boy two rows down said, "But sometimes it does make claims. Like, 'There's a witch in the woods,' or 'Don't go to that lake.' That's either true or not."

"It is either true or not," Adrian agreed. "But what's more important is why a community keeps saying it."

The skeptical student pressed. "So, you don't care if it's true?"

"I care deeply," Adrian said. "But truth is not always where people expect it to be. Folklore isn't a lab report. It's a behavioral record."

That earned a few more notes being taken. People liked language that sounded like it could be quoted.

Adrian turned back to the board and erased everything but the three words. Then he wrote a new phrase.

Ghost Lights.

That got their attention in the way certain topics always did. Anything with the whiff of the supernatural pulled at the same part of the brain that had once made humans stare into fire and wonder what lived beyond it.

"Across the world," he said, "people report mysterious lights in places where there shouldn't be lights. Swamps. Graveyards. Mountains. Desert roads. Forests."

He began listing names as he spoke them, each one a small hook snagging on cultural memory.

"Will-o'-the-wisp. Jack-o'-lantern. Min Min lights. Hitodama."

A few students nodded as they recognized them. One whispered to another, probably repeating a story he'd heard as a kid.

Adrian added one last item to the board and turned the chalk in his fingers.

Brown Mountain Lights.

"Appalachia," he said, "has reported these lights for over two hundred years. Early settlers claimed they were lanterns carried by lost miners. Cherokee traditions describe them as spirits searching for the dead."

The campfire lean in the back row straightened.

The skeptical student raised her hand again. "Isn't that just… swamp gas?"

A few people laughed. There it was. The safe explanation. The joke that let you distance yourself from the discomfort of mystery.

Adrian did not smile this time.

"That explanation has been proposed," he said evenly. "Along with atmospheric plasma, ball lightning, reflections from distant vehicles, trains, brush fires, and the human tendency to misinterpret distance in low visibility."

He let the list sit there, heavy and unimpressive.

"But here's the interesting part," Adrian said, and his voice dropped slightly, not for drama but because he wanted their bodies to lean in.

"The lights don't behave like gas."

That quieted them. Even the students who wanted to laugh again hesitated, sensing that the joke had already been used up.

"They move against the wind," Adrian continued. "They change direction. They stop. They wait. Sometimes they approach witnesses."

He tapped the chalk against the board twice.

"And when people see them," he said, "they do the same thing, over and over, across generations. They follow."

A hand rose in the back row, the boy in the university sweatshirt now fully upright.

"Why would they follow?" he asked. "If it's creepy?"

Adrian looked at him for a long moment. That question, at least, was honest.

"Because the lights don't feel random," Adrian said. "People describe them as if they are responsive. As if they are engaged in the oldest human trick there is."

He paused, and the room felt suddenly still in a way Adrian recognized from field interviews. The moment when someone senses that a story might not be about entertainment at all.

"Invitation," he said.

The skeptical student frowned. "But that's perception."

"Yes," Adrian agreed. "And perception is not nothing. Perception is how humans survive. If a community collectively perceives a place as dangerous, they change their behavior. They build rules. They avoid slopes. They warn children not to whistle at night."

He saw a few students exchange glances at that one. Whistling was a detail. Details tended to stick.

Adrian turned away from the board and leaned his hip lightly against the desk at the front of the room, adopting a posture that signaled he was no longer delivering information but offering something more personal.

"Folklore is what people do with uncertainty," he said. "And when uncertainty repeats, folklore thickens. It doesn't matter if the lights are spirits or plasma or headlights. What matters is that people keep seeing something, and they keep reacting in predictable ways."

The skeptical student's eyes narrowed. "So, folklore is like… data?"

Adrian smiled then, not because it was funny, but because it meant she was finally asking the right kind of question.

"Folklore is a record of human encounters with the unexplainable," he said. "Not reliable in the way historians want it to be. Not clean. Not sterile. But it contains patterns. And patterns, if you know how to read them, can tell you where danger lives."

The bell rang, startlingly loud in the quiet that had settled over the lecture hall. Chairs scraped. Students gathered their things. The room broke back into normal motion, the spell of attention dissolving.

Adrian watched them leave with the familiar mix of satisfaction and frustration. He could give them language and frameworks, he could train them to see structure in story, but he couldn't force them to feel what he felt when he read an old warning and realized someone had once paid for it.

The last few students trickled out. The skeptical young woman lingered near the door as if she wanted to argue again, then thought better of it and left without speaking.

Adrian began erasing the board, chalk dust falling like fine snow.

"Brown Mountain Lights," he murmured to himself, tasting the words as if they were already forming into a new case study. He had no reason, in that moment, to think the mountain would ever matter to him beyond lecture examples and articles.

Then he noticed the man standing just outside the doorframe.

Park ranger uniform. Dark green. Shoulder patch he didn't recognize at first. The man's posture was straight but tired, the kind of tired that didn't come from one long day but from too many nights that refused to end cleanly.

Adrian set the eraser down slowly.

The ranger stepped inside, as if crossing a threshold.

"Dr. Cross?" the man asked.

"Yes," Adrian said, already feeling the shift. The subtle tightening in the air that came when story moved toward you instead of staying safely on the page.

The ranger extended his hand. His grip was firm, cold.

"Evan Mercer," he said. "Pisgah National Forest."

Adrian nodded. He had heard the name before, or something close to it, in the context of Appalachian fieldwork. Rangers remembered things locals didn't say out loud.

"What can I help you with?" Adrian asked.

Mercer hesitated, and in that hesitation Adrian saw something that didn't belong in a routine academic visit.

Fear, carefully managed.

Mercer glanced once at the empty lecture hall, the chalkboard, the erased words still faintly visible in streaks. Then he looked back at Adrian.

"Have you ever heard of the Brown Mountain Lights?" Mercer asked.

Adrian's first impulse was to smile, to keep it light, to treat it like an amusing overlap between his work and a ranger's duties.

He almost did.

Then he noticed Mercer's eyes. Not curious. Not amused. Not skeptical.

Grave.

Adrian's smile faded before it could fully form.

"I've heard of them," Adrian said carefully. "Yes."

Mercer's hand tightened slightly around the strap of his radio, as if the object could anchor him.

"We've had three disappearances in the last year," Mercer said.

Adrian felt the words settle into him like a stone dropped in deep water.

"Disappearances," Adrian repeated. Not missing persons in the abstract. Not a hypothetical. Real names. Real families. Real search grids laid out in cold night forests.

Mercer nodded once, and his voice lowered as if he didn't want the building itself to overhear.

"And every one of them," he said, "started with someone following a light."

Adrian studied Mercer for a moment, recalibrating.

Rangers came to campus sometimes. Usually for benign reasons: a request for help identifying a symbol carved into a tree, a question about local legend variations for an interpretive sign, the occasional invitation to speak at a community event where someone wanted him to tell polite ghost stories without suggesting anything might actually be dangerous.

Mercer had not come for that.

"Three," Adrian said, mostly to give his mind a handhold. "In the Brown Mountain region specifically?"

Mercer nodded. "Within an hour's drive of the ridge. Two tourists, one local. The local was the one that got under my skin."

"Why?" Adrian asked.

"Because he knew better," Mercer said. "He grew up there. His grandmother was the kind of woman who still put salt at the windowsill and wouldn't let you whistle after dark."

That detail landed with a familiar weight. Adrian had mentioned whistling in the lecture almost as a throwaway example, but he'd watched his students' faces at that point. Specific taboos stuck because they implied a specific consequence.

Adrian gestured toward his office down the hall. "Come in. Tell me names."

Mercer followed him past the empty classroom, his boots too loud in the corridor. Adrian unlocked the office, pushed aside a stack of papers on a chair, and waited while Mercer remained standing as if sitting would admit something.

"I can't give you everything," Mercer said. "There's ongoing search documentation, and the families…"

"I'm not asking for a spectacle," Adrian said. He kept his voice even, professional, the way he did when students came to him with grief dressed up as curiosity. "But if you want me to understand why this matters to you, you'll have to let it be more than a campfire phrase."

Mercer exhaled through his nose. "Ryan Dalton," he said, and Adrian felt a small jolt of recognition because the name sounded like it belonged to a person with a university ID and a mother who answered the phone too quickly. "Twenty-one. Went off trail after sunset. Friends said he saw a light across the valley. Said it looked like someone signaling."

Adrian's mind supplied the rest automatically: assumed emergency, assumed human, assumed closeness.

"And the other two?" Adrian asked.

Mercer's jaw tightened. "Hannah Briggs. Thirty-four. Tourist from Richmond, Virginia. She was on a photography trip. Took a series of shots near an overlook. In the last few images you can see a glow behind the tree line. She left her tripod set up and walked down the slope like she was chasing a better angle. That's where the prints stop."

"And the local?" Adrian asked.

"Jesse Pruitt," Mercer said. "Forty-two. Works road maintenance. He went up with his cousin to see the lights, just to prove the stories weren't anything. They stood on the ridge. His cousin told us Jesse started laughing, then went quiet. Like something had caught his attention. Then he stepped off the trail. Just stepped off, like he'd forgotten what the edge meant."

Mercer's hand had drifted to his radio without him noticing. He didn't press any buttons. He just held it, a talisman.

Adrian leaned back in his chair. "And each time, there were lights."

Mercer's gaze stayed steady. "Each time, someone described them as close. Not like distant headlights. Close enough to feel like you could walk to them."

Adrian nodded slowly. "That's a pattern."

Mercer's eyes narrowed slightly. "You talk like it's data."

"It is," Adrian said. "Not scientific data. Human data. The part that gets dismissed until it becomes a body count."

Mercer's mouth pulled into something that was not a smile. "That's what I was afraid you'd say."

Adrian reached for a folder on his desk; one he used for lecture examples. Photocopies of nineteenth-century newspaper clippings. A printout of a field report from Texas. Notes from an interview in rural Japan. He hadn't touched the folder in months, because it was easy to keep ghost lights in the safe category of academic fascination.

He slid it toward Mercer. "Tell me," Adrian said. "When people talk about the Brown Mountain Lights, do they call them anything else?"

Mercer hesitated. "Some do. 'The lanterns.' 'The watchers.' Some people won't say any name. They'll just point. Or they'll say, 'Those things.'"

Adrian tapped the folder. "That's consistent with other traditions."

Mercer looked down at the papers but didn't open them. "Other traditions where people disappear?"

Adrian's answer came without ornament. "Yes."

Mercer's posture stiffened, as if he'd expected the truth to take longer to arrive.

Adrian pulled the folder back, opened it, and began turning pages. "Ghost lights aren't an Appalachian specialty," he said. "They're one of the most persistent categories of global folklore. Different cultures name them differently and explain them differently, but the descriptions rhyme."

Mercer finally sat, though he perched at the edge of the chair. Adrian took that as progress.

"Min Min lights," Adrian said, flipping to a photograph of a dark outback road with a pale orb hovering above the horizon. "Australia. People report them as floating lights that follow travelers. Sometimes they pace a car. Sometimes they lure people off the road. There are scientific proposals, of course. Atmospheric refraction. Headlights distorted by heat layers. But even in places where there are no other cars, no road, no plausible source, the stories persist."

Mercer's gaze sharpened. "Follow travelers how?"

"Like they're curious," Adrian said. "Or like they're herding. And the most striking thing is that witnesses describe the same feeling you just described. Not distant. Personal. Intended."

He turned another page. "Hitodama," he said. "Japan. 'Human souls' in the form of floating flames. In older accounts they appear near graveyards, near places where someone died badly, near lonely roads. People are warned not to chase them because they lead you to places you shouldn't go."

Mercer's eyes flicked up. "People chase them anyway."

"People always do," Adrian said, and regretted how familiar the sentence sounded the moment it left his mouth. He'd heard a version of it in too many interviews. He'd watched it on faces when a story became a temptation.

He continued. "In parts of Louisiana and Texas you get what people call 'spook lights.' Marfa Lights are the famous example. Floating orbs in the desert. Tourists gather to watch them. Researchers set up cameras. Still no single explanation fits every account. Some sightings probably are headlights.

Some probably are atmospheric effects. But then you get reports where the lights split, merge, change direction sharply, appear where there's no line of sight to any road."

Mercer leaned closer. "Change direction, like intelligence?"

"Like responsiveness," Adrian corrected gently. "Folklore doesn't have to prove intelligence to record behavior. It only has to repeat what witnesses keep describing."

He paused and looked at Mercer. "And witnesses, across cultures, keep describing the same trap. The light behaves in a way that makes you feel seen."

Mercer's face tightened as if the word seen hit too close to memory.

Adrian turned another page. "In Scandinavia you have stories of the 'irrbloss,' wandering lights that lead travelers into bogs. In the U.K., will-o'-the-wisp. In many versions the light is described as playful, like it's enjoying the chase. But the ending is consistent: you end up lost, wet, cold, in terrain that kills you quietly."

Mercer stared at the papers, not reading so much as listening to the implication beneath them.

Adrian spoke more carefully now. "There's a consistent moral across these traditions. Don't follow. Don't call out. Don't treat the phenomenon like it exists for you."

Mercer's hand tightened around his radio again. "But why? Why would so many places invent the same warning?"

Adrian's answer was quiet. "Because people in those places encountered something that punished curiosity."

Silence stretched between them. In the hallway outside, the building's radiator clicked, then sighed. The campus continued around them, full of ordinary noise that suddenly felt too soft.

Mercer looked up. "You don't sound like a man who thinks this is all metaphor."

Adrian held his gaze. "I sound like a man who's spent his career listening to communities describe danger in the only language that survives the years."

Mercer swallowed. "Then tell me what you think the lights are."

Adrian let himself breathe before answering. He could feel the old academic instinct trying to protect him: qualify, hedge, defer.

Instead he said, "I think some reports are misidentified lights. Cars. Trains. Distant houses. I think some are atmospheric phenomena. But I also think there's a remainder. A set of accounts that refuse to be explained away because the behavior is too consistent."

Mercer waited.

Adrian tapped the page showing a typed transcript of an interview from West Texas. "In this interview, a woman describes the light stopping when she stops. Moving when she moves. Approaching when she speaks. That is not a description of swamp gas. It's not even a clean description of ball lightning. It's a description of interaction."

Mercer's voice was low. "Like an animal."

Adrian felt a chill at how naturally Mercer had arrived at the same framing. "Like something that has learned how humans respond to a signal," Adrian said. "Like something that understands invitation."

Mercer leaned back slightly, as if making room in his mind for the idea. "If that's true," he said, "then the mountain isn't just dangerous because it's steep."

Adrian nodded once. "No. It's dangerous because it knows what you want to believe when you're standing in the dark. That the light is there for you. That it means help. That it means you're not alone."

Mercer's eyes hardened, and Adrian saw a decision take shape behind them.

"I came here," Mercer said, "because I need someone who will take that possibility seriously without turning it into a circus."

Adrian closed the folder. “Then you did the right thing,” he said. “But if you want my help, you need to understand something.”

Mercer’s gaze stayed fixed.

Adrian’s voice dropped, not for drama, but because it felt like the only respectful way to speak about what he was about to say. “The stories don’t just describe the lights,” he said. “They describe the cost of paying attention to them.”

Mercer stood. “That’s why I’m here,” he said. “Because we’re running out of people to lose.”

Adrian watched him, and felt the shift again, the one he’d felt at the classroom door. Story moving toward him. The boundary between study and participation thinning.

“Show me what you have,” Adrian said. “And then tell me where, exactly, the lights appear.”

Mercer’s answer came without hesitation, as if he’d been carrying the coordinates like a confession.

“Brown Mountain,” he said. “And lately, they’re not staying at a distance.”

Mercer didn’t leave right away.

He stood near Adrian’s door as if the hallway beyond it belonged to a different world with different rules, and he wasn’t sure he trusted those rules to hold.

Adrian watched him, waiting for what came next. The ranger's posture had the rigid economy of a man trained to report only what he could justify, but his eyes kept sliding to the office window as if expecting to see a pale glow in the courtyard below.

"You said," Mercer began, then stopped.

Adrian didn't rescue him. He had learned in interviews that the most important parts came out only when you let the silence do its work.

Mercer tried again. "You said people describe it as invitation."

"Yes."

Mercer's jaw tightened. "I need you to understand what that looks like on the mountain."

Adrian nodded once. "Tell me."

Mercer reached into his jacket and pulled out a folded sheet of paper. Not an official form. Not letterhead. It was creased and soft with handling, like something kept in a pocket too long. He set it on Adrian's desk without ceremony.

Adrian unfolded it carefully.

There were bullet points. Simple sentences. The kind of language people used when they wanted a child to remember something even in fear.

Do not travel the slopes after sundown. Do not answer voices from the trees. Do not follow lights. If a light approaches, lower your eyes and back away. Do not whistle to it. Do not call it by name.

Adrian's fingers paused on the last line.

"What name?" he asked, echoing the question that had formed in his head the moment he read it.

Mercer's face tightened, and Adrian saw the brief conflict: the need to be precise fighting the instinct not to give a thing more shape by speaking it.

"That depends on who you ask," Mercer said finally. "Some folks call them lanterns. Some call them watchers. Some won't call them anything. They'll say, 'those things,' and point like the act of naming is what gets you noticed."

Adrian stared at the paper longer than necessary, letting the weight of it settle. He'd seen rules like this before, in different regions, in different languages. The structure was always the same: specific prohibitions clustered around sound, attention, and pursuit. Don't call. Don't whistle. Don't answer. Don't follow. The rules weren't about avoiding a place as much as avoiding an interaction.

"This is local," Adrian said.

"My grandmother kept one in her Bible," Mercer replied. "She used to say it like a joke when I was a kid. 'Don't you go whistling at night unless you want something whistling back.'"

Adrian looked up. "And now?"

Mercer's eyes didn't soften. "Now I'm not laughing."

Adrian ran a thumb along the crease in the paper. "Where did you get this copy?"

Mercer hesitated. "Church in Jonas Ridge. Someone put a stack on the back table years ago. People stopped taking them. Not because the rules stopped being true. Because nobody wants to admit they still need them."

That made Adrian think of his students laughing. How easy it was to treat old warnings like props when you'd never had to rely on them.

He set the sheet down carefully, like it might break.

"Tell me about Jesse Pruitt," Adrian said. "The local."

Mercer's gaze dropped to the edge of the desk, as if the details were written there. "He wasn't the kind of man who spooked easy. Road maintenance. Worked in all weather. Knew every curve and hollow around that mountain. He grew up hearing stories, but he treated them like you treat lightning. Real, dangerous, but not personal. Something you respected and then went back to work."

"And then he saw the light," Adrian said.

Mercer nodded once. "He and his cousin went up after dinner. Not even late. Dusk. They stood on the ridge near the overlook. His cousin said the lights appeared out over the valley like they usually do. Floating. Drifting. Nothing you can point at and measure, but you can see them clear as day."

Mercer swallowed, and when he spoke again his voice was flatter, as if he'd sanded down the emotion so he could get the facts out.

"Jesse joked about it at first. Said it was car lights. Said it was tourists. Then one of them moved."

"Moved how?" Adrian asked.

Mercer met his eyes. "Sideways. Against the slope. Not along a road. Not down a trail. Sideways, like it had no reason to care about terrain."

Adrian's mind supplied Eli Foster's description from the briefing Mercer had alluded to earlier, and the way that kind of movement snapped a person's certainty in half.

Mercer continued. "His cousin said Jesse stopped laughing. Just… stopped. Like someone turned a switch. And then Jesse said, 'You see that? It's closer than last time.'"

Adrian leaned forward slightly. "Closer."

"Yeah." Mercer's mouth tightened. "That's always what they say. Closer. Like the light is inside their personal space even though it might still be a hundred yards away. Like it's aimed at them."

"And then?" Adrian asked.

Mercer's hand drifted unconsciously to the radio clipped at his belt, the same habitual gesture Adrian had noticed earlier.

"Then Jesse stepped off the trail," Mercer said. "Not stumbling. Not slipping. He stepped like he'd seen a stair. His cousin grabbed his sleeve and Jesse jerked away hard enough to rip the seam. And he didn't look back. He just kept going downslope, straight into laurel."

Adrian listened without interrupting. The pattern was familiar in the way that made his stomach turn. The transition from observer to participant. The sudden narrowing of attention until the rest of the world, including common sense, fell away.

Mercer exhaled. "His cousin said he called after him. Jesse didn't answer. Not once."

Adrian's eyes flicked to the paper again. Do not answer voices from the trees. Do not follow lights. If a light approaches, lower your eyes and back away.

"Did his cousin hear anything?" Adrian asked.

Mercer's face went still. "He said he heard Jesse's footsteps for a while. Then he heard something else. Like… like a clicking. Like stones tapped together. He left the mountain and ran all the way back to the parking lot."

Adrian felt his scalp tighten. "And you searched."

Mercer's gaze sharpened, offended by the implication that he might not have. "All night. Into the next day. Dogs. Drones. Grid. The whole thing. We found Jesse's hat near a ravine. And that's it."

Adrian's throat went dry, not from fear exactly, but from the sensation of standing at the edge of something that refused to be made reasonable.

"So, when you say invitation," Mercer said, "I need you to hear it the way I do. Not poetic. Not metaphor. It's a lure. It behaves like one."

Adrian nodded slowly. "In a lot of traditions, the light is described as a test. It waits to see who will respond."

Mercer leaned forward. "That's the other thing. The waiting."

Adrian's eyebrows rose. "Tell me."

Mercer tapped the folded guidance sheet once, then withdrew his hand as if even touching it too much was dangerous. "People around there will tell you the same rule," he said. "When the light stops, you stop. When it turns, you turn away."

Adrian heard the cadence of oral instruction in it, the kind meant to be memorized.

Mercer's voice lowered. "Because if it stops and you keep going, it knows you're willing. And if it turns and you keep watching, it knows you're interested."

Adrian's stomach tightened at the precision of the logic. It wasn't scientific, but it was consistent. And consistency was what turned story into warning.

"Has anyone ever described it reacting to sound?" Adrian asked.

Mercer's lips pressed together. "Yes."

The answer came too fast, too sure.

Adrian waited.

Mercer looked at the radio on his belt, then back at Adrian. "I had one volunteer last year. Local guy. Good in the woods, thought he was immune to fear because he'd been hunting since he was twelve. He saw the lights and did what people do when they're uncomfortable. He tried to make a joke."

"What kind of joke?" Adrian asked, though he already suspected.

Mercer's voice went hard. "He whistled. Just one sharp little call. Like calling a dog."

Adrian's fingers tightened on the edge of the desk.

Mercer's eyes didn't blink. "He told me later that one of the lights changed direction immediately. Came straight toward him through the trees. And he said, I swear to God, it felt offended."

Adrian felt cold crawl up the back of his neck, not because he believed in offended lights, but because offended implied an entity capable of having expectations.

"What did he do?" Adrian asked.

"He ran," Mercer said simply. "And he never volunteered again."

Adrian glanced again at the line on the paper. Do not whistle to it. He had used whistling as an example in his lecture because it was a detail that showed up so often in global accounts. The fact that it was here too, in a ranger's hand, made his earlier classroom confidence feel naïve.

"So why now?" Adrian asked quietly. "Why come to me now?"

Mercer's gaze held his, steady and bleak. "Because the lights are changing."

Adrian waited.

"They used to stay out over the valley," Mercer said. "A show. A distance. People watched them from overlooks and went home. Now… now we get reports of them in the tree line. Near the trails. Closer to people. Like they're not satisfied with being seen from far away."

Adrian's mind returned to the word he'd used with his students. Invitation. He had meant it as an interpretive frame, a description of how humans experienced a phenomenon. Mercer was describing something else: an escalation. A narrowing of distance.

"And you think," Adrian said carefully, "that if the pattern continues, you'll lose more people."

Mercer's expression didn't change, but something tightened behind his eyes. "I think we already are."

Adrian looked at the guidance sheet again and then at the folder of global accounts on his desk. For years, he had treated the lights as a category. A lecture topic. A research fascination. Something safely placed behind glass by the simple fact that it happened elsewhere.

But Mercer was sitting in his office, bringing elsewhere to him, and Adrian could feel the shift that always preceded fieldwork: the moment a story stopped being something you studied and became something that studied you back.

Adrian folded the guidance sheet along its old creases and handed it to Mercer.

"I'll come," Adrian said.

Mercer's shoulders loosened a fraction, not relief exactly, but the grim satisfaction of a man who had just secured reinforcements.

Adrian continued, "But we do this correctly. I want copies of your reports. Witness statements. Time stamps. Locations. Photos if you have them.

And I want to talk to locals who aren't interested in tourists and cameras."

Mercer nodded once. "I can do that."

Adrian's voice tightened as he reached the edge of what he didn't want to admit, even to himself. "And Mercer?"

"What?"

Adrian held his gaze. "If the lights are an invitation, then we need to treat them like one."

Mercer's expression didn't flicker. "Meaning?"

"Meaning we don't accept," Adrian said. "We don't chase. We don't call out. We don't answer. We observe, and we document, and we keep enough distance that we don't become part of the story."

Mercer's mouth pulled into a humorless curve. "That's going to be hard," he said.

Adrian frowned. "Why?"

Mercer stood, and for the first time since he'd entered the building, he looked tired instead of controlled.

"Because when you see them," Mercer said, "distance is the first thing that starts to lie."

Chapter 3

Academic Warfare

Mercer left Adrian's office with the kind of efficiency that suggested he'd already rehearsed the next steps in his head. He didn't linger in the hallway, didn't turn back for second thoughts. The only trace he left behind was the faint scent of cold air and pine that clung to his jacket, and the paper he had brought, now absent from Adrian's desk but present in Adrian's mind like a list of rules carved into stone.

Do not follow lights. Do not whistle to it. Do not call it by name.

Adrian sat for a long moment after Mercer was gone, listening to the building return to its ordinary noises. A distant door closing. Students talking somewhere on the stairs. The radiator ticking like an impatient metronome. All of it felt staged, as if normal life were a thin set built in front of something else.

He opened the folder Mercer had left behind: photocopied reports, names, dates, fragments of witness statements rendered in the sterile language of liability and procedure. The sort of writing that tried to scrub the world clean of anything it couldn't explain.

But the pattern remained.

A light across a valley. A sense of closeness that made distance lie. A person stepping off trail as if following an instruction only they could hear.

Invitation, Adrian thought again, and this time it didn't feel like a clever interpretive frame. It felt like an accusation.

His phone buzzed with an email notification, something banal from a student asking for an extension. Adrian stared at it without registering the words, then set the phone down and pushed back from his desk.

If he was going to do this, he couldn't do it alone. Not because he feared the mountain, though he would have been lying to himself if he said there was no fear at all. Because fieldwork with a phenomenon like this demanded friction. Checks. Counterweights. Someone who could look at him and say, plainly, you are letting story seduce you.

There was only one person on campus who enjoyed saying that to him.

Marissa Calder's office was on the third floor of the Social Sciences building, which had been renovated within the last decade in a way that made it feel aggressively modern. White walls, glass partitions, furniture designed to look like it belonged in a tech company. Adrian always felt slightly out of place there, like he'd brought dust from old archives into a room that wanted to pretend the past was a solved problem.

He found her door half open. Inside, Marissa sat behind her desk with a tablet propped in front of her, fingers moving rapidly. Her hair was pulled back in a severe twist, and her expression had the controlled focus of someone who would rather cut off a hand than waste time.

Adrian knocked once anyway.

Marissa didn't look up. "If this is about the departmental budget, I already told the dean I'm not accepting another 'shared resource' arrangement that somehow results in my lab paying for your folklore festival."

"It's not the budget," Adrian said.

That got her eyes up. Marissa's gaze was sharp and cool, the gaze of a woman who had made a career out of studying belief without being taken in by it.

"Then what is it?" she asked.

Adrian stepped inside and closed the door behind him, not for secrecy, but because he didn't want her reaction to become hallway entertainment.

"I had a visitor," he said. "A ranger from Pisgah National Forest. Evan Mercer."

Marissa's mouth tightened in faint recognition. "I've heard the name. He gave a talk at a conference panel two years ago about search-and-rescue resource strain."

"He didn't come to talk about resources," Adrian said.

Marissa leaned back slightly, watching him in that measured way she had when she suspected he was about to say something irresponsible. "Adrian, what did you agree to?"

"I haven't agreed to anything yet," Adrian lied, and then corrected himself because she could always hear it in him. "I agreed to go to North Carolina."

Marissa stared at him, silent long enough that Adrian felt the familiar sensation of stepping onto thin ice.

"Why?" she asked at last.

Adrian pulled a photocopy from his bag and set it on her desk. Not the entire guidance sheet Mercer had carried, but a copy Adrian had made before handing the original back. He'd done it on impulse, like a man pocketing evidence before the scene was disturbed.

Marissa glanced down and read. Her eyebrows rose on the line about whistling.

"This is folklore," she said, tone flat.

"Yes," Adrian replied. "Local guidance passed around in churches."

Marissa tapped the paper once, not gently. "This is exactly why I don't like your field when it pretends it's investigative. You take a community's anxiety and you treat it like a map."

Adrian leaned forward slightly. "And you take a community's anxiety and you treat it like a symptom."

Marissa's eyes narrowed. "It often is a symptom. Environmental risk. Generational poverty. Poor infrastructure. Misinformation. Fear as a form of social control."

"This isn't social control," Adrian said. He heard the edge in his own voice and forced it down. "Three people have disappeared. In the last year. Mercer has names. Reports. Time stamps."

Marissa's expression changed by degrees, not softening, but sharpening into a different kind of attention. "Disappearances where?"

"Brown Mountain region," Adrian said.

Marissa gave a small, humorless exhale. "The lights."

He nodded.

She looked back at the guidance sheet and read the lines again, slower this time, as if she were scanning for the mechanics behind them. "Do not answer voices from the trees," she read aloud. "Do not follow lights. If a light approaches, lower your eyes and back away. Do not call it by name."

Marissa lifted her gaze to him. "You see how this spreads, right? How a rule like this becomes a script?"

"A script for what?" Adrian asked.

"For behavior," Marissa said. "A person goes hiking, sees something ambiguous in low visibility, remembers the story, and suddenly their brain fills in the rest. The light becomes an agent. The forest becomes an audience. Their fear becomes a narrative with rules. And then, because the narrative is compelling, they act in ways they otherwise wouldn't."

Adrian didn't argue with the basic premise because it was one of the reasons he respected her work. Belief changed behavior. Behavior created outcomes. Outcomes reinforced belief. A loop as old as language.

But Mercer's voice echoed in his memory: the lights are changing.

"And what about the lights themselves?" Adrian asked.

Marissa held his gaze. "I'm an anthropologist, Adrian. I'm not a physicist. But I'm also not easily impressed by mystery. There are explanations. Optical illusion. Refraction. Headlights. Atmospheric conditions. People misjudge distance constantly in mountains."

Adrian nodded once. "Mercer says they're getting closer to trails. Closer to people."

"Because people are looking for them," Marissa shot back. "Because the story makes them look. You're seeing a classic case of folklore contamination."

"That's not a real term," Adrian said automatically, and hated himself a little for the pettiness.

Marissa's mouth curved. "It is now."

He recognized that look: she was ready to enjoy dismantling him. It was one of the ways they stayed friends. They fought, and the fighting kept them honest.

Adrian reached into his bag again and placed another document on her desk. A printed witness statement Mercer had allowed him to copy, sanitized of names but not of detail. Adrian had read it three times already.

Marissa took it and scanned.

Her eyes paused, then moved back up the page.

"What is this?" she asked, more carefully.

"Volunteer account," Adrian said. "He describes a light responding to sound. To movement. Changing direction."

Marissa's expression remained skeptical, but her fingers tightened slightly on the page. "Witness testimony isn't measurement."

"No," Adrian agreed. "But it's a pattern."

Marissa looked up. "You know what else is a pattern? People telling the same story because they've heard the same story. That's what traditions are. That's what contamination does. It standardizes the experience."

Adrian started to respond, but her door opened without a knock.

Professor Henry Bellamy stepped into the room as if he belonged there, which he often acted as though he did in every room on campus. He was carrying a stack of books pressed against his chest, the spines cracked and annotated, and he wore tweed in a building that smelled like new carpet.

He looked from Marissa to Adrian and sighed, as if walking into their conversations was a burden the universe kept placing on him.

"So," Bellamy said, "I hear you've decided to go ghost hunting."

Adrian stared. "How do you always know?"

Bellamy shifted the books onto one arm and adjusted his glasses with the other. "Because you're incapable of keeping your enthusiasm quiet. Half the faculty lounge heard you ask the departmental assistant if we have travel funds for 'urgent field research.'"

Marissa's gaze flicked between them. "Wait. You're actually doing this."

"Yes," Adrian said. "And before either of you says it, no, I'm not treating it like entertainment."

Bellamy's mouth tightened. "You're treating it like a career move."

Adrian felt heat rise in his chest. "That's not fair."

"It's accurate," Bellamy replied. He set the books down on Marissa's desk with a soft thud, as if anchoring his argument in paper. "You've been chasing the romance of the unverified since you published that ridiculous article about lake spirits and sinkhole deaths."

Adrian's voice went cold. "Ridiculous article that you cited last year."

Bellamy didn't flinch. "To critique, yes."

Marissa leaned back, arms folded. "Bellamy, if you're here to scold, get in line."

Bellamy glanced at her, then at the guidance sheet on her desk. His eyebrows rose, and Adrian could see the precise moment the historian's mind categorized it as cultural artifact rather than warning.

"This is what we're doing now?" Bellamy asked. "Trading in church-bulletin superstition?"

Adrian held his ground. "Three people are missing."

Bellamy's expression softened by the smallest amount, not sympathy, but the recognition that missing persons were harder to dismiss than stories. "People go missing in the mountains," he said. "That is not proof of spectral lanterns."

"No one said spectral," Adrian replied.

Bellamy looked at him pointedly. "You didn't have to."

Marissa's gaze sharpened. "Adrian, tell him what Mercer told you."

Adrian hesitated. He heard Mercer's voice again; distance is the first thing that starts to lie.

He said it anyway, because the only way through academic warfare was to put the weapons on the table.

"Mercer says each disappearance started with someone following a light," Adrian said. "And he says the lights are changing. Getting closer to trails."

Bellamy snorted softly. "Lights don't change. Stories do."

Adrian felt the familiar triangle lock into place: his interpretive hunger, Marissa's skepticism of belief, Bellamy's distrust of anything that couldn't be footnoted.

Marissa tapped the witness statement again. "If this is contamination, then the most important factor isn't the light," she said. "It's the narrative. People are primed to interpret ambiguity as invitation."

Bellamy nodded, surprisingly aligned with her. "Exactly. The Brown Mountain Lights have been folded into tourism for a century. There were newspapers writing about them as early as the early twentieth century. Half the region's economy depends on making visitors feel like they've seen something unexplainable."

Adrian looked from one to the other, irritation mixing with something else, something steadier. They were both providing the counterweight he knew he needed.

"But what if you're wrong?" Adrian asked quietly.

Marissa's eyes narrowed. "About what?"

"About the direction of causality," Adrian said. "What if the stories didn't create the behavior? What if the behavior created the stories? What if there is something there that reliably produces the same human mistake?"

Bellamy's voice turned dry. "And what if it's train headlights?"

Adrian held his gaze. "Headlights don't respond to a whistle."

Bellamy's jaw tightened. "Neither do ghosts. People respond. They panic. They run. They misremember."

Marissa watched Adrian steadily. "You want us to come," she said, not as a question, but as a recognition of where his argument was headed.

Adrian didn't deny it. "I want you there because you won't let me turn this into a fable. And because if Mercer is right and this thing is escalating, then the last thing he needs is one professor wandering into the woods with a notebook and a hero complex."

Bellamy made a sound of reluctant annoyance. "You do have a hero complex."

"I have curiosity," Adrian said.

"Same disease," Bellamy replied.

Marissa picked up the guidance sheet again and stared at the line about lowering your eyes if a light approached. Her face had that thoughtful hardness she got when she was trying to locate the hidden social mechanism in a ritual.

"If we go," she said, "we treat this like fieldwork. Not a séance. We document the cultural framework and the environmental conditions. We interview locals. We track where sightings occur. We map the story as it moves through the community."

Adrian nodded. "Agreed."

Bellamy's eyes narrowed. "And I suppose you'll want to dig into archives too."

"Yes," Adrian said, because that was the truth. "Older reports. Newspaper clippings. Mining records. Anything that shows whether the pattern predates modern tourism."

Bellamy's expression sharpened at the word records, the way it always did. Historians mistrusted mystery, but they loved a paper trail.

Marissa looked at Bellamy. "You're considering it."

"I'm considering preventing Adrian from embarrassing the university," Bellamy said.

Adrian opened his mouth to argue, then closed it. He'd take Bellamy's insult if it got him to North Carolina with someone who could tell him, with irritating precision, when he was making narrative out of thin air.

Marissa set the papers down neatly, aligning the corners the way she did when she wanted control over something that resisted it.

"Fine," she said. "We go. But Adrian, listen to me."

He met her eyes.

"If this is contamination," she said, "then the most dangerous thing in the forest won't be a light. It will be the story you brought with you."

Adrian thought of Mercer's warning. The cost of paying attention.

He nodded once. "Then we'll bring the right kind of attention," he said. "The kind that doesn't chase."

Marissa didn't wait for either of them to change their minds.

She stood, went to the small whiteboard mounted beside her desk, and picked up a marker. The cap popped off with a sharp click that made Adrian think, irrationally, of Mercer describing a clicking sound in the woods.

Marissa wrote one word in clean, hard strokes.

Contamination.

Bellamy shifted his weight and watched her as if she'd just introduced a courtroom exhibit. Adrian remained standing near the door, the printed witness statement still on Marissa's desk, the guidance sheet aligned beneath it like an artifact awaiting interpretation.

"You keep saying that," Adrian said. "Define it."

Marissa didn't turn. "It's not supernatural," she said. "It's social. It's cognitive. It's what happens when a narrative becomes so well-known that it starts shaping the experience it supposedly explains."

She added a second word beneath the first.

Script.

Then she finally faced them, marker still in hand. "People don't just see something," she said. "They see it through a framework. And on Brown Mountain the framework is ready-made. Lights appear. The lights lure. Following the lights is dangerous. People disappear. That story is famous enough that tourists come to reenact it."

Bellamy nodded once, as if the word reenact pleased him. "It has been a performance for a long time," he said. "Newspaper columns, postcards, roadside overlooks. You can buy a T-shirt."

Adrian felt his jaw tighten. "That doesn't account for Mercer's reports. For Jesse Pruitt."

"It accounts for Jesse Pruitt more than you want it to," Marissa said.

Adrian opened his mouth, but she held up the marker, not as a threat but as a pause. "Listen," she said, and her voice softened by a fraction, enough to signal she wasn't trying to win an argument for sport. "I'm not saying there is nothing on that mountain. I'm saying the most reliable mechanism we have is the human brain under low visibility, stress, and expectation."

She turned back to the board and drew a simple loop.

Expectation. Interpretation. Behavior. Outcome.

"Expectation," she said, tapping the first word. "You arrive already primed. You've heard the Brown Mountain Lights story. Or you've heard a version of it. Even if you claim you don't believe it, you know it. The brain stores the shape of a narrative even when it rejects the conclusion."

She tapped the second. "Interpretation. You see an ambiguous light source across a valley. Distance is difficult at night in mountains. Fog compresses depth. A small light can appear close. It can appear to hover. And once you interpret it as meaningful, your attention locks."

Bellamy's expression tightened with familiarity. "Witnesses become unreliable once they've decided the event is extraordinary," he said, as if quoting a textbook.

Marissa didn't disagree. "Behavior," she continued, tapping the third word. "You move. You step off trail for a better view. You leave a safety of the path because the story tells you this is a moment. This is the part where something happens."

Her gaze flicked to Adrian then, direct and pointed.

"And outcome," Marissa said, tapping the fourth. "You get lost. You fall. You hit a ravine. Hypothermia. Injury. Panic. And then the outcome feeds the expectation. Another disappearance becomes another story that reinforces the script."

Adrian watched the loop on the board. It was clean. It was plausible. It made him uneasy precisely because it explained so much without explaining everything.

"You're assuming the light is ordinary," he said.

"I'm assuming the light is not required for the pattern," Marissa replied. "That's the difference. You want the lights to be the agent. I'm saying the agent might be the narrative."

Bellamy leaned forward slightly. "This is why I tried to stop you from turning this into your next monograph," he told Adrian. "You are already granting the phenomenon intent."

Adrian felt heat rise. "Mercer says the lights are changing. Getting closer to trails."

Marissa's gaze didn't waver. "Of course they are. Because people are changing the environment around the story. More visitors. More cameras. More people actively looking for them near the trails at dusk. You create a feedback system. People gather at overlooks. They use flashlights. Headlamps. Phone screens. A light appears, someone points, suddenly you have ten more light sources. Then those photos go online and become 'evidence,' which primes the next group. Contamination spreads."

She walked back to her desk and picked up the witness statement Adrian had brought. She held it at the corner, as if she didn't want to smear the ink of someone else's fear.

"This line," she said, reading. "'It felt like it was waiting. Like it wanted him to come look.'"

Adrian's throat went dry because he'd heard something like it before. Ryan Dalton's friend, in Eli Foster's briefing: like it was waiting.

Marissa looked up. "That's not a description of light behavior. That's a description of perceived social intent. The brain is a pattern machine. It will assign agency to anything that behaves oddly, especially when the story already says agency is there."

Bellamy made a small, approving sound. "Anthropomorphism," he said.

Adrian took a step closer, unable to stop himself. "Then what about the specificity?" he asked. "Whistling. Not calling it by name. Lowering your eyes. Those rules aren't generic. They're not simply 'don't go out at night.' They're interaction rules."

Marissa's mouth tightened. "Interaction rules exist in lots of danger traditions. You don't make noise near a bear. You don't run from a predator. You don't look directly at something you think might be a threat. People formalize what feels like it works. They ritualize caution until it becomes moral law."

Adrian shook his head. "But Mercer says one light changed direction immediately when someone whistled. That's not just 'fear is decorative.' That's a reported stimulus response."

Marissa set the paper down. "Reported," she emphasized. "In a situation with adrenaline, darkness, fog, uneven terrain, and a narrative already planted in the mind. Adrian, I've done fieldwork in regions where everyone believes a particular river bend is cursed. Every drowning happens there, and every survivor describes the water as pulling. Do you know what's actually there?"

"A current," Bellamy offered, smug.

"A submerged concrete slab from an old bridge project," Marissa said. "It creates a localized undertow. The story formed because something real was dangerous. But the story also made people more likely to treat the bend as special. They went there to prove it. They went there to tempt it. That increased exposure. More drownings. Stronger story. That's contamination. It's not fake. It's self-reinforcing."

Adrian stood very still. He understood her point too well, and that was the problem. Folklore had always been a negotiation between the literal and the symbolic. Between the thing that happened and the story that survived. Marissa was arguing that the story had become an accelerant.

Bellamy crossed his arms. "And the mining records?" he asked Adrian, as if daring him to claim they involved subterranean spirits. "You mentioned wanting to see whether the pattern predates tourism. Fine. But be careful what you consider evidence. People in 1890 were not immune to hysteria. They were better at it."

Adrian gave him a look. "You think every report is hysteria."

"I think most reports are human," Bellamy replied. "And humans are suggestible. Especially in groups."

Marissa nodded. "Group dynamics are part of contamination too. Witnesses share descriptions. They standardize language. They correct one another's memories without meaning to. Then when someone later recalls the event, they recall the version the group agreed on."

Adrian's mind flashed to the way Mercer had spoken, controlled and careful, as if he were terrified of sounding irrational. The way he'd carried the guidance sheet as if it were both superstition and procedure.

“And yet,” Adrian said, voice low, “the rules exist. Long before social media. Long before tourism. Someone wrote ‘Do not whistle’ and put it in a church bulletin. Someone decided naming it mattered.”

Marissa’s eyes softened again, the smallest concession. “Yes,” she said. “Which means at some point there was either a consistent set of experiences, or a consistent set of fears. Or both. I’m not saying your work has no value, Adrian. I’m saying that if we go down there assuming the lights are an intelligent lure, we will behave differently. We will create our own contamination.”

That landed hard.

Bellamy looked between them. “So we agree, then,” he said. “If we go, we treat it as an investigation of perception, environment, and historical context. Not a hunt for an entity.”

Adrian felt himself bristle at the word hunt, because it implied sport, and he could still hear Mercer: running out of people to lose.

“You’re both acting like my curiosity is the only hazard,” Adrian said. “But skepticism can be a hazard too. People get killed dismissing a warning because it doesn’t fit their model.”

Marissa's gaze held his. "Agreed," she said. "Which is why I want the model on the table. Not hidden inside your language."

She went back to the board and wrote two more phrases beneath the loop.

Environmental risk. Narrative risk.

"We map both," she said. "We collect reports without leading questions. We document weather conditions. Visibility. Lines of sight to roads, towns, rail lines. We track who has heard which version of the story. Where. From whom. We examine how the community teaches the rules."

Bellamy's eyes narrowed thoughtfully. "And we look for older documentation," he said. "Newspaper accounts. Survey reports. Mining ledgers. If the story shifts over time, I can show you how."

Marissa capped the marker and set it down. "And you," she told Adrian, "do what you're actually good at. You listen. You notice patterns. But you don't make it a creature just because you want one."

Adrian swallowed, then nodded once. He didn't like the framing, but he couldn't deny the discipline of it. If something on Brown Mountain was real and dangerous, then the last thing they could afford was to be predictable.

He reached for his phone and scrolled to Mercer's contact, thumb hovering over the call button.

Marissa watched him. "What are you going to tell him?" she asked.

Adrian looked at the contamination loop on the board one more time and felt, in a way that surprised him, grateful for the argument. It wasn't a dismissal. It was a guardrail.

"I'm going to tell him we're coming," Adrian said. "And that we're not going to chase the story he's scared of."

Bellamy's mouth tightened. "Good."

Adrian hit call anyway, because whatever else was true, there were three missing people whose families didn't care what category the danger fell into.

The phone rang.

And while it did, Adrian thought of the line Mercer had given him, the one that had lodged under his ribs like a splinter: distance is the first thing that starts to lie.

If the story was a contaminant, then the mountain already had the perfect delivery system.

All it had to do was glow.

Mercer answered on the second ring.

"Cross," he said, not quite a greeting, more a confirmation that Adrian had not decided to stay safely academic after all.

"We're in," Adrian replied. He kept his voice neutral, aware that Marissa and Bellamy were listening for any hint of melodrama. "But we're coming as a team, and we're coming with rules."

There was a pause on the line. Adrian could hear faint room noise behind Mercer, the hollow echo of a building with hard floors and too much fluorescent light.

"Good," Mercer said finally. "Because the last thing I need is another person with curiosity and no brakes."

Adrian's mouth tightened in a brief, humorless acknowledgment. "I'm bringing Marissa Calder."

On the other side of the phone, Mercer exhaled. "The anthropologist."

"Yes."

"She's the skeptic," Mercer said.

"She's the guardrail," Adrian corrected.

A sound that might have been Mercer's attempt at a laugh came through the receiver, brief and dry. "Bring her. I'll take guardrails."

Adrian glanced at Marissa. She had her arms folded, expression unreadable, but her eyes were sharp. Bellamy hovered behind her desk, already looking like he regretted agreeing to anything that involved fieldwork.

"And Henry Bellamy," Adrian added.

This time Mercer didn't respond immediately.

"The historian?" he asked, as if Adrian had offered to bring a man made entirely of footnotes.

"He's… thorough," Adrian said.

Mercer made a low sound of acceptance. "Fine. But I'm not babysitting faculty egos on a ridge at midnight."

"You won't have to," Adrian said, though the lie tasted optimistic. "Tell me what you need from us before we arrive."

Mercer's answer came with the clipped efficiency of someone who had been running the same mental checklist for months.

"First, time. If you can get here by tomorrow evening, you'll have a good chance to see them. They've been active almost every night this week. Second, discretion. Don't announce it. Don't post it. Don't turn it into a spectacle. Third, I'm putting you up at the station. I want you close."

Marissa lifted her chin slightly, as if she disliked the idea of being housed under a ranger's supervision.

Adrian said, "Understood."

"And Cross," Mercer added, voice lowering. "I'm not exaggerating the rule about following lights."

Adrian thought of the whiteboard loop in Marissa's office. Expectation, interpretation, behavior, outcome. Thought of how easy it would be to turn that loop into a self-fulfilling disaster.

"We're not chasing anything," Adrian said. "Observation only. Documentation. Interviews. Archive work."

Mercer's silence held for a beat, then softened into something close to relief.

"Good," he said. "Because I need people who can watch without stepping off the trail just because the mountain decides to blink."

They ended the call shortly after. Adrian lowered his phone and felt the strange sensation that always came after committing to fieldwork: a mixture of excitement and dread, braided so tightly he couldn't separate them.

Marissa immediately turned practical, the way she always did when the world threatened to become irrational.

"We need a protocol," she said.

Bellamy made a faint sound of agreement that carried the tone of a man reluctantly conceding there were ways to be foolish and ways to be less foolish.

Adrian nodded. "Mercer's housing us at the station. That helps. Controlled base. We're not improvising lodging in town."

Marissa's eyes narrowed. "Controlled by whom?"

"By the person with jurisdiction and the most experience with missing bodies," Adrian said. "Unless you'd prefer we rent a cabin and pretend we're on vacation."

Bellamy shifted his books against his chest. "Do you have any idea," he asked, "how many liability waivers I am about to violate by accompanying you?"

Adrian looked at him. "You came into Marissa's office on your own."

"Yes," Bellamy said, as if that were the start of his defense. "To stop you."

"And now?" Adrian asked.

Bellamy's mouth tightened. "Now I'm going to make sure your inevitable report doesn't confuse folklore with fact."

Marissa moved back to the whiteboard and, with the same clean strokes as before, added a short list beneath Environmental risk and Narrative risk.

No pursuit. No calling. No whistling. No separation.

She capped the marker and pointed at the last line. "We do not split up. Not on trails, not in towns, not in archives. If Mercer says radios are unreliable in that terrain, then we assume communication failure is normal."

Bellamy raised an eyebrow. "We're applying the premise before we've verified it."

"We're applying safety," Marissa replied. "You can call it premise if you want."

Adrian studied the list. No calling. No whistling. He felt the lines from the church bulletin press against his thoughts like fingerprints. It bothered him that the rules lined up so neatly across sources. It bothered him more that the rules were about attention, as if attention itself was the lever that moved whatever happened on Brown Mountain.

"What about equipment?" Adrian asked.

Marissa was already pulling up a notes app on her tablet. "Audio recorders," she said. "But passive. Not interactive. Environmental sensors if we can borrow them, temperature, humidity, barometric pressure. Cameras with low-light capability. Not phone cameras. And we need a map set that includes roads and rail lines. If Bellamy's train-headlight theory comes up, I want to be able to test sightlines."

Bellamy looked mildly offended at being reduced to a theory, but he nodded. "I'll bring historical maps," he said. "Topographic sheets. Survey reports. Old mine tract plats if I can find them in the library before we leave."

Adrian felt a tug of gratitude despite himself. Bellamy's obsession with paper trails might be their best way to anchor the phenomenon in something older than social media.

Marissa looked at Adrian. "And you," she said. "What are you bringing besides enthusiasm?"

He didn't bristle at the jab. It was earned.

"Interview framework," he said. "Open-ended, non-leading prompts. If we're testing contamination, we need to let people speak in their own terms without us handing them vocabulary."

She nodded once, approving despite herself. "Good. And we need to record who learned the story from where. Family. Church. Tourism. Internet. I want transmission pathways."

Bellamy adjusted his glasses. "And I want documentation prior to the tourism boom," he said. "If there are nineteenth-century references, mining records, early settler journals, anything that indicates the lights were described with consistent behavior before they became a commodity, that matters."

Adrian watched them for a moment, struck by the oddity of the scene: three academics building a field plan around a mountain light that might be nothing more than refraction, and might also be something that made radios go dead and men step off trails as if obeying a private command.

He should have felt ridiculous.

Instead he felt the gravity of it. Mercer had not come to campus because he wanted a debate. He had come because people were vanishing.

Marissa's voice cut into his thoughts. "There's another issue," she said. "Consent."

Adrian frowned. "For interviews?"

"For everything," Marissa said. "If the region is saturated with this story, locals may want to perform it for you. Or they may resent you for asking. Either way, we need to avoid becoming fuel. No sensationalism. No implying we're there to prove ghosts."

Bellamy's mouth thinned. "I never imply ghosts."

"You imply contempt," Adrian said, and then immediately regretted it.

Bellamy stared at him. "Fine," he said after a beat. "I will imply less contempt."

Marissa looked between them. "Good. Because Mercer's priority is search-and-rescue, not our academic posture."

Adrian checked the time. They had less than twenty-four hours if they wanted to arrive by tomorrow evening. He thought of the mountain in October, fog in the hollows, darkness coming early. Thought of Ryan Dalton's name in Mercer's mouth, and how easily a name became a file and then, if you weren't careful, became just another line in a lecture.

"Travel," Adrian said. "I'll book a rental car. One vehicle. We stay together. We go straight to the station."

Bellamy hesitated, and for the first time his reluctance looked less like stubbornness and more like something human.

"I want to make one thing clear," Bellamy said quietly. "I am not doing this because I believe the lights are sentient."

Marissa nodded, almost sympathetic. "Neither am I."

Adrian waited.

Bellamy's gaze held his, steady. "I'm doing it because people are missing. And because if there is an explanation, I'd prefer it be found by someone competent rather than by a tourist with a drone and a YouTube channel."

Marissa's voice softened by a degree. "That," she said, "is the most ethical thing you've said in months."

Bellamy looked vaguely insulted again, which meant the moment of sincerity had passed.

Adrian collected the papers from Marissa's desk, the copied guidance sheet and the witness statement, and slid them into a folder. He felt the weight of them as more than documents. They were fragments of a living tradition, and perhaps also, as Marissa would say, fragments of a script that could make them stupid if they weren't careful.

As they left Marissa's office, Adrian glanced back at the whiteboard.

Contamination. Script. Expectation. Interpretation. Behavior. Outcome.

No pursuit. No calling. No whistling. No separation.

The list looked simple, the way most deadly rules did.

In the hallway, students passed them laughing, backpacks slung over shoulders, busy with ordinary problems. Adrian felt the distance between campus life and the mountain widen and then, strangely, begin to shrink.

Because tomorrow night, if Mercer was right, they would be standing on a ridge in North Carolina with fog in the valleys and dark trees below, watching for something that had no business behaving like an invitation.

And Adrian knew, with an uneasy clarity, that reluctance wasn't the opposite of curiosity.

It was the only thing that might keep them alive.

Chapter 4

Into the Blue Ridge

The rental car smelled like lemon cleaner and someone else's long trip.

Adrian drove because it gave his hands something to do besides fidget. Marissa sat in the passenger seat with her tablet balanced on her knees, the screen throwing a pale light onto her face whenever the clouds thinned and daylight dimmed. Bellamy took the back seat with a tote bag of books and folded maps that looked like they had their own gravitational pull.

They left the flat, familiar geometry of campus highways behind before noon. By midafternoon the land began to rise in slow increments, the kind of elevation change you didn't notice until your ears adjusted and the horizon stopped being a line. The sky had the low, heavy look of October weather deciding whether it wanted to be rain or fog.

Marissa scrolled through a weather feed and spoke without looking up. "Visibility is going to be bad tonight. Low clouds along the ridges, fog in the valleys. Which means we'll get the perfect conditions for people to misjudge distance."

Bellamy made a small sound that could have been agreement. "Or to see exactly what they want to see."

Adrian kept his eyes on the road. Two-lane now, edged by stands of trees that looked darker than the rest of the world. The leaves were past their peak, colors drained toward brown and rust, and the forest had begun to show the bones of winter. Even in daylight it felt old. Not picturesque old. Old in the way stone foundations were old, indifferent to who came and went.

He glanced at the folder in the cup holder. Their printouts and notes. The copied guidance sheet. The witness statement. Marissa's loop written in his mind like a diagram burned into a board.

Expectation. Interpretation. Behavior. Outcome.

No pursuit. No calling. No whistling. No separation.

He heard Mercer's voice again, sharp with the kind of warning that came from repetition. Distance is the first thing that starts to lie.

They drove for a while without talking, each of them sunk into their own preparation. Adrian caught himself watching reflections in the windshield as the road bent, a habit he hadn't had before. Every brief glint on glass made him think of a pale orb hovering where it shouldn't.

Somewhere south of Asheville, the mountains stopped being a distant backdrop and became the whole frame. Blue ridges stacked against each other in layers; the farthest ones faded almost to gray. In the hollows between, mist pooled like trapped breath.

Bellamy leaned forward slightly, peering out the side window. "It's a deceptive landscape," he said.

Marissa looked up. "Deceptive how?"

"Historically," Bellamy said, as if the word was a shield. "People assume Appalachia is empty. It never was. Not in the way outsiders mean it. Every ridge has been walked, worked, cut, and named. Mines, logging, rail spurs. Whole economies folded into these slopes and then abandoned."

Adrian nodded. "And stories grow where abandonment leaves gaps."

Marissa gave him a sideways look. "Don't start narrating the scenery."

"I'm not," Adrian said, though he knew he was.

As the afternoon drained toward evening, they turned onto narrower roads. The lanes tightened, shouldered by rock and trees. The GPS voice began to sound uncertain, recalculating more often as if the mountain roads offended its sense of order. Adrian's hands stayed steady on the wheel, but his body registered each curve as a commitment. There was a feeling of being guided, not by intention but by terrain. You went where the land allowed.

Bellamy unfolded one of his maps in the back seat, paper crackling like dry leaves. "If Mercer's station is where I think it is," he said, "we're approaching the Linville Gorge region. Historically dense with logging routes."

Marissa's eyes returned to her tablet. "And modern sightlines. Roadways across valleys. That matters."

Adrian watched a ribbon of highway appear on the opposite slope, far away, like a scar cut into the trees. A single vehicle moved along it, a small bright speck that flashed once and then vanished behind a bend.

For a moment, the reflection of that moving light in the mist looked like it had floated free from the road.

Adrian's throat tightened.

He reminded himself, firmly, of Marissa's rules. Interpret before you mythologize. Name your variables. Resist the invitation to turn the landscape into a character.

Still, it was impossible not to feel the mountain's presence growing as they closed in. Not an ominous presence, not yet. More like the sensation you got when you approached an old house and realized, too late, that the windows were dark enough to hide anyone watching from behind the glass.

Their phones began to lose signal in pieces. First one bar, then none, then a brief flicker back to life before disappearing again. Marissa noticed and held her phone up in annoyance.

"This," she said, "is going to make data collection harder."

"Or quieter," Adrian replied.

Bellamy snorted. "Nothing about this will be quiet if you're right."

Adrian didn't answer. He didn't know what he was right about anymore. He only knew that Mercer had asked him to come, and that the ranger's fear had felt too practical to dismiss.

They reached Pisgah National Forest in the last hour of daylight. The sign by the roadside looked newly maintained, letters clean, the kind of federal assurance that implied you were entering managed wilderness. But beyond the sign the trees rose in dense ranks, and the road dipped into a corridor of shadow where the sun could not reach.

Marissa went still. "It's different here," she said.

Bellamy looked up from his map. "Different from what?"

"From places that feel like they've been tamed," she said. "This feels… layered."

Adrian understood what she meant. He felt it too. A sense that the forest held more than one version of itself at once: the tourist map version and the older version underneath it, the one that didn't care if you had a permit or a plan.

The ranger station appeared around a bend, set back from the road behind a small gravel lot. It was a low building with plain siding and a porch light already on, the warm yellow glow oddly comforting. A flag hung limp in the damp air. A wooden board near the entrance displayed trail notices and bear warnings. Standard. Ordinary.

And yet Adrian's eyes went to the tree line behind the building, where the forest started abruptly as if it had been waiting for the last human structure to end. The shadows between the trunks already looked thick, and the mist in the distance made depth hard to measure.

A man stepped out onto the porch as Adrian pulled into the lot.

Evan Mercer looked the same as he had in Adrian's office and yet not. On campus he had carried the mountain with him like a weight. Here, he looked more contained, as if the weight had found its proper place again. His uniform was neat, his posture steady, but his eyes flicked over the car with the quick scan of someone counting heads.

Adrian parked and shut off the engine. The sudden absence of road noise made the forest feel louder even though it wasn't. He heard a distant creek. A faint tap of something against the porch railing in the breeze.

Mercer came down the steps and stopped at the driver's side. "You made good time."

Adrian got out, and the cold hit him immediately, clean and sharp. It smelled of wet leaves and pine sap and rock. The air had a thinness to it, not high altitude exactly, but the feeling of a place that didn't retain heat easily.

"We drove straight through," Adrian said. "No detours."

Mercer's gaze shifted briefly to the ridge line visible through the trees. The daylight was fading fast, turning everything into shades of slate.

"You got here before dark," Mercer said. It sounded less like praise and more like relief.

Marissa stepped out next, stretching her shoulders as if she were shaking off the car's confinement. Bellamy followed, unfolding himself from the back seat with a grim expression and his tote bag clutched like a life preserver.

Mercer nodded to each of them in turn. "Dr. Calder. Professor Bellamy."

Marissa's eyebrows rose slightly at the fact that he knew them without introductions.

"I read," Mercer said, anticipating the question. "And I've been waiting for you."

Bellamy's mouth tightened. "That's one of those phrases that sounds worse out here."

Mercer didn't smile. "Get used to it."

He led them toward the station. The porch boards creaked underfoot. On the wall beside the door, a framed aerial photograph of the surrounding forest hung slightly crooked. Adrian saw faint penciled markings along the edge, circles and arrows. Search grids, he realized. The forest rendered into manageable shapes by ink.

Inside, the building smelled of coffee and damp wool. A radio base unit sat on a counter, its display lit, a quiet, constant static whispering from the speaker like an insect trapped in plastic. A bulletin board held missing persons flyers pinned alongside trail closure notices and a laminated map with red lines drawn in thick marker.

Mercer motioned them toward a small meeting room. A table. Four chairs. A stack of folders. A thermos.

"I've got reports for you," Mercer said. "Witness statements, times, locations. Photographs, where we have them. And before you ask, no, it's not everything. But it's enough to see the pattern."

Marissa sat and immediately started arranging her tablet and recorder with methodical care. Bellamy pulled out a pen and set one of his maps beside him, smoothing it flat as if he needed paper contact with the surface to feel stable.

Adrian remained standing for a moment, looking at the static-humming radio.

"Does it always do that?" he asked.

Mercer followed his gaze. "Out here? More often than not."

Adrian thought of Eli Foster's report, the way radios had gone silent all at once on the ridge, and felt the urge to ask a question he didn't want to ask. Not yet. He didn't want to build the story larger by giving it that shape.

Instead, he turned back to Mercer. "You said they've been active almost every night."

Mercer's expression darkened slightly. "Almost."

Marissa looked up. "What does 'almost' mean in this context?"

Mercer hesitated for the first time since they'd arrived. When he spoke again, his voice was lower.

"It means there are nights the lights don't show," he said. "And those are usually the nights we find new tracks where there shouldn't be tracks. Or we get a call from a family saying someone didn't come home."

Bellamy's pen paused above his notebook.

Marissa held Mercer's gaze. "That's correlation," she said carefully.

"I know what correlation is," Mercer replied. His tone wasn't angry, but it carried fatigue. "I also know when a pattern starts to feel like a schedule."

Adrian finally sat. The chair scraped softly against the floor, too loud in the room's quiet.

Mercer set a folder in front of him. The top page held a photo of a young man with a campus smile.

Ryan Dalton.

Adrian's fingers tightened at the edge of the paper, not from sentimentality, but from the sudden awareness of stakes. This wasn't a lecture example anymore. This was a face that had walked off a trail into fog.

Mercer leaned his hands on the table. "Before we do anything," he said, "we go over rules."

Marissa's mouth tightened. "We already have a protocol."

Mercer nodded once. “Good. Then it’ll match mine.”

He looked at each of them in turn, and Adrian saw the thing Mercer had carried into the university now fully at home in his eyes. Not superstition. Not theatrics. The hard-won caution of a man who had watched other people make the same mistake in different bodies.

“No pursuit,” Mercer said. “No calling out to anything you can’t see clearly. No whistling. No separation. If you see a light, you tell me. You do not step toward it, not even one pace, not even for a better view.”

Bellamy’s pen resumed moving, but slower.

Marissa nodded once, as if conceding that sometimes the story and the safety procedure were the same thing.

Adrian thought of the guidance sheet in Mercer’s hand, passed through churches like a sacrament of fear. He thought of how those rules had survived because they were easy to remember and hard to keep.

Mercer straightened. “You’re here now,” he said. “So I’m going to be blunt.”

He glanced toward the window, where the last of daylight had thinned into gray. Beyond the glass the forest stood in silent ranks, patient.

"The mountain doesn't care who you are," Mercer said. "It doesn't care what you believe. But if you give it attention the wrong way, it will take that as agreement."

Adrian felt the hair on his arms lift, not with terror, but with recognition. The word agreement was another version of invitation turned inside out.

Outside, the porch light glowed steadily. Ordinary. Human.

And somewhere beyond that circle of warmth, Brown Mountain waited, unseen in the thickening dusk, like a subject that had finally noticed the researchers were in the room.

Mercer didn't give them time to settle into the safety of fluorescent light and paper.

He let the rules hang for a moment, then pushed a second folder across the table toward Marissa. "Weather logs," he said. "Visibility, wind, cloud ceiling. The nights we've had strong displays, there's a pattern. Not perfect. But it repeats enough that I've stopped calling it coincidence."

Marissa opened the folder and began scanning, her expression doing that subtle recalibration Adrian had come to recognize: skepticism shifting into focus. Not belief, but interest.

Bellamy didn't touch the folders yet. He was watching Mercer instead, as if the ranger might accidentally reveal how much of this was fear and how much was performance.

Adrian asked the simplest question first. "Where are we watching from?"

Mercer stood, already reaching for a set of keys on a hook by the door. "There's an overlook about fifteen minutes from here," he said. "Not the tourist pull-off. A service access point we keep gated. Clear sightline across the valley. If they show, you'll see them there."

"And if they show closer?" Marissa asked.

Mercer looked at her. "Then we leave."

Bellamy's mouth tightened. "That's your professional plan?"

"That's my plan to keep you alive," Mercer replied, and there was no heat in it. Only fatigue.

They layered up in the small entry area of the station. The cold had thickened outside, damp and persistent rather than sharp. Adrian zipped his coat, feeling the scratch of the guidance sheet copy in his inner pocket like a reminder he hadn't earned. Marissa strapped a recorder case across her body and checked her tablet battery twice. Bellamy brought a notebook, a pen, and a small pair of binoculars he seemed mildly embarrassed to own.

Before they stepped out, Mercer opened a drawer and handed each of them a small red lens attachment for their flashlights.

"No white beams unless you have to," he said. "Red preserves night vision. And it doesn't throw as far."

Marissa accepted hers with a nod, as if she'd suggested it first. Bellamy looked at the red lens as though it were a superstitious charm.

"What about radios?" Adrian asked.

Mercer clipped one to his vest. "We'll have them," he said. "But don't count on them. And don't keep keying the mic if you get static. Sound carries out there."

Bellamy glanced up. "Sound carries through rock?"

Mercer held his gaze. "Sound carries," he said simply. "That's all you need to remember."

The drive out was short but winding, the road narrowing into a ribbon of asphalt with trees pressing in close. The car headlights made the forest look like it began and ended in sudden white slices. Beyond them, darkness filled in everything else, thick and uncurious.

Marissa watched the temperature gauge on her tablet. "Dropping," she murmured. "And humidity's high."

"Fog," Bellamy said from the back seat, not entirely mocking now.

Mercer nodded. "In the hollows. On the ridges it comes and goes like it's breathing."

They reached a gate set into a gravel turnout. Mercer unlocked it and drove through, then relocked it behind them. Adrian noticed how the click of the padlock sounded too loud in the surrounding quiet.

They parked near a low wooden barrier and continued on foot along a service path. Their boots crunched softly on gravel, then on packed earth. The forest on either side was dense enough to swallow their shapes if they stepped off the trail by two feet.

Adrian kept his gaze forward, resisting the instinct to scan for movement between trunks. That instinct was old and human and unhelpful. Mercer had warned them: attention the wrong way could be agreement.

The overlook was not dramatic. No railings. No signs. Just a natural opening where the trees thinned and the ground sloped toward a rock outcrop. Beyond it, the valley dropped away into layers of shadow.

The far ridge was a darker line against a slightly lighter sky. A few stars pushed through thin cloud, faint and cold. Below them, fog lay pooled in the ravine like a slow spill, shifting in silent currents.

Mercer gestured them into positions that kept them close but not clustered. "Stay on the path," he said again, as if repetition could carve it into muscle. "No one steps onto the rock lip. The drop is worse than it looks at night."

Bellamy made a small sound of irritation. "I'm aware of gravity."

Mercer didn't rise to it. He set a small tripod on the ground and mounted a low-light camera, then angled it toward the far ridge. The movements were practiced, almost routine, which told Adrian this was not Mercer's first vigil.

Marissa took out a handheld anemometer and held it up, then checked her tablet again. "Wind is minimal," she said quietly, more to herself than anyone. "Cloud ceiling low."

Bellamy lifted his binoculars and peered across the valley. "If there are roads over there," he said, "we may be able to match any appearance with a vehicle movement."

"Good," Marissa said. Her voice was calm, but Adrian could hear the effort behind it. Calm as discipline. "We're not here to be impressed. We're here to observe."

Adrian stood slightly behind Mercer, hands in his pockets, feeling the cold find the gaps around his cuffs. He tried to catalog sensations the way he did in interviews. Smell: wet leaves and pine. Sound: almost none. A distant creek maybe, muffled. No insects. No birds. The absence of small life made the valley feel staged.

Eli Foster's words from Mercer's earlier reports drifted into Adrian's mind: too quiet.

They waited.

Minutes stretched in a way that made time feel less like a line and more like a thickening substance. Adrian found himself checking the edges of his perception, watching for the moment his eyes would start making shapes out of nothing.

Marissa spoke once, very softly. "This is when contamination happens," she said. "The longer you stare into low visibility, the more your brain insists on resolving ambiguity."

Bellamy didn't lower the binoculars. "So if we see something, it might be because we wanted to."

"And if we don't see something," Marissa said, "it might be because the story expects a show and the environment didn't provide one."

Mercer's voice came low and flat. "If we see something, it'll be because it's there."

That ended the discussion for a moment.

Adrian looked down into the fog-filled hollow and felt a faint pressure behind his eyes, like the beginning of a headache. He tried to blink it away. The fog made depth tricky. He could see the suggestion of treetops below, darker masses within darker masses.

Then, far out across the valley, a small white point appeared.

It wasn't bright. Not at first. It was subtle enough that Adrian's first thought was a star sliding through a gap in cloud. But it wasn't in the sky. It was lower, near the line of trees on the far ridge.

Bellamy saw it at the same time. "There," he murmured, and his voice held the careful satisfaction of a man who had waited for his skepticism to be rewarded.

Marissa lifted her tablet, already checking time stamps. Mercer didn't move except to angle his head slightly, as if listening for something that would confirm what his eyes already knew.

The light held steady for several seconds.

Then it moved sideways.

Not along the ridge line in the way a car might travel a distant road. Sideways relative to the tree line, smooth and controlled, as if it didn't care what terrain existed beneath it.

Bellamy lowered his binoculars a fraction. "Refraction," he said, but the word came out less confident than Adrian expected.

A second light appeared several hundred yards to the left of the first. Then a third, slightly lower, hovering at a different height. Each one was a clean, steady glow without a visible source. They did not flicker like fire. They did not sweep like a beam.

The valley began to feel populated.

Marissa's voice tightened, not with fear, but with concentration. "Multiple points. Variable elevation."

Mercer nodded once. "That's how it starts."

Adrian kept his hands in his pockets to stop himself from doing the stupid thing his body wanted to do, which was step forward as if closeness would turn uncertainty into clarity. The lights didn't look close, exactly. They looked present. And he realized, with a faint internal jolt, what Mercer had meant about distance lying. The lights were across the valley, objectively far, and yet his nerves reacted as though they had entered his immediate space.

Bellamy raised his binoculars again and tracked one light as it drifted downward, then paused midair. "If that's a vehicle," he said, "it's driving through trees."

Marissa didn't answer. She was watching a different one, lips parted slightly, as if she were trying not to breathe too loudly.

The lights multiplied gradually, not all at once. A handful became a scattered constellation along the far ridge and just above it, some higher, some lower. Fog caught their glow and softened it, making the air itself look faintly luminous in patches.

Adrian noticed a pattern he didn't want to claim too early: when one light stopped, another would drift closer to it, as if the stopping was a signal.

He thought of the rule from the church bulletin. When the light stops, you stop.

Mercer shifted beside him, and his boot scraped the ground with a soft, accidental sound.

One of the lights, far across the valley, changed direction.

It didn't swing wide. It didn't meander. It turned with an abruptness that made Adrian's stomach tighten, and began moving toward their position, cutting across the dark gap between ridges as if the valley were not a distance but a hallway.

Marissa's head lifted. Bellamy went still. Even Mercer's posture changed, shoulders tightening as if bracing against impact.

"That one," Mercer said quietly, "has been doing that more often."

Bellamy's voice came out low. "Toward us?"

Mercer didn't look away from the approaching glow. "Toward whoever's watching," he corrected.

"It's not always the same person. But it's always someone."

Adrian felt the irrational urge to speak, to announce himself, to do the ancient human thing of trying to control uncertainty with language. He swallowed it down. No calling. No whistling.

The light continued its steady approach. It did not hurry. It did not hesitate. It moved with the patient certainty of something that expected to be met halfway.

Adrian became intensely aware of his own face, as if it were suddenly a vulnerable surface. He remembered Ruth Calhoun's warning from Mercer's earlier mention: do not let it see your face. It learns you.

He hadn't met Ruth Calhoun yet. He hadn't heard those words directly. But the guidance sheet in his pocket might as well have been warm against his ribs.

The light stopped.

It hovered above the near treeline on their side of the valley now, not over the far ridge. The distance it had crossed felt impossible given the time, unless Adrian's perception of its position had been wrong from the start. That was the trick, he realized. The mountain didn't have to break physics. It only had to make you unsure where the physics were happening.

Bellamy lowered his binoculars completely. "That's not a car," he admitted, and the admission sounded like it hurt.

Marissa's voice was barely audible. "Mercer," she said, "how close is that?"

Mercer didn't answer immediately. He did not step forward to measure. He did not raise his voice. He stood exactly where he was, as if the stillness itself were a form of refusal.

"Close enough," he said finally, "that we're done for tonight if it moves any nearer."

The light held steady above the treetops, a pale, watchful presence. It did not flicker. It did not pulse. It simply existed, and in its steadiness, Adrian felt something that unsettled him more than motion would have.

Attention.

Not his attention toward it. Its attention toward them.

Then, as if to prove Mercer's point about escalation, a second light appeared lower, just inside the dark line of trees below the overlook. Not in the valley. Not across the gap. On their side.

Marissa made a small, involuntary sound. Bellamy's hand tightened around his binoculars.

Mercer's voice turned firm. "Back," he said. "All of you. Slow. Stay together. Eyes down."

Adrian took his first careful step away from the edge, and felt the strange, stubborn pull of curiosity trying to anchor him in place.

He moved anyway, because he could feel how easily a story became a script, and how quickly a script became a disappearance.

Mercer led them back along the service path without turning it into a run.

Adrian felt the difference immediately, the way disciplined movement could keep fear from becoming theater. Their red-filtered beams stayed low, painting the ground in muted rust. Gravel, then packed dirt, then a thin mat of wet leaves that made every step sound louder than it should have. The forest still did not answer them with the usual night noises. No sudden scurry. No insect whine. Only their breathing and the faint knock of Bellamy's binoculars against his coat when he forgot to hold them steady.

Behind them, somewhere beyond the outcrop, the pale light held its position above the treeline. Adrian did not look back to confirm. Mercer had said eyes down, and Adrian understood the instruction in a way that bypassed rational argument. Looking back felt like a kind of reply.

Marissa kept close enough that Adrian could hear her exhale through her nose, controlled, measured. Bellamy walked on Adrian's other side, stiff with the effort of not making commentary.

Mercer stopped once at a bend where the trees thickened, raised a hand, and waited until all three of them halted. He listened, head slightly angled.

Adrian listened too, straining for anything. Footsteps that weren't theirs. A crack of branch. A whisper of wind.

Nothing.

Then, soft and almost delicate, something clicked.

It wasn't loud. It wasn't close enough to locate. It reminded Adrian of the sound Mercer had described back on campus, stones tapped together. It might have been a rock shifting in a far-off streambed. It might have been an animal jaw working in the dark.

It might have been neither.

Mercer didn't move for another three seconds. Then he lowered his hand and resumed walking, as if refusing to dignify the sound with reaction.

When they reached the gate, Mercer unlocked it with a practiced speed. The padlock clinked against the metal post, too sharp in the quiet. Adrian flinched at the sound and hated himself for it.

They piled into the vehicle. Mercer started the engine and pulled onto the road without turning on the cabin light. The headlights cut forward into the trees, turning trunks into brief white pillars and then leaving them behind. Adrian watched the side mirror anyway and regretted it at once. The darkness behind the car looked thicker than it should have, as if the night were following at the same pace.

Marissa broke the silence first.

"That second light," she said, voice low. "The one in the trees below us. Was it actually on our side, or did the fog make it look that way?"

Mercer kept his eyes on the road. "It was on our side."

Bellamy cleared his throat. "How can you be sure? Distance is tricky in—"

"I'm sure," Mercer cut in, and there was a finality in it that made Bellamy shut his mouth.

Adrian said nothing. He was replaying what he had felt when the light had approached: not speed, not menace in the usual sense, but certainty. The slow confidence of something that knew humans would translate movement into meaning. He thought again of Marissa's contamination loop, and realized with a tight, unpleasant clarity that whether the lights were natural or not, they behaved in a way that made the loop easier to complete.

Expectation. Interpretation. Behavior. Outcome.

All it took was a small bright point in the wrong place, and a human mind would do the rest.

Back at the station, Mercer parked under the porch light and herded them inside as if he didn't want the night to see them crossing the threshold.

Warm air and coffee smell hit Adrian with sudden relief. The constant hush of the base radio static seemed louder now, like the building itself exhaled on that frequency. Mercer locked the door behind them, then immediately regretted the gesture and glanced at the window as if locks were a superstition dressed up as policy.

Marissa shrugged out of her coat and began setting her equipment on the meeting table with brisk efficiency, as if turning experience into data could keep it from turning into fear. Bellamy dropped into a chair and stared at his hands for a moment before pulling his notebook toward him.

Mercer stayed standing. He looked like a man used to being awake at the wrong hours.

"Time," Marissa said, already recording. "Mercer, confirm. First light appeared at approximately—"

"Twenty-one fourteen," Mercer replied without looking at a clock. "First cluster by twenty-one seventeen. Approaching behavior began about twenty-one twenty-two."

Bellamy's pen moved, scratchy and fast. "And the one below the treeline on our side?"

Mercer's jaw tightened. "Twenty-one twenty-six."

Adrian watched them work and felt a strange dissonance. It was what he always felt when something primal had happened and the intellect rushed in to put it in categories. Part of him wanted to argue about sightlines, refraction, headlights on distant roads. Another part of him remembered the way the light had stopped as if it had reached the correct distance for a conversation.

Marissa set the recorder down and looked at Mercer. "Has it done that before? Approached the overlook like that?"

Mercer hesitated just long enough for Adrian to register the weight behind the answer.

"Yes," Mercer said. "Not every night. But more often lately."

Bellamy's voice came out restrained, careful. "Approached you specifically, or the overlook?"

"The overlook," Mercer said. "Whoever's there."

"Tourists?" Marissa asked.

"Sometimes," Mercer said. "Sometimes us."

Adrian sat and rubbed his hands together, not for warmth but because the movement grounded him. "When it approaches," he asked, "what usually happens?"

Mercer's eyes flicked to him. "Usually, people do what you almost did tonight."

"What I almost did," Adrian repeated.

Mercer nodded once. "Step closer. Just a little. To see it better. To prove something. To take a picture. To make sense of it."

Marissa's gaze sharpened. "That doesn't mean the light is luring them. That means people are curious."

Mercer didn't argue. He looked tired enough to be beyond argument. "Curiosity is the lure," he said. "If you want to call it that."

Bellamy wrote that down, then seemed annoyed at himself for writing it down.

Adrian leaned forward. The question had been forming since the moment Mercer said closer than last time back on campus, since the moment Mercer said some nights they don't show and those are the nights someone doesn't come home. It had been sitting in Adrian like a stone.

He kept his voice even. "Mercer," he said, "I need to ask you something."

Mercer's attention settled on him. "Ask."

Adrian felt Marissa watching him, ready to correct his framing. Felt Bellamy waiting for a question he could dismiss as melodrama.

Adrian asked anyway.

"Have any of the missing hikers been found?"

The room went very still, and the base radio's static seemed to swell, filling the silence like water rising.

Mercer's expression didn't change. But something hardened behind his eyes, the part that had learned how to keep grief from interfering with procedure.

"No," Mercer said.

One syllable. Flat. Final.

Adrian nodded slowly, as if the movement could absorb the meaning. In his mind, names turned into places: Ryan Dalton's keycard clipped into a sleeve, Hannah Briggs's tripod abandoned on a slope, Jesse Pruitt's hat by a ravine. Objects without bodies. Evidence without resolution.

Marissa broke the silence first, because she couldn't tolerate it lingering.

"Not even remains?" she asked, and her voice held the careful tone of someone who knew she was stepping on pain but needed the information.

Mercer shook his head once. "Not a scrap," he said. "No blood. No clothing. No gear. Nothing you can point at and say, yes, this is where the mountain was finished with them."

Bellamy looked up sharply. "That's unusual."

Mercer's mouth twitched in something that wasn't humor. "It's worse than unusual," he said. "It's clean."

Marissa's eyebrows drew together. "Clean how?"

Mercer didn't answer immediately. He walked to the bulletin board near the radio base unit and pulled down a laminated map. Red lines marked search grids. Yellow pins indicated last known points. Adrian recognized one of the labels: Overlook Spur. Another: Ridge Service Gate. Another, further downslope: Lower Ravine Line.

Mercer tapped one pin with his finger. "Ryan Dalton," he said. "We found his keycard and part of his hoodie. No body. Dogs lost scent near the ravine. Drones found nothing. Nothing snagged in brush. Nothing in the creek."

He moved his finger to another pin. "Hannah Briggs. Same pattern. She left her tripod. Prints down the slope. Then nothing. Like she stepped out of the world at a specific line."

Bellamy's voice went quiet. "And Jesse Pruitt."

Mercer's finger paused over the third pin. "Hat near the ravine," he said. "No further signs."

Marissa stared at the map as if she could force it to explain itself. "That could be water," she said, though her tone wasn't confident. "If someone fell in, the current—"

Mercer looked at her. "We searched the water," he said. "We searched it again. And again. We search it every time the lights get active, because we keep hoping the mountain will be ordinary."

Adrian felt a chill slide down his spine that had nothing to do with temperature. Not because the idea was supernatural. Because Mercer's words made it sound like the mountain had choices.

Bellamy set his pen down carefully. "If there are no bodies," he said, "then either the terrain is hiding them extraordinarily well, or… or we're not dealing with the usual failure mode."

Marissa's jaw tightened. "Or we're dealing with human factors we haven't identified. Someone could be using the story to cover—"

Mercer cut her off, not harshly, but with a weary force. "We've considered it," he said. "We've looked for signs of foul play. Tire tracks. Camps. Anything. But the pattern lines up with sightings, and it lines up with behavior that happens fast. People step off trail and they're gone before anyone can stop them."

He paused, then added, quieter, "Like they're answering something."

Marissa looked as if she wanted to argue, then didn't. Adrian saw her swallow it down, the way she'd swallowed her reaction at the overlook. Guardrails, he thought. She was trying to keep her mind from sliding into the same groove the story carved.

Adrian's gaze went to the window. Darkness beyond. Trees crowded with it.

He thought of Mercer's rules. No pursuit. No calling. No whistling. No separation.

And underneath those rules, the older ones, passed around in churches and spoken on porches: When the light stops, you stop. When it turns, you turn away. Do not let it see your face.

He had come here expecting to watch a phenomenon.

Instead, he realized, they were standing at the edge of an absence. A series of missing endings.

Adrian looked back at Mercer. "So, what are we doing tomorrow?" he asked, and heard the ominous second question beneath his own words. Not what is our plan, but what is the mountain's.

Mercer held his gaze, and for the first time since they'd arrived, he looked less like a ranger and more like a man forced into a role by something he couldn't resign from.

"Tomorrow," Mercer said, "we talk to the people who still remember the rules. Then we find out where those rules came from."

He glanced once more toward the window, as if checking whether the night had moved closer.

"And Cross," he added, voice low. "You asked if we've found them."

Adrian nodded.

Mercer's eyes didn't soften. "The better question is whether the mountain means for us to."

Chapter 5

The Rule No One Keeps

Morning came the way it did in the mountains: not with sunrise so much as with a gradual thinning of darkness.

Adrian woke on a narrow cot in a spare room at the ranger station, the kind meant for visiting staff and emergency overflow. The blanket smelled faintly of detergent and old smoke, and the air felt damp enough to make his lungs notice. For a few seconds he lay still, listening for the sounds that usually stitched a morning together. Birds. Wind. A distant engine.

He heard none of those.

What he did hear was the low, constant whisper of the radio base unit out in the main room. Static, almost gentle, like the building was breathing through a clogged throat.

He sat up, rubbed his face, and tried to orient himself by the square of gray light at the small window. The forest beyond it was nothing but vertical trunks and a haze of fog pressed between them. Daylight made everything look less theatrical, and yet it didn't ease the sensation that the night before had left behind something unfinished.

He dressed quietly, pulling on the same clothes he'd worn on the overlook, as if changing them would be a kind of denial. When he stepped into the hall, he found Marissa already awake at the small table in the meeting room, hair pulled back, tablet open, fingers moving in quick, precise taps. A paper cup of coffee sat untouched at her elbow.

She didn't look up right away. "You slept?"

"A little," Adrian said.

Bellamy's voice came from somewhere behind a half-open door. "Some of us slept perfectly well," he called, and Adrian could hear in it the determined cheerfulness of a man trying to prove he was not the type to be unsettled by a light in the trees.

Marissa's eyes lifted briefly. "Lying to yourself doesn't count as rest," she said.

Bellamy made a sound that might have been a scoff, then emerged fully, jacket already on, his notebook in hand as if he feared facts might escape while he blinked. He looked more rumpled than usual, and his glasses had a faint smudge on one lens, but his posture was still stubbornly composed.

"We saw lights," he said, as if summarizing a mildly inconvenient weather event. "We did not see an entity."

"No one said entity," Marissa replied.

Adrian poured himself coffee from the station's battered pot and tasted bitterness strong enough to feel like a warning. "We saw something," he said, keeping his voice neutral. "Something that didn't behave like a car."

Bellamy's mouth tightened. "I said we saw lights."

Before Adrian could respond, the screen door creaked and Ranger Mercer stepped in, bringing the cold with him. His uniform looked the same as it had the night before, but his eyes were sharper, the way they got after too many hours without sleep. He carried a thin folder under one arm and a single sheet of paper in his hand.

"Sheriff's office called," Mercer said. "Nothing new overnight."

Nothing new, Adrian thought, and hated how quickly his mind translated it into nothing worse. As if the absence of fresh disappearance was a kind of blessing.

Mercer set the folder down and looked at them in turn. "Before we go talk to locals, there's something I want you to see."

Marissa straightened slightly. Bellamy's pen appeared in his hand as if conjured. Adrian took a sip of coffee and waited.

Mercer placed the sheet of paper on the table between them.

It was a photocopy, and not a clean one. The black toner had faded in places, and the edges were slightly crooked. At the top was a simple title in block letters:

Guidance for Evening Travel in the Brown Mountain Region

Beneath it were short lines, each one blunt enough to belong in a safety briefing, and yet written with the cadence of something meant to be repeated aloud.

Do not travel the slopes after sundown. Do not answer voices from the trees. Do not follow lights. If a light approaches, lower your eyes and back away. Do not whistle to it. Do not call it by name.

Adrian felt his fingers tighten around his cup.

He had seen the guidance sheet before, on campus, in Mercer's hand. But seeing it here, in the place where the rules were supposedly born, made it feel less like a folkloric artifact and more like a procedure that had outlived the people who first needed it.

Marissa leaned in, eyes scanning the list. "You said this came from local churches."

"Not official churches," Mercer said. "Not denominational leadership. Just… back tables. Bulletins. Women's groups. Old men who didn't want to sound crazy but didn't want to bury another cousin either."

Bellamy frowned at the paper as if it offended him by existing. "This is undated."

"It's been reprinted," Mercer said. "A lot. My grandmother's copy was older than I was. And her mother had one too. Maybe not this exact layout, but the same rules. Same phrasing, mostly."

Adrian traced the lines with his eyes again. Do not answer voices from the trees.

"You've had reports of voices?" Marissa asked.

Mercer hesitated. A small pause, controlled. "Yes."

Bellamy's pen stopped. "Witnesses hearing voices in a foggy forest does not—"

"Bellamy," Marissa cut in, not unkindly, "let him talk."

Mercer nodded once, appreciation flickering and disappearing. "Usually it's distant," he said. "Someone's name, or something that sounds like it. Sometimes it's a call for help. The kinds of sounds that make a decent person turn their head."

Adrian remembered Ryan Dalton's friends describing the light like someone signaling. The overlap was too neat to ignore.

"And the rule about lowering your eyes," Marissa said, tapping that line lightly with one finger. "That's not a common wilderness safety instruction."

"No," Mercer agreed.

Bellamy leaned forward despite himself. "Is it symbolic?" he asked. "A gesture of humility? A religious carryover?"

Mercer's gaze stayed on the paper. "It might be," he said. "Or it might be practical."

Adrian looked up. "Practical how?"

Mercer's jaw tightened. "Because people say that if you look straight at it when it's close, it… fixes on you."

Bellamy let out a small, impatient breath. "And how would they know?"

Mercer's eyes lifted. There was no anger in them. Only the exhausted steadiness of someone who had already asked the same questions and found no comfort in them.

"They know because of what happens afterward," Mercer said. "Because the people who break the rules don't just get spooked. They get gone."

Silence settled over the table. The radio hissed softly in the background, indifferent.

Marissa broke the quiet first, voice careful. "I want to treat this as both, Mercer. Cultural practice and risk response. If these rules persist, it means they've been reinforced. Either by events or by the belief in events. Probably both."

Mercer nodded. "Fine. Call it what you want. But it's kept more folks alive than any trail sign."

Adrian's eyes caught on the line he had never managed to read without feeling a faint internal resistance.

Do not call it by name.

He heard his own voice from the night before, asking about missing hikers. He heard Mercer's reply. The better question is whether the mountain means for us to.

"What name?" Adrian asked now, though he'd asked it before.

Mercer's mouth flattened. "Depends on the family. Some call them lanterns, like the old stories about miners. Some call them watchers. Some call them the wandering. The Cherokee names I've heard, I won't try to pronounce wrong. And some people refuse to say anything at all."

Marissa's eyes narrowed slightly. "Refuse because of fear?"

Mercer considered. "Refuse because of respect. Or caution. Same difference in practice."

Bellamy tapped his pen against his notebook, a small staccato that made Adrian think of the clicking sound on the trail. Bellamy stopped at once, as if he'd made the connection too, and placed the pen down.

Adrian looked back to the list and felt the tug of pattern, the thing his mind always reached for in story. The rules weren't simply avoidant. They were interactive. Don't answer. Don't whistle. Don't call. Don't follow.

Rules about response.

Marissa seemed to reach the same conclusion. "This isn't just 'stay indoors at night,'" she said. "It's an instruction set for encountering something."

Mercer's expression didn't change. "That's how people use it," he said. "Whether that something is real or misinterpreted doesn't matter in the moment. What matters is what the rules keep you from doing."

Adrian stared at the sheet a little longer than he needed to. The language had a plainness to it that didn't feel like tourism. No flair. No storytelling. Just constraint.

"Where did this version come from?" Adrian asked.

Mercer reached into the thin folder he'd carried and pulled out another photocopy, this one showing a church name in faded type at the bottom. "Jonas Ridge Community Church," it read. "Somebody ran off a stack twenty years ago. Maybe more."

Marissa glanced at it, then at Mercer. "And you think the people who still remember the rules will talk to us."

"They'll talk," Mercer said. "Some of them. But you need to understand something before we go knocking on doors."

Bellamy looked up. "Which is?"

Mercer's voice lowered, not for drama, but because it sounded like the natural volume for truth in places that didn't like being overheard. "You're not the first outsiders to come asking. Some folks are tired of being treated like a storybook. Some are tired of being treated like fools. And some are tired of being treated like they're lying when they tell you what they saw."

Adrian nodded. "So, we listen."

Mercer's eyes stayed on him. "And we don't push," he said. "If someone tells you a rule, you don't laugh. You don't argue. You don't bait them into saying a name they don't want to say."

Bellamy's mouth tightened, but he didn't protest.

Marissa folded her hands. "We treat the sheet as an artifact of transmission," she said, more to establish the frame than to contradict Mercer. "We ask when they first heard it, who gave it to them, and what story they attach to each line."

Mercer nodded once. "Good. And Cross?"

Adrian looked up.

Mercer tapped the paper lightly, right on the line Adrian couldn't stop reading.

Do not follow lights.

"You saw how it feels," Mercer said. "That pull. The wanting to step closer. The brain telling you distance is shorter than it is."

Adrian swallowed. "Yes."

Mercer's gaze held his. "That's why I keep calling this the rule no one keeps," he said. "Because it doesn't feel like breaking a rule. It feels like being reasonable. Like you're just taking one step."

Bellamy spoke before Adrian could, voice controlled. "Then perhaps the rule should be more specific."

Mercer gave him a look that was almost sympathy. "You can't out-specify a thing that makes your judgment go soft," he said.

Marissa's eyes flicked to Adrian. "The story becomes a script," she murmured, almost to herself.

Mercer didn't seem to hear her or pretended not to. He gathered the copies back into the folder and slid one across the table to Adrian.

"Keep it," he said. "Not because paper has power. Because it's easy to forget rules when you think you're the exception."

Adrian took the sheet. The toner smudged slightly on his thumb. He folded it carefully, along the creases someone else had made years ago, and slid it into his coat pocket.

Outside, the fog pressed against the windows like a waiting hand.

Mercer picked up his keys. "Finish your coffee," he said. "Then we head into Jonas Ridge. There's a woman there who'll talk to you if she's in the mood. Ruth Calhoun. If you want to know where the rules came from, she's the closest thing you'll get to an answer that isn't written by a tourist bureau."

Bellamy stood, notebook ready. Marissa shut down her tablet screen and slipped it into its case.

Adrian stayed seated for one extra second, fingers on his coffee cup, feeling the paper's shape in his pocket like a second pulse.

Guidance for evening travel, he thought.

Not a legend. Not a metaphor.

A set of instructions for surviving something that, for reasons no one could fully explain, behaved as if it noticed when you responded.

Jonas Ridge looked like a town that had learned how to keep its head down.

The road narrowed as Mercer drove, trees pressing close on both sides, their branches bare enough to show the gray tangle of sky beyond. Fog sat in the low places, not thick like last night's valley fog but persistent, a damp breath that clung to fence lines and the corners of buildings. Brown Mountain itself was not visible from every angle, but its presence was. The land rose and folded in ways that made it feel as though the town had been built in the crease of something much larger.

They passed a small church with a white steeple and a hand-painted sign that listed service times and a fundraiser dinner. A gas station with one pump worked and one that looked like it hadn't in years. A few houses set back from the road under leafless trees. Adrian caught Bellamy staring out the window, his mouth set in the particular expression he wore when he was forcing himself to see people instead of eras.

"This is where your bulletin copy came from," Marissa said, glancing at the church as they passed.

Mercer nodded without taking his eyes off the road. "One version of it."

Bellamy made a noncommittal sound. “There’s always a version.”

“That’s the point,” Adrian said, and felt Marissa’s quick look cut toward him as a warning not to start narrating again. He kept his voice level. “Variation tells you where something is living instead of being archived.”

Marissa didn’t argue, but her lips tightened as if she were filing the sentence away for later dissection.

Mercer parked in front of a diner that looked like it had survived on coffee and habit for decades. The sign above the door was sun-faded, the paint chipped along the edges. A chalkboard by the entrance advertised breakfast specials in thick, uneven letters. Inside, the windows were fogged at the corners, and the smell that hit Adrian as soon as they stepped through the door was a mix of bacon grease, brewed coffee, and something sweet baked too early in the morning.

People looked up.

Not all at once, not theatrically. Just the normal, quick assessment a small town made of unfamiliar faces, followed by the brief hesitation that said these weren’t tourists stopping for pancakes on the way to an overlook.

Mercer led them to a booth near the side wall, one with a view of the front counter and the window.

Adrian slid in first, then Marissa, then Bellamy, who set his notebook beside his coffee cup as if he didn't trust the table not to shift under it.

A waitress approached before they could decide who would speak first. She was narrow and upright, her white hair pinned back tight in a way that made her face look carved rather than simply aged. She poured coffee into their cups without asking, her wrist steady as a surgeon's.

"You're Mercer," she said, not a question.

Mercer nodded. "Morning, Mrs. Hensley."

She didn't greet him back. Her eyes moved to Adrian. "And you're the professor."

Adrian had learned that in some places titles carried weight and in others they carried suspicion. Here it seemed to be the latter.

"Yes," he said. "Adrian Cross."

"The one asking about the lights," she said.

Marissa's posture changed slightly, attentive but controlled. Bellamy looked as if he wanted to protest the premise and decided it would be a poor opening.

"Yes," Adrian said again, because dodging was a kind of answer too.

Mrs. Hensley held his gaze for a beat longer than politeness required, then set the coffee pot down hard enough to make the cups rattle.

"Then ask the old people," she said. "Everybody else just wants pictures."

Marissa offered a small, careful smile. "We'd be glad to hear what you know too."

Mrs. Hensley snorted. "I know enough not to follow them."

Bellamy's pen appeared in his hand. "Ma'am, can you tell us when you first heard of the lights?"

Mrs. Hensley's eyes flicked to him, and Adrian saw the quick classification. Educated man. Notebook. The kind that showed up after.

"I didn't hear of them," she said. "I saw them. I was eight."

The booth seemed to settle, as if even the vinyl seat wanted to lean in.

Mrs. Hensley looked toward the front window, though there was nothing beyond it but the road and fog. "My brother saw one from the upper pasture," she said. "Thought it was Daddy coming back with a lantern. Daddy used to work late, sometimes came home after dark. So, my brother sees this light moving over the slope and he says, 'He's back.' And he starts down the hill."

Marissa's expression softened in that reflexive human way that came with children in stories. Bellamy's pen moved.

"Mama grabbed him by the overalls," Mrs. Hensley continued, and there was no softness in her voice at all, "and whipped him right there in the grass. Didn't even ask questions first."

Bellamy glanced up. "She whipped him for thinking it was your father?"

"She whipped him for stepping toward it," Mrs. Hensley corrected. "For believing it wanted what he wanted. For forgetting he was a child in the dark."

Adrian felt Mercer's stillness beside him. The ranger had gone quiet the way he did when a local voice reinforced what he'd been trying to say in procedure and reports.

Marissa leaned forward slightly. "What did your mother say the light was?" she asked.

Mrs. Hensley's gaze shifted to her, measuring. "She said it didn't matter what it was."

Adrian heard his own lecture in the sentence and disliked the feeling of recognition it gave him.

"What mattered?" he asked.

Mrs. Hensley tapped the table once with a finger, the sound sharp and final. "That it wanted you to think it was meant for you."

Even Bellamy stopped writing.

For a moment, the diner's ordinary noises came through too clearly: a fork clinking against a plate in another booth, a low laugh near the counter, the hiss of a grill. The contrast made Adrian's skin tighten. It was always like this when danger lived inside normal life. The threat wasn't announced. It just waited beneath conversation, patient.

Marissa recovered first. "Did she give a reason for that belief?" she asked, voice careful, as if she were trying not to lead.

Mrs. Hensley straightened, the way people did when they were about to deliver a sentence they'd delivered before. "She gave me the same reason mountain people give for most things," she said. "Because her mother told her. And because her mother's brother didn't listen."

Bellamy's mouth tightened. "That's not evidence."

Mrs. Hensley's expression didn't change, but something in her eyes sharpened. "No," she said. "That's the problem with you educated men. You always show up after the evidence has been buried."

Bellamy looked as if he might argue, then closed his mouth. Adrian saw him swallow down the reflex. It was probably the first wise thing Bellamy had done since agreeing to come.

Mrs. Hensley picked up the coffee pot again and turned slightly as if to leave, then paused.

"You want rules?" she asked, gaze landing back on Adrian.

Mercer's eyes stayed on her. He didn't interrupt.

"Yes," Adrian said. "We want the rules, and we want to know how people learned them."

Mrs. Hensley's mouth pulled into something that wasn't quite a smile. "Most people learn the rules by watching somebody else break them," she said. "Or by getting old enough to realize the folks who made them weren't trying to be interesting."

Marissa nodded. "The guidance sheet," she said. "The one passed around in churches. Is that something you remember?"

Mrs. Hensley made a small sound of acknowledgment. "I remember it on the back table," she said. "I remember women folding it up and sliding it in their purses like a recipe. I remember men pretending they didn't see it and then taking one when they thought nobody was looking."

Bellamy leaned forward, unable to help himself. "Was it always the same wording?"

"Near enough," Mrs. Hensley said. "The rules don't need poetry. They need to stick."

Adrian felt Marissa's attention shift. She was hearing what he was hearing: the difference between a story told to entertain and a set of instructions told to keep someone breathing.

"Do people still hand them out?" Marissa asked.

Mrs. Hensley's gaze went past them, toward the fogged window. "Not like they used to," she said. "People don't like admitting they still need old rules. Makes them feel backward."

Bellamy's voice was quiet. "And do you still need them?"

Mrs. Hensley looked back at him, and the diner felt colder for it. "Ask the families," she said. "Ask the ones who keep a bedroom the same because they can't bury what they can't find."

Adrian's throat went dry. He thought of Mercer's map, the pins, the clean absence.

Mrs. Hensley set the coffee pot down again, softer this time, and lowered her voice slightly. "You want a conversation that'll help you," she said to Adrian, "you don't get it from me. I'm just a woman who pours coffee and minds her business."

"That sounds like a useful kind of witness," Adrian said.

Her eyes narrowed, almost amused, almost warning. "It's useful if you listen," she said. "Not if you argue."

"We're listening," Marissa said, and Adrian believed she meant it.

Mrs. Hensley studied Marissa for a beat, then nodded once, as if granting a small credit.

"There's a house on the western slope," Mercer said quietly, stepping in now. "Ruth Calhoun."

Mrs. Hensley's face shifted, the smallest change in her eyes and mouth that read as respect mixed with fatigue. "Ruth," she repeated, and the name sounded heavy in her voice. "She'll talk if she feels like it."

"We have an appointment," Mercer said.

Mrs. Hensley's gaze slid back to Adrian. "Then don't be late," she said. "Morning's when truth still has some strength in it."

Adrian felt a jolt of recognition at the phrasing, as if the sentence had been circulating here so long it had become part of the air.

"We won't be," he said.

Mrs. Hensley turned to go, then paused again, as if another thought had decided it didn't like being left behind.

"And professor," she added, not unkindly, "if you see a light up close, you don't talk to it."

Adrian didn't ask how she meant close. He didn't ask what she meant by talk. He simply nodded.

Bellamy watched her retreat toward the counter, then exhaled slowly through his nose.

Marissa looked at Adrian, eyes sharp. “You hear the framing,” she said quietly. “Not ‘it’s dangerous,’ but ‘it wants you to think.’ That’s perceived intent.”

“It’s also a consistent description,” Adrian replied.

Bellamy’s pen tapped once, then stopped as if he caught himself. “It’s consistent because it’s shared,” he said. “That is what you both keep ignoring. A shared narrative produces shared language.”

Mercer spoke without looking at either of them. “Shared language doesn’t make people vanish,” he said.

No one had an easy reply to that.

Adrian took a sip of coffee and found it had gone slightly cooler, the bitterness more pronounced. He looked around the diner again. The people eating at tables, talking softly, living inside routines that had learned how to accommodate an unpredictable mountain.

He thought of what Mrs. Hensley had said. The rules don’t need poetry. They need to stick.

And beneath that, the sentence that had landed hardest: it wanted you to think it was meant for you.

Outside, the fog moved in slow, careless swirls along the road.

Mercer stood. "Finish up," he said. "Ruth doesn't like waiting."

Adrian slid out of the booth, feeling the guidance sheet in his pocket like a folded blade. As they walked toward the door, he glanced back once, unable to help himself.

Mrs. Hensley was behind the counter, pouring coffee for a man in a work jacket. She didn't look at Adrian, but her posture was rigid with the kind of certainty that didn't come from belief.

It came from practice.

When they stepped outside, the cold air felt cleaner and less forgiving. Adrian followed Mercer toward the car, and as the diner door swung shut behind them, he had the uncomfortable sensation of leaving the only warm, human-lit place for miles.

Not because the forest was dark.

Because, if the locals were right, the dark could notice when you stepped into it.

The road to Ruth Calhoun's house narrowed until it felt less like a town street and more like a private permission the mountain granted grudgingly. Mercer drove with the steady, unhurried focus of someone who had memorized every dip and soft shoulder. The fog thinned in patches and returned in others, caught in the folds of the land like damp cotton. Adrian watched fence lines appear and vanish, watched bare branches claw at the low sky, and tried not to read intention into weather.

Marissa sat with her tablet dark in her lap, hands folded around it as if she'd decided that, for once, observation needed to be more human than technical. Bellamy stared out the window with the expression of a man determined to treat everything he saw as context instead of omen.

Mercer turned off the main road onto a gravel drive that climbed gently through laurel. The forest pressed close, and the sound of the tires on stone was the loudest thing for a quarter mile. At the top, the trees opened onto a small clearing. A modest house sat back from the drive, older but kept, its porch lined with potted mums gone soft in the cold. A wind chime hung near the door but didn't move. The air smelled like wet wood and smoke that had long since left the chimney.

"She's expecting us," Mercer said, though he sounded less certain of that than he had at the diner.

They stepped out into the chill. Adrian felt the cold in his teeth. Somewhere behind the house, a hound barked once and then stopped, as if it had decided they were not worth the effort.

Ruth Calhoun sat on the porch before they reached the steps, wrapped in quilts that made her look broader than she probably was. A long walking stick rested across her lap. At her feet, a hound lay with its head on its paws, eyes half-open, watching without enthusiasm.

"You're late," she said.

Mercer glanced at his watch. "Mrs. Calhoun, it's ten after eleven."

"That's late for mountain talk." Her voice had the dry firmness of someone who'd stopped negotiating with other people's schedules years ago. "Morning's when truth still has some strength in it."

Adrian felt Marissa shift beside him, attentive, as if filing the phrasing away as both belief and method. Bellamy's mouth tightened, but he said nothing.

Ruth's eyes moved past Mercer and landed on Adrian. The look was not curious. It was assessing, like a woman deciding whether a tool was likely to break in her hands.

"You're the lore man," she said.

"I am," Adrian replied.

Her gaze slid briefly to Marissa, then to Bellamy, then back to Adrian. "You listen better than the others?"

Marissa opened her mouth, but Adrian answered first.

"I try to."

That seemed to satisfy Ruth more than any credential could have. She gave a single nod, small but decisive.

"My grandfather used to say there was a rule no one keeps anymore," she said, and tapped the walking stick once on the porch boards. The hound didn't move. "Used to be children learned it before they learned the Lord's Prayer."

She lifted a finger toward the ridge line, though the mountain itself was hidden behind a thinning veil of fog.

"When the light stops, you stop," Ruth said. "When it turns, you turn away. And if it comes close enough to show interest, you do not let it see your face."

The air seemed to tighten around that last sentence. Adrian felt the instinctive, useless urge to glance around, as if the mention of interest might summon it the way whistling supposedly did.

Marissa frowned. "Why the face?"

Ruth's eyes moved to her, sharp with something like impatience. "You anthropologist?"

Marissa blinked once. "Yes."

"You ask questions like somebody who thinks fear is decorative," Ruth said.

Bellamy made a sound that might have been a laugh and immediately disguised it as a cough.

Adrian kept his voice careful. "Mrs. Calhoun, why the face?"

Ruth held his gaze for a long moment. The silence didn't feel like suspense. It felt like decision. The hound lifted its head as if even it understood that something important was being weighed.

"Because," Ruth said softly, "it learns you."

Marissa's expression changed by degrees, skepticism tugged into something more cautious. Bellamy looked away, irritated at the effect the words had in the space between them. Mercer stood very still, his shoulders slightly raised, as if he'd been bracing for that line.

Adrian nodded slowly. The statement landed in him as both folklore and warning, the kind of double-purpose sentence Appalachian traditions seemed to excel at. He tried to translate it into Marissa's loop: expectation, interpretation, behavior, outcome. If you believed something learned your face, you would behave differently. You would refuse eye contact. You would not engage. The rule would keep you from becoming part of whatever pattern followed attention.

Ruth shifted the quilts on her lap and looked past them toward the tree line. "You want to know where the rules come from," she said. It wasn't a question. "You don't get them from paper. Paper comes after. You get them from people who watched somebody not come home."

Mercer cleared his throat. "Ruth, they're trying to help."

Ruth's eyes flicked to him, and for a moment her expression softened, not into kindness exactly, but into recognition. "I know who you are, Evan Mercer," she said. "You've been trying to carry this like it's your duty and not your curse."

Mercer didn't deny it.

Ruth looked back at Adrian. "Come inside," she said. "If you're going to ask, you might as well ask where the walls can hold the sound."

Inside, the house was cooler than the porch but felt warmer in a different way, dense with the presence of years. The air smelled faintly of cedar and old fabric. Photographs crowded the walls, frames layered close together: weddings, baptisms, hunting trophies, graduation portraits. Ordinary proof that the family had kept living even while the mountain kept taking.

Marissa moved slowly, respectful, as if her usual briskness would be an offense here. Bellamy's eyes flicked from frame to frame with the habitual hunger of a historian, but he kept his hands to himself.

Adrian drifted toward a set of older photographs near the hallway. One, faded into a gray softness, showed a group of men posed beside a timbered opening cut into a slope. Their clothes were dark with coal dust; their faces set in the patient seriousness of people who had been required to become practical. Behind them, the mine mouth was a shadow.

Adrian leaned closer, and his stomach tightened.

In the darker part of the photograph, near the edge of the mine entrance, there were three pale spots. They could have been damage to the print. They could have been dust caught in the camera's old lens.

Or they could have been lights.

Bellamy stepped beside him. "Mine workers," he murmured. "Late nineteenth century, I'd guess."

Adrian pointed without touching the glass. "Those."

Bellamy squinted, then straightened a fraction, his skepticism forced into a more careful shape. "Could be deterioration," he said, but he didn't sound convinced.

Ruth's voice came from behind them. "That was before the closing," she said.

Adrian turned. "What closing?"

Ruth's mouth tightened. "The lower shaft."

Bellamy's head lifted sharply. "There was a mine on this property?"

"Not on this property," Ruth corrected. "On the tract over. But the men who worked it lived all around here. My grandfather's brother worked down there for three years. He came home one night white as flour and wouldn't speak to anybody for two days."

Marissa's eyes narrowed, not in disbelief, but in focus. "What happened?"

Ruth's gaze shifted, as if looking at something only she could see. "After the screaming," she said.

The word hung there, heavy and plain.

Bellamy's pen came out automatically, then stopped as if he remembered Mercer's warning about baiting. "What screaming?" he asked anyway, unable to help himself.

Ruth looked at him with genuine irritation, as if he'd interrupted a prayer with a footnote.

"Well, Professor," she said, "if I knew that, I'd be writing your books."

Bellamy shut his mouth. His cheeks reddened slightly, whether from the rebuke or from the uncomfortable possibility that he had just been given a piece of history he couldn't categorize.

Adrian turned back to Ruth. "Is that where the rules started?" he asked. "In the mine?"

Ruth's eyes narrowed. "Rules start wherever people realize they're not the biggest thing in the dark," she said. "The mine was just where men had to keep going back even when their bodies told them not to."

Mercer shifted, his gaze moving to the floor, then to the walls, as if the house itself had become a witness stand. "Ruth," he said quietly, "they saw the lights last night. Close."

Ruth's expression didn't change, but her attention sharpened. She looked at Adrian. "Close enough to make you want to step toward it?"

Adrian felt a flush of honesty creep into his throat. "Yes," he admitted.

Ruth nodded once, like a judge confirming what she'd already known. "That's the part people don't understand," she said. "You don't follow because you're stupid. You follow because it makes it feel reasonable. Like there's an answer waiting in the next tree."

Marissa spoke softly. "And the face?"

Ruth's eyes went to her again. "You want everything to be about belief," she said. "About culture. About stories people tell themselves." Her voice wasn't cruel. It was simply tired. "But some stories are shaped around a thing that doesn't care whether you believe. It just cares whether you respond."

Bellamy's jaw worked as if he wanted to object and couldn't find a clean opening.

Ruth continued, voice low. "You keep your eyes down when it comes close, not because it's magic and not because it's manners. Because you don't give it more of you than it already has."

Adrian felt the guidance sheet in his pocket like a second skin. Do not follow lights. If a light approaches, lower your eyes and back away.

"Do people still keep the rules?" Adrian asked.

Ruth's mouth pulled into something that wasn't a smile. "They keep them until they don't," she said. "And then someone else has to learn the hard way."

Mercer looked at Adrian, and Adrian heard the unsaid in the look: this is why I called you. Not to argue about what the lights are, but to find out how long they've been training people to make the same mistake.

Ruth glanced back at the old mine photograph and then away, as if she couldn't bear to look at it too long. "You want to know where to dig," she said. "You go to the county records. You find the papers nobody reads anymore. Not the tourist stories. Not the newspaper fluff. The work stoppage reports. The insurance letters. The things written by men who didn't benefit from sounding scared."

Bellamy's eyes sharpened at that, the first sign of genuine interest he hadn't had to defend with sarcasm.

"And when you read them," Ruth added, her voice lowering another notch, "pay attention to the rules that show up where they don't belong. The little ones. The ones too specific to be invented for fun."

Adrian thought of Mercer telling them not to key the radio too much because sound carried. Thought of Mrs. Hensley's warning not to talk to a light up close. Thought of the line on the guidance sheet that made his throat tighten every time he read it: do not call it by name.

Ruth's gaze fixed on Adrian again. "And lore man," she said, "when you go back up on that ridge tonight or tomorrow, you remember something else."

Adrian waited.

Ruth's voice was quiet but firm. "It doesn't need you," she said. "It doesn't need your questions. It doesn't need your bravery. If you're there, it's because you stepped into its country. And the only advantage you've got is the rules you keep."

Mercer exhaled through his nose like a man who had been holding his breath for years.

Marissa nodded slowly, as if she could feel the warning's shape and was deciding how to frame it without blunting it.

Bellamy looked down at his notebook, then back up. He didn't argue. Not this time.

Adrian felt, for the first time since arriving in Jonas Ridge, that the mountain's presence was not only out there in the fog. It was in here, in the way people arranged their lives around a set of instructions that had outlasted explanations.

He thanked Ruth, and the words felt inadequate.

As they stepped back out onto the porch, the hound lifted its head again and watched them go with the weary patience of an animal that had seen too many humans walk away believing they were in control.

Mercer led them back toward the car. The fog had thinned slightly, and through the trees Adrian thought he could just make out the darker rise of a ridge line.

Marissa climbed into the passenger seat and didn't speak for a full minute.

Then she said, quietly, "If contamination is shaping the story, it's shaping it around something older than tourism."

Bellamy's voice came from the back, reluctant. "At the very least," he said, "it's shaping itself around a paper trail."

Mercer started the engine. "County records office opens in an hour," he said. "If Ruth told you to look there, you look there."

Adrian stared out at the trees as they pulled back down the drive and felt the warning settle into him in the only way warnings ever truly did.

Not as belief.

As behavior.

Chapter 6

The Archive of Unreliable Things

The county records office sat behind the courthouse in a low brick building that looked like it had been added as an afterthought and then quietly forgotten. The parking lot was half gravel, half cracked asphalt, with a line of bare maples along the fence that clicked their branches together in the damp.

Inside, the air hit them like a closed book left too long in a basement.

Paper. Dust. Old glue. Radiator heat that never quite warmed anything, only made the smell more intense. The fluorescent lights above were too bright for the narrow hallway, turning every surface the color of tired bone.

Bellamy drew in a breath that might have been disgust if Adrian hadn't seen the faintest lift at the corners of his mouth.

"This," Bellamy said, adjusting his glasses as he took in the shelves behind a glass partition, "is where facts go to survive bad memory."

Marissa glanced at him, unimpressed. "And to be misfiled for a century."

Mercer stood just inside the doorway, one hand still on the knob as if he wanted a quick exit. His ranger uniform looked out of place in a room that belonged to clerks and stamps and quiet. "We've got an hour before lunch," he said. "Maybe two if they're in a good mood."

A woman at the front desk looked up from a computer and assessed them with the same practiced suspicion Mrs. Hensley had shown in the diner, only this version came with bureaucratic authority.

Mercer stepped forward first, polite and familiar. "Morning, Linda."

"Morning, Evan." Her gaze slid to Adrian and the others. "You bring friends."

"Researchers," Mercer said. "They're looking for historic mining records. Work stoppage reports. Anything from the eighteen-nineties around the Brown Mountain tract."

Linda's expression tightened, the way it did when a sentence landed too close to a rumor she didn't want attached to her workplace. "We've got newspapers on microfilm. County plats. Some corporate filings, if they were recorded here. You want mine records, that's usually Raleigh."

Bellamy leaned in slightly, voice smoother than it had been at Ruth Calhoun's house. "We're not expecting full ledgers," he said. "Just local documentation. Notices of closure. Death certificates. Coroner's reports. Property disputes. Anything that would have required county involvement."

Linda looked at him for a beat, then reached under the desk and pulled out a clipboard. "Sign in," she said, and slid it toward them. "No bags beyond the reading tables. Pencils only. If you need copies, you pay per page."

Bellamy accepted the clipboard like it was a sacred object.

They signed, surrendered their bags to a set of dented lockers, and were led into a long room lined with shelves and filing cabinets. A few tables sat beneath the harsh lights. On one wall, a row of microfilm machines waited like squat gray animals, their screens dark.

The quiet inside wasn't peaceful. It was enforced.

Adrian lowered himself into a chair and felt the old wood creak under him. Somewhere behind the shelves, a heater clicked, then settled back into its dull, overworked hum.

Marissa set her tablet on the table but didn't turn it on yet. "Protocol still stands," she said, low enough that only they could hear. "We're not here to find a monster. We're here to track transmission. Documentation. Changes over time."

"I know," Adrian said.

Bellamy was already moving toward the microfilm cabinets, scanning labels. "Newspaper first," he said. "Local papers will report what companies won't."

Mercer stayed standing, eyes drifting over the shelves as if the room itself made him uneasy. "If you find a name," he said, "tell me. I can check it against our missing persons. Families that are still here. People keep stories alive longer than records."

Adrian nodded and stood, joining Bellamy at the cabinets. The drawers rasped as Bellamy pulled them open. Inside, black reels sat in neat rows, each one marked with white stickers that had yellowed at the edges.

Bellamy read labels aloud under his breath. "Morganton Herald. Lenoir News-Topic. Burke County Ledger…" He paused, then selected one. "Eighteen ninety-one."

Marissa looked over from the table. "You're starting before the collapse Ruth mentioned."

"I'm starting before anyone had reason to invent a collapse," Bellamy replied, then seemed faintly annoyed at himself for sounding like Adrian.

They loaded the reel into the microfilm machine. The plastic cover clacked shut. Bellamy's fingers worked the knobs with the comfort of habit, and the screen flickered to life, casting a pale light across his face.

Adrian took the chair beside him and watched the first page slide into view: dense columns, small print, advertisements for patent cures and farm equipment, the past presented as commerce and routine.

He reminded himself of Ruth's instruction. The things written by men who didn't benefit from sounding scared.

Bellamy's voice was brisk. "We're looking for mentions of Brown Mountain, Jonas Ridge, Linville, or the mine company name if we can find it."

Adrian leaned closer. "And anything that describes lights without using the tourist vocabulary."

Marissa, from across the table, finally turned on her tablet and began making a list. "Track dates," she said. "Track wording. Track whether the same phrasing repeats. That's how you see contamination. Even in print."

Bellamy made a small approving sound and rolled the reel forward.

Weeks passed in minutes on the screen. Local politics. Crop failures. A church picnic. A fire.

Then a small item near the bottom of a page caught Adrian's eye, not because it was dramatic, but because it tried so hard not to be.

"Hold it," Adrian said.

Bellamy stopped the reel and angled the focus. The article was brief, tucked beside a notice for a mule sale.

Adrian read softly. "Strange illuminations were again observed above Brown Mountain on Saturday evening…"

Bellamy exhaled through his nose. "Again," he said. "So, by eighteen ninety-one it's already established enough to be 'again.'"

Marissa got up and moved closer, her chair scraping the floor. "Read the rest."

Adrian continued. The item described "wandering lights" seen by several townspeople, dismissed by the editor as likely "distant lanterns" or "mist magnifying ordinary sources." The language was cautious, apologetic, as if the paper feared being accused of fueling nonsense.

Mercer leaned in behind them, expression unreadable.

Bellamy rolled forward again.

Eighteen ninety-two.

A mining accident made the front page in larger type. Two dead, names printed without flourish, survived by wives and children. One missing. The paper described a collapse in a lower cut, rescue efforts hampered by unstable supports.

Mercer's jaw tightened. "That's the year Ruth's family would've been talking about," he murmured.

Marissa's voice was steady. "What's the company name?"

Bellamy pointed. "Brown Mountain Mining and Reduction Company." He sounded pleased, like a man who had just been handed a thread.

Adrian wrote it down in his notebook, then forced himself to keep reading rather than rush ahead. The story's details were familiar in structure, even if the century made them feel distant: men went down, the mountain shifted, someone didn't come back up.

But it was the follow-up item three weeks later that made the room feel colder.

Bellamy stopped the reel again, less theatrical this time. The article was smaller, placed deeper in the paper. It noted a second incident, another collapse, and added a line about "labor unrest" and "refusal to reenter the lower shaft."

"Read," Marissa said.

Adrian leaned toward the screen until he could make out the tight print.

"Several laborers refused to reenter the shaft," he read, "claiming to have seen lights moving below ground where no flame had been carried."

Mercer went very still behind them.

Bellamy spoke first, reflexively. "Panic contagion."

Marissa didn't argue, but her brow tightened. "Bad air," she said. "Ventilation issues can cause hallucination. Hypoxia. Gas exposure."

Adrian's eyes caught the next line.

"Wait," he said, and pointed. "There."

He read it aloud. "One foreman described the lights as responsive to speech and movement."

The sentence sat on the screen like a stain.

Bellamy stared at it, and Adrian could see him trying to force it into a comfortable category. Marissa's lips parted slightly, then closed. She didn't look at Adrian. She didn't look at Mercer. She looked at the sentence as if it might change if she stared long enough.

Mercer's voice came low. "Responsive how?"

Adrian read the quoted description beneath.

"They dimmed when the men held still," he said, "and gathered when they shouted."

Silence thickened at the table. Across the room, a clerk turned a page with a dry whisper that sounded indecently loud.

Bellamy finally spoke, but his voice had lost some of its earlier certainty. "Group perception," he said. "Stress. Darkness. Confined space. Sound echoing, making distance hard to judge. The mind assigns pattern."

Marissa nodded once, but it wasn't agreement so much as an attempt to hold onto method. "That's still consistent with environmental explanation," she said.

Adrian didn't argue with either of them yet. He was thinking of the guidance sheet in his pocket, the line about not calling to them, and Mercer's warning about sound carrying. He was thinking of Mrs. Hensley's story about her mother whipping a child for stepping toward a light that looked like a father coming home.

A century apart, and the rules were still about response.

Mercer straightened and moved away from the microfilm machine as if the glow of the screen itself had become suspect. He walked to the nearest window, though there was nothing outside but a slice of foggy daylight and the courthouse lawn.

"Keep going," he said, voice tight. "See what happens after."

Bellamy rolled the reel forward again.

Eighteen ninety-three.

A notice about the mine's closure. Short. Vague. No dramatic explanation. Just a formal statement that operations in the lower cuts had been suspended indefinitely due to "unsafe conditions" and "unrecoverable loss."

Unrecoverable. Adrian felt the word press into him. Not found. Not brought back.

Bellamy tapped the screen with the eraser end of his pencil. "They don't name the missing man," he said, irritation returning. "They name the dead, but not the missing."

Marissa's gaze flicked to Adrian. "Because naming makes it stick," she said quietly.

"Or because the company didn't want a paper trail tying them to liability," Bellamy countered.

"Both can be true," Adrian said.

He sat back, rubbing his thumb over the edge of his notebook. He felt a familiar shift inside himself, the point where a scatter of details started to align into shape. Not an answer. But a path.

There were lights reported over the mountain before tourism could monetize them. There were lights reported underground, where headlights and distant trains couldn't reach. There were men refusing to go back down, and a closure that didn't bother to explain itself to the public.

Mercer turned from the window. "So, it's not new," he said. It wasn't triumph in his voice. It was something closer to grim confirmation.

Marissa inhaled slowly. "If the mine reports match the modern rule set," she said, "then either the story has been remarkably stable, or the stimulus that produces it has."

Bellamy's eyes narrowed. "Or the paper is repeating rumor."

Adrian looked at him. "Then we find something that isn't meant for print," he said. "Work stoppage reports. Insurance correspondence. Anything internal."

Bellamy's attention sharpened immediately, pulled back toward his element. He stood. "Linda said there might be corporate filings," he said. "And if the county recorded any disputes, they'd be in the clerk's back files."

Mercer moved toward the door with him, as if the thought of going deeper into this paper maze made him want to keep motion on his side. "I'll ask," Mercer said. "They'll listen to me faster than they'll listen to you."

Marissa stayed at the table, already typing. "Log everything," she said without looking up. "Dates, language, placement in the paper. And note the editorial tone. Dismissive, cautious, mocking. That matters."

Adrian watched Bellamy and Mercer disappear into the hallway, then glanced back at the microfilm screen, where the old article still glowed faintly.

Lights moving below ground where no flame had been carried.

He thought of Ruth Calhoun's face when she'd said the word screaming. He thought of her warning, almost gentle in its bluntness: pay attention to the rules that show up where they don't belong.

Adrian lowered his voice, though no one else was close enough to hear.

"Paper doesn't lie," he murmured.

Marissa looked up at him, eyes sharp. "Paper lies all the time," she said. "It lies by omission. It lies by agenda. It lies by what it chooses not to name."

Adrian nodded slowly. "Then maybe," he said, "this is an archive of unreliable things."

Marissa's gaze held his for a beat, and in that look he saw the shared understanding that was beginning to form despite their arguments.

Whatever was on Brown Mountain, it had left traces in more than one kind of record.

Not enough to explain it.

Enough to prove it had been there long before any of them arrived, and long before anyone had learned how to sell it.

Bellamy and Mercer returned a few minutes later. Bellamy's expression had shifted into something Adrian recognized: reluctant excitement disguised as annoyance.

"There's a folder," Bellamy said. "Not much. But it's something. Internal communications, a couple of statements. They'll bring it out."

Mercer's face was set. "And Linda says we can have it for an hour," he added. "No copies unless we pay."

Marissa stood, closing her tablet case with a snap. "Then we don't waste a second," she said.

Adrian felt his pulse pick up, not with fear, but with the particular tension of approaching a door that had been shut for a hundred years and was about to open on a crack.

Somewhere in the back of the building, a file drawer slid out with a long, protesting rasp.

And Adrian couldn't shake the thought that, if Ruth was right, the most telling things in that folder wouldn't be the dramatic claims.

It would be the small, specific rules.

The ones too practical to be written for fun.

The folder arrived in Linda's hands like something she didn't want to touch for long.

It was thin, the kind of manila that had softened at the corners from decades of being moved and put back, moved and put back, each time handled by someone who thought it might matter and then decided it probably didn't. A strip of faded red tape held the flap shut, brittle with age. Linda set it on the table with a firm, controlled motion and then stood with her hands clasped in front of her as if daring them to waste her time.

"One hour," she said. "No pens. You tear it, you pay for conservation. You take pictures, you do it without flash."

Bellamy looked offended by the implication that he would behave like a tourist, which was exactly why Linda had said it.

Mercer nodded. "Thanks, Linda."

She didn't soften. "Evan," she said, and her eyes moved briefly over the three academics. "Don't make me regret it."

Then she walked away, heels tapping down the hallway, leaving them alone with the smell of old paper and the hum of the lights.

For a moment none of them reached for the folder.

Adrian realized, with a kind of quiet irony, that this was the closest thing they'd had so far to a threshold. Not the mine entrance itself, not the ridge at night, but a set of documents that had been kept out of ordinary circulation. The mountain's shadow translated into bureaucracy.

Marissa broke first, as she usually did when hesitation risked becoming ritual. She pulled on the thin archival gloves Linda had tossed onto the table and slid one pair toward Adrian, another toward Bellamy. "Photograph each page," she said. "Even if we can't copy it, we can document it."

Bellamy was already putting on the gloves with practiced irritation. "I know how to handle paper," he muttered.

Mercer stayed standing behind them, leaning forward slightly. His eyes never left the folder. Adrian could see the tension in his jaw, the way he held himself when he was bracing for something that couldn't be helped.

Adrian lifted the flap carefully. The red tape cracked in two places but held. Inside were fewer pages than he'd expected, and they weren't neatly arranged. Some were typed, others handwritten. A couple were carbon copies with the lettering blurred and faint, like a voice trying to speak through cloth.

Bellamy pulled the first page free and held it close to the light, angling it so the faded ink could be read.

"Brown Mountain Mining and Reduction Company," he said softly, and the satisfaction in his tone surprised Adrian. A name on a page did something to Bellamy's mind. It made uncertainty feel less personal.

The document was a typed memorandum, dated October 4, 1892, addressed to a superintendent whose name was partially smeared, as if someone's thumb had wiped at it long ago.

Bellamy read aloud, voice clipped. "Notice of temporary cessation of work in Lower Cut Shaft B pending investigation of structural integrity and worker conduct."

Marissa leaned closer. "Worker conduct?"

Bellamy's eyes moved down the page. His mouth tightened. "It's written like discipline," he said. "Like the men were the problem."

Mercer's voice came low from behind them. "They always write it that way."

Adrian reached for the second page, a handwritten statement on lined paper, the kind used for schoolwork. The date matched the newspaper mention they'd found: late 1892. The handwriting was careful at first and then grew hurried, as if the writer had tried to stay professional and failed.

At the top: Statement of Foreman J. Hale.

Adrian read, slowly.

"On the evening of September 28, I descended with shift laborers to the lower cut. Lanterns were lit and normal. At approximately 8:40 p.m. there was a sudden cold draft and a dimming of lamps not attributable to wind. Several men reported seeing intermittent glows deeper in the passage, though no flame had been carried beyond the work line."

He paused, eyes flicking to Mercer. The ranger's face didn't change, but his shoulders had lifted slightly, as if the paper itself had made the room colder.

Adrian continued. "At 8:45 p.m., laborer Thomas Vick called out into the passage, saying he saw movement. I instructed him to hold and return to the group. At this time the glows appeared to gather at varying heights and locations, not fixed to the floor. Men became agitated."

Bellamy leaned in closer, the historian's skepticism shifting into a more reluctant attention.

The phrase varying heights snagged him the same way it had snagged Adrian on the microfilm.

Adrian's throat tightened as he read the next lines.

"Lanterns failed simultaneously, as if the air had swallowed them. Three laborers fled without instruction. Mr. Vick did not return. He was last heard shouting for a light."

Marissa's hand went to her mouth, not theatrically, but as if her body had reacted before she could decide whether she believed the words.

Mercer exhaled once through his nose. "Vick," he said quietly. "So that was his name."

Bellamy reached for the next page with gloved fingers that suddenly seemed less steady. "There's another statement," he said, and Adrian could hear the shift in him: this wasn't folklore anymore, not in the way Bellamy liked to dismiss. This was the language of men trying to protect their jobs and still leaving traces of fear.

Bellamy read the second statement, shorter and more blunt, signed by a man named R. M. Sutton, likely another supervisor.

"Men claim luminous phenomena responsive to speech and movement," Bellamy read. "They assert it dims when stillness is kept and increases when noise is made. I cannot speak to the truth of the matter but can speak to the effect: we have lost control of the workforce. They will not reenter."

He looked up at Marissa, as if daring her to call it contamination. She didn't. Not yet.

Marissa picked up her tablet and began typing, eyes fixed on the page as if she could pin it down by recording it fast enough. "Responsive," she murmured. "Stillness reduces. Noise increases."

Adrian felt a pulse behind his eyes. He thought of Mercer's warning the night before: don't keep keying the mic. Sound carries out there. The rule in the guidance sheet: do not answer voices from the trees. The way Ruth Calhoun had said it cares whether you respond.

He forced himself to keep reading rather than let the pattern run ahead of the evidence.

A third document was folded in half, tucked under the statements. It was on company stationery, the edges browned. The signature line was blank, but the tone was unmistakably managerial, the voice of a man who had decided that whatever happened underground was less important than the appearance of control.

Adrian unfolded it carefully. The ink was darker here, as if written with more pressure.

"We cannot have the workers spreading stories of spirits and mountain tricks," Adrian read. "This harms recruitment and invites inspection. Though I put no stock in such talk, I will note for the sake of liability that the luminous phenomena displayed a curious tendency toward pursuit when men attempted to withdraw."

He stopped, the words settling in his chest like a weight.

Displayed a curious tendency toward pursuit.

Marissa went still. Bellamy's face had tightened in a way Adrian recognized: the look of a man encountering a sentence he would never put in his own writing because he didn't want to be laughed at, and therefore couldn't easily dismiss in someone else's.

Mercer's hand came down on the back of a chair, fingers curling around the wood as if he needed something solid. "That's what it does now," he said. His voice didn't rise. It didn't need to. "It approaches. It closes distance."

Marissa looked up at him. "That letter could still be exaggeration," she said, but the argument sounded thinner than it had earlier in the day. Not because she believed in ghosts. Because the words matched too neatly with what they'd already seen.

Bellamy cleared his throat, a small, involuntary act of discomfort. "Liability language," he said. "He's covering himself. He's implying the men panicked because something chased them, rather than because the mine was unsafe."

Adrian nodded slowly. "Maybe," he said. "But why choose that phrasing at all? Why not write 'the men fled due to fear'? He writes pursuit."

Marissa's eyes narrowed, not at Adrian but at the paper, as if she were trying to separate mechanism from meaning. "If the men perceived the light as pursuing," she said, "it would intensify panic. Which makes them more likely to run blindly, causing injury, making the mine more dangerous. It would also make the story stick."

Adrian didn't argue. He could hear her working, doing what she always did: building a model that explained behavior without granting intent to the phenomenon. But he also saw the flicker behind her eyes, the place where she could not deny the recurring specificity.

Mercer shifted his weight. "Keep going," he said.

Adrian reached deeper into the folder and pulled out the final item: a rough map on thin paper, the kind a foreman might sketch on a clipboard. It showed the main tunnel line, a branching lower cut labeled B, and a handful of notes in cramped handwriting. Several areas were crosshatched with pencil, indicating collapse or danger.

Bellamy leaned over Adrian's shoulder, breath warm in Adrian's ear. "That's not an official plat," he said. "That's field-made. Which means it's closer to what they actually used."

Marissa moved to Adrian's other side, her skepticism now translated into full attention. "Look at the markings," she said.

Adrian's eyes caught on a section that had been circled repeatedly, the pencil so dark it nearly tore the paper. Next to it, along the margin, was a note written in a different hand, heavier strokes, as if the writer had been angry or afraid.

The sentence was short. Too short to be an explanation. Too specific to be a general warning.

Do not whistle below this point.

Adrian stared at it and felt something in him go very still.

Across the table, Bellamy's expression shifted into the reluctant recognition that this was exactly what Ruth had told them to watch for: a rule showing up where it didn't belong, smuggled into a practical document like contraband.

Marissa's voice dropped. "That's… the same rule," she said.

Mercer leaned closer, eyes fixed on the words as if they might rearrange themselves into something safer if he looked long enough. "Do not whistle," he repeated. "In a mine."

Bellamy let out a slow breath. "Miners whistled," he said, almost to himself. "To signal. To keep rhythm. To steady nerves. That's—"

"A response," Adrian said, and surprised himself with how certain it sounded.

Marissa looked at him sharply, the guardrail ready. "Or a superstition," she countered automatically, but her voice lacked its earlier force.

Adrian didn't take the bait. He kept his eyes on the map, on the circled section, on the handwritten warning pressed into the margin like an afterthought that had refused to stay quiet.

Outside the records office, the day continued in its foggy normalcy. Cars moved. People ate lunch. Somewhere a clerk stamped forms.

Inside, at the table, the four of them leaned over a century-old sketch that carried the same rule Mercer had handed them in a church bulletin format: do not whistle to it.

And Adrian understood, with a clarity that unsettled him, why the folder felt like a threshold.

Because whatever had happened below ground in 1892 hadn't stayed there.

It had climbed out into the stories, into the rules, into the way people moved on trails at night, eyes down, refusing to answer voices from the trees.

Bellamy straightened slowly, as if his back had begun to ache under the weight of implication. "If this is authentic," he said carefully, "then the warning predates modern tourism by decades."

Marissa's fingers hovered over her tablet screen. "And it suggests the same interaction pattern," she said. "Sound. Attention. Response."

Mercer's gaze moved from the map to Adrian. "You wanted where the rules came from," he said quietly. "That's where."

Adrian nodded once, unable to find a more honest gesture.

The folder lay open between them, thin and insufficient and somehow heavier than any stack of newspapers. The mine's dark history wasn't a single catastrophe. It was a set of traces that pointed to something ongoing, something that had taught people, again and again, that the most dangerous moment wasn't the first sighting.

It was the moment you answered back.

Adrian photographed the map three times, changing angles each time to catch the graphite lines and the darker pencil circle without glare. Even without flash, the micro-texture of the paper showed in the image: fibers worn flat where hands had pressed too often, a faint crease that suggested it had once been folded and carried in a pocket.

Marissa leaned close enough that Adrian could feel her breath on his shoulder.

"Get the margin," she said.

"I am," Adrian replied.

He framed the warning again.

Do not whistle below this point.

The sentence looked wrong on the page in a way that had nothing to do with grammar. It was too plain. Too practical. It had the feel of an instruction scrawled in haste, the kind meant to stop a mistake that had already happened.

Bellamy, still gloved, traced the tunnel line with his eyes without touching the paper. "If this map is accurate, that circled section would be deeper than the work line," he said. "Past the area they considered stable enough for regular descent."

Mercer's gaze remained fixed on the words, as if he were trying to decide whether it was better to have proof or to be left with uncertainty. "Below this point," he echoed.

Marissa's tablet clicked as she locked her screen and looked up. "The phrasing matters," she said.

"Not 'don't whistle in the mine.' Not 'don't whistle at night.' It's bounded. Spatially specific."

Bellamy's mouth tightened. "Superstitions often are."

Marissa didn't flinch. "Yes. And those boundaries usually correspond to something. A dangerous current, a bad patch of ice, a bend in a road where people crash. Culture draws lines around risk."

Adrian kept the phone steady and took one last photo, then carefully slid the map back into the folder. The paper made a soft, dry sound as it settled, and he hated how loud even that felt.

He glanced toward the doorway. Linda stood at the front desk, watching them with the detached patience of a woman timing strangers. The records office quiet had a weight to it, as if the building itself preferred what was filed to stay filed.

Adrian closed the folder flap and looked at the others. "We've got what we need," he said.

Bellamy's eyes flicked to the folder, reluctant to let it go. "We have photographs," he corrected. "We have evidence of documents. Which is not the same as having the documents."

Mercer stepped forward, the decision already in his posture. He carried the folder back to Linda and set it down with the care of someone returning an object that could cut.

Linda's eyebrows rose slightly. "Done already?"

"We got what we came for," Mercer said.

She opened the folder and scanned the contents quickly, making sure nothing had been slipped into a pocket. When she was satisfied, she closed it and tucked it away beneath the counter.

"You find what you were looking for?" she asked, and her tone implied she already suspected the answer.

Mercer paused just long enough that Adrian could feel the question's hook. "We found old paperwork," Mercer said finally.

Linda nodded once, as if that was all she wanted to hear. "Mm-hm."

They retrieved their bags from the lockers and stepped back into the daylight, which was still the washed-out gray of fog refusing to fully lift. The air smelled cleaner outside, but the damp clung to the skin the same way the folder's contents clung to Adrian's thoughts.

In the parking lot, Bellamy stopped beside the car and pulled his notebook out again, as if movement might shake loose the exact sentence he needed. "Miners whistled for signaling," he said. "For coordination in low visibility. For morale. There are entire accounts of it as a tradition. If someone wrote that warning, it implies whistling produced a predictable consequence."

Marissa's gaze went sharp. "Or it implies someone believed it did."

Bellamy bristled. "You keep making my arguments for me."

"Because they're not wrong," Marissa said. "But neither is the opposite conclusion. That's the problem. The same data supports both if you're sloppy with causality."

Mercer unlocked the vehicle and got in behind the wheel. "Argue in the car," he said. "Not out in a lot where people can hear the word mine and start remembering things they don't want to remember."

Adrian slid into the front passenger seat. The heater came on with a dry rattle, pushing lukewarm air that smelled faintly of dust from the vents. He watched fog drift past the windshield and tried to keep his mind in the present rather than sliding down the old tunnel lines on that map.

Marissa climbed in beside Bellamy in the back, still holding her tablet but not looking at it. She sounded thoughtful now, not combative. "If the mine warning and the church bulletin warning are linked," she said, "then we're looking at an unusually stable transmission. Same rule, same phrasing, two contexts separated by a century."

Bellamy nodded once, grudging. "Which suggests a common source."

Mercer drove without hurry, hands steady on the wheel. "You're missing the part that matters," he said.

Marissa leaned forward slightly. "Which part?"

Mercer's eyes stayed on the road. "That the rule is about sound," he said. "About response. It's not 'don't go down there.' It's 'don't do this specific thing down there.'"

Adrian felt that settle into him with uncomfortable familiarity. It matched everything: the guidance sheet's list of don'ts, the old articles about lights gathering when men shouted, the way Mercer had told them not to key the radio too much because sound carried.

A thought rose in Adrian's mind, uninvited and persistent: if the phenomenon responded to sound, then a whistle was a kind of beacon. Not because it was mystical. Because it was a clean, high-frequency signal that cut through other noise. Easy to localize. Easy to follow.

He didn't say it yet. He wasn't sure whether speaking it would make it more true, or merely make it easier for his mind to see the pattern it wanted.

Bellamy's voice came tight. "So,/ what are you proposing?" he asked Mercer. "That we go into a collapsed mine because a margin note told us not to whistle?"

Mercer didn't answer immediately. The road narrowed as they left town and moved back into forest. Trees pressed close, wet bark dark as old bruises. The sky was a low, uniform lid.

Mercer finally said, "I'm proposing we go to the entrance. We don't go in today. We look. We map the approach. We check for recent activity. Tourists. Campers. Anyone who might have decided the story was an invitation."

Marissa's brow furrowed. "Why would anyone go there?"

Mercer gave a short, humorless exhale. "Same reason people step off trail. To see it better. To prove something. To feel like they're part of the mountain instead of just looking at it."

Bellamy leaned back. "You're assuming people know it exists."

Mercer's jaw tightened. "People know everything exists," he said. "They share coordinates. Old mine openings end up on forums. 'Hidden places.' 'Forgotten history.' Someone always wants a door that says keep out."

Adrian stared out the window as the forest thickened. The sense of being funneled returned, the land guiding them with indifferent authority. The roads here didn't feel designed so much as permitted.

He felt Marissa watching him, and when he looked back, her expression was careful.

"You're thinking about going in," she said quietly.

Adrian didn't deny it. "I'm thinking about what happens if someone else already has," he replied.

That shut Bellamy up for a moment. It was one thing to argue about theories. It was another to consider the possibility that their work had a ticking edge to it, that while they discussed contamination loops, someone might be down a dark passage testing a rule with a careless whistle.

They parked at a rusted chain barrier where the road had given up pretending it was maintained. Mercer cut the engine. The sudden silence felt like a pressure change.

They got out and continued on foot.

The forest here was denser than the overlooks and service paths, laurel and young pine crowding in until the trail felt like a narrow corridor cut through green. The ground was soft with leaf mold. Every step gave a quiet, wet sound. Adrian smelled minerals beneath the decay, a cold metallic note that reminded him of coins and old tools.

Bellamy walked behind Mercer, scanning the trees as if expecting to see the past pinned to a trunk. Marissa stayed close to Adrian, her gaze alternating between the ground and the spaces between branches. Mercer led without hesitation, as if he'd walked this route before and didn't like remembering it.

After ten minutes, the trail dipped slightly, then rose toward a slope that looked subtly wrong, the way earth looks wrong when it has been cut and rearranged.

Mercer slowed. "There," he said.

The mine entrance lay half-concealed in laurel and young pine, a dark opening framed by old timbers that had gone gray with age. Collapsed rock narrowed the mouth, but not enough to seal it. The darkness inside looked thick, not simply unlit. Cool air flowed outward in a steady breath, carrying dampness and the faint, stale scent of stone that hadn't seen sun in decades.

Mercer stopped several yards back, as if there was an invisible line he refused to cross.

"I've been here before," he said.

"And?" Adrian asked, keeping his voice low without knowing why.

Mercer's eyes stayed on the entrance. "I never went in."

Bellamy swallowed and tried to make practicality sound like dominance. “Those beams could fail.”

“That,” Marissa said, “is the first sensible thing any of us have said all day.”

Adrian crouched near the mouth without stepping into it and angled his light toward the ground. He expected animal tracks, maybe evidence of rain runoff. What he saw made his chest tighten.

Boot prints.

Not old impressions softened by time. Recent. At least one set, maybe two, where the leaf litter had been disturbed and the soil beneath had been pressed hard. The steps were spaced carefully, placed with the caution of someone aware that they might be noticed.

Adrian reached out and touched the edge of one print lightly, then pulled his hand back as if the ground might be warm.

“Someone’s been here,” he said.

Mercer swore under his breath. “Tourists.”

Adrian shook his head slowly, still studying the pattern. “Not tourists.”

Mercer looked at him sharply. “How can you tell?”

Adrian pointed to the depth and placement, the way the prints avoided loose gravel, the way they angled toward the narrowest part of the opening rather than the most obvious approach.

"Too careful," Adrian said. "Too measured. Whoever came here knew they weren't supposed to be noticed."

Bellamy stared at the prints with a look that mixed irritation and unease. "And you know that how?"

Adrian lifted his gaze to the mine mouth. The darkness inside seemed to absorb the beam of his flashlight rather than reflect it back.

"Because I would've done the same thing," Adrian said.

For a moment none of them spoke. The forest held its quiet, and the mine breathed cold air into the day like a reminder that the mountain had layers.

Mercer's voice came low, controlled. "No one goes in," he said.

Adrian didn't argue. Not yet.

But as he stood, he felt the warning from the map tighten around his thoughts, no longer an artifact in a folder but a living boundary drawn across a place.

Do not whistle below this point.

And the worst part was how clearly Adrian could imagine someone doing exactly that, somewhere in the dark beyond the timbers, to see if the old rule still meant anything at all.

Chapter 7

Below the Mountain

Mercer's "No one goes in" hung in the air like a posted sign, the kind people pretended to respect until curiosity gave them a reason not to.

Adrian kept his flashlight angled down, as if the mine entrance might react to being looked at too directly. That was ridiculous, he told himself. And then, as quickly, he remembered how many of their rules had once sounded ridiculous until the pattern repeated often enough to become policy disguised as superstition.

Marissa shifted beside him, boots sinking slightly in the soft leaf mold. She stared at the opening with a scientist's caution and a human being's unease, the two instincts pulling against each other in her posture. Bellamy stood back with his arms tight across his chest, as if he could physically hold the past at bay by refusing to step closer.

Mercer didn't move. He watched the darkness the way he'd watched the treeline the night before, as though he expected something to lean forward out of it.

"We should mark this," Marissa said finally, voice low. "Photograph the prints. Document the approach. Then we call the sheriff and ask if anyone has been reported missing since last night."

Mercer nodded once. "I already texted him when we left Jonas Ridge. No answer yet. Signal's spotty."

Bellamy gave a humorless laugh. "Convenient."

Mercer's head turned just enough that Adrian caught the look. Not anger. A kind of exhausted warning. Bellamy had a habit of treating every inconvenience as a clue, and in a place like this that habit could become its own trap.

Adrian pulled out his phone and took a series of photos of the boot prints, placing his glove beside them for scale. The disturbed leaves made a sharp contrast against the darker soil beneath, and the neatness of the impressions bothered him. A careless trespasser left scuffs and half-steps. Whoever came here had walked like someone trained to move quietly.

"Mercer," Adrian said, keeping his voice even, "if it's not tourists, who is it?"

Mercer's jaw tightened. "People who think they can handle it."

"And you think they came recently," Marissa said.

Mercer crouched, not at the prints but a few feet to the right and brushed aside leaves with a gloved hand. Adrian watched him reveal a shallow gouge in the soil where something heavy had been dragged.

"Someone carried gear," Mercer said. "Not camping gear. Too narrow. Something like a case."

Bellamy's eyes sharpened despite himself. "Camera equipment?"

"Maybe," Mercer said. "Or something else they thought would help."

Marissa's gaze flicked to Adrian, then back to the entrance. "If someone went inside with equipment and didn't come out—"

"We don't know they didn't come out," Bellamy cut in quickly, as if the sentence itself was dangerous. "We know they were here."

Adrian stood and looked at the mine mouth again. The timbers framing it were old enough that the grain stood out like muscle under skin. Moisture darkened the lower edges where the ground met wood. The rock fall at the entrance had narrowed the opening to a hunched passage that felt deliberately unwelcoming, as if the mountain had attempted to close it and failed.

A cold breath slipped outward, steady and continuous.

Marissa noticed it too. "Airflow," she said, more softly than she intended. "So, it's not sealed."

Mercer straightened and stepped back, drawing a line with his body. "We don't go in," he repeated. "This is exactly how it starts. People see a door and decide the rule is for everyone but them."

Adrian met his eyes. "Then what's the plan if someone's already inside?"

Mercer hesitated. Adrian saw the conflict there, the collision between training and experience. Rangers didn't abandon people. But rangers also didn't walk into hazards blind.

Marissa held her recorder case against her chest like a shield. "We can call in a formal search," she said. "Get a mine rescue team."

Mercer shook his head. "Not fast. Not here. The nearest team is hours out, and nobody mobilizes for 'maybe someone trespassed.' Not without a missing report. Not without proof."

Bellamy's voice went tight. "So, we do nothing."

"No," Mercer said, and the sharpness surprised all of them. Then he exhaled, forcing control back into his tone. "We do what we can do without becoming the next set of names."

Adrian understood that sentence in his bones. It was what Mercer had been doing all year: measuring help against the way the mountain erased people.

Mercer reached into his vest pocket and pulled out a small roll of bright survey tape. He tore a strip and tied it to a low branch near the mine opening. The fluorescent color looked obscene against the wet greens and browns.

"Marker," Mercer said. "So, nobody loses the entrance in fog. And so if someone comes while we're here, we'll see movement."

Marissa frowned. "Are we staying?"

Mercer didn't answer immediately. He looked at each of them in turn, weighing what they were and what they could handle. Not academics. Not skeptics and believers. Bodies. Balance. Breath.

"If we hear something," Mercer said, "we back out. No hero behavior. No chasing echoes."

Bellamy scoffed, but it lacked energy. "And if we hear nothing?"

Mercer's gaze returned to the darkness. "Then we decide if we can afford to leave without checking," he said.

Adrian felt his stomach tighten. This was the threshold Ruth had warned them about, and not only the physical one. The moment when principle met consequence. If they walked away and someone was inside, they might be leaving a person to die. If they went in and the mountain did what it did, they might be multiplying the problem.

Marissa spoke carefully, as if choosing each word for how it might land in a report later. “A limited entry,” she said. “Just the first section. We stay within line of sight of daylight. We don’t split up. We don’t call out. We don’t whistle. We don’t do anything that adds sound.”

Bellamy stared at her. “You’re proposing we enter a collapsed nineteenth-century mine because you think it’s safer to be inside the hazard than to admit we can’t control it.”

“I’m proposing,” Marissa replied, voice tightening, “that if someone went in there, the ethical thing is to verify whether they’re still alive. But we do it under strict constraints.”

Mercer looked at Adrian last. “Cross?”

Adrian felt the guidance sheet in his pocket, remembered the line that had started all of this: do not follow lights. It was too easy to recast what he wanted as duty. He did not want to be the man who confused curiosity for responsibility.

But the prints were too careful. The drag mark suggested equipment. And the mountain had a habit of making absence look clean.

"I don't want to go in," Adrian said, and heard the honesty in it like a confession. Then he added, because it mattered: "But I don't think we can pretend this is just a historical site anymore."

Mercer nodded once, grim. "All right," he said. "Limited entry. Ten yards, maybe twenty. No deeper. We look for signs, we listen, we leave."

Bellamy's mouth tightened. "This is how people die."

Mercer didn't argue. He simply said, "That's why I'm setting rules."

He made them check their gear like it was a ritual with a purpose. Headlamps on, red filters available. Flashlights charged. No loose straps that could snag. Boots tight. Marissa's recorder stayed off, not because data didn't matter, but because Mercer had already decided sound mattered more. Bellamy protested that he needed notes, and Mercer told him to write them afterward.

"Inside," Mercer said, "the mountain doesn't care about your documentation."

Marissa glanced at Adrian and then away again, as if she didn't want to admit she agreed with Mercer on that point.

Mercer went first. He didn't step directly into the opening. He leaned in and angled his light across the floor, scanning for collapse, for animals, for anything that moved. The beam disappeared into the dark as if the darkness had texture.

Adrian followed close behind, and Bellamy and Marissa brought up the rear in a tight line.

The moment Adrian crossed under the timber frame, the temperature dropped. It wasn't just cooler. It was a different kind of cold, damp and mineral, as if the air had been stored in stone.

The daylight behind them shrank instantly, turning into a pale rectangle cut out of the world. The forest sounds, faint as they were, softened further until even their breathing seemed intrusive.

Mercer stopped just inside and held up a hand.

Adrian froze. He felt the old wood above him, not touching him but present, as if weight had a radius. He smelled damp rock and something else beneath it, old oil and rusted metal and rot that had never fully dried.

Mercer pointed his light downward.

Old rails, half-buried in debris, ran into the mine like a set of ribs. Broken boards and splintered crates lay scattered along the sides. The floor was uneven with rubble, and water had carved shallow channels through the dirt.

Adrian's headlamp caught a faint smear on the wall at shoulder height. He leaned closer, then stopped himself before he got too close. The smear wasn't recent. It looked like soot or charcoal, rubbed into the rock by a hand that had needed to leave a mark.

A cross, half blurred.

And Adrian felt, without knowing why yet, that the mine had its own version of the guidance sheet. Not printed. Not handed out in church. Pressed into the walls where men had worked until fear forced them into instruction.

Mercer lowered his voice to the smallest workable volume. "We stay together," he said. "We don't talk unless we have to. And if any of you feel that pull," he paused, as if choosing a word that wouldn't make it bigger, "you tell me."

Marissa's response was equally quiet. "Pull like last night."

Mercer nodded once.

Adrian looked ahead into the narrowing dark and realized the threshold wasn't behind them anymore. They had crossed it, and the mine had accepted them with the same indifferent patience the ridge had shown.

It breathed cold air into their faces.

And deeper in, somewhere past the reach of their lights, water dripped steadily in the dark like a clock that didn't measure time so much as it measured how long people stayed where they shouldn't.

They moved in a slow, careful line, the way you moved through a place that could punish you for haste.

The first few yards were almost disappointing. Broken rails. Rotting boards. Rusted metal that had once been equipment and was now only debris. The mine smelled like damp stone and old iron, and Adrian's mind tried to slot it into an ordinary category: abandoned industrial site, structurally compromised, unsafe but explainable.

Then the passage angled slightly downward and the air changed again. The cold wasn't just temperature, it was presence. It sat against the skin like wet fabric. Adrian felt it in his teeth, in the shallow ache behind his sinuses.

Mercer kept his light low and swept it across the floor before each step. He wasn't searching for answers. He was searching for the next stable place to put his boot. Marissa followed close enough that Adrian could hear the small, controlled breath she took before stepping, as if she'd turned herself into a machine that could not afford to flinch. Bellamy stayed behind them, rigid and quiet, the kind of quiet that wasn't calm so much as contained.

They did not speak.

The mine made sound anyway.

Not voices. Not anything dramatic. Just the slow, persistent drip of water somewhere deeper in, and the softer sound of their own movement echoed back at them wrong. Adrian had expected echoes to be obvious, a repeat you could recognize. Instead it was subtler: a thin resonance that seemed to cling to each footstep and then trail off in a different direction than the one it came from. Like the mine didn't reflect sound so much as reroute it.

Mercer stopped after ten yards and raised a fist.

All four froze.

Adrian's headlamp beam trembled slightly on the wall, and he hated that his body had betrayed him in such a small way. He forced the light steady and listened. In the sudden stillness, the drip became louder, not because it changed, but because his brain had nothing else to hold onto.

Mercer angled his head, listening with the practiced focus of a man used to locating a noise in the woods before it became a problem. He waited long enough that Adrian's legs began to ache from holding tension.

Then Mercer lowered his hand and moved again.

Adrian saw what had stopped him.

On the ground, half covered by wet grit, a fresh scrape cut across the dirt like someone had dragged a hard edge through it recently. Not a collapse mark.

Not the random scuff of an animal. It was too straight.

Mercer pointed his light at it, then at the rail line. "Something heavy," he breathed, not quite a whisper but close.

Marissa leaned in, careful not to step off the narrow strip of firmer ground near the wall. She didn't touch the mark. "A case," she murmured.

Adrian felt a small, cold weight settle in his stomach. The drag mark outside had been a suggestion. This was confirmation.

Bellamy, behind them, made a small sound that Adrian recognized as a swallowed comment. The historian wanted to speak, to anchor the moment in explanation, but Mercer had warned them: inside, sound carried.

Adrian thought of the letter in the records folder. The luminous phenomena displayed a curious tendency toward pursuit when men attempted to withdraw. He'd read it as a description of movement. Now, in the quiet, it also felt like a description of something else: attention triggered by response.

A little farther in, the passage narrowed and forced them into single file, close enough that Adrian could smell Bellamy's aftershave when Bellamy exhaled. The mine walls were rough, chiseled stone scarred by tools. In places, moisture had darkened the rock into streaks that looked like old smoke trails.

Adrian's shoulder brushed the wall once, just a light contact, and the sound it made was too loud. A soft scrape that shot down the tunnel and returned in thin fragments, not one echo but several, as if the noise had been caught and thrown into different pockets of the mine.

Mercer stopped again, instantly.

Adrian froze with his hand half-lifted, as though he could take back the sound by holding still.

Mercer didn't look at him, but Adrian could feel the reprimand anyway. Not anger. A reminder: your body is louder than you think down here.

Mercer moved on, slower.

They reached a place where the wall on Adrian's right showed a series of parallel scratches. At first he thought they were old tool marks. Then he realized they ran too evenly, too long, and they were at shoulder height. He angled his headlamp toward them, and the beam caught the grooves like thin black lines.

Marissa saw them and went still. Her scientific composure had not cracked yet, but it strained. "Those aren't from picks," she said.

Bellamy leaned forward, then checked himself and stayed where he was. "Could be cart damage," he whispered.

Mercer's light swept the scratches and then kept going, refusing to give them the dignity of too much attention. "Keep moving," he said, voice tight.

The passage opened slightly and then dipped again. The drip sound changed, not in volume but in rhythm, as if they were nearing a place where water fell into a different chamber. Adrian found himself tracking it the way you tracked a voice in a crowd. The drip became a metronome for their intrusion.

He tried to measure their distance from the entrance, but the mine made distance unreliable. The pale rectangle of daylight behind them had shrunk into something that felt less like an exit and more like a memory of one.

Mercer slowed at a branching point where the main tunnel split.

Two passages, each narrower than the one they'd been in, each slanting down into a different dark. Wooden supports framed the split like ribs. The timbers were older here, darker with age and damp. On one beam, Adrian saw a faint charcoal mark.

A cross, smeared and half-erased.

Below it, a line of writing.

He stepped closer without meaning to, drawn by the simple human urge to read. Then he stopped himself before his boots crossed the line Mercer had been walking.

Mercer noticed anyway. He angled his light.

The writing was shakier than the cross, as though made by a hand that had not wanted to linger.

DO NOT CALL TO THEM

Bellamy's breath caught, audible despite his effort to keep it quiet.

Marissa stared, her face pale in the beam. "This is… old."

Mercer didn't answer. He didn't need to. The warning belonged to the same category as the one scrawled on the mine map in the county records: too specific, too practical, too ashamed to be theatrical.

Adrian felt the pattern align again, a straight line drawn from paper to stone. Do not answer voices from the trees. Do not whistle. Do not call it by name. Do not call to them.

Whatever had been here had trained people, not with explanation, but with consequence.

Mercer unfolded the copied mine map from his pocket, the photograph printout they'd made from Adrian's phone. He held it close to his light, squinting at the lines. "Left should lead toward the lower cut," he murmured. "Right is supposed to dead-end in a storage chamber, if the sketch is even close."

Bellamy's voice was tight and unwilling. "We're already beyond 'ten yards.'"

Mercer met his eyes briefly. "I know," he said. "But we're not wandering. We're checking."

Marissa's gaze stayed on the warning on the timber. "Do not call to them," she repeated softly, and there was an edge to her voice now, not fear exactly, but the recognition that the rule had survived because it had to.

Adrian looked down the left passage and felt, with surprising clarity, the same pull he'd felt on the ridge the night before. Not a physical force. Something more intimate and insidious: the sense that an answer existed just out of sight, and that one more step would make the uncertainty resolve.

He didn't move.

Instead, he forced himself to focus on the soundscape. The drip. Their breathing. The faint creak of old wood settling under its own weight. And underneath it all, the mine's thin resonance, like a held note you couldn't quite hear but could feel in your jaw.

Mercer kept his voice low. "We go right first," he said. "If it's a dead end, we confirm no one's there. Then we back out."

Bellamy seemed relieved by the idea of a dead end. Marissa nodded once, and Adrian recognized the relief in her too: a bounded space meant fewer unknowns.

They turned into the right passage.

It tightened quickly, forcing them close to the wall. The floor grew rougher, scattered with smaller rock and old splinters of timber. The air smelled more stagnant, and the drip sound shifted again, farther away, less regular.

Adrian's headlamp caught something pale on the ground. For a second his mind made it a bone, and his stomach lurched. Then the beam steadied and he saw it was only a strip of cloth, bleached by damp. He crouched, careful, and touched it with a gloved finger.

Synthetic.

Not nineteenth century. Not linen or wool.

Modern fabric.

Marissa crouched beside him, her discipline slipping just enough to show urgency. "That's recent," she said.

Mercer's light snapped down. He didn't touch the cloth. He simply stared at it as if it proved what he'd been trying not to say out loud since they'd seen the prints outside.

Someone had been here.

Not long ago.

Bellamy swallowed. "We should leave," he whispered.

Mercer nodded once, sharp. "We check the chamber," he said. "Then we leave."

They moved the last few yards and the passage opened into a low space choked with rubble. The ceiling had partially collapsed long ago, leaving a mound of broken rock and timber that filled half the chamber. The rails ended here, bent and half-buried like snapped bones. It was a dead end, as the map had suggested.

And yet the dead end didn't feel empty.

The air was colder here. Not in a way that suggested a draft, but in a way that made Adrian's skin prickle. He realized, with a small shock, that the drip sound had stopped. Not faded. Stopped.

Mercer held up his hand again.

They froze, four figures in a pocket of darkness, lights pointed down, bodies trying to become quiet enough to be ignored.

Adrian listened until his ears seemed to strain. He could hear his own pulse. He could hear Bellamy's shallow breath, trying not to be heard and making itself more obvious.

Then, faint and delicate, something clicked.

Once.

A sound like two small stones touched together.

It came from somewhere beyond the rubble, in a space that should not have existed, a space the collapse should have sealed.

Mercer's head turned slightly, trying to locate it. His posture tightened. His hand remained raised, not just a signal to stop moving, but a command to stop being human.

Adrian's throat went dry. He remembered Mercer's instruction before they entered: if any of you feel that pull, you tell me.

He realized he wasn't feeling it now.

He was feeling something worse.

The certainty that sound had traveled farther than it should have, and that whatever had made the clicking had heard them arrive.

For a long moment none of them moved.

Mercer's raised hand held them in place, but it was the click that really pinned them. A sound small enough to be nothing, and yet too deliberate to dismiss.

Adrian kept his headlamp angled low, trying not to brighten the collapsed wall as if light itself counted as attention. The beam showed only broken stone, jagged timber, and the bent rails vanishing under rubble. A dead end.

And still, the click had come from beyond it.

Marissa's eyes tracked along the debris field as if mapping weak points, searching for some slit or breathing gap the collapse had left behind. Bellamy stood stiff, his jaw working, as if he was trying to chew his way back into rational explanations without making a sound.

Mercer lowered his hand slowly, not as permission to move, but as a warning that any movement should be chosen.

"We're leaving," Bellamy whispered, the words barely shaped.

Mercer didn't answer immediately. He leaned his head a fraction, listening again. Adrian watched the ranger's posture, the way his shoulders were slightly raised, his weight balanced on the balls of his feet. Ready to back out without turning it into panic.

Another click came, softer than the first. Not in the same place, Adrian realized. Or maybe the mine made location unreliable. The sound seemed to drift, as if it didn't need a straight line.

Marissa's mouth was close to Adrian's ear when she spoke. "There has to be an opening behind that collapse. A void. Something that connects."

Adrian didn't respond. He was thinking of the wording in the old foreman statement: varying heights and locations, not fixed to the floor.

Mercer gestured with two fingers toward the passage they'd come in through. Back. Slow.

They began to retreat, boots placing themselves carefully in the grooves they'd already made in the grit. Adrian kept his breathing shallow, not from fear of suffocation, but from the strange, animal urge not to announce himself in a place where sound behaved wrong.

Halfway back down the narrow passage, his headlamp beam swept across the stone and caught a faint shimmer near the ground.

It was so slight he almost dismissed it as moisture reflecting light. Mines were full of slick rock and wet surfaces. Any beam could bounce.

Then the shimmer moved.

Not like water. Not like a reflection dragged by his own motion. It slid, sideways, against the logic of his headlamp.

Adrian stopped so abruptly Bellamy nearly bumped into him.

Mercer's light snapped toward the spot. "Don't," Mercer breathed. Not don't look, Adrian realized. Don't move.

The shimmer resolved into a pinpoint glow, pale and steady, hovering just above the mine floor near a scatter of small stones. It wasn't bright enough to throw light onto the rock around it. It was light without illumination, a presence more than a lantern.

Adrian felt his stomach tighten with a recognition that didn't want to form words.

The glow dimmed slightly as all of them held still.

Marissa's eyes widened. She didn't speak, but Adrian saw her swallow, the motion loud in his imagination.

The glow brightened again, just a fraction, as Bellamy exhaled a little too hard.

And then it moved toward them.

Not fast. Not darting. It slid with that same patient certainty they'd seen across the valley, as if it understood distance better than they did and knew exactly how close it wanted to be.

Mercer's voice was barely audible. "Back," he said.

They backed up one step in unison, four bodies obeying one impulse: leave without making it a chase.

The light stopped when they stopped.

Adrian felt the hair lift on his arms under his sleeves. It wasn't the light's movement that terrified him. It was the timing. The way it behaved like an animal that had learned a rule.

When you stop, it stops.

When you move, it follows.

Another glow appeared, higher up, about chest height near the wall to Adrian's right. This one was fainter at first, as if it had been there all along and only now decided to be seen. It hovered in place, and Adrian had the irrational sensation that it was watching their faces, cataloging features the way Ruth Calhoun had warned.

Because it learns you.

Marissa's gaze flicked toward it and then dropped quickly, as if her body remembered the rule even as her mind argued with it.

"Mercer," she whispered, "how many?"

Mercer didn't answer the question directly. He didn't count. Counting was a human act, a way of turning threat into data.

He said, "No calling. No names. No whistles."

A third glow blinked into existence near the ceiling timbers, tucked between two supports like a pale knot of light caught in old wood. Adrian couldn't see a source. There was no flame, no spark, no visible object carrying the brightness. Just the brightness itself, suspended as if it belonged to the air.

Bellamy's lips parted. Adrian knew he was about to speak, to do what humans always did when confronted with the incomprehensible: narrate it into manageable shape.

Mercer cut him off with a look that said, do not give it your voice.

Bellamy shut his mouth.

The first light near the ground drifted closer by another foot, then stopped. The second light at chest height shifted slightly, angling as if it was repositioning for a better view of the group.

And in the silence between drips and breath, Adrian heard it again.

A click.

This time it was closer. Not behind the collapse anymore. Around them.

The lights brightened subtly, the way eyes adjust when something of interest moves.

Adrian realized with a sick certainty that the dead-end chamber had not been the point. It had been the trigger. The moment they entered, the moment the clicking began, the mine had started arranging itself around their presence. Not stone. Not timbers.

The phenomenon.

Marissa's face had gone pale in the narrow tunnel. Her voice, when it came, was controlled and thin. "If it's responding to sound," she whispered, "we have to reduce output. Even breathing."

Adrian wanted to tell her the obvious problem: you can't be alive quietly enough in a place like this.

Mercer began to guide them backward again, leading with his shoulders rather than his voice. One slow step.

The ground light moved with them, maintaining distance.

One more step.

It followed again.

Mercer stopped.

The light stopped.

Adrian felt the pattern lock into place like a mechanism. It wasn't random. It wasn't drifting like gas. It wasn't behaving like distant headlights misread through fog.

It was tracking.

Bellamy's hand rose slightly, perhaps to adjust his glasses, perhaps to point. The motion was small, but it was motion.

The chest-height light glided toward him instantly, closing the space by several feet with a smoothness that looked wrong in the stale air. Bellamy froze mid-gesture, fingers half-curled.

The light halted so close that Adrian could see it wasn't a simple orb. Its edge was not crisp. It had a subtle shimmer, like heat distortion, as if something translucent sat around the light and bent the air. Adrian's mind tried to supply a form: membrane, film, thin structure moving too quickly to resolve.

Bellamy's eyes went wide behind his glasses. He didn't scream. He didn't speak. But his breath hitched, and that involuntary sound seemed to act like a signal.

The light pulsed once, brighter.

Mercer snapped his fingers sharply, once, low at his side, the smallest sound that still carried command. Not for the lights, Adrian realized. For Bellamy. Freeze and breathe through it.

The pulsing stopped when Bellamy steadied.

Marissa's gaze was down, fixed on the dirt and the rails as if she could anchor herself to something that obeyed physics. But Adrian saw her hands trembling slightly near her recorder case. Fear, disciplined but present.

Adrian thought of the old newspaper line they'd read in the records office, the foreman's observation that had sounded ridiculous until now: they dimmed when the men held still and gathered when they shouted.

He could see it happening in real time. Stillness reduced interest. Movement and sound intensified it.

Mercer began backing them toward the junction again, the place with the charcoal cross and the warning on the timber. Adrian felt a desperate gratitude for that sign, absurd as it was. The mine had instructions, pressed into wood by hands that had survived long enough to write them.

DO NOT CALL TO THEM.

At the junction, Mercer paused and angled his light down the left passage, the one he'd avoided at first. The air coming up from it felt colder, as if the mine exhaled from deeper lungs there. Adrian saw the slope of the floor dip away, a throat leading down.

A faint glow pulsed in that darkness, far below the reach of their beams.

Then another.

Then a third, at a different height, floating above the descending cut like pale seeds suspended in water.

Marissa made a small, involuntary sound, a breath that wasn't quite a gasp.

The lights in the right passage reacted immediately.

The ground light brightened and slid closer. The chest-height light that had approached Bellamy shifted position, as if flanking. The timber-light above them moved, drifting toward the junction like a slow, curious star.

Adrian felt the pull again, stronger now, and it didn't come from wonder.

It came from a terrible, instinctive urge to resolve the situation by doing something, by stepping toward the new lights as if proximity meant control. The same urge that made hikers leave trails. The same urge that turned rules into tragedy.

Mercer's voice, when he finally used it, was barely more than breath. "Eyes down," he said. "We go out. Now."

They began to retreat toward the faint rectangle of daylight that still existed somewhere behind them.

The lights followed.

Not rushing. Not attacking.

Keeping pace with the patience of something that had learned, over a century of mountain nights and underground shifts, that humans always made more noise when they were trying to leave.

And in the dim, mineral cold of the tunnel, with pale glows rearranging themselves around their movement, Adrian understood the cruel brilliance of the phenomenon's oldest trick.

It didn't need to chase at first.

It only needed to teach you that you were being watched.

Then wait for you to react.

Chapter 8

The Things That Pursue

They backed up in the same careful rhythm Mercer had set, one step at a time, bodies turned half-sideways in the narrow passage so they wouldn't brush the walls. Adrian kept his head down, but the lights still burned at the edges of his vision, pale afterimages that seemed to hang in the air even when he blinked.

The rectangle of daylight behind them was no longer visible. Not because it was gone, but because the mine had bent and turned enough that the exit existed only as an idea. The tunnel swallowed light the way fog did on the ridge, softening distance, making direction feel less like a line and more like a suggestion.

A click sounded close to Adrian's left ear.

He flinched before he could stop himself. The sound had no breath behind it, no throat, no human shape. It was too clean, too small, and it carried the wrong kind of intention. Not speech. Not warning. A signal.

The ground-level glow brightened immediately, as if his movement had been a raised hand in a dark room.

Mercer's hand came up again, palm low, his fingers spread in a command that meant become stone.

They froze.

The lights did what they had been doing all along. They froze too.

Adrian's mind snagged on the impossibility of that, even as his body accepted it. This was not drifting. This was not gas catching a draft. It was an interaction, a script that required both sides to participate. And the mine itself seemed designed to make participation inevitable. You could not move without sound. You could not breathe without motion. You could not turn fear off like a lamp.

Mercer began to back them again, barely shifting his weight.

The lights slid with them.

Not closing in. Not falling back. Maintaining a distance that felt chosen.

Bellamy's shoulders were tight under his jacket, his head angled down the way Ruth Calhoun had instructed without ever seeing this place. Marissa kept her gaze fixed on the rails and dirt, but her hands were clenched hard around the recorder case strap, knuckles pale.

Another click, farther away, answered the one near Adrian's ear.

Then another.

The mine was no longer quiet enough for Adrian to pretend the sounds were isolated. The clicking was moving around them, not as echoes, not as random settling of rock. It was patterned. A soft, irregular chorus that suggested multiple sources, communicating or coordinating in a way their brains could feel without being able to translate.

Mercer stopped again, and for a second Adrian thought they might actually get out like this: slow, controlled retreat, no shouting, no sprinting, no panic. A ranger's method, applied to something that was not an animal but behaved like one when it came to attention.

Then Bellamy's foot slipped.

It was small. His boot found a patch of loose grit beside the rail and skated an inch. But the scrape was loud in the mine's thin, rerouting acoustics, and Bellamy's instinctive intake of breath came with it, sharp and involuntary.

The effect was immediate.

The lights did not simply brighten.

They surged.

The chest-height glow snapped forward with a smooth, unnatural speed, crossing several feet of tunnel in less than a second. It stopped short of Bellamy's face, close enough that Adrian saw the shimmer around it intensify, as if the air had thickened. Bellamy froze mid-recovery, one hand half-raised, eyes wide behind his glasses.

The ground-level light shot forward too, not toward Bellamy but toward the scrape mark his boot had made, as if the sound had a physical location it could taste.

The timber-light above them dropped lower, sliding down through the stale air until it hovered just above Marissa's shoulder.

Marissa jerked instinctively, her body rebelling against her discipline.

The light lunged with her movement, and Adrian heard a new sound beneath the clicking: a wet flutter, like thin material flexing rapidly, too fast to be a wing and too organic to be an echo. For a flicker of a second, the glow distorted and Adrian thought he saw a translucent fold around it, like membrane catching light.

Mercer hissed, "Stop."

But it was too late. The script had changed.

The lights were no longer testing them for reaction. They were reacting.

One of the glows from the left passage, the deeper cut they'd only glimpsed, drifted up into the junction behind them, joining the cluster as if called by the commotion. Then another followed. The clicking increased, not louder in volume but denser in frequency, filling the air in a way that made Adrian's jaw feel tight, like his teeth were responding to it.

Mercer's head snapped toward the direction they'd come from, as if checking whether they were being boxed in.

They were.

The corridor ahead of them, the way out, was still open. But the mine no longer felt like a straight line. It felt like a throat tightening.

Mercer made a decision so quickly Adrian felt it as a shift in the air.

"Move," Mercer said, a whisper forced into a command. "Now. Slow, but move."

They began backing faster, still trying to place each step carefully, still trying to keep their bodies from brushing the walls. But the surge had done something to them. Their control was no longer clean. It had been cracked.

Bellamy's breathing was audible now, an uneven rasp he couldn't help. Marissa's boot struck the rail with a dull clang and she winced, head dipping lower as if she could apologize to the mine by making herself smaller.

The lights tightened their spacing.

They were no longer keeping a respectful distance. They were closing the ring by degrees, glows repositioning like scouts, brightening and dimming in quick pulses that seemed to correspond to the rhythm of human error.

Adrian felt the pull again, that sick, unreasonable urge to turn and look directly at them, to get information, to understand. It was the same instinct that made someone turn toward headlights even when they knew they should get off the road. The mind's belief that vision could solve what fear could not.

He kept his eyes down and hated how hard that was.

The clicking moved closer.

A glow darted past Adrian's left side, so near his cheek the cold hit him like damp breath. The rotten-sweet smell followed it, faint but real, and Adrian's stomach lurched. The air did not move like wind. It was heavier than that, a cold that carried moisture and decay.

Adrian's throat tightened around a sound. He forced it down.

Do not call to them.

Do not answer voices from the trees.

Do not whistle below this point.

All the rules, all the paper and porch talk and dismissive arguments, reduced to this: do not feed it response.

But response was not only voice.

Response was motion. Response was breath. Response was the involuntary noise of fear.

Mercer's shoulder bumped Adrian's as the ranger adjusted position, putting himself slightly between the nearest glow and the others. Adrian saw Mercer's hand go to the radio on his vest out of habit, then stop short as if he'd touched a hot surface. The ranger let it drop. No transmissions. No sound offered into the stone.

They turned a bend in the tunnel and the pale rectangle of daylight reappeared, faint and distant, the mouth of the mine like a memory made real. Relief hit Adrian so hard he almost stumbled. It was a dangerous relief, the kind that made the body loosen at the wrong moment.

The lights sensed it. Or perhaps they sensed the subtle increase in human speed, the way hope made people careless.

Two of them shot forward, passing Adrian and Mercer and Bellamy, gliding toward the visible exit as if to cut it off. They hovered in the center of the tunnel, brighter than before, their edges shimmering in rapid motion that made the air around them look like it was boiling.

Marissa made a small sound, not a word, but a broken inhale that turned into something like a whimper.

The lights pulsed.

The clicking became frantic.

Adrian's mouth went dry as he realized, with sudden clarity, that the phenomenon did not need the mine to trap people. It used the mine because it magnified what it needed: panic, noise, confined motion. The mountain didn't just hide it. The mountain helped it hunt.

Mercer reached behind his hip, fingers fumbling for something in his pack, and Adrian saw the strap shift, heard the faint rattle of gear.

The nearest glow snapped toward the sound with startling speed.

Mercer swore, not loud, but sharp, a single syllable that shot through the tunnel like a flare of its own.

The lights surged all at once.

No more patient sliding. No more measured tracking. They came forward as a cluster, a rush of pale, strobing glows that filled the corridor from floor to shoulder height, darting in irregular angles that made the air seem alive with them. Adrian caught flashes of translucent structure around the light, thin articulated folds that flexed and collapsed, appearing only when the glow changed speed. Membrane. Joint. Something that was not a simple orb.

Marissa stumbled backward into Bellamy, and Bellamy grabbed her arm too hard, trying to steady her and steady himself. Their contact made another scrape, another involuntary cascade of sound.

The cluster accelerated.

Adrian's fear finally broke into action. He found himself moving without permission, half-turning, trying to shield his face with his shoulder, trying to keep his eyes down while still seeing enough not to fall.

Mercer yanked something free from his pack.

A cylinder. A flare.

Adrian saw it in Mercer's hand in the same instant he saw the lights close the final gap, their cold presence rushing into the space around them with that wet fluttering sound, as if thin bodies were flexing in excitement.

Mercer brought the flare up, his arm shaking, and Adrian understood that they had reached the point in every old story where the rules stopped being enough.

Now it would be whatever worked. Whatever burned. Whatever the mountain hadn't taught the lights to ignore.

And the pursuing things, bright and clicking and suddenly furious, were already within reach.

Mercer's thumb found the cap of the flare by feel, fumbling once, then gripping harder as if force could substitute for steadiness. The cylinder trembled in his hand.

The lights were everywhere now, close enough that Adrian could no longer pretend they were separate points in space. Their glow bled across the stone, strobing in broken pulses that made the tunnel look like it was breathing. The clicking had risen into a nervous, overlapping chatter, and beneath it that wet flutter kept returning, an organic flexing sound that did not match any animal Adrian could name.

Mercer brought the flare up between them and the oncoming cluster.

"Down," he rasped.

It wasn't a shout. It was worse than that, a voice forced through clenched teeth. It still seemed to punch through the mine like a signal.

Adrian dropped instinctively, knees slamming into grit beside the rail. Marissa folded down too fast and hit her shoulder against the wall. Bellamy crouched awkwardly, one hand braced on stone, his glasses reflecting pale light in a way that made his eyes look briefly unhuman.

The nearest glow snapped forward.

For one terrible instant Adrian thought it would reach Mercer before he could do anything. The cold, damp presence washed across Adrian's face like a hand dipped in creek water. The rotten-sweet smell thickened. Something moved inside the light, a translucent fold tightening and releasing, as if the glow was only what leaked out around a body.

Mercer struck the flare.

The ignition was not a clean spark. It was a violent, scraping flare of friction, followed by a sudden blossom of red fire that hissed into life with a sound like tearing cloth. The tunnel filled with a harsh, chemical burn smell that cut through damp stone and rot.

The effect was immediate and absolute.

The lights recoiled.

Not drifted back. Not dimmed. They jerked away as if yanked by an invisible line, the clicking breaking into a higher, frantic rhythm. Several glows shot toward the ceiling timbers, slamming themselves into the upper dark and then bouncing away in erratic angles as if the red light had become a physical barrier.

One of them, too close to the flare when it ignited, flashed brighter for a split second, and Adrian saw more than shimmer. He saw the edge of a thin, membranous structure curl inward, like a translucent fin snapping shut. Then it vanished backward, swallowed by darkness beyond the flare's reach.

Mercer lifted the flare higher, arm shaking from the effort and the heat. Red light washed over the tunnel walls, turning the mine's damp stone into something raw and newly wounded. Shadows jumped and twisted. The rails gleamed like wet bones.

"Move," Mercer said. This time it was a command with momentum. "Now. Now."

They went.

Adrian pushed up, slipping once on grit, then catching himself on the rail. His palm came away smeared with cold mud. Marissa grabbed Bellamy's sleeve and hauled him forward as he stumbled, his body moving like it had forgotten the order of steps. Bellamy's mouth was open, drawing too much air, and each inhale sounded loud enough to summon the whole mountain.

The flare hissed and spit. Mercer held it out and slightly behind them like a torch held against pursuing wolves.

The lights kept their distance, but they did not leave.

They hovered beyond the red glow's edge, pulsing in and out like pale eyes refusing to blink. The clicking continued, uneven now, circling. Adrian couldn't always tell where it came from. The mine rerouted sound, smeared it, made it impossible to trust direction.

They ran anyway, as much as the uneven tunnel allowed. It wasn't a full sprint. The rails and rubble would have punished that. It was a frantic, half-controlled flight, boots thudding, shoulders brushing stone, breath turning into an involuntary broadcast.

Do not call to them, Adrian thought, but the rule had expanded now, in his mind, into something broader and more desperate.

Do not give them anything.

A glow darted sideways across the tunnel ahead, stopping in the center of their path like a floating obstruction. For a split second Adrian's body tried to react the way it would to a living creature blocking a trail: slow down, assess, decide. The impulse to look up, to lock eyes with it, surged hard.

Mercer thrust the flare forward.

The red light hit the pale glow and the pale glow snapped backward as if struck, flickering violently. The clicking spiked, and the glow retreated to the side, leaving the corridor open again.

Marissa made a sound that was almost a laugh and almost a sob, her voice breaking. She clamped her mouth shut immediately as if ashamed to have made any noise at all.

"Eyes down," Mercer repeated, though it sounded more like he was reminding himself. "Don't stare at them."

Bellamy's voice came out thin, disbelieving. "It hates the flare."

"It reacts to it," Marissa said, and there was something fierce in her tone now, a scientist's anger at being forced into the language of fear. "It's not about hate."

Adrian didn't answer. He was watching the flare's red halo as if it were a shrinking circle of safety. The hiss had a rhythm. The flame's intensity wasn't constant. It surged and softened, surged and softened, and each softening made the pale lights inch forward, testing.

Behind them, a crack sounded overhead.

Not a click. A crack. Dry wood shifting under stress.

The mine reminded them that it had its own ways of killing.

Mercer didn't slow. He lifted the flare higher, and the red light painted the timbers above them. Adrian saw old beams bowed and damp-blackened, the grain split in places like scars. He imagined the whole ceiling giving up, imagined being trapped under stone while pale lights hovered just beyond reach, patient.

The thought nearly stole his balance.

They rounded a bend and the pale rectangle of daylight widened ahead, no longer a memory but an actual opening. The sight hit Adrian like oxygen. Outside was fog and cold and forest, but it was open space. It was distance. It was sound that didn't bounce back and trap you inside it.

The lights sensed it.

They surged again, not into the flare's radius, but into positions that made Adrian's stomach drop. Two glows darted toward the entrance, hovering near the mouth of the mine as if they could hold the threshold the way a door held a room. Others clustered behind, pulsing like signals passed along a line.

The clicking became dense, urgent.

Mercer swore again, and this time it was louder, scraped raw by panic. The cluster responded instantly, several glows snapping closer, their cold presence pressing into the tunnel air.

Mercer whipped the flare in a short arc, forcing the red light across the corridor.

The pale glows recoiled, but only just enough. They were learning too, Adrian realized with horror. They were adjusting their distance, figuring out how close they could get without crossing into whatever the red flare did to them.

A bright pulse flared near Marissa's shoulder. She jerked away, slammed into the wall, and her boot struck the rail with a metallic clang.

The response was immediate. A pale glow lunged, so fast Adrian saw only a streak.

Mercer shoved the flare toward it, almost touching.

The pale glow convulsed backward, and Adrian heard, very distinctly, a sound like thin material snapping wetly, like a membrane pulled too tight. The rotten-sweet smell intensified for a second, then faded as the glow retreated beyond the flare's edge.

Marissa's eyes were wide, fixed on the ground. Her jaw clenched as if she were trying to force her body to stop betraying her.

"Move," Adrian said, and hated that he spoke at all, hated that his voice shook, hated that the mine took it and threw it back in fragments. But the word was already out, and it was for Marissa, not the lights.

She moved.

They reached the last stretch to the entrance, and daylight flooded in around the fog, turning the mine mouth into a harsh silhouette. The forest outside looked unreal after the tunnel's strobed dark: laurel leaves slick with damp, trunks rising straight and indifferent, fog hanging in layers like breath caught in the branches.

Mercer pushed out first, flare held high. The red light looked obscene against the gray daylight.

Adrian stumbled out behind him, boots sliding on wet leaves. Bellamy and Marissa followed, half-falling into the clearing like people ejected from a bad dream.

For one second Adrian thought it was over.

Then, behind them, inside the mine, the clicking continued.

Not muffled. Not distant.

Close enough to make his skin tighten.

Mercer didn't lower the flare. He backed away from the entrance slowly, eyes locked on the dark opening, his posture wide and braced like a man keeping a wild animal from charging.

Adrian stood beside him, chest heaving. Every breath felt too loud, too full of information.

In the mine mouth, pale light bloomed again.

One glow hovered just inside the timber frame, held back by the red flare's radius. Another appeared higher up, near the top beam, pulsing as if tasting the air. They did not rush out into daylight. They didn't have to. They simply held position, watching, patient as hunger.

Marissa's voice came out hoarse. "They won't cross."

Bellamy stared, eyes flicking between the pale glows and the flare. His face had gone ashen, the color of old paper. "Or they don't need to."

Mercer's arm shook, and the flare hissed harder, spitting sparks. Adrian saw with sudden dread that the flare was burning down faster than his mind wanted to admit. The red light was a finite resource. The mine's darkness was not.

Mercer glanced at Adrian, and in his eyes Adrian saw the same calculation he'd heard in his voice at the entrance: how to help without becoming another disappearance.

"We go," Mercer said. "Back to the truck. No running. Stay together."

Adrian nodded, though his legs wanted to bolt. The instinct to sprint away was overwhelming, a primitive need to put distance between skin and cold light. But he remembered the rule set as behavior, not belief: panic made noise, noise made pursuit.

They began moving away from the mine mouth in a tight cluster, Mercer backing first, flare still held out like a boundary line.

The pale glows remained inside the entrance, hovering, clicking softly, as if conferring.

As Adrian stepped backward into the foggy forest, the red flare painting wet leaves and tree trunks in violent color, he realized the cruelest part of what they'd learned.

The mine had not been a cage for the lights.

It had been a tool.

And now that they had brought red fire into its dark, the mountain knew exactly where they were.

The fog swallowed them within three steps of the mine entrance.

It wasn't the thick, theatrical fog tourists liked in photographs. It was the kind that made distance uncertain, that softened edges and stole reference points. The clearing around the mine was small, choked by laurel and young pine, and as soon as the gray air folded between them and the opening, Adrian realized how easy it would be to lose the exact location of the mouth again if Mercer hadn't tied the strip of survey tape.

Mercer moved backward, flare held out and slightly up, his arm extended like it was bracing against something that pushed back. The red light pulsed against wet leaves and dark trunks, turning the forest into a series of blood-colored flashes. Sparks hissed and died in the fog before they could fall.

Adrian stayed close on Mercer's left, eyes low, scanning the ground for roots and loose stone. Bellamy and Marissa kept tight behind, their bodies pulled inward, shoulders high, like they were trying to make themselves smaller in a world that had proven size didn't matter.

"Don't run," Mercer said again, quieter now. "If you run, you fall. If you fall, you scream."

No one argued. They didn't have the breath for it.

Behind them, from the direction of the mine, the clicking continued. It came and went as the fog shifted, sometimes sounding muffled, sometimes close enough that Adrian's neck tightened as if he could feel it on his skin. He couldn't tell if the sound was traveling through air or through the strange way the mine had rerouted noise, spilling it into the trees like a leak.

Marissa's voice came thin. "How long does that flare last?"

Mercer didn't look at her. "Not long enough."

Adrian could see it himself. The flare's length had already shortened, the burning end creeping closer to Mercer's fist. The red fire was still bright, still aggressive, but it had a different quality now, less like a wall and more like a countdown.

They reached the chain barrier where the old road began. The truck was beyond, half-hidden by fog and branches. Adrian had never been more grateful to see a dull government vehicle.

Bellamy's breathing hitched, and in that involuntary sound Adrian heard the beginning of panic. Bellamy's mind had been built for archives and arguments, not for things that reacted to a slip of a boot.

Mercer slowed and turned his head just enough to catch Bellamy in his peripheral vision. "Professor," he said, and the use of the title was deliberate, a reminder of identity, of control. "Stay with me."

Bellamy swallowed hard and nodded once.

They moved again, stepping around puddles that reflected the red flare like torn-open wounds. The fog made every tree look closer than it was. The forest was too quiet in the way it had been on the ridge that first night, that hollow quiet where sound didn't belong to the living world so much as it belonged to whatever listened.

Adrian tried not to look back.

He failed.

Over Mercer's shoulder, he could just make out the mine's direction by the darker cut of the slope and the obscene little strip of survey tape shining like an insult. For a moment he saw nothing else. Then, near where the mine mouth should have been, a pale point blinked in the fog.

It didn't illuminate the trees around it. It didn't throw light the way a headlamp would.

It simply existed.

Adrian felt his body tighten, the old instinct to stare at danger. He forced his eyes down again, but the afterimage of it remained on his retina, a ghost spot.

"It's out," Marissa whispered.

Mercer didn't ask what she meant. He'd heard it in her tone.

"Keep moving," he said.

The clicking rose again, and this time it didn't sound like it was coming only from behind. It sounded as if it had stepped into the woods with them, broken into separate points, some nearer, some farther, a scattered pattern that made Adrian's skin itch with the urge to locate and name.

Do not call it by name.

The rule came back with cruel clarity. Naming wasn't only speech. It was attention. It was the mind reaching out and offering a shape.

They reached the truck.

Mercer yanked the driver's door open without letting the flare dip. Adrian could see the interior briefly, dim and ordinary, and the ordinariness felt like a lie the world told to make itself bearable. Mercer shoved the flare toward the open space beside the truck, holding it away from the vehicle as if the red fire might be the only thing keeping the pale lights from sliding closer through the fog.

"Keys," Mercer said, and Adrian realized Mercer's hands were too occupied to retrieve them.

Adrian dug into his coat pocket with clumsy fingers, pulled out the key ring Mercer had handed him at the records office earlier when they'd swapped vehicles to avoid parking issues, and jammed it into Mercer's palm.

Mercer took them without looking and made a sharp motion with his chin. "Bellamy, back seat. Marissa, other side. Cross, front. Now."

They moved with the jerky obedience of people whose bodies were ahead of their minds. Marissa climbed in first, then Bellamy, nearly tangling their legs as they scrambled across the bench seat. Adrian slid into the passenger seat, his hands shaking enough that the door handle felt slick. He slammed it shut and immediately regretted the noise.

The clicking spiked outside, quickened, as if the sound of the door closing had been a signal.

Mercer was still out there.

He leaned over the hood and looked past it into the fog, flare held high. His face in the red light looked carved and exhausted, eyes too bright. Adrian saw the moment Mercer understood the flare was almost spent. The burn had reached the halfway mark, the heat close enough to make Mercer's grip shift.

Marissa pressed her forehead against the glass of the back window, trying to see past Adrian's headrest. "Mercer," she said, voice breaking. "Get in."

Mercer's jaw clenched. He didn't move.

He was watching something.

Adrian turned slightly in his seat, and through the windshield he saw a pale glow to the right, just beyond the tree line. Then another, higher up. The lights were faint in daylight fog, but they were there, hovering between trunks like patient punctuation marks. They didn't rush. They didn't drift randomly.

They held position as if mapping the truck.

Bellamy's voice came tight and disbelieving. "They followed us out."

"Quiet," Mercer snapped, sharper than he'd been all day. Bellamy shut his mouth immediately.

Mercer swung the flare in a slow arc. The red light swept over the nearest pale glow. It recoiled, not vanishing but pulling back into thicker fog, like an animal stepping out of a spotlight. The clicking faltered, then resumed.

Mercer moved fast then, opening the driver's door and climbing in, flare held awkwardly out the open window so it wouldn't scorch the cab. The heat pushed into the vehicle anyway, harsh and chemical.

"Windows up," he said.

Adrian hit the button on his door. The glass rose with a soft whine that felt obscenely loud in the hush. Marissa did the same. Bellamy's window rose last, and Adrian saw Bellamy's fingers trembling on the switch.

Mercer jammed the key into the ignition.

The engine turned over once, then stuttered.

Adrian's heart dropped into his stomach.

Mercer swore, the sound clipped and raw. He tried again.

The engine coughed, hesitated, and then caught, roaring to life loud enough to make the fog shudder.

Outside, the pale lights brightened.

Not dramatically, not like a flare of anger, but like interest. Like recognition.

Mercer put the truck in reverse, backing hard down the old road. The tires slipped in mud, then found purchase. The vehicle lurched. Adrian grabbed the dash, his knuckles whitening.

In the side mirror, Adrian saw one pale glow drift closer to the road, keeping pace along the tree line. It moved smoothly, as if the underbrush didn't exist for it, as if it was skimming just above the ground without touching it.

Another glow appeared higher up, among the branches, tracking the truck's movement the way the mine lights had tracked their steps.

Mercer kept the flare out the window, and the red light flared and spat, throwing sparks that vanished in the fog. The pale glow nearest the road edged away each time the flare swung in its direction, but it did not leave.

It followed.

The old phrase from the letter came back like a line written in blood: a curious tendency toward pursuit.

Mercer hit the end of the old road and swung onto the narrow paved cut that led back toward Jonas Ridge. Trees rushed past in gray streaks. The fog thinned slightly as they gained elevation, giving the world a little more distance.

The pale lights stayed with them for another quarter mile.

Adrian watched in the mirror as long as his eyes could handle it, forcing himself not to stare directly into the brightness when it slid between tree trunks. The last one hovered at the edge of the road, just inside the forest, keeping pace even as the truck climbed.

Then Mercer rounded a bend where the road widened and a strip of open sky appeared, a lighter gray above the ridgeline.

The pale glow stopped.

It held position for two seconds, hovering like a question.

Adrian had the sudden, irrational certainty that it could see through the glass, that it was learning the shape of their faces anyway, recording them the way Ruth Calhoun had warned.

Because it learns you.

Mercer swung the flare toward it one last time, and the glow recoiled deeper into the trees. The clicking, faint as a memory now, cut off abruptly.

Mercer didn't slow down. He didn't speak. He kept driving until the mine tract was well behind them, until the fog thinned enough to show more of the road, until the forest looked like ordinary forest again, just wet and cold and indifferent.

Only then did he pull the flare inside long enough to drop it into a metal coffee can he kept in the footwell, the kind rangers used for makeshift fire safety. The flare hissed angrily as it burned down the last inch, red light reflected in the can's dull interior like a trapped sunset. When it finally sputtered and died, the cab felt instantly colder.

No one spoke for a full minute.

Adrian realized his hands were still clenched. His jaw ached.

Marissa's voice came at last, quiet and precise, as if she could keep herself together by making language behave. "That wasn't a hallucination."

Bellamy's laugh was small and broken. "No," he said, and then, as if the admission offended him, he added, "but it doesn't mean it was supernatural."

Mercer kept his eyes on the road. "Call it whatever you want," he said. "It followed us."

Adrian stared out at the trees sliding by and tried to reconcile the mine's dark with the daylight's gray. He couldn't. The mountain didn't care about the difference.

He thought of Ranger Eli Foster in the prologue, radios dead, lights drifting patient across a valley, and the scream from the trees that had ended the conversation. He thought of the careful boot prints leading into the mine. The modern fabric scrap. The drag marks.

Someone else had been down there.

Someone who might not have had a flare.

Adrian swallowed and finally said the thing that had been building like pressure since the engine first stuttered.

"We need to find out who went in," he said. "Now. Before the mountain decides it's finished with them."

Mercer nodded once, tight. "Back to the station," he said. "Then we make calls."

Bellamy's voice came from behind, quieter than Adrian had ever heard it. "And if the calls don't bring anyone?"

Mercer's gaze stayed forward. "Then," he said, "we start counting disappearances we used to pretend were accidents."

The road climbed, and the forest thickened again, and Adrian felt the terrible certainty settle into him like cold water soaking through cloth.

They had gotten out.

But the mountain had let them out the way a predator sometimes let prey run, not because it had lost interest, but because it had learned something worth remembering.

And whatever lived in the mine had now learned them too.

Chapter 9

Aftermath and Arguments

The ranger station looked different when they came back to it.

In the morning it had felt like a staging point, a place where plans could be made at a safe distance from the ridge. Now it felt like a thin, bright shell they had crawled into, carrying the mine's cold on their clothes.

Mercer drove too fast up the last stretch of gravel and braked hard in front of the building. The tires spat stones. The sudden stop rocked them forward in their seats.

No one spoke as the engine ticked and cooled.

Adrian's hands were still stiff from gripping the dash. When he flexed his fingers, the skin across his knuckles pulled tight, smeared with dried mud. He could still smell the flare on his jacket, a harsh chemical tang that clung to fabric like a warning.

Mercer opened his door and stepped out first. He moved around the front of the truck and looked back down the road they'd come from, as if expecting the fog to cough something pale into view.

Nothing followed them into the station yard. No clicking. No hovering glow in the treeline.

That absence wasn't comforting. It felt like a pause.

"Inside," Mercer said.

The word came out rougher than his usual tone. He sounded like a man who had held himself together by rule and training and now needed walls to finish the job.

They filed in. The station's fluorescent lights were too clean, turning their faces the color of paperwork. The air was warmer than outside, and the warmth made Adrian aware of how cold he'd been. As his body began to thaw, a tremor ran through him that he couldn't entirely hide.

Marissa noticed and looked away quickly, as if acknowledging it would make it worse.

Bellamy's glasses were fogged at the edges. He wiped them with the hem of his sweater, hands still unsteady. He tried to reclaim his usual posture, shoulders squared, jaw set, but he kept glancing toward the windows like he expected to see the mine's dark mouth reflected there.

Mercer went straight to a metal utility sink near the back, turned on the tap, and shoved his hands under the running water as if he could rinse off what had touched the air around them. He didn't wash like someone cleaning dirt. He washed like someone performing a ritual he didn't believe in but couldn't stop doing.

Adrian set his flashlight on a counter and stared at it. The object looked ordinary. Plastic. Scuffed. Useful. It had been useful in a place where usefulness had nearly gotten them killed.

Marissa lowered her recorder case onto a chair with deliberate care, then immediately pulled it back into her lap, fingers tightening on the handle.

"Everyone good?" Mercer asked.

It was a ranger question, the kind that expected "fine" as a reflex. But his eyes scanned them anyway, taking inventory.

Adrian swallowed. "I didn't get hit. If that's what you mean."

Marissa's voice came quieter than usual. "My shoulder's bruised. I'm fine."

Bellamy opened his mouth, then closed it as if he couldn't decide whether honesty would shame him. Finally, he said, "I'm not injured."

Mercer nodded once, not satisfied but moving on because there wasn't time to linger on feelings. He turned and crossed to the desk, grabbed a corded phone, and began dialing from memory.

Adrian watched his hands. They'd stopped shaking now that he had a task.

"What are you calling in?" Marissa asked.

Mercer didn't look up. "Sheriff first. Then district. Then, if I have to, state."

Bellamy let out a thin breath that might have been a laugh in another context. "And what exactly are you telling them? That we went into an unstable mine because of a scrap of fabric and found… luminous predatory phenomena?"

Mercer paused mid-dial and looked at him.

Bellamy's spine stiffened, ready for a fight.

Mercer's voice stayed low. "I'm telling them there are signs of recent entry into a restricted hazard site. Drag marks. Modern material. And," he added, eyes narrowing slightly, "that I personally observed lights behaving in a way consistent with prior reports."

Bellamy's lips pressed together. He didn't have a clean counterargument to that. Not one that didn't sound like denial.

Mercer finished dialing. The call rang.

No answer.

He hung up and dialed again, this time a different number.

Marissa shifted in her chair. "You're going to put this in writing."

"Yes," Mercer said, and the word had weight. "I have to."

Adrian sat heavily at the edge of a table, the station's plain wood pressing into the backs of his thighs. "If someone went in there with equipment," he said, "they weren't just sightseeing."

Marissa's eyes cut to him. "You think they were studying it."

"I think they were prepared," Adrian replied. "And I think preparedness is what gets people killed faster, because it gives them permission to go deeper."

Bellamy made a sound of irritation. "Or it was a photographer. One of those 'urban explorer' types. Cameras in cases. Tripods."

Mercer's phone call connected. "Yeah," he said into the receiver. "It's Mercer. I need the sheriff to call me back as soon as he's available. This isn't a routine lost hiker. It's the mine tract."

He listened, jaw tightening. "No, I'm at the station. Yes, now."

He hung up and immediately dialed another line.

In the quiet between the buttons, the station seemed to amplify small noises. The hum of the overhead lights. The faint rattle of a heater vent. The distant sound of a truck passing on the main road outside.

Adrian's mind kept trying to map those sounds onto the mine's acoustics, as if his body had learned to distrust any noise that didn't behave.

Marissa stood suddenly and went to the window. She peered out into the gray afternoon, then down at her own reflection. For a moment Adrian thought she was checking for pale glows behind her.

She turned back. "We should document everything while it's fresh," she said, and the sentence sounded like her grabbing the edge of a cliff. "Time in. Time out. Environmental conditions. The sequence of responses."

Bellamy seized on that, relief evident in the way he straightened. "Yes," he said too quickly. "A timeline. That's how you make this useful instead of… hysteria."

Marissa gave him a look that wasn't kind. "Don't say hysteria."

Bellamy's face flushed. "I meant it as a descriptor, not an insult."

"You meant it the way men always mean it when they're trying to put a woman's fear in a jar," Marissa said, voice sharp now, her old energy returning because anger was easier to hold than dread.

Mercer spoke into the phone again, but his eyes flicked toward them. “Not now,” he said, half to them and half to whoever he was calling. “I need a patrol routed toward the old mine tract. Today. If you can’t do that, I’ll do it myself, but I’d rather not.”

He listened, then exhaled through his nose. “Fine. Then put it in the log. Put it in writing. I’m filing too.”

He hung up and turned toward them fully. “We have a gap,” he said.

Adrian frowned. “What gap?”

“A missing report,” Mercer answered. “No one officially missing from that tract today. Which means nobody mobilizes. They’ll treat it as trespassing until a family calls crying.”

Bellamy spread his hands. “Then we wait for something concrete.”

“No,” Adrian said, more forcefully than he intended.

All eyes turned to him.

Adrian steadied his voice. “We saw fresh evidence inside,” he said. “Modern fabric. The drag mark. Someone is playing with a rule set they don’t understand. That’s concrete.”

Bellamy's gaze hardened. "And what do you propose? We go back? With another flare? That's not a plan, Cross, that's a compulsion dressed up as ethics."

Marissa's mouth tightened, but she didn't immediately side with Bellamy. She looked at Mercer instead, and her voice softened into something more careful. "If we do anything, it has to be controlled," she said. "We need distance. Observation. Not another entry."

Mercer rubbed a hand over his face. In the harsh station light he looked older than he had in Jonas Ridge. "I'm not taking you back in there," he said flatly. "Not without proper rescue support. Not without rope, helmets, a second vehicle, and a plan that doesn't rely on me waving fire around like a medieval priest."

Adrian nodded, because he knew Mercer was right, and because the memory of the flare burning down to nothing was still lodged under his ribs like a splinter.

But his mind wouldn't let go of the thing that mattered most, the thing that sat behind every argument.

"Then we find out who it was," Adrian said. "The boot prints. The care. The equipment case. That kind of person tells someone where they're going. Or they post it. Or they brag. There's a digital trace."

Bellamy scoffed. “Now you want to hunt social media.”

“Now I want to keep a human being from becoming a story,” Adrian shot back.

Mercer’s radio, sitting on its charger, crackled suddenly.

All four of them froze at once, bodies reacting before reason.

The speaker hissed, then a voice pushed through in broken fragments, stressed and strained. “Station… this is Foster… you copy?”

Mercer’s head snapped toward the radio. He crossed the room in three strides and grabbed it, thumb pressing transmit. “Foster, this is Mercer. Say again.”

Static chewed at the reply. The voice came back, thinner, like it was traveling through a long, narrow throat. “Lost contact with Team Two… lights on the opposite ridge… they moved… not headlamps.”

Adrian felt his stomach drop.

Marissa’s eyes widened, and this time she didn’t try to hide it.

Bellamy’s mouth opened, but no sound came out.

Mercer leaned closer to the radio. “Foster, where are you? Do you need assistance?”

A pause, then the faintest sound behind the static that made Adrian's skin tighten.

Click.

Foster's voice returned, breathless. "They're following it. I told them not to. I told them—"

The transmission dissolved into a long, empty hiss.

Mercer pressed transmit again. "Foster? Eli, respond."

Nothing.

Mercer tried again, voice rising despite his effort to keep it steady. "Foster, come in."

Only static answered.

For a moment the station was silent except for the hum of the fluorescent lights and the distant, ordinary sound of the world outside. Adrian stared at the radio as if it had become another mine passage, an opening into a dark place where rules failed.

Mercer set the radio down slowly, as if a sudden movement might make it worse.

Marissa's voice came out in a whisper. "That was today."

Mercer nodded once, his face hardening into the expression of a man watching his worst expectations become procedure. "That was on the ridge," he said.

"And now it's not just our problem in a hole in the ground."

Bellamy swallowed. "Who is Foster?"

"District ranger," Mercer said. "Search lead. Good at his job."

Adrian felt the prologue scene snap into place with sick precision: the hollow quiet, the drifting lights, the scream from deep in the trees, the radio falling silent.

He looked at Mercer. "So, it's happening again," he said.

Mercer met his eyes. "It never stopped," he replied. Then he turned back toward the phone, already reaching for it with the grim clarity of a man forced into action.

"We're not regrouping anymore," Mercer said. "We're responding."

Mercer kept the phone in his hand for a second without dialing, as if the weight of it could steady the room.

Bellamy broke first, because Bellamy always broke silence by turning it into a problem he could argue with.

"That click," he said, voice tight, "we didn't actually hear it on the radio. That could have been interference. A clipped consonant. Anything."

Marissa's eyes snapped to him. "You heard it."

"I heard something," Bellamy insisted. "A sound in static. Don't turn it into—"

"Into what?" Adrian asked. His own voice surprised him with its roughness. He hadn't meant to raise it. He felt like he'd been shouting in his own head for minutes. "Into the same sound we heard in the mine? Into the same patterned clicking that started before the lights appeared?"

Bellamy's nostrils flared. "Correlation is not causation. You of all people should respect that."

Marissa let out a breath that wasn't quite a laugh. "He respects it when it's convenient," she said, and there was a brittle edge to her tone that Adrian had not heard in the classroom. "Right now we have two field events. One underground, one on a ridge. And the same set of behavioral rules showing up in both. You can call it coincidence if that makes you feel safer, Henry, but it won't make it less real."

Bellamy's jaw worked. He looked, briefly, not at Marissa but at Mercer. Like a man appealing to the authority in the room.

Mercer didn't give it to him. He was already flipping open a weathered notebook on the desk and writing, not elegantly, but fast.

"Time," Mercer murmured, more to himself than to them. "Transmission received, 2:41 p.m. Foster reports lost contact with Team Two. Mentions lights moving, not headlamps. Then silence."

Adrian watched the ranger's handwriting and felt a small, cold recognition: Mercer was building a paper trail. The same kind Bellamy trusted. The same kind the mountain had already swallowed a hundred times.

Marissa moved to the table and opened her tablet case with a snap. "We need to document our mine incident too," she said. "Not just for ourselves. If we're going to push for resources, the district and the sheriff will want a coherent narrative."

Bellamy bristled at the word narrative, as if it were a contaminant. "A coherent narrative," he repeated, skeptical. "That's your solution? Turn it into a story?"

Marissa didn't look up. "No. Turn it into a report that doesn't get laughed out of a conference room."

Adrian rubbed his thumb against a smear of dried mud on his knuckle. His body kept trying to return to normal. His mind refused.

Mercer hung up the phone receiver he'd been holding without dialing and turned to them. "Listen," he said, voice low. "You can argue taxonomy later. I need to know what you saw, how it behaved, and what triggers it. Because if Foster's team is out there right now and the lights are doing what they did to us, someone is about to make the worst possible choice."

"No following," Adrian said automatically.

Mercer nodded. "Yeah. And what else?"

Marissa's fingers paused above her tablet. She looked up, and for a moment Adrian saw how hard she was working to keep fear from becoming belief. "Response," she said. "Sound. Movement. It reacts to changes. It escalates when people panic."

Bellamy lifted his chin. "Or people panic because they believe it escalates. That's my point. Folklore drives behavior. The more a witness has heard about predator-like lights, the more likely they are to interpret ambiguous stimuli as pursuit."

Adrian felt anger flare, sharp and bright as the flare Mercer had used. "Ambiguous," he repeated, and couldn't keep the disbelief out of his voice. "Henry, it slid toward us when we moved. It stopped when we stopped. It pulsed when Bellamy—when you—gasped. It repositioned around us. That's not ambiguous."

Bellamy's face flushed. "And you think the only explanation is that it's alive?"

"I think," Adrian said, forcing himself to slow down, "that it behaves like a living thing. Whether it is a living organism, a physical phenomenon with feedback response, or something else entirely, it behaves with intent."

Marissa's eyes narrowed at the word intent. "Careful," she said.

"I said behaves with intent," Adrian corrected. "Not that it has intent in the human sense."

Mercer's pen scratched. He underlined something in his notebook and looked up. "Feedback response," he said. "Explain."

Marissa leaned forward, her posture shifting into teaching without her meaning to. "If it responds to stimulus, and sound is a stimulus, then any communication attempt is a lure. Radio chatter. Shouting. Whistling. It's a high-salience signal. Easy to locate. Easy to track. That fits with the older rules too."

Bellamy's lips tightened. "Fits," he said. "Or the rules were built after the fact to assign control to an uncontrollable situation."

Adrian looked at him. "Then why the mine?"

Bellamy hesitated.

Adrian pressed. "How do you get headlights in a mine? Train lights in a mine? Swamp gas in a mine? Even atmospheric plasma doesn't do coordinated movement in confined tunnels. And it sure as hell doesn't recoil from a flare."

Marissa's gaze flicked to Adrian. "The flare part bothers me too," she admitted, and that admission had weight. Marissa didn't give ground easily. "A chemical flare produces intense red light and heat. It also produces smoke, different ionization, different wavelengths. If the phenomenon is plasma-like, certain wavelengths might destabilize it."

Bellamy seized on that. "Exactly," he said. "A physical mechanism. Not spirits."

"No one said spirits," Marissa snapped.

Adrian almost smiled at that. Almost. The humor died before it could form.

Mercer held up a hand, stopping the argument before it could become the only thing in the room. "I don't care whether it's physics or folklore," he said. "I care what keeps my people alive. Foster said Team Two is following it. If they're chasing a light through the trees, they're making noise. They're talking. They're calling out. They're doing exactly what the rules say not to do."

Bellamy's voice went quieter. "What rules, exactly? The church sheet? Ruth Calhoun's advice? At some point, Evan, you're asking trained rangers to follow folklore."

Mercer's eyes hardened. "I'm asking trained rangers to follow field-tested survival guidelines. I don't care where they came from."

Adrian felt something settle in his chest at that. This was the point where folklore stopped being a story and became a tool, or at least tried to.

Marissa's tablet clicked as she began typing. "We need to be precise," she said. "If this goes to district, the wording matters. We can't write 'predator lights' in an official report."

"I can," Mercer said.

Marissa looked at him. "And it will be buried," she replied, and her tone was not unkind. It was pragmatic. "It will be marked as stress response. It will be treated as a ranger seeing what the public expects him to see. We need language that forces them to engage."

Bellamy exhaled through his nose. "Finally," he muttered, "something sensible."

Marissa ignored him. "Write it as an anomalous luminous phenomenon with demonstrable responsive behavior," she said. "Stimulus: sound and movement. Observed reaction: approach, reposition, escalation. Mitigation: high-intensity red flare appeared to deter proximity in enclosed environment."

Mercer stared at her for a beat. "You've done incident reports before."

"I've done fieldwork in places where people died because academics thought being correct mattered more than being clear," Marissa said, and Adrian heard something personal in it. Something she hadn't shared before.

Bellamy's expression softened a fraction, then hardened again as if softness were dangerous. "And the folklore angle?" he asked, as though the word tasted bad. "You're going to omit it entirely?"

Adrian leaned forward. "No," he said. "We include it because it predicts behavior. The rules exist because people observed a pattern. Sound increases interest. Stillness reduces it. Don't call. Don't whistle. Don't let it see your face."

Marissa's eyes flashed. "We did not verify the face part," she said.

"No," Adrian agreed. "But we verified the learning part."

Bellamy snapped, "We did not verify learning."

Adrian looked him dead in the eye. "Then explain why it adjusted to the flare," he said. "Explain why it held at the edge of the red light and tested distance. Explain why it blocked the tunnel near the exit. That's not a moth around a bulb. That's not gas."

Bellamy's mouth opened, then closed. His gaze dropped to the desk. When he spoke again, his voice was quieter, more honest. "I can't," he said. "Not yet."

The room went still around that admission.

Mercer nodded once, as if that was all he needed from Bellamy: not belief, just the willingness to stop pretending the mountain was simple. He reached for the radio again.

"Foster," he said into it, thumb on transmit. "Eli, this is Mercer. If you can hear me, do not follow the lights. Repeat: do not follow. Stop moving, stay together, minimize radio traffic. Respond with one click if you copy."

He released the button.

Static.

Then, so faint Adrian wasn't sure at first if his mind had inserted it, a sound threaded through the hiss.

Click.

Marissa's head lifted sharply.

Bellamy went pale.

Mercer didn't move for a second, as if moving might break the connection. Then he pressed transmit again, voice steady by force. "Eli, if you can hear me, stay where you are. We're coming to you. Do not chase anyone who leaves the trail. Do not call out. Use your flare if you have it."

He released the button and looked at the three academics.

"That's it," Mercer said. "Science can wait. Folklore can argue with it later. Right now we go to the ridge and we keep them from feeding it anything else."

Mercer was already moving, snatching his jacket from the back of a chair and shrugging into it as if speed could seal the crack that had opened in the day. He yanked a cabinet drawer open and started pulling gear out by muscle memory: an emergency pack, two road flares, a headlamp strap, a coil of bright survey tape.

Adrian watched him for a beat too long, caught between the relief of having a clear directive and the sick understanding that the directive came from the same place as the mine's rules. Not policy. Pattern.

Marissa stepped in front of the cabinet, not blocking it entirely, but forcing Mercer to meet her eyes.

"Evan," she said, and the use of his first name was deliberate. It wasn't a colleague's tone. It was the tone she'd used on students before they did something stupid. "We need to slow down and decide what we're doing before we go charging up a ridge in fog."

Mercer didn't stop packing. "I'm not charging. I'm responding."

"You are responding based on a click in static," Bellamy said, voice tight, and there it was again: his need to make the world obey categories. "That is not a reliable communication method."

Adrian looked at Bellamy. The historian's face had the strained composure of a man who'd just admitted ignorance and hated the aftertaste. His hands were still slightly unsteady, but he kept them folded as if that could disguise it.

Mercer snapped the cabinet shut harder than necessary. "A click is all I asked for," he said. "One click if he copies. He clicked."

"That could be anyone," Bellamy said. "Or anything. It could be some artifact in the frequency."

Marissa's eyes flicked between them. "Henry, not now."

Bellamy's chin lifted. "No. This is exactly now. If we're going to risk another field incident, I want to know what standard of evidence we're using. We are not trained for search operations. You are."

Mercer's gaze hardened. "Then come or don't."

The bluntness landed like a slap. For a moment the station felt too small for four people with incompatible definitions of duty.

Adrian stepped forward, forcing his voice into calm. "Everyone's running on adrenaline," he said. "We just came out of a mine with something that behaved like it wanted us to panic. Let's not do its work for it in here."

Marissa exhaled sharply through her nose, the closest she came to agreement. "He's right," she said. Then, to Mercer, "You need to tell us what you want from us on the ridge. Not just 'come.'"

Mercer shifted the pack onto his shoulder, and Adrian noticed the way he kept his body angled toward the door, as if standing still was a kind of risk. "I want eyes," Mercer said. "I want additional people who can observe and then write it down in a way district can't ignore. I want you two," he nodded toward Marissa and Adrian, "because you can document and because you've seen it. And I want you," he looked at Bellamy, "because you won't let anyone exaggerate what happened."

Bellamy's mouth tightened. "You mean I'll be your internal skeptic."

"I mean you'll keep us honest," Mercer said, and there was a tired edge to it. "Even when honesty is uncomfortable."

Bellamy didn't answer immediately. He glanced toward the window, toward the fog-lidded line of trees beyond the station yard, as if he expected pale light to be waiting there like an accusation. Then he said, "There is a difference between honesty and recklessness."

Marissa cut in, voice clipped. "Fine. Then set parameters. On the ridge, we do not split. We do not chase. We do not add noise. Minimal radio. If we can't safely reach Foster, we mark and withdraw."

Mercer nodded once, sharp. "Agreed."

Adrian felt a small pulse of relief. It was a plan, even if it was a plan made with inadequate tools against an inadequate enemy.

Bellamy shook his head slowly. "This is absurd," he said. But his voice had less heat now and more fear. "We're saying 'we do not add noise' like we're in a laboratory. You know what happens during a search? People shout names. They call back and forth. They coordinate."

"That's what got Team Two in trouble," Mercer said.

"That's what saves people," Bellamy snapped. "You can't conduct a search in silence."

Mercer leaned closer, just enough that Adrian heard the controlled anger in his breath. "You can if calling out is what brings it in," Mercer said. "You can if the old rules exist because people died every time they did the sensible thing."

Bellamy flinched, and Adrian saw that it wasn't the content that stung. It was the certainty.

Marissa folded her arms. "Henry," she said, and her voice softened a fraction, "you saw it in the mine.

You saw it change when we changed. That isn't a metaphor. That's an observed behavior."

Bellamy's eyes flashed. "And your conclusion is that folklore is correct."

"My conclusion," Marissa said, careful, "is that the behavioral prescriptions embedded in the local tradition align with a real stimulus-response pattern. We can argue why later. Right now, the safest choice is to treat the pattern as true."

Bellamy's laugh came out thin and humorless. "We are going to risk our lives because an old woman said don't let it see your face."

Adrian felt his stomach tighten. Ruth Calhoun's voice rose in memory, not dramatic, just tired: Because it learns you.

He kept his own voice level. "We're not doing this because of Ruth," Adrian said. "We're doing it because we saw the same mechanisms the stories describe. The stories might not explain it, but they predict it."

Bellamy's gaze swung to Adrian. "And you're enjoying that," he said, and the accusation was small but sharp. "This is your field finally being validated by something you can point to. You get to say, see, the legends were right."

Adrian felt a flare of anger that surprised him with its clarity. "Enjoying?" he repeated. He took a step closer, not threatening, but refusing to be backed into the role Bellamy wanted. "Henry, I nearly got us killed in that mine because I thought we could do a limited entry. I'm not enjoying anything."

Marissa watched them, eyes narrowed, as if she was tracking escalation the same way she tracked the lights. Bellamy's face went rigid, and for a second Adrian thought he might double down, might keep pushing because it was easier than admitting how frightened he was.

Instead Bellamy said, quieter, "You want to chase it."

Adrian opened his mouth, then closed it, because there was truth there and it sickened him. He did want to chase answers. He'd built a career on chasing what other people called nonsense. And the mountain had just proven that the nonsense could chase back.

"I want to stop it," Adrian said finally. "Or at least stop pretending it's only stories while rangers disappear."

Mercer's radio crackled softly from the desk, a brief burst of static that made all three academics stiffen. Mercer didn't. He picked it up with the reflex of someone who'd already accepted the day's shape.

"Foster," Mercer said, thumb on transmit, voice controlled. "Eli, give me one click if you're still on."

Static stretched.

Then, faint but distinct: click.

Marissa's eyes widened. Bellamy went pale again, as if his body accepted what his mind resisted.

Mercer didn't gloat. He didn't look at them as if to say I told you so. He simply nodded once to himself, the way a man nods when he's confirmed the direction of a storm.

"Still there," Mercer murmured. He pressed transmit again. "Eli, stay put. Do not move toward the lights. If Team Two is moving, do not follow them. One click if you understand."

A pause. Then: click.

Mercer set the radio down, but not on the charger. He kept it in his hand like a tether. "That's our confirmation," he said. "He's alive. He's holding position. Now I have to get to him."

Bellamy stared at the radio as if it had betrayed the universe. "This is insane," he whispered. "He's communicating in clicks because… because sound matters."

"Yes," Marissa said, and her voice was brittle with the strain of being right about something she didn't want to be right about. "Sound matters."

Mercer moved toward the door. "Last chance," he said. "You're not obligated. I won't hold it against you if you stay."

Bellamy hesitated, and Adrian saw the fracture line run through him: pride on one side, self-preservation on the other, with curiosity and shame mixed into both.

"I'm coming," Bellamy said at last, and the words sounded like defeat.

Marissa picked up her recorder case, then stopped, fingers tightening on the handle. She looked at Mercer. "No audio," she said, as much to remind herself as to ask permission.

Mercer nodded. "No audio."

Adrian grabbed his coat from the chair and patted his pocket unconsciously, feeling for the folded church bulletin Mercer had shown him that morning. The paper was soft now from being handled, the edges bent. A list of rules that had seemed quaint twelve hours ago.

As they stepped out into the fog, the station door closing behind them with a soft click that made Adrian's skin prickle, Bellamy spoke again, voice low and strained.

"If this goes wrong," he said, "this will ruin all of us."

Mercer didn't turn. He walked ahead, boots crunching gravel, his silhouette already blurring into gray. "If this goes wrong," Mercer said, "it'll ruin Foster. It'll ruin Team Two. The rest of us can worry about reputations later."

Marissa fell into step beside Adrian. "He's right," she murmured.

Adrian watched Mercer's back, watched the fog swallow the ranger's outline in slow increments, and felt the team's new shape forming under pressure. Not united by agreement. United by the simple, brutal fact that the mountain had taken the argument out of their hands.

They followed Mercer to the truck, and each of them carried a different fear.

Mercer feared losing his people.

Marissa feared being forced to believe in something she couldn't control.

Bellamy feared being made ridiculous by the truth.

And Adrian feared the most personal thing of all: that the mountain had finally given him a story that was not just a story, and that wanting it might be the same weakness the lights had always counted on.

Chapter 10

Patterns in the Past

The ridge road climbed into fog so thick it made the world feel unfinished. Trees appeared and vanished at the edge of the headlights. Mercer drove with both hands locked on the wheel, jaw set, radio in his lap like a live thing.

No one spoke unless they had to. Even Bellamy seemed to understand that his usual arguments would turn into noise, and noise had become something else in their minds: not just sound, but bait.

Mercer kept the truck's interior light off. The dash glow was enough to show the hard lines of his face and the way his eyes kept flicking to the mirrors.

Adrian's mind did what it always did under stress. It reached for structure. Sequence. Cause. A way to turn fear into something that could be studied without being swallowed.

Mine: clicking, then lights, then pursuit.

Radio: static, then clicking, then a man holding position like he'd learned a new language the hard way.

Ruth Calhoun's porch voice returned, quiet and absolute. When the light stops, you stop. If it comes close enough to show interest, you do not let it see your face.

Adrian hadn't believed a light could see at all. After the mine, he wasn't sure what "see" meant anymore.

Mercer eased the truck into a pull-off and killed the engine. Silence fell so fast it felt like pressure. The fog outside glowed faintly in the headlights, a pale wall.

"From here," Mercer said, barely above breath, "we walk."

Marissa nodded once. Her tablet and recorder case were in her backpack, zipped and silent. Bellamy's hands were shoved into his pockets, shoulders drawn up against the cold and against something else.

Mercer handed each of them a road flare. Adrian looked down at the red cylinder in his glove and felt a grim gratitude. It wasn't a solution. It was a boundary. A way to say no in a language the phenomenon appeared to understand.

"Do not light unless I tell you," Mercer said. "We keep them as last resort. The red is a deterrent. But it's also a beacon."

Bellamy swallowed. "A beacon for what?"

Mercer's gaze held him. "For anything paying attention."

They stepped out into the fog.

The ridge trail was slick with damp leaves and loose gravel. Mercer led with a headlamp on its lowest setting, angled down. Adrian followed close, matching his pace. Behind him, Marissa moved like she had in the mine: controlled, economical. Bellamy brought up the rear, his boots careful, his breathing shallow.

Mercer lifted the radio once, thumb poised, then didn't press transmit. He raised it to his mouth anyway and made a single, soft click with his tongue.

The sound was small enough Adrian almost didn't register it. But Mercer did it deliberately, like a knock.

They waited.

For a few seconds there was only fog, the wet hush of the mountains, and the faint sound of their own blood moving in their ears.

Then, from somewhere ahead and off to the right, came a click in answer.

Marissa's head turned sharply. Bellamy froze so hard his coat creaked.

Mercer didn't speak. He clicked again, two quick beats. Pause. Then one beat.

A code, Adrian realized. Not Morse exactly, but something close. Something invented under pressure.

The answering click came again, nearer now. Followed by another, and another, irregular, as if the responder was struggling to keep control.

"That's him," Mercer breathed, and the relief in his voice was immediate and dangerous. Relief made you hurry. Hurry made you loud.

Mercer steadied himself. Slower, he signaled with his hand for them to keep moving, and they followed the clicks the way sailors followed a distant bell through fog.

As they advanced, Adrian began to see faint white points out in the trees. Not bright at first. Easy to mistake for droplets catching headlamp spill. Then one slid sideways between trunks, steady as thought.

Mercer stopped instantly and held up his fist.

All four froze.

The point of light held position, hovering at the edge of visibility. Another appeared above it, higher up, as if the first had summoned company.

The lights didn't rush. They watched.

Adrian tried to keep his eyes down, but he couldn't keep the lights out of his peripheral vision. They made the fog feel inhabited. Not haunted. Monitored.

Mercer made a single click. Pause. Another click.

A moment later, the answering clicks returned, closer and more urgent. Then a faint shape materialized through fog: a man crouched low beside the trail, one hand pressed to his radio, the other holding an unlit flare.

Ranger Eli Foster looked like he'd aged several years since the last time Mercer had seen him. Mud streaked his pants and jacket. His face was pale, eyes bloodshot, mouth tight like he'd been clenching it for hours to keep himself silent.

He lifted his chin toward Mercer and made one click.

Mercer exhaled, controlled. "Eli."

Foster's mouth opened as if to speak, then shut again. He shook his head sharply, a warning.

Marissa stepped closer, careful, and held up both hands, palms slightly out, as if showing she wasn't a threat. She kept her voice low but it still sounded too loud in the fog. "Are you hurt?"

Foster didn't answer with words. He tapped his chest twice, then held up two fingers and pointed into the fog off-trail.

Team Two.

Mercer's expression hardened. He didn't need clarification.

Bellamy whispered despite himself, "Are they alive?"

Foster's head turned toward Bellamy, and his eyes flashed with something like anger. Not at the question. At the noise.

Foster raised his hand and made a sharp, downward gesture. Quiet.

Bellamy shut his mouth. His face tightened with shame.

Mercer leaned close to Foster, speaking barely above breath. "Where are they?"

Foster pointed again, then traced a line in the air that slanted down, off the ridge into thicker forest. Then he held up his hand and made a walking motion with two fingers, followed by a circling gesture.

Following.

He mimed a light drifting ahead of those fingers, then mimed a person stepping toward it.

Mercer's jaw worked. "They went off trail."

Foster nodded once, then made another gesture: a hand to his mouth, opening and closing like shouting. He followed it with a flinch and a recoil, as if something had surged toward him.

Adrian's throat tightened. The same script. Sound and movement feeding response.

Marissa crouched beside Foster and pulled a small notepad and pen from her pocket, the paper already creased from the day. She wrote quickly, then held it up for him to see: Can you lead us without talking?

Foster read it, then looked out toward the lights, and shook his head. He pointed to himself, then to the lights, then made a small sweeping motion across his face.

Don't let it see you.

Adrian felt the old woman's warning strike him in a new way. Not metaphor. Not superstition. Procedure.

Mercer made a decision that Adrian recognized with dread as the same kind of decision they'd made at the mine entrance: help weighed against becoming part of the pattern.

"Eli," Mercer whispered, and even the whisper seemed like too much. "We're not going after them off trail in this fog."

Foster's eyes flared. He made a tight fist and pointed hard into the trees again, then to his radio, then dragged his finger across his throat.

He mimed radio chatter, then cut it. Like he'd watched Team Two talk themselves into being followed.

Marissa wrote again: They're still out there.

Foster nodded.

Then he did something that made Adrian's skin go cold. Foster held up his radio and, very carefully, turned the volume knob. Not up. Down. Until even static was nearly gone. Then he held up the radio and tilted it toward them as if showing them a weapon he'd disarmed.

Adrian understood. Foster had been surviving by reducing every trace of himself. Light. Voice. Even the comfort-noise of static.

Mercer glanced back at the pale points hanging in the fog. They had shifted positions while Foster communicated, sliding slightly closer, like careful animals circling a campsite.

Mercer's hand tightened around his flare. He didn't light it. Not yet.

Adrian leaned toward Marissa, his mouth close to her ear. "Old warnings," he breathed. "New evidence."

Marissa's eyes stayed fixed on the lights, but her face tightened as if she'd been forced to concede something she hated. "It's operational," she whispered back. "It isn't belief. It's an adaptive protocol."

Bellamy, voice barely present, said, "Protocols don't come from nowhere."

Adrian looked at him. Bellamy's skepticism wasn't gone, but it had shifted. It wasn't trying to erase what they'd seen. It was trying to find where it had been seen before.

Mercer gestured with two fingers: back. The universal signal.

Foster's shoulders sagged with exhausted, furious relief. He rose slowly, keeping his head angled down. The group tightened into a close formation, Mercer in front and Foster beside him, Adrian and Marissa in the middle, Bellamy behind.

They retreated toward the truck without running.

The lights tracked them the way they had tracked in the mine: not charging, not vanishing, simply holding the boundary of attention. Every time someone's boot slipped on wet gravel, one of the lights brightened a fraction. Every time they stopped, the lights stopped too.

When they reached the truck, Mercer opened the doors with controlled care and got them inside without slamming anything. Only when all four were seated did he strike a flare and hold it out the driver's window, keeping the red glow outside like a fence.

The nearest pale point in the fog recoiled, shifting back into the trees.

Foster finally spoke once they were moving, once engine noise could cover him and once distance had made the lights less immediate. His voice was rough, as if he hadn't used it in hours. "I told them," he said. "I told them not to follow."

Mercer kept his eyes on the road. "What did they say?"

Foster's laugh was short and broken. "They said it was probably a headlamp. They said the missing hiker might be carrying one. They said they had to check."

Marissa's hands were clenched in her lap. "And the lights?"

Foster stared out the window, not focusing on anything visible. "They waited until the moment someone stepped off trail," he said. "Like they knew the rule better than we did."

Adrian sat back and felt the day's fragments align into something that looked too much like a design.

Rules passed through churches. Warnings carved into mine timbers. A note in a corporate file: Do not whistle below this point. A modern ranger reduced to clicking into a radio to stay alive.

The old warnings hadn't been poetic. They had been field notes.

And now they had new evidence, the kind that didn't stay in archives.

Mercer drove faster, and the flare burned down in its metal can, painting Foster's tired face red in pulses. In that harsh light, Adrian saw what frightened him most: not that the phenomenon was real, but that it was consistent.

Consistency meant pattern.

And pattern meant it could be learned.

By them.

Or by whatever was learning them back.

Mercer didn't take them back to the station.

He took them to Jonas Ridge first, as if putting a few miles and a handful of familiar buildings between them and the fog-choked ridge might make the day's logic less contagious. The truck rolled into town under a sky that had darkened early, the mountains swallowing light the way the mine swallowed sound.

Foster sat rigid in the passenger seat, flare smoke still clinging faintly to his jacket. He had spoken once on the road, just enough to tell them Team Two had stepped off trail and then vanished into the trees after a drifting white glow. After that, his silence had become its own statement: there were no more words that could make it better.

Mercer parked behind the diner, out of the way of the single-file evening traffic. "We don't have enough information to go off trail," he said, voice low. "Not in fog, not at dusk, not with whatever that was adapting to us."

Bellamy's jaw tightened. "So we get information from coffee and gossip."

"We get information from people who have survived here longer than we have," Adrian said.

Marissa glanced at Foster. "Only if we can ask without turning it into theater."

Foster's mouth twitched, not quite a smile. "Ask," he said hoarsely. "Just don't do it loud."

Inside the diner, the air was warm with fryer grease and coffee, and for a moment Adrian's body tried to pretend it was an ordinary evening. The illusion didn't last. The waitress recognized them instantly. Her eyes flicked to Foster's mud-streaked pants, to Mercer's tense posture, to the way all four of them moved like they were still in a narrow tunnel.

"You found one," she said, not a question.

Mercer nodded. "Eli Foster."

Her gaze sharpened. “Then you lost others.”

No one answered fast enough to deny it, and the silence did the work.

The waitress set four cups down without asking what they wanted. Coffee appeared like a small, stubborn ritual. “Sit,” she said. “Back booth. Not by the window.”

They slid into the booth she indicated, half-hidden from the front door. Foster sat with his back to the wall. Mercer remained angled toward the entrance anyway, habit and vigilance refusing to negotiate.

The waitress leaned in, lowering her voice. “Who’d you lose?”

“Team Two,” Mercer said. “Two volunteers and a ranger tech.”

She made a sound that was mostly air. “And they went after the lights.”

Foster’s hands tightened around his cup so hard the styrofoam creaked. “They thought it was a headlamp,” he said. “They thought it was the missing hiker.”

The waitress looked at him with something that wasn’t blame, exactly. It was the tired anger of someone who’d watched the same mistake repeat under new names. “People always think it’s meant for them,” she said, and Adrian felt the sentence land with the same shape as her earlier words: it wanted you to think it was meant for you.

Marissa opened her mouth, then closed it again, as if she'd decided not to lead with a theory. Adrian respected that. She finally asked, quietly, "Do you know where they would go if they left the ridge trail? Any old paths, any cuts?"

The waitress's eyes flicked to Mercer. "You want a map," she said.

"We want them back," Mercer replied.

She straightened and called toward the kitchen, "Hank, cover me five minutes."

Then she slid into the booth beside Adrian as if she had always been part of their group and had simply waited for them to become serious.

"People like to talk about the lights like they're up there," she said, nodding vaguely toward the darkened window. "But the old folks didn't treat it like a sky thing. They treated it like a ground thing. Like it had places it liked."

Bellamy's pencil appeared from his pocket despite Mercer's earlier rule about noise. Bellamy did not click the pen. He wrote anyway, carefully, the lead scratching faintly.

The waitress noticed. "You write quiet," she said, and it might have been approval.

Adrian asked, “Places like the mine tract?”

Her eyes narrowed. “You went in there?”

Mercer didn’t answer, and the waitress’s face told Adrian she didn’t need the answer.

She took a sip of coffee, then spoke like she was reciting something she’d heard enough times to memorize. “There’s a hollow west side,” she said. “Locals call it Devil’s Stairs sometimes, though the church people don’t like that. It’s steep and it’ll twist your ankle, but that ain’t why folks avoided it. There’s an old cut that runs down off the ridge, not marked on your pretty forest service signs. It goes toward the lower shaft area and the creek. If somebody follows a light, that’s where they end up, because it’s the easiest wrong way.”

Marissa’s face tightened. “Easiest wrong way,” she repeated softly.

Foster stared into his cup. “That’s where they went,” he said. His voice was flat, like he’d been holding the line against that truth for hours and it had finally slipped through. “I could hear them moving off trail. I could hear them talking, and then I heard them stop talking, like someone put a hand over their mouths.”

Mercer’s gaze snapped to him. “You didn’t say that part.”

Foster's eyes lifted, bloodshot and furious. "You think I want to say it?" he rasped. "You think I want to put it into words where it can follow me?"

The waitress held up a hand, palm down. "Don't," she said gently. Not don't argue. Don't keep giving it language.

Adrian felt his throat tighten with a sudden understanding of why the old rules were so strict about sound. It wasn't only bait. It was exposure. It was making the phenomenon real in the air between people.

Marissa asked, "Who else should we talk to?"

The waitress didn't hesitate. "Ruth Calhoun," she said. "And if she'll speak on it, Reverend Pike. He's got the old bulletins and the funerals to match. And there's a man named Seth Harper, lives out past the old timber road. His granddaddy worked the mine before it shut, and he's got things put away you won't find in county records."

Bellamy's head lifted at that. "Things?"

The waitress's expression hardened. "Photos," she said. "And a ledger. Mine company men wrote down what they could admit and left out what they couldn't. Families kept the rest."

Mercer pushed his coffee aside untouched. "We don't have time for three visits," he said. "It's getting dark."

"You don't have time to be polite either," the waitress replied. "But you're trying. That's why you'll go to Ruth first. She'll tell you whether you should even bother with the others."

Marissa leaned forward. "We need specifics. If Team Two went down the west cut, we need to know where it meets water, where the ground breaks, where people disappear. We need a route we can search in daylight."

The waitress looked at Marissa like she was reassessing her. "You're the one that don't believe," she said.

"I didn't say I don't believe," Marissa replied. Then, after a beat, she added, "I said I don't want belief to do our thinking for us."

The waitress gave a single nod, as if that distinction mattered. "Ruth'll like that," she said.

Mercer stood. "We go now."

Foster rose too, but he swayed slightly. Mercer caught his elbow.

"I'm coming," Foster said immediately, the words sharp with pride and something like fear.

Mercer's grip tightened. "You're coming to a porch," he said. "Not a ridge."

Foster's eyes flickered, and Adrian saw the conflict there: the ranger instinct to return to the field, and the survival instinct that had kept him alive by becoming quieter than his training allowed. Finally Foster nodded once.

They paid quickly. The waitress waved away Mercer's attempt to leave money. "Buy batteries for those flares," she said. "Or whatever you think helps."

Outside, the fog had thinned slightly in town, the streetlights turning it into a soft amber veil instead of a white wall. The mountain remained a darker shape beyond, watching without outline.

Ruth Calhoun's porch light was on when they arrived, a small yellow bulb that made the yard feel both safer and more exposed. The hound raised its head as the truck doors closed. Ruth sat in the same chair as before, quilts around her shoulders, walking stick across her lap, as if she had never moved since morning.

"You brought him," she said, eyes on Foster.

Foster's throat worked. "Ma'am," he managed.

Ruth's gaze shifted to Mercer. "How many now?"

Mercer didn't correct her. Didn't say missing, not dead. He simply said, "Three off trail. Team Two."

Ruth nodded slowly, and Adrian felt the weight of generational arithmetic. Not names. Not faces. Numbers added to an old sum.

Marissa spoke first this time, careful and respectful. “Mrs. Calhoun, we need to know where people end up when they follow the lights. Not just stories. Paths. Water. Old cuts. We need to search in daylight.”

Ruth studied her for a long moment. Then she looked at Adrian. “Lore man,” she said. “You still listening better than the others?”

“I’m trying,” Adrian said.

Ruth’s eyes returned to Foster. “Did you call to them?” she asked him.

Foster flinched. “No, ma’am,” he said. “I didn’t. I… clicked. Like you said. Like you would for a dog in the dark.”

Ruth’s mouth tightened. “And you kept your face down?”

Foster hesitated, just a fraction.

Mercer’s voice went quiet. “He did what he had to do.”

Ruth nodded, as if that was enough.

Then she lifted her walking stick and tapped the porch plank once, a single decisive beat that silenced even the hound’s breathing.

“Here’s your testimony,” she said. “The lights ain’t lost souls. Lost souls don’t learn.”

Adrian felt the words move through him like cold water.

Ruth continued, voice steady. "They take the easiest wrong way, like that waitress told you. Down the west cut. They always favor water, because water carries sound and keeps folks from hearing their own steps right. And when a person thinks they're close enough to see where it's coming from, that's when it stops. That's the part that makes them step forward."

Marissa swallowed. "Why?"

Ruth's gaze held hers. "Because they want you to choose it," she said. "Not by force. By your own feet."

Bellamy's voice came out rough. "Mrs. Calhoun… what do you call them?"

Ruth looked at him with a tired irritation that made Adrian almost wince. "We don't," she said. "That's the rule you educated men keep trying to turn into a question."

She shifted her stick and pointed it toward the dark slope beyond her yard. "But my granddaddy called them the watchers. Not because they watch the mountain. Because they watch you."

Mercer drew a slow breath. "Can you show us where the west cut begins?" he asked.

Ruth nodded once. “In daylight,” she said. “Not tonight. Tonight you’ll stay put and you’ll keep your people from making noise they can’t take back.”

Foster’s hands curled into fists. “They’re out there,” he said, and the words sounded like pain.

Ruth’s face softened, just a fraction. “I know,” she said. “And you’re still here, which means you did one thing right.”

She leaned forward, quilts shifting, and her voice dropped lower, forcing them closer to hear. “You want patterns in the past,” she said. “Then you listen to this: every time the mountain takes somebody, it leaves something behind for the next one to find. A scrap of cloth. A boot print. A story. That’s not mercy. That’s instruction.”

Adrian felt his stomach tighten as he saw the mine’s fabric scrap again in his mind, pale on damp stone.

Ruth tapped her stick once more. “You go see Seth Harper in the morning,” she said. “He’s got a page from a ledger that ain’t in the county office. It’s got names and marks beside them. And it’s got where they were last seen, written down by men who didn’t want to admit they believed their own eyes.”

Marissa’s eyes narrowed. “A list,” she murmured. “Locations.”

"A map," Adrian said quietly, the next step forming in his mind even as dread followed it. "A map of avoidance."

Ruth nodded. "Now you're thinking like a mountain person," she said. "Not brave. Not stupid. Practical."

Mercer looked at the darkening sky, then back at Ruth. "We'll come at first light," he said.

Ruth's gaze sharpened. "Bring red," she said simply. "And keep your faces to yourselves."

As they walked back to the truck, Foster lagged a half-step behind Adrian.

"Watchers," Foster murmured, testing the forbidden name like it might burn his tongue.

Adrian kept his voice low. "Don't use it," he said.

Foster swallowed. "I know," he replied. "I just… needed to know the shape of what I'm up against."

Adrian thought of Ruth's line, hard and clean as a carved warning: lost souls don't learn.

He looked toward the mountain's black outline beyond town and felt the pattern tightening, not only around the missing team, but around all of them. Testimonies weren't stories now. They were field notes passed hand to hand across generations.

And in the morning, if Seth Harper's ledger held what Ruth promised, they would have something more dangerous than belief.

They would have coordinates.

Morning came thin and gray, like the day itself was reluctant to look at the mountain too clearly.

Adrian woke in the spare room of the ranger station with the stale smell of flare still caught in his jacket. For a few seconds he lay still and listened for clicking, as if the sound might have followed them into sleep. There was only the hum of the heater and the far-off murmur of a road.

When he stepped into the main room, Mercer was already up, pouring coffee into a travel mug with the rigid efficiency of a man who had decided fatigue was a luxury. Marissa sat at the table with her tablet open, hair pulled back, posture straight. Bellamy leaned against the counter, staring into a paper cup as if it contained a better explanation than any of them had found so far.

Foster was there too, slumped in a chair by the window. His eyes looked bruised from lack of sleep. He didn't greet Adrian. He just lifted his cup slightly, the smallest acknowledgment.

Mercer spoke first. "Ruth said first light. We're already behind."

"We're not behind," Marissa said, voice clipped but controlled. "We're alive. That's not nothing."

Mercer didn't argue. He took it as permission to move. "Seth Harper's place is out past the old timber road. Ruth said he's got a page from a ledger. If it's real, it's more than stories. It's a record."

Bellamy's mouth tightened. "Or it's a family heirloom that's been embellished for a century."

Marissa didn't look up. "Everything is embellished. The question is whether the embellishment preserves a pattern."

Adrian watched Bellamy absorb that. It was the closest Marissa had come to agreeing with Adrian since they'd arrived, and it landed on Bellamy like an unwanted concession.

Foster's voice came rough from the chair. "If there's a pattern," he said, "it doesn't bring Team Two back by itself."

"No," Mercer said. "But it keeps us from stepping where people always step right before they vanish."

They drove out of Jonas Ridge with fog still caught low in the trees, the mountain a darker mass beyond it. The road Mercer took was narrow and broken, fringed with wet leaves that clung to the shoulder like warnings. As they climbed, the town fell away, and the forest closed in with the same indifferent patience Adrian had felt at the mine tract.

Seth Harper's house sat back from the road behind a sagging fence and a yard scattered with old equipment: a rusted wood splitter, a trailer with one flat tire, a stack of cut logs silvered by rain. A hound barked once from under the porch and then went quiet, as if even dogs learned what noises were worth making out here.

Harper came out before they reached the steps. He was in his late sixties, lean and rope-tough, wearing a faded jacket and a cap pulled low. His face was weathered into lines that looked carved rather than aged.

He looked at Mercer first, then at Foster. His gaze sharpened. "You're the one that stayed," he said to Foster.

Foster stiffened. "Yes, sir."

Harper nodded once, as if that mattered more than any introduction. Then his eyes moved to Adrian and lingered a fraction longer than comfort. "And you're the lore man," he said.

Adrian didn't ask how he knew. He'd learned that news traveled here in ways that didn't involve phones. "I am."

Harper's gaze slid to Marissa and Bellamy. "And you brought the two that don't like it," he said.

Bellamy bristled. "We didn't come to like or dislike anything. We came to—"

"To what?" Harper cut in, not loud, but sharp enough to stop the sentence. "To understand it? You don't understand a thing that hunts by giving it a good argument."

Marissa's mouth tightened. "We came to keep people alive," she said.

That seemed to satisfy him. Harper stepped aside and motioned them onto the porch. "Then don't stand out in the open," he said. "Come in."

Inside, the house smelled like wood smoke and old paper. The living room walls held photographs in mismatched frames: family portraits, hunting shots, a black-and-white image of men standing in front of a timbered mine entrance that made Adrian's skin tighten in recognition. On a shelf under the photos sat a row of mason jars filled with nails and screws, practical things arranged like a small, stubborn defense against chaos.

Harper didn't offer them seats. He went straight to a cabinet and pulled out a flat metal box the size of a briefcase. He set it on the table and flipped the latches.

"This belonged to my granddaddy," he said. "He didn't keep it for company pride. He kept it because men started disappearing and the company started pretending they hadn't."

Bellamy leaned forward despite himself. "You have company documents?"

Harper's eyes narrowed. "I have what came home in lunch pails and jacket pockets. And what was copied before it could be burned."

He lifted out a folded sheet protected by brittle wax paper. The page was yellowed and creased, the ink browned with age. It looked like it had been handled too many times by hands that wanted it to mean something different each time.

Adrian felt a jolt of recognition when he saw the header, faint but legible: a company ledger format, lines and columns, the kind Bellamy loved because it made human lives look like entries.

Harper laid it flat. "This is one page. Not the whole book. The rest got locked up, or lost, or thrown into a stove when a man decided paper couldn't hurt him if it was ash."

Mercer leaned over the table, careful not to touch. "Ruth said there were names."

Harper pointed with a thick finger. "Here. And here. And here."

The names were listed down the left margin. Some had neat marks beside them, as if they'd been paid and logged. Others had a different notation: a small, dark symbol like a tilted cross or a simple circle, repeated with grim consistency.

Adrian's throat tightened. "Missing," he said.

Harper didn't deny it. "Sometimes they wrote 'not recovered.' Sometimes they wrote nothing at all. Just that mark. Like a man could be turned into punctuation."

Marissa's voice came careful. "And locations?"

Harper tapped the far right margin. There, written in a smaller, tighter hand, were brief notes: Lower Cut B. West slope path. Creek bend. Devil's Stairs. Near the old laurel stand. Above the water shelf. Words that were half directions and half local vocabulary.

Bellamy's skepticism shifted shape. It didn't leave his face, but it stopped looking amused. "This is real," he said quietly.

Harper gave a humorless smile. "It's paper. It's as real as men make anything."

Adrian scanned the notes and felt the pattern begin to show itself, not as a story, but as repetition. The locations weren't random. They clustered.

Mercer saw it too. "Most of these are west side," he murmured.

Harper nodded. "Easiest wrong way," he said, echoing the waitress without knowing it or proving he did. "People think the ridge is the danger because that's where you see the lights. But the ridge is just where you get invited. The west cut is where you accept."

Marissa pulled her tablet closer, but she didn't start typing. She simply looked, eyes narrowing as if she could turn ink into terrain. "Can you show us on a map?" she asked.

Harper walked to a drawer and pulled out something rolled and tied with twine. He spread it across the table with both hands.

It was an old topographic map, but not the clean kind sold at outdoor stores. This one was patched with tape and had handwritten marks along the margins. Pencil lines traced certain paths with deliberate emphasis. Other areas were shaded faintly, as if someone had rubbed graphite into the paper to darken whole sections.

Adrian felt a chill. "Avoidance," he said before he could stop himself.

Harper looked at him. "That's what Ruth called it?"

"She didn't use the word," Adrian said. "But it's what she described."

Harper nodded once, approving. "My granddaddy called it the no-go map. My daddy called it common sense. I call it proof the mountain teaches."

He pointed to the west slope where a faint, shaded band ran like a bruise along the contours. "These hollows," he said, "they aren't harder to travel. Some of them are easier. That's the point. Men like easy. So the lights like easy too."

Mercer leaned closer. "These shaded areas," he said, "they match the ledger notes."

"They match the stories too," Harper said. "But you don't want stories." His gaze flicked briefly toward Bellamy. "So look at your ink."

Bellamy didn't argue. He simply stared, and Adrian saw something shift behind his eyes: the reluctant understanding that history did not always sanitize itself into train headlights and mistaken lanterns. Sometimes history stayed messy and specific.

Marissa traced a finger above the map without touching it. "This path here," she said, "it skirts the west slope. It detours."

Adrian recognized it from the county office maps. "The old route," he said. "The one that predates the mining cuts."

Harper nodded. "Cherokee path," he said. "Or older. Folks argue about who walked it first like it matters. What matters is it bends away from places that look harmless."

Foster, who'd been silent, spoke suddenly. "Devil's Stairs," he said, voice tight. "That's where Team Two went."

Harper's finger moved to a steep contour line where the shading thickened. "That's your west cut," he said. "It drops fast, and it's loud underfoot. Gravel, leaf slip, water noise. You can't hear yourself right, and you can't hear anyone else right. It makes people call out."

Mercer's jaw tightened. "And calling out brings them in."

Harper didn't say yes. He didn't need to. He tapped the map once, a decisive beat like Ruth's walking stick on porch planks. "If you go after them," he said, "you don't go straight down that cut."

Marissa looked up. "Then how?"

Harper's finger slid along the detour path, the older route that curved wide around the shaded hollow before narrowing again near a creek bend. "You go the long way," he said. "You come in from the side. You keep your footing. You keep your breath. And you keep red where you can reach it."

Mercer stared at the map as if committing it to memory. "This gives us an approach corridor."

"It gives you a chance," Harper corrected. Then his eyes lifted, and his voice dropped lower, forcing them to lean in. "But don't mistake a chance for control. The map doesn't tell you where they are. It tells you where people stop coming back from."

Adrian felt the words settle heavy in his chest. A map of avoidance wasn't a treasure map. It was a list of borders drawn by grief.

Bellamy finally spoke, quiet and careful. "Why keep this? Why not give it to the forest service?"

Harper's expression hardened. "Because they'd file it and forget it," he said. "Or they'd come asking questions loud enough for the mountain to hear. Or they'd decide it makes the county look bad and bury it in a drawer. Families keep what families need."

Mercer nodded slowly. "We need it now," he said.

Harper looked at him for a long moment, measuring. Then he reached into the metal box again and pulled out a smaller sheet of paper, freshly copied, the map section traced by hand in dark pencil.

"You can have this," Harper said. "Not the original."

Mercer took it with both hands like something fragile. "Thank you."

Harper's gaze moved across them, lingering on Foster. "And you," he said to Foster, "you did right staying put."

Foster's throat worked. "It didn't feel right."

Harper's mouth twitched. "Right and easy don't have much to do with each other on this mountain."

As they rolled the copied sheet carefully and prepared to leave, Adrian looked once more at the shaded hollows on the old map. The shape of avoidance was unmistakable now. It wasn't random fear. It was accumulated data, a tradition built from repeated outcomes. Folklore with a backbone of geography.

He thought of Ruth's words the night before: every time the mountain takes somebody, it leaves something behind for the next one to find. Not mercy. Instruction.

Outside Harper's house, the fog had lifted just enough to show Brown Mountain's ridge line in the distance, dark against a paler sky. Adrian felt, with a clarity that made his stomach clench, that they had crossed another threshold.

Not into a mine, not onto a ridge, but into a kind of knowledge that changed what responsibility meant.

Mercer tucked the copied map into his jacket. "We go in daylight," he said, more to himself than to them. "We use the long approach. We don't shout names. We don't chase. And if we see the lights, we don't let them make the decisions."

Marissa looked toward the mountain, jaw set. "A map of where not to go," she murmured, "is still a map."

Adrian heard the dread beneath her steadiness. A map meant routes. Routes meant action. Action meant the phenomenon would have something new to learn.

Bellamy climbed into the truck without speaking, his face tight and pale, his mind clearly wrestling with the fact that the past had left them something more damning than a legend: a pattern precise enough to draw.

Foster shut his door and stared straight ahead, as if he could already see the west cut dropping away into the hollow.

Adrian held the copied sheet in his mind like an afterimage. Avoidance wasn't cowardice. It was an old intelligence shaped by survival. And now they were about to do the one thing the map implied was always dangerous, even when done carefully.

They were going to enter the borderland on purpose.

Chapter 11

Night Watchers

By late afternoon the copied map sheet had softened at the folds from being opened and closed too many times. Mercer kept it in his jacket anyway, close to his chest as if paper could absorb intent. The four of them drove back toward the station in a thin, working silence, each mile carrying them away from Seth Harper's porch and closer to the truth that none of the ledger marks had been made in daylight.

At the station Mercer spread the traced section on the conference table beneath fluorescent lights that made everything look too clinical to be trusted.

"We go in the morning," he said again, as if repetition could turn it into a rule the mountain had to honor. He traced the detour line Harper had indicated, the long approach that curved wide of the shaded hollows and came in from the side near a creek bend. "We come in here. We don't drop straight down Devil's Stairs. We don't take the easiest wrong way."

Foster stood with his arms folded, shoulders still hunched from exhaustion. His eyes tracked Mercer's finger, then flicked toward the windows as the wind pushed fog against the glass.

Marissa sat with her tablet closed, hands wrapped around a mug she wasn't drinking. Bellamy hovered near the edge of the table like he didn't trust himself not to smudge the ink.

Adrian watched the map while his mind did something it hated doing: it imagined night as a variable. The ledger marks didn't say "night," but every story they'd heard did. Every disappearance started with someone seeing a light in the dark and thinking it meant something.

Mercer finally looked up. "But we're not doing nothing until then."

Bellamy's head lifted sharply. "You just said we go in the morning."

"We do," Mercer said. "Search in daylight. Off-trail in daylight. That's the plan."

"And now?" Marissa asked. Her voice stayed controlled, but there was an edge under it, the edge of someone who had watched the same decision-making loop tighten. "What do you mean, not nothing?"

Mercer's jaw flexed. "I mean we keep eyes on the ridge tonight."

Foster's gaze snapped to him. "No."

Mercer didn't blink. "Yes."

Foster took a half-step forward and stopped himself, as if movement itself could be an argument now. "You saw what happened," he said, voice raw. "They don't need a trail. They don't need a mine. They just need somebody to react."

"That's exactly why," Mercer replied. "Because the lights are up there, and Team Two went off the ridge after them. If they're still alive, they're somewhere down that west cut, maybe trying to climb back, maybe trying to signal, maybe doing the exact thing Ruth warned against because it's what people do when they're scared."

Marissa's mouth tightened. "Calling out."

Mercer nodded once. "Calling out. Whistling. Shouting names. Radio chatter. All the things we've been trained to do."

Bellamy's voice came out careful, strained. "So your solution is to… what? Sit on a ridge and watch lights?"

"My solution is a controlled presence," Mercer said. "A vigil. We don't chase. We don't talk. We don't go off trail. We sit where we can see the valley and we document. If we see anything that suggests Team Two is moving back toward the ridge, we're there to intercept them before they follow something else."

Adrian felt his stomach tighten at the word intercept. Like the lights were a suspect and the rangers were setting a perimeter. Like any of this obeyed law.

Marissa looked from Mercer to Foster. "Eli?"

Foster's eyes were bloodshot and furious, but his anger was exhausted too, the kind that didn't have enough fuel to burn clean. "A vigil is how people end up staring into the dark," he said. "And staring is attention. Ruth said don't let it see your face."

"We keep our lights low," Mercer said. "We keep our heads down unless we have to look. We stay behind the rock outcrop near the overlook. If something approaches, we back away. We have flares."

Bellamy's laugh came out thin. "Flares. Like medieval wards."

Marissa's gaze cut to him. "Don't."

Bellamy shut his mouth, but the tension in his shoulders didn't change.

Adrian spoke quietly, surprising himself with the steadiness of his own voice. "If we do it," he said, "we do it like fieldwork. Minimal variables. Clear objectives. Clear stop conditions."

Mercer nodded at that, a small acknowledgment. "Exactly."

Marissa's eyes narrowed as she thought. "Objective one: observe lights without provoking response. Objective two: listen for non-light indicators. Movement. Voices. Anything human."

Foster's mouth tightened. "Listening is dangerous too."

Marissa didn't disagree. "Yes," she said. "But not listening hasn't worked either."

Bellamy leaned on the table, looking down at the shaded band on the map. "And if you hear someone calling?"

No one answered for a beat. The question landed like a trap.

Mercer finally said, "We don't answer."

Foster's eyes closed for a second, long enough to look like prayer. When he opened them again, he looked older than he had that morning. "People will call," he said, voice low. "They always do. They call because they think it proves they're still human. They call because silence feels like giving up."

Adrian remembered the mine, the instinct to speak just to break the pressure of the dark. He understood too well.

Mercer reached into a cabinet and pulled out a small dry-erase board from the wall, the kind used for visitor notices. He set it on the table and uncapped a marker.

"We make a script," he said. "Like we did with clicks."

Bellamy flinched at the word script, as if it confirmed the thing he'd been resisting: that there was a pattern, and patterns could be exploited by both sides.

Mercer wrote, blocky and blunt:

No names spoken. No whistling. No radios unless emergency. If approached, eyes down. If followed, retreat to truck. Flares only on my call.

He drew a line under it, then added:

If we hear a voice, we do not respond.

Marissa stared at the last line. "Even if it's Team Two."

Mercer met her gaze. "Especially if it's Team Two. Because if it is them, answering might kill them faster."

Foster's jaw clenched so hard the muscle jumped.

Adrian said, "We can use clicks," and felt the sick irony of it. Scholars and rangers reduced to the language of tapping insects. "If we absolutely have to signal."

Mercer nodded. “Clicks only. One click means ‘hold.’ Two means ‘move back.’ Three means ‘flare.’ No improvising.”

Bellamy opened his mouth, then closed it. He looked like a man watching his own training fall apart and be replaced by something older, something he’d spent a career calling superstition.

They ate quickly before sunset, standing at the counter with protein bars and lukewarm coffee because no one wanted to sit down. At dusk Mercer loaded the truck with extra flares, a thermal blanket, and a coil of tape. Marissa left her recorder behind on purpose and carried only her tablet, its brightness turned down until the screen looked almost black. Bellamy brought a notebook and a pencil, then hesitated and put them back, as if the scratch of graphite might count as noise.

Foster came with them despite Mercer’s earlier attempt to keep him off the ridge. He didn’t argue. He simply got in the truck, face set, hands folded tight in his lap. Adrian wondered if Foster could even sleep with the sound of clicking in his head.

The ridge road was clearer tonight, less fog, but the air had the same hollow quiet Adrian had felt in the mine and in the prologue memory that wasn’t his. The mountain seemed to hold its breath when night arrived, as if listening for the first mistake.

Mercer parked at the same pull-off they'd used the day before and killed the engine. Darkness poured in around the truck immediately, thick and damp. In the distance the valley was a layered shadow, ridgelines stacked like folded cloth.

They walked the last hundred yards to the overlook without headlamps at first. Mercer led by feel and memory, boots careful on gravel. When they reached the rock outcrop, he lifted a hand and made a single click with his tongue.

The sound was tiny, almost nothing.

Adrian waited for an answering click out of habit and felt his skin prickle when none came. Of course none came. Foster was beside them, not out in the fog.

Mercer signaled them down, crouched behind the rock so the skyline wouldn't silhouette their bodies. They settled into a tight cluster: Mercer at the left edge where he could see the trail behind them, Foster beside him, Adrian and Marissa in the center, Bellamy on the right.

For a few minutes there was only the valley and the dark.

Then a pale point appeared across the gap, low over the trees on the far ridge. It was small, steady, and so bright against the black that Adrian's eyes watered.

It hovered.

Another appeared higher up, and another farther down the line, like stars rearranging themselves into a pattern only the mountain understood.

Bellamy's breath caught, audible in the hush. Foster's hand snapped up and pressed lightly against Bellamy's sleeve, not a reprimand, a reminder: still.

The lights drifted slowly along the treeline, not bobbing, not jittering the way a flashlight beam would. They moved like intent made visible.

Marissa leaned closer to Adrian until her shoulder brushed his. Her voice, when it came, was barely there. "They're earlier tonight."

Adrian didn't answer with words. He simply watched, forcing himself to look and not look at the same time, keeping the lights at the edge of his vision the way Ruth's rule demanded. Direct attention felt like leaning over a cliff.

Mercer lifted the map copy from his pocket, unfolded it by touch and kept it low between them. He pointed without speaking to the west shaded band, then out toward the valley as if aligning paper to terrain. Even in darkness, the gesture was clear: those hollows were down there, somewhere under the lights' slow drift.

Foster's face was angled down, eyes fixed on the rock at their feet. Adrian wondered if the lights could see faces from this distance, or if the rule was about something else: recognition, identity, the moment you became more than movement and sound.

Across the valley one of the lights stopped.

It held perfectly still for several seconds, brighter than the others.

Then it turned, not drifting with wind, but pivoting as if it had chosen a new direction.

It began moving toward them. Slowly, deliberately, crossing the dark space above the trees as if the valley were not a barrier at all, only distance.

Adrian felt the old, unreasonable urge to stand, to get a better look, to understand. The same urge that had pulled hikers off trail and miners deeper into a shaft.

Mercer made two clicks, soft and quick.

Move back.

They shifted as one, retreating a foot behind the rock without standing, bodies low, faces turned slightly away. No scrambling, no sudden movements. Just a controlled withdrawal, like a tide pulling back from a shore.

The approaching light paused again, as if recalculating. It hovered, pulsed faintly, then drifted sideways instead of forward, rejoining the line of other lights along the far ridge.

Adrian realized his hands were clenched so tightly his nails bit through his gloves.

They held the vigil for another hour, watching lights appear, drift, cluster, and separate. Sometimes they seemed to trace the valley contours as if following invisible paths. Sometimes they stopped, held still, and then moved again with the same patience that had filled the mine mouth when the flare burned down.

No one spoke. Not because there was nothing to say, but because every word felt like it might become a signal.

And somewhere down the west slope, beyond the reach of their eyes, three members of Team Two were either waiting in silence or making noise in the dark and teaching the mountain exactly where to find them.

When Mercer finally signaled for them to withdraw, he did it with one click and a slow hand gesture, as if even deciding to leave needed to be done carefully.

As they backed away from the overlook toward the truck, Adrian kept his face angled down, but he could feel the lights in the valley the way you could feel a stare at the back of your neck.

Night watchers, Ruth had called them.

Adrian understood now that the phrase was incomplete.

They weren't only watching the mountain.

They were watching for the moment a human being forgot the rules.

They were almost back to the truck when Foster stopped so abruptly that Marissa nearly ran into him.

Mercer's hand lifted at once, fist tight in the dark.

Hold.

No one moved. The forest around the pull-off was a thick wall of trunks and laurel, the kind of dense edge that made the open road feel like a fragile ribbon laid through something older. The air carried the sharp smell of wet leaves and cold soil. Somewhere far off, a creek murmured, steady and indifferent.

Adrian had his eyes down, fixed on the pale gravel at his feet, but he felt the shift in the night the way you felt a change in pressure before a storm. The valley had been full of lights. Here, away from the overlook, there should have been nothing but darkness and the dim outline of Mercer's truck.

A click came from the trees to their right.

Not Mercer's tongue click. Not a radio click.

A small, clean sound, like two pebbles tapped together.

Bellamy's shoulders drew up. Adrian saw his throat move with a swallow he was trying to make silent.

Mercer turned his head slightly, careful not to swing his face toward the sound. He raised two fingers and moved them in a slow, downward motion.

Stay low.

They crouched. The gravel pressed into Adrian's knees through his pants. He became acutely aware of how loud bodies were even when they tried not to be: joints shifting, fabric whispering, breath trying to turn into speech.

Another click, nearer this time, answered the first.

And then, between two trunks about twenty yards off, a pale light appeared.

It was smaller than the ones across the valley, but it had the same wrong steadiness. It did not throw a beam. It did not illuminate branches or leaves the way a flashlight would. It simply existed, a floating point of white in the dark understory.

Marissa's hand found Adrian's sleeve and tightened, not to pull him, but to anchor herself to something human.

The light held position.

A second pale point winked into existence higher up, among the branches. It drifted sideways without bobbing, without any sign of weight. It moved like a thought changing its mind.

Mercer made a single click with his tongue.

Hold.

Foster's head dipped even lower, almost to his chest, as if lowering his face could erase him. His hands were clenched so tightly Adrian could see the tendons in his fingers.

The first light pulsed once, faintly, and Adrian felt the instinct to look directly at it rise like nausea. Vision wanted to solve it. The urge was physical. He fought it by staring at the road's edge, at a strip of broken leaf litter, at a beer can crushed flat and half-buried in damp gravel.

People come here for pictures, he thought. People come here to stare.

The lights, patient as hunger, had all the time in the world for staring.

A third point of light appeared, lower to the ground, hovering just above a patch of fern. It drifted forward a few feet and then stopped, as if it had found the line where their hearing began.

The clicking began again, a loose pattern now, not loud but layered. Not echoes. Not settling wood. A kind of soft conversation carried on in a language made of contact and distance.

Bellamy's breathing hitched.

Foster's hand shot out and caught Bellamy's wrist with a grip that was both warning and plea. Bellamy froze, eyes wide in the dark, his lips pressed together so hard they blanched.

Mercer's hand slid slowly to the pack at his side. Adrian saw the outline of a flare in his grip, unlit. Mercer did not move to strike it yet. He was listening, measuring how close the lights were willing to come before they met resistance.

The nearest glow drifted one careful foot toward them.

Then another foot.

It stopped again, hovering at about chest height, exactly where a person's face would be if they stood.

Because it learns you.

Ruth's words came back with brutal clarity, and Adrian understood, in a way he hadn't in daylight on a porch, that the rule about faces wasn't mystical. It was practical. If this thing learned by attention, then giving it a face was giving it a person. A specific person. An identity it could carry forward the way it carried patterns.

Mercer raised two fingers and gave a slow, backward wave.

Back.

They retreated in a tight, crouched cluster, each step placed with a care that bordered on ritual. Gravel shifted under Adrian's boot and he felt panic flare, then forced his body to soften, to reduce the urge to catch himself too sharply.

The lights followed.

Not rushing, not surging like they had in the mine, but moving in the same controlled increments, maintaining their chosen distance as if they were herding.

Adrian realized with a sick jolt that they weren't blocking the path to the truck.

They were coming with them.

The road appeared ahead, a paler strip of open space. The truck was there, a dark shape at the pull-off, its metal reflecting faint starlight. It looked absurdly ordinary.

Mercer made two quick clicks.

Move back.

They edged toward the vehicle. Mercer reached it first and placed his palm on the door, not opening it yet. He kept his head angled down, body turned slightly sideways so he could watch without staring.

The lights hovered at the treeline, just inside the forest. Three, maybe four now, and one higher up that drifted between branches as if branches were only suggestions.

Mercer lifted the flare an inch.

The nearest light pulsed again.

And then, from somewhere behind them on the ridge trail, a human voice spoke.

"Mercer?"

It was faint. Not shouted. Not close enough to be immediate danger.

But it was a voice, in the dark, saying a name.

Every muscle in Adrian's body tensed. Names spoken, Mercer had written. No names spoken.

Foster went rigid like he'd been struck.

Mercer did not answer. He didn't turn his head. His hand, still on the truck door, tightened.

The voice came again, a little clearer.

"Evan Mercer? Hey."

Bellamy's eyes flicked upward despite himself, searching for a shape. His mouth opened a fraction, then closed as Foster's grip on his wrist tightened until it must have hurt.

Marissa's hand slid to her own throat, fingers pressed there as if she could physically stop sound from escaping.

Adrian felt his mind scramble for explanations. Another ranger? A volunteer? A local? Someone coming up the trail unaware?

Then the voice did something wrong.

It repeated itself, but not like a person repeating because they hadn't been heard. It repeated with the same cadence, the same spacing, like an audio recording played twice.

"Evan Mercer? Hey."

The exact same tone. The exact same pause.

Mercer's eyes, in the faint light, narrowed. He did not look back. He made a single click, sharp and controlled.

Hold.

Adrian stared at the gravel. He could feel his heartbeat thudding in his ears, loud enough to be a signal. He tried to slow it. Tried to make himself smaller without moving.

From the forest at their right, the clicking increased, denser now, and one of the lights drifted closer to the road's edge as if to listen.

The voice spoke again. This time it wasn't Mercer.

"Marissa?"

Marissa flinched so hard her shoulder bumped Adrian. The sound was tiny, but in the open road it seemed to carry.

The nearest glow brightened.

Adrian felt cold climb the back of his neck. Only a few people would use her first name like that. Adrian did. Adrian heard it in his own voice sometimes. Bellamy usually said Dr. Calder. Mercer used Calder or Marissa depending on stress. Foster had barely spoken to her at all.

The voice in the dark behind them sounded close enough to be one of them.

And that was the point.

It wanted you to think it was meant for you.

The waitress's words and Ruth's warning overlapped in Adrian's mind, forming a single, ugly truth: the phenomenon didn't only lure with light. It lured with recognition. With the intimate hook of a name spoken at night.

"Marissa?" the voice said again, and this time it had a faint edge of impatience, a human emotion pasted on like a mask.

Marissa's lips trembled. She didn't speak, but Adrian saw the reflex in her eyes, the urge to respond to being called, the way humans were trained from childhood to answer their names.

Mercer's hand lifted the flare higher.

Three clicks, quiet and absolute.

Flare.

Adrian's fingers closed around his own unlit cylinder, but Mercer struck his first. The flare ignited with a violent hiss, red light tearing open the dark. Smoke poured upward, sharp and chemical.

The response was immediate. The nearest pale glow recoiled backward into the treeline, sliding fast and wrong between trunks. The higher light among the branches jerked away as if it had been swatted. The clicking spiked, suddenly frantic, and then thinned as the glows retreated to the forest's deeper shadow.

Behind them on the ridge trail, the voice cut off mid-breath, as if someone had hit a switch.

Silence fell hard.

Red light washed over the road, the truck's door, Mercer's knuckles white around the flare. The smoke made Adrian's eyes sting. In that harsh red, Foster's face looked hollow, his skin stretched tight over fatigue and fear.

Mercer opened the truck door with controlled care and jerked his chin.

In.

They climbed in without slamming anything, moving like people who'd learned that noise was a currency the mountain accepted gladly. Mercer stayed outside half a second longer, holding the flare out and turning slightly, sweeping the red light across the treeline as if drawing a boundary.

No pale glows remained visible.

But Adrian did not feel safer. He felt watched by something that had simply stepped back to think.

Mercer got in and pulled the door shut softly. The cab filled with the flare's harsh smell. He held the burning cylinder out the cracked window, keeping the red glow outside as much as possible.

No one spoke for several seconds. It was Foster who finally broke the silence, voice rough, low.

"It's doing it now," he said.

Marissa's hands were clenched in her lap so tightly her knuckles shone. "Doing what?" she whispered, though she knew.

Foster swallowed. "Using us," he said. "Using what we say. What we answer to."

Bellamy's face was pale in the dash glow, his eyes fixed on the windshield as if he expected a light to bloom there, inches from the glass. "It said your names," he managed. The words sounded like an accusation against reality itself. "It said them correctly."

Adrian tasted metal at the back of his mouth, the body's old response to dread. He kept his gaze down, staring at the texture of the glove in his hands, at the fine grit embedded in the fabric from the mine.

"It doesn't need to see our faces to learn us," Adrian said quietly. "Not if it can learn our names."

Mercer's jaw tightened. "Then we stop giving it anything," he said.

He put the truck in gear and drove, not fast, not yet. As they pulled away from the overlook, Adrian looked once in the side mirror.

At the edge of the pull-off, just inside the trees, a pale point of light appeared again.

It did not follow.

It hovered in place, steady and calm, like a punctuation mark at the end of a sentence.

Then it pulsed once, faintly, as if acknowledging that it had been heard.

And Adrian realized, with a cold certainty that settled deep, that the vigil had not been a watch to see whether the lights would return.

The lights had already been there.

They had been watching to see whether the humans would.

Mercer didn't drive all the way back to the station.

He took them down off the ridge road and into a small gravel lot beside a closed picnic area, a place the forest service used in summer when families needed bathrooms and maps and a reason to believe the woods were friendly. Tonight the tables were stacked and chained. The information board was a black rectangle of glass that reflected the truck's dim dash lights and four pale faces that didn't look like themselves.

He killed the engine and let the silence settle, heavy as wet wool.

No one moved at first. The flare Mercer had struck on the pull-off had burned down in its coffee can, and without it the cab felt exposed in a way Adrian couldn't name. Not unsafe exactly. Just open, as if the night had more ways to get in than through windows.

Foster was still staring straight ahead. His hands were locked together in his lap like he was holding himself in place by force.

Marissa's voice came finally, quiet and tight. "That wasn't Team Two."

Bellamy exhaled through his nose, brittle. "Congratulations. We have reached consensus."

Mercer didn't take the bait. He leaned forward slightly, elbows on his thighs, and kept his voice low as if the forest could hear through glass. "It said my name first," he said. "Then yours. It's not random."

Adrian felt his mind reach for the same structure it always wanted. Stimulus. Response. Escalation. In the mine it had been sound and motion. On the ridge it had added something else.

Recognition.

"It repeated itself," Adrian said. "Like a recording."

Marissa shook her head once, a sharp denial. "It sounded like impatience. Like it wanted me to answer."

"That's mimicry," Bellamy said, and Adrian heard the effort it took to keep the word academic. To keep it from becoming a confession of fear. "Birds do it. Some mammals do it. Even if— even if this is something physical, not biological, mimicry can be functional. It can be a strategy."

Foster's throat worked. He spoke without looking at anyone. "Team Two answered the radio," he said.

The sentence dropped into the cab like a stone.

Mercer turned slightly toward him. "Eli."

Foster finally looked over, eyes bloodshot, expression flat with exhaustion and the kind of guilt that didn't care about reason. "I heard them," he said. "Not close. Not clear. But I heard them call back. They kept saying, 'You see it? You see it?' like they were excited. Then one of them said the tech's name. Just like we always do. Like it mattered. Like it anchored them."

Marissa's fingers tightened around her own wrist. "And then?"

Foster swallowed. "Then the chatter stopped. Not gradual. Like a switch. Like somebody took the sound away."

Adrian remembered what Foster had said in the diner, that he'd heard them stop talking as if a hand had gone over their mouths. He'd thought it might be metaphor, the brain trying to describe a thing it couldn't properly name.

Now he wasn't sure.

Mercer stared out through the windshield into the dark, where the road bent away and disappeared behind trees. "We can't search off trail tonight," he said. It wasn't a decision now so much as a boundary line. "And we can't sit on the ridge letting it practice our names."

Bellamy's laugh came out small and pained. "Practice. As if it's studying for an exam."

Adrian's mouth went dry. Practice was exactly the word that fit. The voice hadn't been a single lure tossed into the dark. It had been a demonstration, careful and calibrated. Name. Pause. Repeat. Then a different name. See what moved. See what answered.

A field test.

Marissa glanced toward the side mirror, then away again, as if the habit of checking for pale light had become involuntary. “We should go,” she said. “Back to the station. Write it down while it’s still precise.”

Mercer nodded, but he didn’t start the engine yet. He reached for the radio on the dash and turned the volume even lower. Not off. Never fully off. Adrian understood the instinct now: silence felt safer, but total silence meant you couldn’t hear the moment danger decided to speak.

Mercer clicked the transmit button once, but didn’t speak. A soft, controlled click with his tongue.

They waited.

Static answered. No click back. No faint signal. Nothing that sounded like Foster’s earlier communication pattern.

Mercer’s jaw tightened. He clicked again, a simple rhythm they’d used before.

Nothing.

Foster’s hands clenched. “He won’t be answering,” he said, and Adrian realized with a jolt that Foster wasn't talking about himself. He was talking about Team Two.

Mercer tried one more time, thumb on transmit, voice barely a thread. "Team Two, this is Mercer. If you copy, one click. One click only."

The radio hissed softly, empty.

Then, so faint Adrian almost dismissed it as interference, a sound slipped through the static.

Click.

Marissa went still, her whole posture tightening like a wire pulled taut.

Bellamy's head snapped up. "That was—"

Mercer raised a hand, silencing him without a word. He pressed transmit again, voice the lowest Adrian had ever heard from him. "Who is this? One click for yes."

A pause.

Click.

Foster's face drained of what little color it had left. "No," he whispered, and the word was not argument. It was pleading, like he could deny a thing into being false.

Mercer didn't answer with his own name. He didn't say Team Two again. He didn't offer language.

He clicked once, then twice. A simple instruction, the code he'd invented because it carried less bait.

Hold. Then move back.

Static. Silence.

Then, too cleanly, too neatly, the radio produced another click. Exactly one. Like a correct response.

Adrian felt cold move under his skin. The timing was wrong. It wasn't the delayed, struggling click of a man crouched in fog trying not to die. It was immediate, confident. It sounded like something that wasn't afraid of being heard.

Mercer stared at the radio as if it had become the mine mouth again, an opening that let the wrong thing breathe into the room.

He leaned in and spoke anyway, controlled but unmistakably tense. "What's your position?"

Static. Then a voice, low and broken, threaded through the hiss.

"Mercer…"

It wasn't loud. It wasn't shouted. It sounded like someone trying to whisper and failing. Like throat muscles that didn't remember the shape of words.

Marissa's hand flew to her mouth.

Foster made a sound that wasn't quite a sob, and his eyes squeezed shut hard, as if he could keep the voice from getting in that way.

Bellamy's face had gone ashen. His lips moved without sound, forming a silent no.

The voice came again, clearer now, and the cadence made Adrian's stomach turn.

"Mercer. Hey."

The same phrase as on the ridge trail. The same spacing. The same false casualness. As if it had been rehearsed.

Mercer's thumb hovered over transmit. Adrian expected him to answer, to demand a name, to demand proof. The ranger in him would want to lock on, to make contact, to turn this into a rescue operation with coordinates and procedure.

Instead Mercer did something Adrian hadn't expected.

He turned the radio off.

The sudden lack of static made the cab feel hollow. For a second Adrian thought he'd made a mistake, that he'd just cut off the only thread they had.

Then, in the silence that followed, Adrian heard something else.

A click.

Not from the radio.

From outside the truck.

Close. Too close.

Marissa's eyes widened, and she looked at Mercer with a terror that wasn't abstract anymore. It was immediate, physical, and furious at being confirmed.

Bellamy's breath hitched, and Foster grabbed his wrist again by reflex, as if holding onto a human pulse could keep the rest of the world from rearranging.

Another click came from the darkness beyond the passenger-side window, followed by a faint, wet fluttering sound that Adrian had hoped never to hear again outside the mine.

Mercer didn't move fast. Fast was noise. Fast was panic. He lifted his hand slowly, reached down between his seat and the door, and brought up a flare.

He didn't strike it yet. He held it ready, listening.

Adrian stared at the glass, at his own faint reflection layered over the dark. For a moment he thought he saw a pale smudge out there, just beyond the window's edge, like a star caught between branches. Then it drifted, smooth and deliberate, into a position level with the cab.

Chest height. Face height.

As if it knew exactly where a person sat.

Foster's voice came out in a rasp, barely audible. "It followed the radio."

Marissa shook her head once, small and frantic. "Or it used the radio to bring us to a place it could reach."

Bellamy's whisper was almost prayer. "This is impossible."

A light bloomed outside the windshield, a pale point hovering near the picnic board's glass surface. It didn't illuminate the lot. It didn't cast shadows the way a lantern would. It simply made itself visible, like an eye opening.

Another appeared near the driver's side, higher up, as if it had climbed the air.

The clicking increased, not loud, but layered. Coordinated. A loose chorus that suggested more than two, more than three.

Adrian's heart pounded so hard he was sure it could be heard.

And then, from somewhere in the darkness beyond the truck, a human voice called softly, almost gently, as if trying not to startle them.

"Marissa?"

The sound came from outside, not through the radio. Close enough that it carried the shape of breath.

Marissa went rigid. Her eyes filled, not with tears, but with the reflex to answer. Humans were made to respond to their names. It was one of the first rules the world taught.

Mercer's voice came low, tight as wire. "Do not."

Marissa's lips trembled. She didn't speak.

The voice repeated, with the same cadence as before, the same synthetic patience.

"Marissa. Hey."

Adrian felt the full horror of it settle into place. The disappearance repeated itself not as an event, but as a method. Light to draw you. Sound to hook you. Name to claim you. The mountain didn't need new tricks. It only needed you to be human, to do the human thing.

Foster's eyes were squeezed shut, his face angled down. "Don't let it see you," he whispered, and Adrian didn't know whether Foster meant their faces or their fear.

Mercer struck the flare.

Red fire erupted in the cab's narrow space through the cracked window, hissing violently. The chemical stink filled Adrian's nose and made his eyes sting. Mercer held the flare outside the driver's window, arm rigid, sweeping the red glow across the lot in a slow arc.

The pale lights recoiled instantly, sliding back into the trees, jerking away from the flare's radius with that wrong, living precision. The clicking spiked into frantic density, then thinned as the lights retreated.

The voice stopped mid-word, cut off as cleanly as a recording.

Mercer shoved the key into the ignition and started the engine. It caught immediately, a roar in the quiet lot that felt like profanity. He put the truck in gear and pulled out without turning the overhead light on, without slamming anything, without giving the night a chance to collect details.

Adrian looked back through the rear window.

At the edge of the picnic area, just beyond where the gravel gave way to leaf litter, a pale point of light hovered in place. It did not chase the truck. It didn't need to.

It held position and pulsed once, faintly, as if acknowledging a successful experiment.

Marissa's voice broke at last, hoarse and furious. "It used Team Two's radio discipline against them."

Bellamy stared forward, unblinking. "It used us," he said. "It used our names. Our voices. Our procedures."

Foster's hands shook openly now, the control finally gone. "That's what happened to them," he whispered. "They followed it because it sounded like us. They answered because it sounded like someone needed help."

Adrian swallowed hard, throat burning with the urge to speak and the certainty that speech was dangerous.

Mercer drove faster, flare still burning outside the window like a red boundary dragged through the night. "It wants repetition," Mercer said, voice hard. "It wants the same mistake, again and again, until it doesn't have to work for it."

Adrian watched the dark road unfold ahead and realized the mountain didn't have to take new people in new ways.

It only had to wait for the old human reflexes to reassert themselves: answer your name, respond to a call for help, follow the light that seems meant for you.

And somewhere out there, down the west cut, three members of Team Two had likely heard a familiar voice in the dark and stepped toward it.

A disappearance repeated, not because the mountain was cruel in a new way, but because it had learned the oldest way to make someone come closer.

Chapter 12

Buried Truths

The station felt smaller after the picnic lot.

Not physically, but in the way a room shrank when it could no longer pretend it was a boundary. Mercer pulled the truck into the gravel beside the building and killed the engine without ceremony. For a moment none of them moved. The heater ticked as it cooled. The faint smell of flare smoke clung to their jackets like a second layer of skin.

Foster was the first to open his door. He stepped out stiffly, as if the act of standing upright in the world required permission. Under the station's porch light his face looked scraped raw by fatigue.

Mercer followed, carrying the burnt coffee can that had held the flare. He set it on the steps with exaggerated care, like he didn't want to make a sound loud enough to be remembered.

Inside, the fluorescent lights turned their silence into something procedural. Marissa went straight to the table and sat, shoulders squared, hands clasped as if she could hold herself together by grip alone. Bellamy stood near the counter and stared at the sink, not using it, just looking at something solid and ordinary.

Adrian took off his coat, then put it back on. He couldn't shake the sensation that removing layers was the first step in being exposed.

Mercer didn't ask if they were okay this time. He already knew what the answer would be.

"We're done with night," he said.

Foster's head snapped up. "We were done with night before we went up there."

Mercer didn't argue. He moved to the desk and pulled Seth Harper's copied map and ledger page from his jacket. He laid them flat and smoothed the paper with his palm as if he could press out the century.

Bellamy drifted closer despite himself, the way he always did when paper entered a room. His fear didn't cancel his instincts. It just rode on top of them.

"That voice," Marissa said finally, her words clipped. "It's not random mimicry. It's targeted. It used our names in a sequence. It repeated phrases with identical cadence. It's either recording, or it's imitation with a very specific selection mechanism."

Foster's laugh was dry and short. "You make it sound like a grant proposal."

Marissa's gaze went to him, not sharp, just tired. "I'm trying to keep it from becoming a story people tell wrong."

Adrian looked down at the ledger page. The brown ink, the cramped notations, the small symbols that turned names into outcomes. Earlier, in Harper's living room, it had felt like proof of pattern. Now, after hearing a voice speak from outside the truck, it felt like a list of warnings that had been ignored because the warning didn't use the right language.

Bellamy pointed at one of the marks beside a name. His finger hovered, not touching. "These aren't standard accounting symbols," he said. "They're not tally marks for pay. They mean something else."

Mercer nodded. "Harper said missing."

"Not recovered," Adrian murmured, remembering the phrasing from the county file. A man reduced to a liability statement.

Foster pulled out a chair and sat heavily. "The mine is where it started," he said, and his voice had the rough certainty of someone clinging to a timeline because timelines were the only things that didn't drift.

Marissa turned her head slightly. "What do you mean, started?"

Foster looked at the papers. "Out here," he said, "everyone talks like the lights have always been a sky thing. But Ruth doesn't talk like that. Harper doesn't either. They talk like it has places. Like it has routes. Like it learned the mountain from below and then learned how to invite people from above."

Adrian felt his stomach tighten. He thought of the mine chamber, the pale cluster rising fast, the smell of rotten-sweet cold on his face. He thought of the warning on the timber beam: DO NOT CALL TO THEM.

"Below and above," Adrian said quietly. "Same behavior. Same response."

Bellamy's eyes flicked to him. "If we're going to talk about the mine," he said, "then we need to talk about what happened to the miners. Not the folklore version. The real version. There was an incident severe enough to close operations permanently. That doesn't happen because men get spooked."

Mercer's gaze didn't leave the ledger. "Tell that to the men who ran."

Bellamy swallowed, then pushed on anyway because that was what he did when fear crowded in. He turned it into research. "We have fragments," he said. "A company letter mentioning pursuit. Notes warning against whistling. A missing laborer, Thomas Vick. But there should be more. If a mine closed, there were inquests, compensation claims, church funerals, maybe even a state inspection. Paper trails don't vanish on their own. Someone makes them vanish."

"Cover-ups," Marissa said, but the word didn't sound like she enjoyed being right. It sounded like she was bracing for an ugly kind of predictable.

Mercer leaned back, exhaling slowly through his nose. "We need daylight to go after Team Two," he said. "But we also need the mine story. If we understand what happened down there, we might understand what it does now."

Foster's hands were still shaking, just slightly, a tremor that refused to be disciplined away. "I don't want to understand it," he said. "I want it to stop."

Adrian looked at him. Foster had spent his whole career making the woods behave according to maps and rules and training. The mountain had just shown him a rule set that didn't care about ranger authority.

"Understanding is how we get leverage," Adrian said gently. "Even if it's small."

Foster didn't answer. But he didn't argue either, and that silence was its own kind of permission.

Mercer picked up the phone and called Reverend Pike.

The reverend's voice came through on speaker, low and wary, like he already knew why the call was coming. Mercer kept it brief, careful. No mention of voices. No mention of lights. Just the mine, the old closures, the deaths.

There was a pause on the other end long enough that Adrian heard the faint scrape of a chair, as if Pike had stood.

"You're asking about the men," Pike said finally.

"Yes," Mercer replied. "The ones who didn't come back."

Another pause. Then, quieter, "The ones who did."

Marissa's posture changed immediately. "The ones who did come back?"

Pike didn't answer her directly. "Be at the church at eight," he said to Mercer. "Side door. Not the front. And don't bring a crowd. Those records aren't for sightseeing."

Mercer nodded even though Pike couldn't see him. "We'll be there."

When the call ended, the station's fluorescent hum filled the gap.

Bellamy spoke first. "The ones who did," he repeated, as if tasting the phrase. "That implies survivors. Not just fatalities."

Adrian's mind pulled at that. Survivors weren't just evidence. They were witnesses. And witnesses could be contaminated, not by folklore, but by whatever had followed them out.

At eight the church in Jonas Ridge looked like every other small mountain church from the road: white siding, narrow windows, a steeple that tried to point the building toward heaven whether heaven wanted it or not.

But the reverend didn't take them into the sanctuary.

He met them at the side door and led them down into a basement that smelled of damp concrete and hymnals stored too long. A single fluorescent light flickered overhead.

Reverend Pike was thinner than Adrian expected, with pale eyes that kept moving, not nervously, but as if he had learned that attention could be a form of invitation. He didn't shake hands. He didn't offer greetings.

He carried a cardboard box sealed with old tape.

"These aren't county records," he said. "These are family deposits. People bring things to the church when they don't know where else to put them. They think the walls make it holy enough to be safe."

He set the box on a folding table and peeled the tape back carefully, avoiding the ripping sound.

Inside were envelopes, brittle notebooks, a few folded newspapers, and a small cloth sack tied with twine. Pike reached past all of it and withdrew a narrow ledger book with a cracked spine, not the company's official ledger but something copied by hand. The ink was dark in places, faded in others, as if different entries had been made under different kinds of fear.

Bellamy leaned forward. "Who wrote this?"

Pike's mouth tightened. "A man named Edwin Sutter. He was a clerk for the mine office, and he was also a deacon. Those two loyalties don't mix when men start disappearing."

He opened the book to a page marked with a strip of cloth. Adrian's stomach turned when he saw the cloth was the same pale color as the scrap they'd found in the mine, as if fabric had become a language of warning all its own.

Pike ran a finger down a list of names.

Thomas Vick was there.

So were others Adrian didn't recognize: Hale, Darnell, McCreary, Rusk. Beside some names were the same symbols Harper's page had shown. Beside others were words written small, as if the writer didn't want the page to overhear.

Came up wrong.

Would not speak.

Kept clicking teeth.

Would not look at wife.

Refused lantern light.

Marissa drew a slow breath through her nose. "These are behavioral notes," she said, and her voice had gone very quiet.

Bellamy's face had drained of color. "This is... this is medical," he whispered, though the words were not medical in any formal sense. They were the vocabulary of a community trying to describe post-trauma symptoms without the concept of trauma.

Foster's jaw clenched. "Clicking teeth," he said, and Adrian saw him swallow hard. The wet, clicking flutter in the mine wasn't just sound. It had become an echo that could take root in human bodies.

Pike turned another page.

Here the handwriting changed, more hurried. A date. 1893.

Pike read aloud, his voice flat and controlled, as if emotion would make it more dangerous.

"'Lower Cut B, third shift. Men report glows again, low in the shaft where water stands. Foreman orders them on. Men refuse. Foreman descends with three. Lanterns fail. Sutter hears shouting from below, then silence. Later, a voice calls up from the dark in the foreman's tone. Uses names. Says, come down, I found him.'"

Adrian felt cold move under his skin.

Marissa's hand pressed against the table edge, knuckles whitening. "Uses names," she repeated, barely audible.

Pike's eyes lifted. "You've heard about the lights," he said. It wasn't accusation. It was weary recognition. "So you know why this book stayed down here."

He looked at Foster. "You know why the old folks taught children not to answer voices from the trees."

Foster didn't speak. He couldn't, not without making it real in the air.

Bellamy forced himself to ask, voice rough. "What happened to the men who went down?"

Pike turned one more page. The ink here was smeared, as if the writer's hand had been shaking.

"'Two came out at dawn. No third. They would not say where he was. They would not say what they saw. One kept his face turned away from the sunlight like it hurt. The other would not look at anyone, not even his own mother. When his wife spoke his name, he flinched like he'd been struck. They sat on the church steps and did not move until dusk. When asked why, Edwin Sutter wrote: Because they said the lights learn a man by his face and call him by his name.'"

Silence filled the basement like water filling a shaft.

Adrian looked at the copied words until they blurred, not from tears, but from the sensation of his eyes trying to refuse what they were taking in.

This wasn't just a mining accident. It wasn't just bad air or collapse or panic contagion. It was the oldest shape of the thing they'd already encountered: light, then response, then pursuit, then mimicry, then the intimate hook of recognition.

The miners' fate was not simply that some died.

It was that some came back carrying rules in their bodies, rules strict enough to pass down through churches and porches and family maps, and still those rules weren't kept, because every generation believed it would be different for them.

Mercer's voice was low, steady with effort. "And the missing one?" he asked.

Pike closed the book slowly. "Not recovered," he said, using the same phrase the county file had used, and now it sounded like a kind of cowardice. "But that wasn't the part that made people stop working."

Marissa lifted her eyes. "What made them stop?"

Pike's gaze held hers, and for the first time his control cracked enough that fear showed through, not loud, not dramatic, just old and settled.

"The ones who came back," he said. "Because the mine can take a man and the mountain can take a man and folks will call it tragedy. But when a man comes home and won't look at his own child, when he jerks at his name like it's a leash, when he starts to answer voices that aren't there…"

He shook his head once, small and final.

"Then people realize the mountain doesn't only take," Pike said. "It teaches. And sometimes it sends a lesson back up."

Pike didn't put the book back in the box right away.

He held it closed with both palms, as if keeping the pages shut was the only thing preventing their contents from spilling into the room. The flickering fluorescent light above them made his knuckles look bloodless.

Mercer's gaze stayed on the ledger's cracked spine. "You said there were family deposits," he murmured. "More than this."

Pike's eyes shifted to the cardboard box, then back to Mercer. "People brought what they could carry," he said. "What they could hide. What they could live with not burning."

Bellamy finally found his voice again, but it came out careful, almost respectful. "That passage," he said. “The foreman’s tone. The names. If this is accurate, then mimicry was documented in 1893.”

Marissa’s jaw tightened. “Not documented,” she corrected softly. “Confessed.”

Pike gave a small nod, as if that distinction mattered more than most people would think. He opened the ledger again, not to the story he’d just read, but to the inside cover. There, pressed into the paper like an old bruise, was a faint imprint of something that had once been folded and kept there for years.

Bellamy leaned closer. “There was an insert.”

“There was,” Pike said. “It’s not in the book anymore.”

Foster’s shoulders lifted with a breath he couldn’t seem to finish. “Where is it?”

Pike’s expression went tight. “Some things don’t stay in the same place,” he said. “Not if they’re dangerous.”

Mercer’s voice lowered. “Reverend, we’ve got three people missing right now.”

Pike’s eyes held his for a long moment. Then he reached into the box and pulled out an envelope, the paper thick and yellowed, sealed with wax that had cracked. A name was written across the front in careful script.

Sutter.

Pike didn't hand it over. He set it on the table, kept it between himself and Mercer like a boundary marker. "This didn't come from the mine office," he said. "This came from Edwin Sutter's granddaughter. She brought it in forty years ago after her father died. She said her family had carried it like a sickness and she wanted it somewhere that wasn't her house."

Bellamy's eyes flicked to the envelope. "What is it?"

Pike hesitated, then slid a finger under the flap and lifted it without tearing. Even now, he avoided unnecessary noise. He drew out a folded sheet, thinner than the ledger page, covered in tight writing that grew more frantic toward the end.

Adrian leaned in, heart beating hard, not from excitement but from the old human reflex to reach toward information even when it bit.

Pike read silently for a few seconds, lips barely moving. Then he looked up at them as if weighing whether he should give the words air.

Mercer didn't rush him. That restraint was new, Adrian realized. Or perhaps it had always been there and the mountain had finally demanded it.

Pike cleared his throat once, softly. "Sutter wrote this to the mine superintendent," he said. "But he never sent it. Or if he did, the superintendent never admitted receiving it."

Bellamy's voice went sharp with instinct. "A suppressed report."

Pike didn't react to the historian's hunger. He began reading, his tone controlled.

"'Sir, you will dismiss what I say as nerves, and I pray you do, but I cannot in good faith remain silent. The glows are not like lanterns nor like gas. They have a manner of attention. They gather when spoken to and they retreat from the red flare the foreman used in jest. They do not cast light upon the walls in the expected way. They sit in the air as if the air were water.'"

Adrian felt Marissa's shoulder stiffen beside him. The words were too close to what they'd seen in the mine, too close to how the pale points hung without illuminating their surroundings.

Pike continued.

"'The men say they hear a clicking and I have heard it too, though I could not say if it comes from the rock or from the glows themselves. When we shouted into the shaft, the glows rose as if pulled upward by sound. When we held still, they dimmed. When we stepped, they shifted to keep pace.'"

Mercer's jaw flexed. Foster's eyes were on the table, but his hands had curled into fists, knuckles whitening.

Bellamy swallowed. He didn't interrupt. Adrian could almost see the historian's mind recalibrating, reluctantly building a new category: not superstition, not misinterpreted headlights, not mass hysteria, but a behavior consistent enough to be described by an office clerk who clearly wished it weren't true.

Pike's voice tightened slightly as he reached the next lines.

"'I must also state, with a shame I cannot put away, that voices have come from below when no man was below. We heard Mr. Hale call up to us in his own manner. He used our names. He said, "Come down, I found him." It was Mr. Hale's voice, but I do not believe it was Mr. Hale speaking. The men near me answered without thinking, as a person answers when called.'"

Marissa closed her eyes for a brief moment, then opened them again, forcing herself to look at the paper. Adrian recognized it as her version of refusal and control at once.

Pike lowered the letter slightly. "That part," he said quietly, "is what broke the mountain people. Not a collapse. Not a death. A voice that knew your name."

Adrian's throat went dry. The ridge voice had been wrong in the same way: too clean, too rehearsed, and yet close enough to human cadence to pull the reflex like a hook.

Mercer spoke softly. "What else is in it?"

Pike resumed reading.

"'There is a list in the company ledger, and there is another list that is not in the company ledger. I have copied what I can. The places are repeated. The west cut path. The water shelf. The laurel stand. The bend where the creek runs loud. It is always where a man cannot hear his own steps well and must call to his fellows. It is always where a light can be seen ahead but not reached. It is always where a man takes one more step to prove he is not afraid.'"

Adrian's mind flashed to Harper's shaded map and the phrase everyone had repeated without knowing they were quoting one another: the easiest wrong way.

Bellamy's voice came out low, strained. "He's describing lure points."

Marissa looked at him. "He's describing decision points," she corrected. "Places where human behavior becomes predictable."

Pike lowered the paper fully and rubbed the bridge of his nose, as if the act of reading had cost him. "Sutter's copy," he said. "The one he says he made. That's what's missing from the ledger. The insert that used to be in the cover. That list had names and places together. The company kept the names and hid the places. The families kept the places and hid the names. Because names make people curious."

Bellamy's mouth tightened. "And curious people become entries."

Foster finally lifted his eyes. "Where is the list now?" he asked. His voice was rough, but it held, and Adrian understood what it took for him to speak at all in this room.

Pike looked at Foster for a long moment. Then he reached back into the box and pulled out a second notebook, smaller than the ledger, its cover made of oilcloth. It had no title, only a faint cross scratched into the surface, as if someone had tried to bless it by force.

"This isn't the list," Pike said. "Not the whole thing. But it's part of what came afterward. The church did what the company wouldn't. It kept track, quietly. Not for gossip. For warnings."

He opened it to a page marked by another scrap of pale cloth, frayed and soft with age.

Adrian's stomach turned at the repetition of fabric as a bookmark, as if cloth had become the safest way to touch these stories without speaking.

Pike pointed at the page. There were columns, like an accountant's mind couldn't be fully escaped even in a church basement. Names. Dates. Last known locations. And then a final column with terse notes written in different hands over decades.

Does not answer to name. Refuses lantern. Keeps head down. Clicks in sleep. Will not speak after dark.

Adrian felt something cold settle into him. This wasn't just a record of disappearances. It was a record of partial returns.

Bellamy's face tightened. "How many," he whispered.

Pike didn't answer directly. He traced a finger down the page. "Not many," he said. "Most don't come back. The ones who do…" He stopped, as if searching for language that didn't give the phenomenon too much shape. "The ones who do are the reason the old rules got so strict."

Mercer leaned in. "Are there any notes about what stops it?" he asked. "Anything besides flares?"

Pike's finger moved to a line that was underlined twice. The name was smudged, as if written by a hand that didn't want to commit. The note beside it read: Would not look at wife. Would not look at child. Said, keep your face.

Marissa's voice went very quiet. "That's not just fear," she said. "That's deliberate prevention."

Foster's jaw worked. "They thought it recognized faces."

Pike nodded once. "Or they knew it did," he said.

Adrian stared at the notebook until the words blurred. He kept thinking of the pale light outside the truck window at the picnic area, hovering at face height, as if it had mapped the inside of the cab without needing eyes.

Bellamy spoke, and the effort showed in the way he shaped the question. "Reverend," he said, "is there any indication the company tried to study it? Not just cover it up. Study it."

Pike's eyes narrowed. "Why would they?" he asked, but the question sounded more like a warning than curiosity.

"Because mines aren't just holes," Bellamy said. "They're assets. If something threatened production, they'd try to mitigate it. If something could be exploited…" He trailed off, but Adrian heard what he didn't want to say: if the phenomenon had any value, someone might have tried to use it.

Pike's mouth tightened. He reached into the box again and pulled out a folded newspaper clipping, edges browned. He laid it flat and smoothed it.

It was a short article from the early twentieth century, the ink faded but legible.

Private interests to reexamine abandoned shaft for mineral potential.

Under that line, someone had written in pencil, hard enough to dent the paper: They went in quiet and came out quieter.

Adrian felt a jolt of recognition. “Someone tried to reopen it.”

Pike nodded. “Twice,” he said. “And both times the men who went in didn’t talk about why they stopped. They just stopped. The second time, a man came to me, not this church, another one down the road, and he asked the same question you just asked.”

Bellamy’s eyes sharpened. “Who?”

Pike’s gaze held his. “A company man,” he said. “With clean boots and polite words. He wanted to know what the old folks knew. He called it local intelligence.”

Marissa’s expression hardened. “And you told him.”

“I told him nothing,” Pike said. “I told him the mountain doesn’t like being treated like a resource.”

Mercer’s voice went tight. “Did he go anyway?”

Pike’s silence was answer enough.

Adrian felt the pieces align with a sick inevitability. Fresh boot prints at the mine entrance. Careful steps. Equipment case fabric. Someone who knew they weren't supposed to be seen. Someone who went in quiet.

Not tourists.

Preparations give people permission to go deeper.

His own words from the station came back, bitter now.

Foster's eyes flicked up to Mercer. "You think someone's back in the mine," he said.

Mercer's face didn't change, but something in his posture did. A subtle tightening, like the ranger part of him had been waiting for this conclusion to become unavoidable. "I think someone never stopped," Mercer said quietly. "And I think Team Two might have followed a light that wasn't meant to be a rescue at all. It might have been a route."

Marissa's voice went sharp. "A route to what?"

Adrian stared at the notebook's columns of names and symptoms and last locations. He thought of the way the phenomenon had used their names, practiced their cadence, tested their reflexes. He thought of the mine warning: DO NOT CALL TO THEM. And of the note in the old corporate file: luminous phenomena displayed a curious tendency toward pursuit.

"Not to what," Adrian said, the answer forming like ice. "To who."

Bellamy's face tightened in reluctant agreement. "Someone who knows how to feed it," he said. "Or someone who thinks they can control it."

Pike closed the notebook and began returning papers to the box with slow, deliberate movements. "You wanted secrets in the ledger," he said. "There they are. Names tied to places. Places tied to behavior. Behavior tied to survival. And the part nobody says out loud in daylight."

He looked at Mercer, then at all of them. "The mountain learns," he said. "But men learn too. Sometimes the worst thing on Brown Mountain is not the lights."

Mercer picked up Seth Harper's copied sheet from his jacket pocket, the traced approach line and shaded hollows, and held it as if it had gained weight in this basement. "We search in the morning," he said, voice steady by force. "We take the long approach. We keep silent. We keep red. And we don't answer anything that knows our names."

Pike nodded once. "Good," he said. Then, after a beat, he added, quieter, "And if you find one of yours down there, and he comes back wrong…"

Foster's hands clenched, and Marissa's eyes flashed as if she wanted to reject the possibility with anger alone.

Pike finished the sentence anyway. "Don't try to talk him back into himself," he said. "Get him into light. Get him into safety. And keep your own face turned away until you're sure what followed him out is only fear."

Adrian felt a cold, terrible clarity: the ledger didn't just hold the past. It held instructions for what came next.

And they were already following them.

Pike walked them back up the basement stairs without saying much, the cardboard box cradled against his chest like something fragile and dangerous. The church above was dark, pews invisible beyond the faint spill of light from a hallway bulb. Adrian felt the urge to glance toward the sanctuary doors, as if the empty room might hold a pale point hovering between hymnal racks.

Pike stopped at the side entrance and held the door for them one at a time. The night air outside was colder than Adrian expected, and it carried the scent of damp leaves and wood smoke from somewhere down the road. The mountains were a darker shape beyond the churchyard, and the darkness felt crowded now, not empty.

Mercer lingered last on the steps. "Reverend," he said quietly.

Pike's hand stayed on the door. "Don't ask me to come with you," he said. It wasn't rude. It was a boundary set long ago and maintained by practice.

"I wasn't going to," Mercer replied. "I was going to ask if there's anyone still alive from the ones who came back. Family members. Somebody who remembers."

Pike's gaze shifted, a small movement like someone checking a corner before stepping into it. "There's always somebody," he said. "The mountain doesn't just take people. It gives families a shape. A set of rules. A silence."

Bellamy, standing at the edge of the churchyard, spoke carefully. "Do you know anyone who will speak to us?"

Pike's mouth tightened. "Most won't," he said. "Not because they don't have words. Because they do. Too many. And once you start, you feel like you're calling it."

Marissa's voice came quiet, more controlled than gentle. "We're not here to collect ghost stories."

Pike looked at her for a long moment, and Adrian saw something like approval flicker across the reverend's face. Not belief. Recognition. "No," Pike said. "You're here because a list became a map and a map became a plan. That's how it always goes."

He shifted the box under one arm and reached into his coat pocket with the other. He pulled out a scrap of paper, already folded small as if it had lived there for a while. He didn't hand it to Mercer immediately.

"This name," Pike said, "belongs to a woman who doesn't come to church anymore because she got tired of people asking her to testify. Her brother came back wrong in 1954. Not from the mine, from the west cut. He lived another thirty years, and he never once answered when someone said his name at night."

Foster flinched at that, a brief tightening around the eyes.

Pike held the paper out finally. "Mrs. Lenora Sutter," he said. "Edwin's kin. Not direct granddaughter, not the one who brought the envelope. Another branch. They all scattered, but they kept the same habits. If anyone has the missing insert list, or knows what became of it, it's her."

Mercer took the paper with both hands as if it could cut him. "Will she talk to us?"

"She might talk to a ranger," Pike said. "She won't talk to a crowd. And she definitely won't talk to a man with a notebook out like a shield."

Bellamy's lips pressed together, but he didn't argue.

Pike's gaze moved across all four of them, resting briefly on Adrian. "And you," he said. "You're the one who likes the old words. Be careful with them. Some words are hooks."

Adrian nodded. "I understand."

Pike looked unconvinced, then turned his eyes toward the road as if ending the conversation before it became an invitation. "Go home," he said. "Get what sleep you can. Daylight isn't protection, it's just honesty. It shows you where you're standing when you make the wrong choice."

They drove back to the station in near silence. Mercer didn't turn the radio on. Foster seemed relieved by the absence of static, but Adrian noticed his eyes kept darting to the side mirror as if he expected a pale point to appear in it, calm and patient. Bellamy stared out his window, jaw set, and Marissa sat very still, hands folded in her lap with deliberate care.

At the station, Mercer spread Seth Harper's copied map again on the table, along with the ledger page copy and the few notes Marissa had typed earlier. Under fluorescent light the shaded hollows looked almost harmless. Pencil graphite. Contour lines. A neat representation of a place that had already proven it didn't care about representation.

Mercer tapped the corner of the paper Pike had given him. "We see her now," he said.

Foster's head lifted. "Tonight?"

"Not night," Mercer said quickly. "Now. It's late, but it's not deep night yet. And tomorrow at first light we go down that approach corridor. If there's anything in this family that can narrow where Team Two might be, we need it before we step into the west slope."

Marissa nodded once. "A location refinement," she said. "Not a theory."

Bellamy's voice came out rough. "We're leaning heavily on family memory."

"We're leaning on survival," Mercer replied.

They left the station again with one vehicle and no radio chatter, the habit of quiet settling in like a second uniform. Lenora Sutter's address led them out of Jonas Ridge toward a cluster of older homes tucked along a narrower road where the trees grew closer and the shoulders dropped off into black ditches.

Her house sat at the end of a gravel drive. A single porch light burned, weak and yellow. No decorations. No wind chimes. No porch swing that could creak. The place looked built around the principle of minimizing uninvited sound.

Mercer walked up first. He didn't knock immediately. He stood on the porch step and waited, head slightly bowed as if listening for movement inside before making any.

Adrian found himself mirroring the posture without meaning to. It wasn't superstition. It was the new protocol their bodies had adopted: slow, careful, with the constant awareness that any sudden noise might ripple outward into the dark.

Mercer knocked once, firm but not loud.

A long pause followed. Then a bolt slid back. The door opened a few inches.

A woman's face appeared in the gap. Lenora Sutter was older than Adrian expected, her hair white and pulled back tight, her eyes sharp and weary. She didn't look afraid. She looked practiced.

"I don't do interviews," she said immediately.

Mercer kept his voice low. "Mrs. Sutter, I'm Ranger Mercer."

Her gaze flicked to his uniform, then to Foster behind him. It lingered there a beat longer, as if she could read the strain in Foster's posture and recognize it as familiar.

"You found one," she said, the same words the waitress had used, as if the town only had one sentence for this kind of night.

"We did," Mercer replied. "But we lost others. Team Two."

Her eyes narrowed. "They went after the lights."

Foster's throat worked. He didn't speak, but the truth was in his face.

Lenora opened the door wider. "You better come in," she said. Then, after a beat, she added, "And shut it gentle."

Inside, the house smelled like old wood and something medicinal. The living room was neat to the point of severity. No television. No radio. A clock on the wall with its battery removed, hands frozen at an arbitrary hour.

Marissa noticed it too. Her eyes flicked to the clock and back without comment.

Lenora watched them watching. "Clocks make noise," she said, as if explaining a choice that needed no defense. "And people start thinking time matters more than rules."

She motioned them toward chairs, then remained standing herself, arms folded. "Talk," she said. "But don't dramatize it."

Mercer nodded. "We were shown a church ledger," he said. "We were shown records of men who came back changed. We heard about Edwin Sutter."

Lenora's expression tightened at the name, not with grief exactly but with fatigue, as if family names were burdens carried as much as honors.

"My great-uncle," she said. "He was a careful man. Careful enough to be called coward, which usually means you outlived somebody else."

Adrian spoke, gentle. "Reverend Pike said there was a list that went missing. A copied insert from the company ledger."

Lenora's eyes sharpened on him. "Lore man," she said, like Ruth and Harper had, and Adrian felt the odd, unsettling continuity of that label moving from porch to porch like a token. "You're the one that listens and thinks it makes you safe."

Adrian didn't deny it. "No, ma'am," he said. "I listen because people left instructions in their habits. We're trying to keep a search team alive."

Lenora's gaze drifted to Foster again. "Your men," she said to Mercer.

"Three missing," Mercer replied.

Lenora exhaled slowly through her nose, then turned and walked to a small cabinet in the corner. She unlocked it with a key on a string around her neck, the motion practiced. From inside she pulled out a flat folder wrapped in oilcloth.

Bellamy straightened instinctively, drawn by paper the way a moth was drawn to light, then checked himself as if remembering that not all attraction was safe.

Lenora set the folder on a table but didn't open it yet. Her hand rested on it, palm down, claiming it. "You want family legacies," she said, and her voice had turned hard. "Here's one. We keep what the company tried to bury. We keep it, and we don't show it to anyone who comes up the mountain looking entertained."

Mercer's voice stayed steady. "We're not entertained."

Lenora studied his face, then nodded once as if deciding. She opened the folder.

Inside was a single page, brittle and brown at the edges, with a hand-drawn map and a list of names written in tight script down the side. Next to each name were marks and short notes, the kind Adrian had seen in Pike's notebook: last places, behavior, the simplest possible words for complicated harm.

Bellamy inhaled sharply despite himself, then forced the sound back down. "That's it," he whispered. "The insert."

Lenora's eyes flicked to him like a warning. "Don't get excited," she said. "That's how it starts."

Marissa leaned forward, voice controlled. "Mrs. Sutter, can you show us where Team Two would be likely to end up if they followed a light off the ridge? We have an approach corridor, but we need a tighter search area."

Lenora's finger moved across the hand-drawn map with certainty. It stopped at a curve marked with a blunt note: creek loud here.

"Here," she said. "That's where my uncle said the mountain takes men who think they're being careful. Water noise. Gravel slip. You can't hear your own feet. You call out, and then you can't take it back."

Foster's face tightened. "Devil's Stairs," he rasped.

Lenora nodded once, not looking at him. "And the shelf below it," she said, tapping again. "Flat rock. People stop there because it feels like a break. That's where lights wait. That's where voices come from below like they're someone you know."

Mercer leaned in. "Is it marked in the forest service maps?"

Lenora gave a humorless smile. "No," she said. "That's another legacy. The official maps show you how to travel. The family maps show you how to survive."

Adrian looked at the page and felt the same cold clarity he'd felt in the church basement: tradition wasn't decorative here. It was data passed down through fear, rewritten into rules and kept alive by people who never wanted to become examples.

Lenora lifted her eyes to Mercer. "You go in daylight," she said. "You keep quiet. And when you hear someone say your name down there, you remember this."

She tapped the list of names once. "Every one of those men answered," she said. "Not because they were stupid. Because they were human. That's what the mountain counts on. Family legacies aren't stories. They're what's left after you learn the hard way what being human costs on Brown Mountain."

Mercer's jaw tightened. He nodded once, controlled. "May we copy it?"

Lenora's hand pressed down harder on the page. "No," she said. "You can look. You can memorize. You can draw your own. But this stays in my house. Because paper travels, and curiosity follows it."

Bellamy swallowed and nodded, chastened.

Mercer bent his head over the map and began to trace the lines with his eyes, committing the creek bend and shelf to memory. Marissa watched too, lips pressed tight, her mind already turning it into coordinates without saying the word. Foster stood behind them, shoulders drawn up, as if the room itself were a narrow tunnel.

Adrian stayed back half a step, looking at the list of names and marks, at the tight handwriting that had crossed generations. He understood then what Pike meant by families being given a shape. This was the shape: a locked cabinet, a silent clock, a map that didn't promise rescue, only the best chance of not becoming another line.

When Mercer finally straightened, Lenora closed the folder and locked it away with the same deliberate care.

"You got what you came for," she said. "Now go."

Mercer hesitated at the door. "Thank you," he said.

Lenora's face didn't soften. "Don't thank me," she replied. "Bring somebody back. That's the only gratitude that counts."

Outside, as they walked back down the porch steps, Adrian felt the night press close again, full of damp air and unseen distance. The road was empty. The trees were still.

But he could not stop thinking about the frozen clock inside Lenora Sutter's house.

Time, removed of its ticking, reduced to a silent face.

A family legacy built not on what happened once, but on what kept happening, until people learned to take the noise out of their own lives.

Mercer drove them back toward the station without a word. In Adrian's mind, the hand-drawn map and its creek shelf settled into place beside

Harper's shaded hollows and Pike's list of partial returns.

The legacies weren't just warnings.

They were routes through a world that had learned their names.

Chapter 13

Theories and Threats

By the time they returned to the station, the night had thinned into something that wasn't quite morning but wasn't fully dark either. The sky was a heavy slate above the trees. Mercer killed the engine and sat for a moment with both hands on the steering wheel as if he needed the pressure to keep his thoughts from drifting.

Inside, the fluorescent lights snapped on with a hard buzz that felt too loud after Lenora Sutter's quiet house. Adrian found himself listening for the tick of a clock that wasn't there. The station's wall clock did tick, and the sound made Foster's shoulders tighten until Mercer reached up and pulled the battery without comment. The second hand stuttered and died. Silence settled in like a new rule.

Marissa set her tablet on the conference table and didn't turn it on. Bellamy stood near the counter, rubbing his hands together as if washing off the church basement and Lenora's locked cabinet with sheer friction. Foster sat with his elbows on his knees, head angled down, eyes fixed on the floor in a way that looked less like exhaustion and more like compliance with a protocol his body now understood.

Mercer spread out the map copy from Seth Harper and his own hand sketch from memory of Lenora's page. The drawing was crude, but he'd captured the important shapes: the west cut dropping steep, the loud creek bend, the flat shelf below Devil's Stairs where people stopped because stopping felt safe.

"Daylight search at first light," Mercer said, voice steady by force. "Long approach. No names. No radio unless it's life or death."

Bellamy's gaze lifted. "It's all life or death."

Mercer didn't look at him. "Then we keep our definitions tight."

Adrian expected the conversation to turn immediately to tactics, but Marissa spoke first, her tone clipped, almost resentful of the fact that she needed to speak at all.

"We need hypotheses," she said. "Not to soothe ourselves. To constrain what we do next. If we treat this like an intelligent predator and it turns out to be a physical phenomenon with emergent patterning, our strategy changes. If we treat it like atmospheric plasma and it turns out to be something that can learn our names, we die."

Foster let out a sound that might have been a laugh if it hadn't been so dry. "It already knows our names."

Marissa's eyes flicked to him. "It used our names. That's not the same thing as knowing."

Adrian watched the way she chose her words. She wasn't retreating into skepticism. She was trying to build a narrow bridge between terror and analysis.

Bellamy finally moved to the table. "Scientific hypotheses," he repeated, as if tasting the phrase. "All right. Let's begin with what people always begin with, because it's the easiest story to tell. Misidentified distant light sources."

Adrian said, "Train headlights," and heard the bitterness in his own voice.

Bellamy nodded once. "Yes. The 1913 Geological Survey conclusion. Headlights, brush fires, lanterns, cars on the far ridge. It explains some sightings. It does not explain lights in a sealed mine shaft with lanterns failing simultaneously. It does not explain approach behavior. It does not explain mimicry."

Mercer's mouth tightened. "Good. So we can stop pretending it's somebody's Jeep."

Marissa leaned forward, elbows on the table. "Second category. Atmospheric and geophysical light phenomena. Ball lightning, St. Elmo's fire, piezoelectric discharge."

Bellamy's eyes sharpened slightly. This was his preferred terrain: explanations that didn't require belief.

Marissa continued. "Quartz-bearing rock under strain can produce electrical discharges. The Blue Ridge has quartz. Stress, seismic microfractures, even changes in groundwater pressure could create conditions where charge accumulates and releases."

Adrian pictured the pale points hanging in the mine's lower passage like stars underwater, and the way they recoiled from the flare as if red light was a kind of pain.

"Would that produce sustained, moving orbs?" Mercer asked.

"In a simplistic sense, no," Marissa admitted. "But we don't actually know what shape those discharges take in a humid, particulate-heavy environment like fog or a mine with suspended dust. If the charge ionizes local air, you could get luminous plasma. Plasma can move with electromagnetic gradients."

Bellamy added, "And gradients can change around conductors. Old rails. Wet timber. Mineral seams."

Foster's head lifted slightly. "So the mine is a battery."

“Something like that,” Marissa said, not looking at him like he was foolish. “A system. Not a ghost.”

Adrian kept his voice low. “A system that responds to sound.”

Marissa’s jaw tightened. “That’s the sticking point.”

Bellamy spoke carefully, as if the words were fragile. “Acoustic coupling. Infrasound can induce disorientation, fear, a sense of presence. It can also make people interpret ambiguous stimuli as directed.”

Adrian thought of the urge to look directly at the lights, physical as nausea, and of the way human reflexes reached outward for confirmation. He could imagine infrasound turning the body into its own unreliable witness. He could not imagine it speaking Mercer’s name.

Marissa tapped the table once, controlled. “There’s also the possibility of a layered mechanism. One phenomenon produces light. Another produces the clicks. And then humans provide the rest: pattern completion, meaning assignment, the irresistible reflex to answer.”

Bellamy’s gaze went to Mercer’s hand sketch. “Which would make the west cut’s environmental features relevant. Loud water. Gravel slip. Reduced proprioception. People can’t hear their own steps, so they call out. Calling out becomes a trigger for escalation."

Mercer stared at the map, jaw clenched. "A trigger for what we saw outside the truck?"

Marissa held his gaze. "We haven't earned certainty yet."

Foster's hands tightened together. "We earned something," he said, and for the first time his anger had a direction other than inward. "We heard it say our names. We heard it repeat phrases like it had them saved."

Bellamy's voice dropped. "Mimicry exists in nature."

"Not like that," Foster snapped. The outburst made him flinch immediately after, as if he regretted the sound. He lowered his voice, forcing it flat. "It wasn't a crow. It wasn't a parrot. It was close. It was right behind us. And it stopped when the flare went up like something yanked a leash."

Silence followed. Mercer's pencil hovered over the paper, then lowered without making a mark. Even the idea of scratching graphite felt too loud.

Adrian felt the conversation turning toward the place they'd all been trying not to step: if a physical phenomenon could mimic, then either their model of physical phenomenon was incomplete, or something else was involved.

Marissa spoke again, and this time her voice had the careful tone of someone walking along a ledge.

"Third category," she said. "Human agency. Someone is out there doing this."

Bellamy's eyes narrowed. "With what? Drones?"

"Maybe," Marissa said. "Or something we don't recognize as technology because we aren't looking for it. Directed speakers. Hidden radios. A system of lures designed to exploit search-and-rescue behavior. If someone has studied the local rules, they'd know what makes people break them."

Mercer's face hardened. "Like the boot prints at the mine. The careful ones."

Adrian remembered Pike's story about the company man with clean boots and polite words, and the pencil note on the clipping: they went in quiet and came out quieter.

"Yes," Adrian said. "And like whoever Pike refused to help."

Bellamy frowned. "But that still doesn't explain lights in the 1890s."

Marissa didn't argue. "No. It doesn't. Which means either the human-agency hypothesis is wrong, or it's parasitic. Someone exploiting a preexisting phenomenon."

The word parasitic sat in Adrian's mind with unpleasant clarity. The lights didn't need a person to exist, perhaps, but a person could learn to use them the way a hunter learned the habits of an animal.

Foster's voice came rough and immediate. "Team Two could've been led," he said. "Not by the lights. By somebody who knows how to make them move, or where to stand so it looks like they're moving."

Mercer's gaze snapped to him. "You're saying someone took them."

"I'm saying," Foster replied, "that the mountain isn't the only threat anymore."

That landed hard. The station felt suddenly smaller, not because the walls had moved, but because the world outside had grown. A thing that lured with light was dangerous. A thing that lured with light and had a person behind it, someone who could choose targets and times, was worse.

Bellamy spoke with reluctant precision. "If a person is involved, they may be using the flare response as conditioning. Drive the lights away from themselves. Or herd people into specific areas."

Marissa's eyes sharpened. "Or they're avoiding the red because they've learned the same rule we did."

Mercer leaned over the table, palms flat, and his voice went low. "Here's what I know. The lights react to sound. They react to movement. They recoil from red flares. They can mimic voices, or something can. And they prefer the easiest wrong way down into loud water."

He looked at each of them in turn, and Adrian saw that Mercer was doing what rangers always did in crisis: turning chaos into a checklist. Not because it made it less frightening, but because checklists gave the hands something to do besides shake.

"We build our plan on what we can test without dying," Mercer said. "Marissa, you want hypotheses, fine. But we do not run experiments in the west cut. We do not try to provoke response. And we do not answer anything that calls us by name."

Bellamy's mouth tightened. "That means if Team Two is alive and calling, we—"

"We don't answer," Mercer said, cutting him off. "We find them in daylight, by terrain, not by voice."

Foster's shoulders rose and fell with one slow breath. "And if they come back wrong," he said quietly, repeating Pike's warning as if the words had lodged in him.

Mercer didn't flinch. "Then we get them into light," he said. "We get them into safety. And we keep our own faces to ourselves until we're sure what followed them out is only fear."

Adrian felt the station's silence shift. Not comfort. Not calm. A kind of grim alignment, like a team finally admitting what kind of field they were actually in.

Marissa reached for her tablet at last, brightness still dim, and began typing without turning on any sound. "Working model," she said. "Multi-factor system. Environmental light phenomenon with responsive behavior, whether intrinsic or emergent. Strong interaction with sound and attention. Possible overlay of human exploitation. Threat level extreme."

Bellamy looked at her. "You're writing it like a report."

"I'm writing it like something we can hand to someone else if we don't come back," she said. Her voice didn't shake. "Folklore became field notes. Now field notes become warnings."

Adrian watched her screen reflect faintly in her eyes and thought of Lenora's locked cabinet, the oilcloth folder, the map that couldn't be copied because curiosity followed paper. Marissa was doing the opposite, and maybe she had to. Maybe the only way to break a cycle was to make the warnings too public to bury.

Mercer folded the map and slid it back into his jacket. "Get whatever rest you can," he said. "We step off at first light."

As they dispersed, Adrian lingered at the table a moment longer, looking at the crude lines of the west slope and the marked creek bend where water ran loud. Scientific hypotheses could name the parts: ionization, discharge, acoustic coupling, mimicry, human exploitation.

None of them, Adrian thought, explained the oldest fact that sat beneath every theory like bedrock.

The phenomenon didn't merely occur.

It invited.

And now, with Team Two missing and the mountain practicing their names, invitation had become threat.

Adrian didn't go to the spare cot Mercer had offered.

He sat alone at the conference table after the others drifted to their corners of the station, jackets still on, boots still laced, bodies refusing the vulnerability of sleep. The fluorescent lights hummed overhead. The wall clock, newly dead, stared at them with its hands pinned in place. Outside the windows the forest was a single dark mass, and Brown Mountain was somewhere beyond it, patient enough to wait for dawn.

Adrian spread his notebook open without clicking a pen. He didn't write at first. He stared at the blank page and felt an old, stubborn discomfort: the sense that language, his tool, had become bait.

Folklore is what communities remember after history forgets.

He'd said it a hundred times in lecture halls. It had always felt like a defense of his discipline, a tidy phrase to correct smug undergraduates who thought legends were the opposite of evidence.

Tonight it felt like an admission.

The rules weren't metaphors. They were procedures.

Do not whistle below this point. Do not call to them. Do not answer voices from the trees. Keep your face. Do not call it by name.

Adrian heard Ruth Calhoun's porch-voice in his head, flat and absolute: Lost souls don't learn.

At the far end of the room Foster sat in a chair by the window, his posture folded inward like he was trying to reduce his surface area. His eyes were open but unfocused, fixed on the glass as if he expected his own reflection to speak.

Marissa moved quietly at the counter, refilling water bottles without letting plastic crinkle. Bellamy stood near the sink again, hands braced on the edge, as if he needed something solid under him to keep his skepticism from sliding away entirely.

Mercer came back from the supply room carrying a small box of spare batteries and two additional flares. He set them down gently, then looked at Adrian.

"You're not sleeping," Mercer said. It wasn't a reprimand. It was a statement of fact in a place where facts were rare and valuable.

Adrian shook his head. "I'm trying to reframe," he said softly.

Marissa turned from the counter. "Reframe what?"

Adrian tapped the blank page. "Folklore," he said. "Not as belief. As an interface."

Bellamy's mouth tightened. "An interface between what and what, exactly?"

Adrian glanced toward the windows. "Between people and whatever this is," he said. "Between a set of environmental triggers and human reflex."

Marissa's eyes narrowed. "So you're saying the rules are behavioral engineering."

"I'm saying they're a user manual," Adrian replied. "Written by survivors who didn't have our vocabulary. They didn't say mimicry. They said don't answer voices. They didn't say attention as stimulus. They said don't look at it. They didn't say conditioning response to wavelength. They said red keeps it back."

Mercer leaned a hip against the table. "And 'don't call it by name,'" he added.

Foster's jaw worked. His voice came out rough, barely audible. "The watchers."

Adrian looked at him sharply, but he didn't correct him this time. The name had already been spoken in Ruth's yard and again in his own mind. The taboo had teeth, but it wasn't a spell. It was a preventive measure. A way to stop people from turning the phenomenon into something familiar enough to invite into conversation.

Marissa took a slow breath. "Names increase salience," she said. "They make a thing more cognitively present."

Bellamy's eyes flicked to her. "You're adopting his language."

"I'm adopting what works," Marissa said, then paused as if she was choosing how much to concede. "The old warnings look like superstition until you match them to observed behavior. Then they become… protocols."

Adrian heard something in her tone he hadn't heard since this started: not belief, but respect for non-academic knowledge. The mountain had forced it out of her the way pressure forced water through stone.

Mercer said, "So what does folklore tell us that science didn't?"

Adrian finally began to write, the pencil moving carefully, minimal sound. "It tells us where people die," he said. "And it tells us why they make the choice that gets them there."

Bellamy exhaled, short. "Desperation. Fear. Poor visibility."

"Yes," Adrian said, "but also something more precise. The rules keep repeating one word without saying it. Recognition."

Marissa's face tightened. She didn't need him to explain. They'd heard the false voice outside the truck. They'd heard it use Mercer's name. Then hers. They'd felt the reflex to answer.

Adrian continued, "Folklore doesn't preserve the physics. It preserves the moment of failure. The trigger moment. The human hinge."

He wrote a list as he spoke.

Light approaches. Do not follow. Voice calls. Do not answer. Face offered. Keep it.

Then he added, almost reluctantly: Sound attracts. Reduce it.

Mercer watched him write. "You're making a new bulletin," he said. "Like the church sheet."

Adrian looked up. "Because the old ones are right," he said. "And we keep acting like they're quaint."

Bellamy pushed off the sink and stepped closer. His voice was quieter than usual. "There's a problem," he said. "If these are protocols, they came from repeated contact. That implies the phenomenon has been consistent over time. And yet it also implies something else."

"What?" Mercer asked.

Bellamy hesitated, and Adrian realized how hard it was for the historian to say it. Bellamy's entire profession was built on the assumption that human motives explained most patterns.

"If it has been consistent," Bellamy said finally, "then it has been studied. Not just by families. By someone with resources. Company men. Private interests. People who believe everything can be monetized or controlled."

Marissa's eyes sharpened. "That aligns with Pike's clipping. The attempts to reopen the shaft."

"And the boot prints at the mine," Mercer added, voice hardening. "Careful. Measured."

Adrian nodded. "Folklore also preserves this," he said. "The part Pike said out loud: sometimes the worst thing on Brown Mountain is not the lights."

Foster stirred, the chair creaking despite his effort. He winced at the sound and went still again. "If someone is using it," he said, "they're using our training against us."

Mercer's jaw clenched. "Search teams call out. They use names. They respond to voices because it might be someone in trouble."

Marissa's voice went flat. "That reflex is a feature, not a flaw. In normal conditions it saves lives."

"In these conditions," Foster whispered, "it gets you taken."

A silence settled that felt different from the earlier fear. This was the silence of a team realizing they couldn't rely on their default ethics without adaptation. Even rescue could become a lure.

Adrian looked at Mercer. "Folklore addresses this too," he said. "It doesn't say be brave. It says be careful with what makes you human."

Marissa's mouth tightened. "That's a grim way to put it."

"It is," Adrian agreed. "But it's accurate."

Bellamy's eyes flicked to Adrian's notes. "You said interface," he murmured. "Between human reflex and—"

"And an adaptive system," Marissa finished, surprising Adrian with the phrase. She stared at the table as if she could see the west cut's steep contours under the laminated wood. "If it learns, then the rules are not only for what the phenomenon does. They're for what we do when we're being observed."

Mercer nodded once. "So folklore is operational security."

Adrian almost laughed, but the humor died before it formed. "Yes," he said. "A century of opsec passed around in church basements and kitchen drawers because official channels wouldn't carry it."

Foster swallowed. "And we broke it," he said. "We went to the overlook at night. We listened to it say our names. We taught it a new target set."

Marissa's gaze softened by a fraction. "Eli," she said quietly, "it didn't need us to be reckless. It already had the pattern. It just confirmed what it could do."

Bellamy spoke without looking at anyone. "It's not only that it mimics," he said. "It's that it times the mimicry. It waits for a situation where responding is socially mandatory."

Adrian wrote that down too: It exploits obligation.

The phrase felt ugly on the page. It made the phenomenon seem like a strategist, and Adrian still didn't know if calling it strategy was accurate or anthropomorphic. But the outcome was the same either way: people were being manipulated by their own decency.

Mercer picked up one of the spare flares, rolled it slowly in his hand. "So what does your field tell us to do next?" he asked Adrian.

Adrian looked at the list of old rules, then at the rough hand sketch Mercer had made of Lenora Sutter's map: creek loud here, the flat shelf where people stopped, the place voices came from below. He felt the weight of responsibility shift in a way he hadn't expected. Folklore wasn't entertainment now. It was triage.

"It tells us to respect the boundary between daylight and night," Adrian said. "And it tells us not to let urgency bully us into breaking protocol."

Foster's eyes squeezed shut for a moment. "Urgency is all I have left," he whispered.

Mercer's voice softened, not much, but enough. "Then we turn urgency into discipline," he said. "That's the only way we go down there and don't add four more names to a list."

Marissa looked at Adrian's page. "There's something else," she said. "The old rules about faces. The idea it learns you."

Adrian nodded. "That's the one I used to dismiss as superstition," he admitted. "Now it's the one I can't stop thinking about."

Bellamy frowned. "A face is a signature," he said slowly, as if feeling his way through an unfamiliar corridor. "A pattern. Humans are very good at recognizing faces. If it is too, then showing your face is giving it a stable identifier. Something it can track across context."

Marissa's eyes flicked toward the windows. "And names are stable identifiers too," she said. "Which means our discipline has to include not only silence, but anonymity."

Mercer's expression hardened with decision. "Then tomorrow," he said, "we don't say Team Two's names in the field. We don't call. We don't respond. We search by ground, by tracks, by cloth, by anything that doesn't require giving the mountain a voice to copy."

Foster flinched at that, but he didn't argue. Perhaps because he finally understood the shape of the trap: when you called out to save someone, you also announced yourself.

Adrian set the pencil down and looked at the page again. It was a new kind of document, one he hadn't expected to write. Not a paper for a conference. Not a lecture note. A set of rules to keep living people alive.

Folklore reconsidered, he thought, wasn't about believing in ghosts.

It was about admitting that survival knowledge could be accurate without being comfortable.

Mercer gathered the flares and the batteries and began packing them into his field bag again with quiet efficiency. "Try to rest," he said to all of them. "Even ten minutes. Dawn isn't far."

As the station settled back into its uneasy silence, Adrian stared at his list of rules and felt a strange, cold gratitude for every old person who had ever been mocked for being cautious.

The mountain had been teaching for a long time.

The only question now was whether they could learn fast enough without paying the same tuition.

The station never truly went quiet again after midnight. It only shifted into different kinds of silence.

Adrian sat at the conference table with his pencil laid flat beside his notebook, hands clasped to keep himself from writing more words into the air than necessary. Across the room, Mercer finished packing his field bag with the same careful economy he'd used in the truck: batteries, flares, tape, a small first-aid kit, water. Marissa had settled into a chair near the counter with her tablet face-down, as if even a dim screen was too much invitation. Bellamy hovered by the window, shoulders drawn tight, eyes fixed on the black glass. Foster had not moved from his chair, head angled down, as though he could obey Ruth Calhoun's rule even indoors.

The wall clock remained frozen where Mercer had killed it. Without the tick, time felt thick, almost viscous. Adrian found himself measuring the night by other cues: the heater's cycling hum, the soft shift of someone's weight, the distant, indistinct hiss of wind through trees.

He was thinking about Lenora Sutter's finger on the map, the blunt certainty of creek loud here, when headlights swept across the station windows.

Mercer stiffened instantly. So did Foster. Even Bellamy's posture changed, as if the light from outside had the same gravity as the lights on the ridge.

A vehicle door shut, too hard. The sound snapped through the night like a branch breaking.

Mercer's jaw tightened. He moved toward the front door without turning on any additional lights. Adrian rose with him, an instinctive, useless solidarity. Marissa stood too, quiet and ready. Foster didn't stand until the second knock came, louder than the first.

Mercer opened the door and stepped into the porch light. "Sheriff," he said, his voice controlled but not friendly.

Sheriff Delaney stood at the bottom of the steps with a deputy beside him and two men Adrian didn't recognize. They were dressed like locals who'd been pulled from sleep and dressed in whatever was nearest: jeans, boots, heavy jackets, knit caps. One of them held a handheld radio. Its indicator light blinked green in the dark.

"We got a call," Delaney said. He didn't bother lowering his voice the way Mercer had learned to. "A woman down in Jonas Ridge says she heard her boy."

Mercer didn't move. "At this hour?"

Delaney nodded toward the darkness beyond the station. "From the slope. From the west side. She said it was him. Same phrase he always says when he wants help with his truck. She said she knows her own son."

Adrian felt the words settle into his stomach. Same phrase. Recognition. The phenomenon didn't need to invent whole conversations. It only needed one familiar hook.

Marissa's face tightened. Bellamy looked down, as if refusing to see the sheriff's mouth forming the dangerous words.

Mercer said, "Who's missing is Team Two. Two volunteers and a ranger tech. Nobody goes down that slope at night."

Delaney exhaled sharply. "We're not waiting for professors to get comfortable."

Mercer's eyes flashed. "This isn't about comfort."

One of the local men stepped forward, impatience in his posture. "My cousin's on that team," he said. "We can't just sit. If they're calling, we answer."

Foster made a small sound, half breath, half pain. His hands had clenched into fists at his sides.

Mercer kept his voice level. "Do not answer voices from the trees," he said. "Do not answer anything that calls your name. Those rules aren't folklore. They're survival."

Delaney's mouth tightened as if he'd expected this speech. "I've lived here fifty years," he said. "I know the stories."

"Then you know what happens when people ignore them," Mercer replied.

The deputy shifted uncomfortably. The handheld radio in the local man's hand hissed softly with faint static, the volume turned too high for anyone who had spent the last day learning what sound could do.

Delaney nodded toward the radio. “We’ve got comms. We’ve got lights. We’ve got more bodies than you do. We’re going in now.”

Marissa spoke, quiet but edged. “The lights react to radios. They react to voices. They react to names. We saw it.”

Delaney glanced at her like she was a nuisance, not a warning. “We’ve got three men missing,” he said, as if repeating it could bulldoze the mountain into obedience. “Dawn’s still hours off.”

Mercer’s hands stayed at his sides, but Adrian could see his restraint working like a clamp. “You go in quiet,” Mercer said. “No calling. No whistling. No names over radio. No chasing lights.”

The local man with the radio scoffed. “How do you find somebody without calling?”

“You don’t,” Foster said suddenly. His voice was rough and low, but it cut cleanly through the porch light’s brittle calm. Everyone looked at him.

Foster’s eyes were bloodshot, his face hollowed by the hours he’d spent learning a new kind of discipline. “You don’t find them by voice,” he said. “You find them by ground. Tracks. Cloth. Signs in daylight. If you call, you aren’t just calling them. You’re calling it.”

The porch went still.

Delaney's gaze narrowed. "You're the one Mercer found on the ridge," he said. It wasn't admiration. It was accusation. "You're spooked."

Foster's expression didn't change. "I'm alive," he said simply.

For a moment it seemed as if the sheriff might actually absorb that. But urgency was a kind of arrogance too. It made men think they could trade rules for speed and win.

Delaney turned his head slightly, addressing his people instead of Mercer. "We go down Devil's Stairs," he said. "Fast. We call out. If they answer, we lock on. If they don't, we keep moving."

Mercer stepped down one stair, putting himself closer, not larger. "Sheriff," he said, and there was a hard patience in his voice. "You do not go down Devil's Stairs in the dark. That's the easiest wrong way."

Delaney's mouth twisted. "You got that from a waitress and some old women?"

"I got it from a ledger of names and a century of people not coming back," Mercer said.

The local man with the radio raised it as if to prove a point. "Team Two, this is—"

Mercer moved before the name could be spoken. His hand came up fast and clamped over the radio's speaker grille, muffling the static. The local man jerked in surprise, anger flaring. Delaney's eyes hardened.

"Don't," Mercer said, low and sharp. "Not here. Not like that."

Delaney's voice lifted, finally losing its attempt at calm. "Get your hands off my people."

Mercer released the radio immediately, but he didn't back away. "I'm trying to keep your people from becoming another mark beside a name," he said.

The deputy shifted again, gaze flicking toward the tree line behind the station. Adrian followed the look before he could stop himself.

The forest beyond the porch light was a wall of black, but black didn't mean empty anymore. Adrian had learned that.

A faint click sounded from somewhere off to the right, out past the corner of the building.

Not loud. Not dramatic.

Precise.

Marissa went rigid. Bellamy's shoulders lifted as if he'd been hooked by a string.

Delaney didn't seem to register it. Or maybe he did and refused to. "Wind," he said dismissively, though no leaves were moving near enough to explain it.

Then, beyond the station's parking area, a pale point of light appeared between two trunks.

Adrian's throat tightened. It wasn't far away. It wasn't across a valley. It was close enough that its wrong steadiness felt intimate.

The local man with the radio sucked in a breath. "You see that?"

Mercer didn't answer. He didn't look directly at it. He angled his face down, as if demonstrating the rule with his body.

The pale point hovered at about chest height.

Another appeared higher, just beyond it, and drifted sideways with the same deliberate smoothness Adrian had seen near the truck at the picnic lot. The clicking came again, two soft taps, like something testing a boundary.

Delaney stared at the lights, and for the first time uncertainty crossed his face. It wasn't fear yet. It was the discomfort of being confronted with something that didn't fit the toolbox he'd arrived with.

"Could be somebody with a lamp," the deputy offered weakly.

"No," Foster said, quiet and flat. "It doesn't throw a beam."

As if in response to the attention, the lower light pulsed once, faintly, then slid a foot closer.

The local man took a half-step forward without thinking, drawn the way people were drawn. His hand lifted slightly, palm open, a gesture of greeting or caution. An instinctive human offering.

Mercer said, “Back,” not loud, but urgent. The word itself felt dangerous, but he couldn’t stop it.

The man didn’t back up.

He raised the radio again, voice rising with relief and adrenaline. “Hey! If that’s you, we’re here!”

Adrian felt his blood turn cold. Too many words. Too much presence.

The pale light brightened.

And from the darkness behind the lights, somewhere deeper in the trees, a human voice spoke. Soft. Familiar in its casualness.

“Sheriff Delaney?”

The sheriff’s head snapped toward the sound.

Adrian’s stomach clenched hard enough to hurt. A name used correctly. A voice shaped like someone local, someone who knew how to address him. It wasn’t shouted. It was pitched exactly to make him lean closer.

Delaney’s mouth opened.

Mercer’s hand went into his bag.

Foster’s eyes squeezed shut.

Marissa's fingers curled against her own throat as if she could physically hold sound in.

Delaney said, "Who's—"

Mercer struck a flare.

Red fire erupted with a violent hiss, a harsh, chemical scream of light that tore the porch and parking area open. The pale points recoiled instantly, sliding back into the tree line with that wrong, living precision. The clicking spiked, rapid and wet for half a second, then thinned as the lights retreated.

The voice cut off mid-syllable.

Silence slammed down.

In the flare's red wash, Delaney's face looked suddenly older, his authority rendered small by the simple fact of reaction. The local man with the radio stood frozen, the anger gone from him, replaced by a wide-eyed confusion that was almost childlike.

Mercer held the flare steady, arm rigid. Smoke curled upward in red-lit coils. "That," Mercer said, voice low and hard, "is why we don't go in at night."

Delaney swallowed. His gaze flicked from the retreating darkness to Mercer's flare. Pride warred visibly with fear.

"We're still going," Delaney said finally, and the stubbornness in the words felt like a prayer he didn't believe but needed anyway. "We can't do nothing."

Mercer's jaw clenched. "Then you go quiet," he said. "No radio chatter. No names. No calling. You stay on the detour route, not Devil's Stairs. You wait for daylight."

Delaney nodded once, too quickly, as if nodding could substitute for understanding. The deputy looked unconvinced, but he didn't argue with his sheriff.

They turned toward their vehicles.

As they moved off the porch, the local man muttered, "If they're out there, they'll want to hear us."

Mercer didn't answer him. Adrian could see the moment Mercer decided that persuasion had reached its limit. A warning could be offered. It could not be forced into someone's bones.

Delaney climbed into his SUV and started it. The engine noise felt obscene in the new discipline the station had adopted. Headlights swept the trees, and Adrian caught a brief glimpse of nothing but trunks and wet leaves.

But absence didn't mean safety. It only meant the phenomenon had stepped back to think.

Mercer watched them pull away with the flare still burning, red light snapping and hissing in his hand. When the vehicles disappeared down the road, he finally lowered it into the coffee can by the steps.

Foster exhaled, a shaky release that sounded like it hurt. "They didn't listen," he said.

Marissa's voice was tight. "They heard. They just didn't believe the cost applied to them."

Bellamy stared down the road, face pale. "That was the warning," he murmured. "And they ignored it."

Adrian looked into the darkness beyond the parking lot, beyond the reach of the porch light, where a pale point had hovered as if it belonged there.

He thought of Ruth's arithmetic, numbers added to an old sum. He thought of the ledger marks and the way a name could become punctuation.

Mercer's voice came quiet, controlled, and final. "We leave at first light," he said. "Not later. Not after a meeting. Not after we hear something else we want to believe. We go the long way in. We search the shelf by the creek. And if Delaney's people start calling out down there…"

He didn't finish the sentence. He didn't have to.

The mountain had already demonstrated what it did with voices, with names, with the human reflex to answer.

Adrian stood in the station doorway and felt the cold truth settle deeper than fear.

Warnings weren't failing because they were unclear.

They were failing because urgency always sounded more reasonable than caution, right up until the moment it became another disappearance repeated.

Chapter 14

Descent Once More

Dawn did not arrive like relief. It arrived like exposure.

The sky behind the trees lightened from black to a thin bruised gray, and with it every sound seemed to sharpen: the soft creak of the station's porch boards, the faint hiss of tires on wet pavement far down the road, the heater cycling on and off like an anxious breath. Mercer had finally allowed the flare to die in its coffee can, but the chemical smell remained, clinging to their clothes and hair. Adrian wondered if the mountain remembered scent the way it remembered names.

Mercer stood at the conference table with both hands braced on the edge, staring at the hand sketch he'd drawn from Lenora Sutter's map. He had copied only what mattered: the detour route that curved wide and came in near the creek bend, the steep drop of Devil's Stairs marked in his mind with a hard no, and the flat shelf below where people stopped because it felt like the world gave them permission to rest.

Marissa sat across from him, eyes ringed with exhaustion but focused, her tablet open now with the brightness still dimmed almost to nothing. Bellamy hovered near the table but kept his hands off the paper, as if touch itself might count as a kind of claiming. Foster remained by the window, posture tight, face angled slightly away from the glass even though the lights would fade with the night.

Mercer broke the silence first. His voice was low, but there was a new quality to it, something clipped and deliberate, as if he were making himself into an instruction manual.

"New plan," he said.

Bellamy's gaze flicked up. "It was already a plan."

"It was a plan before Delaney decided to turn the slope into a live-fire exercise," Mercer replied. He didn't say the word night. None of them were eager to put it back into the room.

Marissa's fingers paused above her tablet. "Do we know if they went in?"

Mercer nodded once. "They left the station. That means they went in, or they're parked somewhere arguing about whether to. Either way, they're on the mountain with radios and urgency."

Foster's throat worked. "If they start calling out…"

He didn't finish, and Adrian didn't want him to. The sentence had a shape now, a predictable ending. This is what it does with sound. This is what it does with names.

Mercer pointed at the map sketch. "We don't chase them. We don't try to manage Delaney from inside his own bad decisions. Our mission stays the same: find Team Two in daylight by terrain."

Bellamy's mouth tightened. "Daylight didn't stop it from being at the mine."

"No," Mercer said. "But daylight gives us two things: footing and honesty. Pike said it. Daylight shows you where you're standing when you make the wrong choice. I want to see the wrong choices before we step into them."

Marissa glanced toward the front door, then back. "We're going to the creek shelf."

Mercer nodded. "Long approach. We come in from the side, just like Harper's detour and Lenora's map. We avoid Devil's Stairs. We do not go straight down the line where people always go when they think speed is the same thing as rescue."

Adrian watched Mercer's finger trace the route in the air without touching the paper. Mercer had learned the same habit Lenora had: paper drew eyes, and eyes drew curiosity. Curiosity made people lean in.

Mercer continued, "Objective one: locate any sign of Team Two near the shelf and the creek bend. Tracks. Gear. cloth. Anything. Objective two: if Delaney's people are down there, we keep them from turning themselves into bait."

"That implies we'll find them in time," Marissa said.

Mercer's jaw flexed. "It implies we try without sacrificing the plan."

Bellamy gave a short, humorless exhale. "You're making it sound like a tactical operation."

Mercer didn't look at him. "It is. Only the enemy doesn't care about jurisdiction."

Adrian found himself thinking of the old church bulletin Mercer had shown him: Guidance for Evening Travel in the Brown Mountain Region. It hadn't been written by people who wanted to be dramatic. It had been written by people who wanted their children to come home.

Marissa tapped her tablet once. No sound. Her eyes stayed on Mercer. "Rules," she said.

Mercer nodded. He reached for the dry-erase board again, the one he'd used before the vigil. He didn't bother writing everything. They all knew the list. But he wrote the parts that mattered now, in block letters that looked like a warning sign.

No names spoken. No calling out. No radios unless emergency. Clicks only. Eyes down if approached. Red only on my call.

He paused, then added a line beneath it, slower.

Do not answer.

Foster's shoulders lifted with a silent breath. Adrian could see the effort it took him not to look relieved at the simplicity. A rule was something you could hold onto when everything else moved.

Bellamy stared at the board. "How do we coordinate search spacing without speaking?"

Mercer looked at him. "We stay tight," he said. "No wide sweep. We're not covering miles. We're following a known lure corridor. That shelf is a funnel. That creek bend is a funnel. We move together, slow, and we read the ground."

Marissa's eyes narrowed. "If Team Two is alive and they hear us…"

"They'll want to answer," Foster said quietly.

Adrian looked at him. Foster wasn't theorizing. He was remembering the radio chatter, the excitement that had turned to silence like a switch.

Mercer's voice softened a fraction. "If they're alive, they may be doing what the old ones did. Keeping quiet. Keeping faces down. Not answering anything that calls."

Bellamy swallowed. “And if they’re calling for help?”

No one answered immediately. The question wasn’t academic. It was a blade.

Marissa’s voice finally came, controlled but thin at the edges. “If they’re calling, we risk pulling the thing toward them by answering. If we answer, we also identify ourselves.”

Adrian nodded slowly. “Recognition is the hook,” he said. “It doesn’t need us to be loud. It needs us to be specific.”

Bellamy’s gaze moved between them, unwilling but listening. “So what do we do if we hear them?”

Mercer pointed at the board. “Clicks,” he said. “One click means hold. Two means move back. Three means flare. If we hear a human voice, we do not answer with words. If we have to signal that we’re there, we use a click. Nothing else.”

Foster’s jaw clenched. “And if the voice says our names?”

Marissa’s eyes flicked to him. “Then it’s not them,” she said, and said it like a decision she was forcing into reality.

Mercer nodded once. “Then it’s not them.”

Adrian felt the weight of that settle. Humans used names as care. The mountain used names as leverage.

They were going to have to treat the difference like a life-and-death diagnostic.

Mercer turned from the board to his field bag. He began laying out equipment with quiet efficiency. Not much. They had learned that tools created their own temptations. Too much gear made people think they could afford mistakes.

Two flares in easy reach, not buried. One headlamp each, but kept off unless necessary. A length of tape for marking a return route, but used sparingly. Water, but no crinkling wrappers. First aid.

Marissa watched the flares. "Red again."

Mercer nodded. "It recoils. That's not a superstition, that's observed. But we don't wave them around like torches. We use them to create space when the thing is close. Not to chase it. Not to make it angry."

Bellamy's voice went dry. "As if anger is an emotion it has."

Adrian didn't correct him. He understood Bellamy's need to keep the phenomenon from becoming a person in their minds. But he also understood the opposite risk: dismissing intent because it didn't wear a human face.

Mercer finished packing, then looked at each of them in turn. His gaze lingered on Foster.

"You sure you're coming?" Mercer asked quietly.

Foster's eyes lifted. There was no bravado in them, no ranger pride. Just a tired stubbornness that had been stripped down to its core. "If it's my team," he said, voice rough, "then I'm not sitting here."

Mercer nodded once. "Then you follow my hand signals. You don't freelance. You don't call out. You don't use your radio."

Foster's mouth tightened. "I know."

Mercer glanced at Adrian. "And you," he said. "No field lectures."

Adrian almost smiled, but it didn't reach his face. "Understood."

Marissa stood and slid her tablet into her bag. "We should also plan for the worst," she said.

Mercer's expression didn't change, but Adrian saw something in his eyes harden. "Say it," Mercer replied.

Marissa inhaled once. "If Delaney's group gets themselves in trouble, we don't split," she said. "We don't chase voices. We don't turn the search into a rescue for the rescuers. We stick to the shelf and the creek bend. If we have to pull back, we pull back."

Bellamy looked like he wanted to argue, but he didn't. Perhaps he'd finally learned that moral instinct and tactical reality weren't always allies.

Mercer nodded. “Agreed.”

Foster’s hands clenched. “That’s going to be hard,” he whispered.

“Yes,” Mercer said, not unkindly. “Hard is better than dead.”

They moved toward the door with the kind of quiet that no longer felt unnatural. It felt learned. Adrian noticed, with a small jolt, that the station sounded different when they all behaved this way. The building itself seemed to settle, as if less noise meant less invitation.

Outside, the air was cold and damp. The first thin light of morning turned the fog into a low gray veil between the trees. Brown Mountain was still mostly a shape, but not a black one now. It was a deep green mass under a pale sky, ancient and indifferent, like something that had watched too many dawns to care about this one.

Mercer paused on the porch step and looked out toward the road, listening. No engines. No voices. No calling.

Adrian wondered where Delaney and his people were. Somewhere down the slope, perhaps, moving too fast, speaking too much, trying to do the heroic thing the mountain counted on.

Mercer lifted his chin slightly, a signal to himself as much as them. “We go in quiet,” he said. “We go in together. We follow the family map, not the easy route. And we bring them back without teaching the mountain anything new."

Adrian stepped off the porch behind him. As his boots hit the damp ground, he felt the strange, unwelcome truth of the new plan settle in.

It wasn't a plan to win.

It was a plan to survive long enough to learn what the mountain had been hiding under all those lights.

The detour route felt wrong in the way careful things often did. It was longer, flatter, and less direct, a looping approach that made urgency itch under Adrian's skin. The forest service trail they started on was narrow and damp, edged with laurel that held yesterday's fog in its leaves. Their boots sank softly into old pine needles, muffled enough that Adrian could imagine the mountain listening and finding nothing worth tracking.

Mercer kept them tight, close enough that a hand signal didn't need to become a sound. He led without headlamp, using the thin, colorless morning light and a memory of the slope that seemed carved into him. Foster walked just behind, shoulders hunched as if he could make himself smaller by will. Marissa carried her tablet in her bag and looked at the ground with the practiced attention of someone turning fear into observation. Bellamy, stripped of his usual commentary by necessity, watched the terrain like it might suddenly reveal a footnote.

They moved for nearly forty minutes before the land began to tilt downward. Not the obvious drop of Devil's Stairs, but a subtle change that made every step require a decision. The sound of water began as a suggestion, then grew into a steady rush, a creek running hard over stone somewhere below them.

Mercer lifted a fist.

Hold.

They stopped as one. Adrian felt the silence tighten around them, not empty, but braced.

Mercer pointed ahead with two fingers, then angled them down: the shelf.

They came to it by degrees. The flat rock was exactly what Lenora had described, a broad slab that jutted out beside a bend in the creek, worn smooth in places by decades of boots and rain and foolish rests. The water here ran loud enough to erase the fine sounds of movement. It was the kind of noise that made people raise their voices without thinking. It made the world feel less precise.

Adrian understood why the old lists always circled places like this. The creek did the mountain a favor. It made humans clumsy and talkative.

Mercer crouched near the edge of the shelf and studied the ground. He didn't touch anything yet. He only looked, letting his eyes do the work first.

There were tracks.

Not just one set. Several, overlapping, pressed into the damp grit at the shelf's edge where mud had collected in shallow pockets. Boot treads. Some narrow, some wide. Adrian felt his stomach tighten as he recognized the pattern of too many people moving too fast.

Delaney.

Mercer's jaw flexed. He looked back at the others and held up two fingers, then pointed to his eyes. Watch. Then he pointed to the tracks and made a slow circling motion.

More than us.

Marissa leaned in, careful not to let her boots scrape. She studied a print with a precision that looked almost absurd in a place built for panic. Then she pointed to another impression slightly off to the side, a deeper tread set apart from the cluster.

Solo movement. Careful placement.

Adrian's mind flashed to the mine entrance days earlier and the measured boot prints there. Too careful. Too deliberate. Not tourists.

Bellamy saw what she was indicating and swallowed, his skepticism forced into a smaller box. He gestured toward the creek bend, then the slope beyond it, as if asking without words where those careful steps had gone.

Mercer answered with a single hand motion: forward, but low. Proceed.

They moved off the shelf along the creek bank, hugging the quieter side where the water didn't slap as hard against stone. It helped only a little. The creek's roar stayed in their bones, encouraging the throat to work. Adrian caught himself wanting to speak just to prove he was still there.

He forced his lips closed and followed Mercer's back.

Twenty yards downstream they found the first sign that was not a track.

A strip of bright orange survey tape had been tied to a rhododendron branch at shoulder height. It was fresh, the knot too clean and the plastic too new for it to be anything old.

Delaney's people marking their path.

Mercer's eyes narrowed, and he lifted two fingers, then tapped them together twice in a motion that meant nothing official and everything practical: noise. Too much movement. Too confident.

Foster's face tightened, and Adrian saw him glance toward the loud bend of water where the sound thickened. It was where, on Lenora's map, voices were said to come from below like they belonged to someone you knew.

As if the mountain had a script and liked this part.

They rounded the bend and the terrain changed. The bank rose into a steep, root-laced incline that forced them single file. The laurel thickened, closing their sightlines. The air felt cooler here, damp and mineral, as if the creek's breath carried something older than water.

Mercer stopped again and held up his fist.

Hold.

He crouched and pointed to something caught on a thorn bush: a snag of fabric, dark green, torn cleanly as if ripped by force rather than worn away.

Mercer didn't pull it free immediately. He looked at Foster.

Foster's throat worked. He didn't say a name. He didn't need to. The fabric was the right color for a ranger's outer layer.

Marissa reached slowly and pinched the cloth between two fingers, lifting it just enough to see the torn seam. Her expression didn't change, but Adrian saw the tension jump in her jaw.

Bellamy's eyes flicked up the slope, then back to the torn cloth. His face carried a hard question he couldn't voice: if Team Two had been here, where had they gone?

Mercer raised two fingers and moved them in a gentle backward wave.

Back to the shelf. Then up.

Not up the stairs. Up the detour.

They climbed with slow discipline, leaving the creek behind until its roar softened into background and then into a memory. The forest here was quieter, and the quiet was more dangerous. Adrian felt the difference immediately: without the water's constant masking, every footstep became information.

The mine tract was farther than it had felt on the drive. The ground rose and fell in shallow folds that made the distance deceptive. But when the air began to change again, taking on that damp stone smell that lived under mountains, Adrian knew where Mercer was leading them before he saw it.

The mine entrance appeared through laurel like a mouth half-hidden by vegetation.

The timbers were still there, dark and old, the opening narrowed by collapse but not sealed. Cool air breathed out. Not a gust, not a draft from weather, but the steady exhale of a space that did not care about time.

Mercer held up a fist and dropped into a crouch.

Hold.

They clustered behind him, low and tight, faces angled down by habit now, not superstition. Adrian's eyes fell to the ground at the entrance.

Fresh tracks.

Many.

Not the older impressions they'd seen before. These were new, edges sharp, mud still wet in places. Delaney's boots had been here. The deputy's. The two locals'. Perhaps more.

And among them, again, those careful prints. Measured. Purposeful. The kind that avoided stepping on loose stone.

Adrian felt cold rise under his skin. Someone else had been using this entrance. Someone who walked like the mountain belonged to them.

Mercer's gaze swept the ground, then the timber frame, then the blackness beyond. He lifted two fingers and pointed into the mine, then drew them back toward his chest.

They went in.

Bellamy's face tightened, and for a second Adrian thought he might argue anyway, break the discipline with a burst of logic. But Bellamy only swallowed and nodded once, as if accepting that the past had stopped being something you could study from the outside.

Marissa's hand went to the strap of her bag and shifted it higher on her shoulder. Her eyes met Adrian's briefly, and in that glance he saw her balancing two terrors: the nonhuman logic of the lights and the very human possibility of Delaney's group trapped below.

Foster stared at the entrance without lifting his chin. His posture looked like prayer, but it was the mountain's protocol: keep your face.

Mercer reached into his bag and pulled out a flare, not striking it, just holding it ready like a knife. Then he lifted his other hand and made one click with his tongue.

Hold.

He pointed at each of them in turn, then touched two fingers to his own eyes and angled them down.

Eyes down. No staring.

He pointed to his ear and shook his head once.

No listening for voices. No answering.

Adrian understood, with a bleak clarity, that this was the part where every rescue instinct became bait. If Delaney or Team Two called from below, the natural human reflex would be to answer. And answering would make them specific. Names. Voices. Recognition.

Mercer moved into the mine first.

The light outside fell away fast. Within ten feet the world narrowed into headlamp beams kept low and tight. Their boots found the old rails half-buried under grit. The air became colder, and the smell of damp stone and old oil thickened, carrying that faint metallic edge that made Adrian think of blood even when there was none.

The first chamber was still the ordinary kind of abandoned. Broken crates. Rotting beams. Splintered timber. But something had changed since their last descent.

On the wall near the left branch point, where the main tunnel divided, there was fresh tape. Orange survey tape, tied in a quick knot and hanging like a flag.

Delaney marking a way forward.

Mercer's hand hovered near it, then pulled back without touching. He pointed down the left passage.

Lower shaft.

Adrian's mouth went dry. The lower shaft was where the old warnings clustered, where the mine's breath felt colder, where the lights had gathered and surged upward like hunger given motion.

Mercer lifted his hand again, fingers poised.

Two quick clicks.

Move back, but inside the gesture it meant something else now: tighten up. Stay close enough that silence could be shared.

They went left.

The walls narrowed, forcing them into single file. Adrian felt the rock close around them, not pressing, not moving, but present in a way daylight never was. Old scratches at shoulder height caught his headlamp's low beam, the same parallel scoring they'd seen before. He didn't stop to examine them this time. He already knew they were wrong.

A faint sound drifted up the passage.

Not a voice. Not yet.

A muffled clatter, distant and irregular, like a boot striking rail or rock. A human mistake echoed by stone.

Foster went rigid. Mercer lifted his fist.

Hold.

They froze, and in the sudden stillness Adrian heard the mine breathing. Drip. Drip. A distant trickle of water. The thin resonance of their own blood in their ears.

Then, from farther down the left passage, came another sound.

A soft click, clean and precise, as if two stones had been tapped together deliberately in the dark.

Adrian felt his stomach knot. It was the same sound they'd heard near the truck. The same language the mountain had used when it wanted to test whether humans would answer.

Mercer did not click back.

He only lifted the flare slightly, unlit, and angled his head down another fraction, showing them with his body what his rules demanded.

They moved again, slower now, deeper into the lower shaft, following the orange tape Delaney had left behind like breadcrumbs into a place that didn't respect maps.

The passage ahead swallowed their light.

And somewhere in that darkness, something had already learned that people always came looking.

The orange tape led them deeper, each strip tied with the same hurried confidence. Mercer didn't touch the markers. He followed them the way you followed footprints in fresh snow: as evidence, not invitation.

The tunnel dipped, and the air changed again, colder and wetter, carrying that rotten-sweet undertone Adrian remembered from the first descent. Their headlamps stayed low, cutting short wedges of pale light along the rails and the grit between them. The farther they went, the more the mine seemed to drink the light instead of reflecting it.

Another click sounded ahead.

Not loud. Not frantic. A clean contact sound, like a signal meant for ears that had learned to listen.

Mercer stopped and lifted his fist.

Hold.

They froze in a tight cluster, shoulders nearly touching. Adrian stared at the rail at his feet, at the flecks of rust and stone dust, forcing his gaze to stay anchored. He could feel the urge to look down the passage, to see what was making the sound, rise in him like nausea. He swallowed it.

A faint clatter followed the click. Something metallic, far ahead, struck stone and rolled once before settling.

Human.

Marissa shifted her weight, controlled, and Mercer's hand lifted in a slow downward motion.

Still.

The mine answered their stillness with its own: drip, drip, the thin, arrhythmic water sound that made time feel unreliable. Then, faintly, a second clatter.

A boot scuff, maybe. A person trying to move quietly and failing.

Foster's breath hitched, barely audible, and he visibly fought to steady it.

Mercer lowered his fist and raised two fingers, then curled them back toward his chest.

Close. Tighten.

They began moving again, slower than before, placing feet with deliberate care. The tunnel narrowed further, then widened into the low chamber they'd reached on their last descent, the one with the half-buried rail line and the braced cut dropping into the darker passage below. Adrian recognized the shape of it before his headlamp revealed the details. Memory and geometry lined up in his bones.

The timber beam with the old warning was still there, the charcoal cross smeared and the letters like a shaky scold from another century.

DO NOT CALL TO THEM.

Someone had added something beneath it.

Not words. A strip of orange survey tape tied around the beam, bright as a wound.

Delaney's people had stood here long enough to mark it and keep going.

Mercer crouched near the edge of the drop, scanning the rubble and the darker cut beyond. He didn't step down. Not yet. Adrian saw the carefulness in the way Mercer held his shoulders: a man forcing his body to be quieter than fear.

Marissa leaned close, her headlamp angled toward the floor, and pointed.

A flashlight lay near the rail, half-covered in dust. Not an old mining lantern. Modern. The kind a deputy might carry. Its casing was scuffed as if it had been dropped hard.

Bellamy's eyes flicked to it and then away, like he didn't want to claim ownership of any object down here. He gestured, two fingers toward the flashlight and then toward Mercer.

Delaney.

Mercer nodded once, a small, grim confirmation. He reached out and nudged the flashlight with the tip of his boot instead of his hand. It rolled slightly. No light came on. Dead battery or switched off. Either way, silence preserved.

Foster stared at the darkness below the cut. His posture tightened, and Adrian knew what he was thinking without words. Team Two had gone missing after following lights. Delaney's group had marched in with radios and urgency. This was where both paths could intersect, and where both could end.

Another click echoed up from below.

This time it was followed by something else, a soft fluttering wetness, like a tongue clicking against teeth or thin membranes tapping together. Adrian's stomach tightened. The sound didn't belong to a human mouth, and it didn't belong to rock.

Mercer's hand moved into his bag and closed around the flare, unlit. He didn't look at the others; he didn't need to. He raised two fingers and drew them down.

Down. Low.

They crouched.

The lower passage breathed up at them, a steady cold exhale. Adrian kept his eyes on the grit near his knees, but he could feel the blackness below like an open throat. The instinct to call out, to announce themselves, to demand a response, pressed against the inside of his teeth. He forced it down. Names were hooks. Voices were bait.

From the darkness below came a faint sound that might have been a cough.

Human and wrong, as if the throat making it didn't remember how.

Foster jolted forward an inch before stopping himself. Mercer's hand snapped up, palm flat.

No.

The cough came again, and then, so softly it might have been imagination if their nerves weren't tuned raw, a voice rose from below. It didn't shout. It didn't plead.

It said, conversationally, like a man speaking across a room, "Sheriff?"

Delaney's title. Not a name, but close enough. Familiar enough.

Marissa's shoulders went rigid. Bellamy's throat moved with a swallow.

Mercer did not answer.

The voice continued after a pause, as if waiting for the reflex and not getting it.

"Sheriff Delaney? You down here?"

The cadence was wrong, the timing too even, too measured. It carried the same unsettling sameness as the voice at the picnic lot and on the ridge trail, the quality of something repeating a learned phrase rather than improvising speech.

Adrian felt cold rise behind his ribs. It was doing the social thing again. Asking a question that demanded response. Creating obligation.

Mercer shifted slightly, angling his body so his headlamp stayed low, and pointed down into the cut with two fingers. Then he curled them inward again.

We go, but careful.

He pointed at Foster, then at himself, then down. Foster nodded once, jaw clenched, eyes still angled downward, face kept deliberately out of the beam.

They began descending.

The slope into the lower passage was narrow, braced with old timber that creaked faintly under pressure, not loud enough to be a scream but loud enough to feel like risk. Adrian's boots found the same worn spots others had used, the same places where fear had put weight over decades. He focused on that practical thing, on footing, because thinking about anything else made the dark feel closer.

At the bottom the air was colder, damp enough that it beaded on Adrian's upper lip. Their headlamps picked up mineral sparkle in the stone, tiny flecks that caught light and gave it back like false stars.

The orange tape continued here too, tied to a timber brace with a knot that had been pulled too tight. A second tape marker lay on the ground, torn free, its plastic strip twisted as if someone had grabbed it while stumbling.

They moved forward.

The lower passage opened into a broader chamber, the ceiling low, the rock walls slick with moisture. Adrian recognized it with a jolt: this was where they had first seen the pale glow last time, faint and distant, before it gathered.

The Chamber of Lights.

It didn't wait to be found this time.

A pale point hovered near the far wall at about waist height, steady and cold. It did not illuminate the damp stone around it. It existed like a presence, like an eye opened in the dark.

Then a second point blinked into view above it.

Then a third, farther left, lower to the ground.

They were not drifting randomly. They were positioned.

Marissa froze, then slowly crouched lower, her headlamp beam held tight to the ground. Bellamy's breath caught, a small sound he swallowed immediately.

Mercer lifted his fist.

Hold.

The lights pulsed faintly, as if their brightness were a kind of listening. Adrian kept his gaze on the rock at his feet, using his peripheral vision to track the pale points without meeting them directly. Even so, he could feel the pull in his eyes, the urge to look straight at them and solve the shape.

The clicking began again, multiple taps now, layered. Not frantic. Coordinated. A loose chorus that made Adrian think of the way Mercer had described the lights as if they were herding.

One of the lights slid a few inches closer.

Another shifted sideways, maintaining a spacing, like a formation adjusting.

Foster's hands tightened into fists at his sides. His posture was all restraint, a man fighting every rescue instinct he'd ever learned. Adrian knew what Foster was seeing in his mind: Team Two, missing somewhere beyond this chamber. Delaney's men, possibly down here too. And these pale points, patient and calm, between them and any human voice.

A shape lay on the ground near the left edge of the chamber, half in shadow.

A boot.

Adrian's stomach dropped. It was modern, leather and rubber, not mine gear. The foot was still inside it. The leg above it disappeared into the darkness beyond the headlamp spill.

Marissa's fingers flexed at her side as if she wanted to reach for the person, to check a pulse, to do anything. She didn't move.

Mercer crouched even lower and inched forward, slow enough that it felt like moving through water. He kept his head down, eyes scanning the ground rather than the lights. His hand came up, palm flat, and he made a small guiding motion to the others.

Stay.

He moved alone toward the body.

The lights reacted instantly. Not by surging, not yet, but by repositioning. Two of them slid to the left, one to the right, as if making space for Mercer while still keeping him bracketed. The clicking tightened, becoming denser for a moment, and Adrian felt the pattern change the way you felt a predator's attention sharpen.

Mercer reached the booted foot. He did not touch it. He angled his headlamp down and swept the beam over the ground, revealing more.

A deputy's uniform pant leg. The fabric torn at the knee, damp with something dark that Adrian refused to name.

A hand splayed palm-up in the grit, fingers curled slightly as if they had tried to grab rock and found only dust.

The deputy's face was turned away, half-hidden by his own shoulder. Not a mercy. A rule. Keep your face, the old warnings had said. Adrian couldn't tell if the man had followed that rule or if the mountain had arranged him that way.

A faint sound came from deeper in the chamber, beyond the points of light.

A low, rough inhale. Someone alive, trying to stay quiet, failing.

Mercer went still. His head turned a fraction, careful not to lift his face. He did not answer with words. He made a single click with his tongue, small and controlled.

Hold.

The lights pulsed brighter. The clicking answered, faster, as if irritated by the sound.

Adrian felt the chamber tighten around them. The pale points shifted again, and this time one of them slid upward toward face height, hovering exactly where a standing man's head would be, as if reminding them what it preferred.

From the darkness beyond, the voice came again, closer now, and it chose its hook with ugly precision.

"Evan?"

Mercer didn't move, but something in his posture stiffened, a involuntary flinch the rest of his discipline caught and smothered. Adrian's heart hammered hard enough he thought the lights might be able to hear it.

The voice continued, gentle, coaxing.

"Evan Mercer. Hey."

Same phrase. Same cadence.

The Chamber of Lights held its breath, waiting for the oldest human reflex in the world.

Mercer's hand closed tighter around the unlit flare.

And Adrian understood, with sudden, brutal clarity, that whatever was speaking had learned something new since 1893.

It didn't just know names.

It knew which one would make a man turn his face toward the dark.

Chapter 15

The Predator's Game

Mercer stayed crouched beside the deputy's outstretched hand, so still Adrian could have mistaken him for another piece of mine debris if not for the tension in his shoulders. The voice from the darkness had done what voices were built to do. It had reached for the name that carried authority, responsibility, reflex.

"Evan Mercer. Hey."

It wasn't shouted. It didn't have to be. It had the easy familiarity of a colleague calling across a parking lot. It was pitched at the exact level that made a man want to tilt his head and answer, just to clear up the misunderstanding.

Adrian's mouth went dry. His brain offered explanations out of habit, as if taxonomy could reduce risk. Recording. Mimicry. A person in the dark playing a cruel game. None of them mattered. The effect was the same: a hook thrown into Mercer's nervous system.

Mercer's body gave the smallest tell, a tightening at the base of his neck. Then he forced it down, the way you forced down a cough.

The pale points held their positions like pieces on a board. One hovered at about knee height near the chamber's center; another at waist height; a third just above head height, as if claiming the space where faces lived. They did not cast a beam across the rock. They did not behave like light in any honest way. They were simply there, cold and present, like eyes that did not blink.

The clicking fluttered again, quick and wet, layered from multiple directions. Adrian felt it in his teeth. He had the irrational urge to press his tongue to the roof of his mouth, to keep it from accidentally answering.

Behind him, Foster shifted his weight, and gravel whispered under his boot. The nearest light slid toward the sound instantly, not drifting now but gliding with deliberate purpose. It stopped just short of where Foster's knees would be if he were standing.

Foster froze.

Marissa's hand lifted slightly, palm down, the universal gesture of steady. She didn't touch him. Touch could become a signal. Everything was a signal here.

Mercer did not look up. He did not give the chamber his face. He moved one hand slowly, not a wave, not a command, just a small motion close to his body that Adrian recognized as the new language they'd built in the station.

Back. Tight.

Adrian began to shift backward, inch by inch, keeping his head angled down. Bellamy followed, jaw clenched so hard Adrian could see the muscle jumping. Marissa moved with them, controlled and careful, as if she were trying to prove to herself that fear did not get to dictate her motor skills.

Mercer stayed where he was, one hand closed around the flare, the other braced lightly against the grit for balance. Adrian wanted him to move. Wanted him to come back with them. Wanted to whisper, Now, now, now.

He did none of it. Words were bait.

From deeper in the chamber came a different sound: a slow scuff, like someone dragging a boot. Then a breath, rough and wheezing, too ragged to be a perfect imitation.

A human being was alive down there. Or something close enough to make the difference dangerous.

The voice tried again, and this time it changed tactics.

"Evan," it said, softer, almost hurt. "Come on."

The phrase was so ordinary it made Adrian's stomach turn. It was the kind of thing you said when you were trying to coax a friend into helping you, when you believed the friend owed you care.

The lights pulsed brighter in response, a faint increase that felt like attention sharpened into a point.

Mercer made no sound. He shifted his knee a fraction, testing balance, and then, without raising his head, he reached out and pinched the deputy's sleeve between thumb and forefinger.

He didn't pull. He only confirmed what Adrian already suspected: dead weight. Limp fabric. No resistance.

The deputy's radio, clipped to his vest, was visible now in the low spill of Mercer's headlamp. Its screen was dark, and a thin crack split the casing. Even broken, it looked obscene, a tool built for calling out.

Mercer's fingers hovered over it for a beat, then moved away.

No names. No radio. No answering.

The voice from the dark shifted again, more insistent.

"Sheriff's hurt," it said. "We need you."

Adrian felt Marissa's shoulders tighten. The hook wasn't just Mercer's name anymore. It was obligation. It was the shape of emergency that made rules feel immoral.

Bellamy's eyes flicked up despite himself, and one of the lights, the highest one, slid sideways to align with his face. It stopped there, hovering at the perfect height to be met by a direct look.

Bellamy jerked his gaze down, too late to hide the reflex.

The light pulsed once, almost pleased.

Adrian understood then what Ruth Calhoun had meant, the blunt porch sentence that had sounded like superstition until the mine gave it teeth.

It learns you.

It didn't need a photograph. It needed patterns. The angle of a head when someone listened. The way shoulders lifted before speech. The micro-movements that preceded a turn, a response, a face offered to the dark.

Mercer released the deputy's sleeve and shifted backward an inch. The lights repositioned instantly, maintaining a loose bracket around him. One slid to his left, another to his right, as if ensuring his retreat stayed controlled.

Herding, Adrian thought. Like cattle. Like prey.

Foster's hands had curled into claws at his sides. He couldn't save Team Two by calling. He couldn't even say the deputy's name. Every rescue instinct he had was being used against him, squeezed into the exact shape that would make him step forward and speak.

Marissa's mouth opened slightly, then closed again, the motion so tight it looked painful. Adrian could almost hear the thought behind her eyes: If we don't answer, we abandon them. If we answer, we become them.

Mercer made another small motion, a quick downward wave.

Down. Lower.

They all crouched more deeply, shrinking their silhouettes, keeping faces angled away. Adrian's knees ached, and the ache felt like a gift. Pain anchored him to his body. Pain kept him from drifting into the hypnotic pull of the lights.

The clicking fluttered rapidly now, as if the chamber were full of wet teeth.

Then, from the darkness beyond the lights, something moved.

Not a full shape. Not a body stepping into view. A ripple, a suggestion of translucent membrane catching faintly in their headlamp spill and then vanishing again. Adrian's skin tightened with revulsion, an old mammal response to something not meant to exist in air.

The lowest light slid forward, crossing a patch of damp rock, and Adrian realized it wasn't simply approaching them. It was checking their distance, calibrating.

A step. A pause. A pulse.

Observed and pursued, he thought, and the phrase landed in his mind with the weight of an old truth. Predators watched first. They learned. They tested.

The voice took advantage of the pause.

"Marissa," it said.

Marissa flinched so hard Adrian saw her shoulders jump. Her eyes went wide, and for a fraction of a second she looked up, pure reflex, toward the dark that had spoken her name.

The highest light darted half a foot toward her face, fast enough to be a threat but controlled enough to feel like a correction.

Marissa snapped her gaze down again, breathing hard through her nose, lips pressed tight. She did not speak.

Adrian felt cold spread through him. It wasn't just choosing names at random. It was cycling through them, looking for the one that cracked discipline first.

Mercer's hand closed hard around the flare. Adrian saw his thumb find the striker, the readiness in the small movement.

Mercer did not ignite it yet.

Instead, he did something Adrian hadn't expected. He made a single click, sharp and deliberate, not toward the dark but toward his own team, the same way a handler might use a sound to reset a dog's attention.

Hold.

It was their word, their signal, a reminder of protocol. And it worked. Foster steadied. Marissa's breathing slowed by force. Bellamy's shoulders dropped a fraction, eyes still down.

The lights pulsed in response, and the clicking surged, as if irritated that Mercer had used sound without giving it speech.

One of the lights shot forward, close enough that Adrian felt a sudden damp chill on his cheek, that rotten-sweet cold that did not belong to air. His vision flashed white at the edge of his peripheral sight.

He fought the urge to recoil. Recoiling was movement. Movement was information. Everything gave it more to work with.

Mercer struck the flare.

Red fire exploded into the chamber with a violent hiss, the harsh light turning damp rock into blood-colored shine. Smoke curled upward, thick and chemical.

The effect on the lights was immediate and unmistakable.

They recoiled.

Not drifting away, not fading. They snapped backward as if yanked by invisible cords, their positions breaking, formation fracturing into scattered points that retreated deeper into the chamber.

The clicking turned frantic for half a second, rapid and wet, like agitation. The voice cut off mid-breath.

Mercer held the flare low and out to the side, creating a boundary of red that widened the space between them and the points of pale light.

He made a fast hand motion now, no subtlety, no debate.

Go. Now.

Adrian rose from his crouch with stiff knees and moved backward, careful not to turn fully, careful to keep his face angled down and away. Bellamy stumbled once on the uneven grit and caught himself on a timber brace, the wood groaning softly. Marissa grabbed his sleeve and steadied him without a word.

Foster hesitated, his gaze flicking toward the deputy's body near the chamber edge. He didn't move toward it, but Adrian saw the impulse like a physical struggle.

Mercer, still near the deputy, reached out and hooked his fingers under the man's vest strap. He pulled, not dragging the body fully, just shifting it a foot toward the slope they'd descended, as if refusing to leave the evidence exactly where the lights had arranged it.

The pale points hovered at a greater distance now, clustered in the dark beyond the red flare's radius. They did not disappear. They waited, their brightness steadying again as if regrouping.

Adrian understood the coldest part: the flare did not defeat them. It only bought seconds.

Mercer backed up, dragging the deputy's body another foot. It was slow, awkward, and it made gravel rasp. Each rasp felt like a shout.

The lights reacted, drifting laterally, tracking.

Not attacking. Watching. Measuring the red boundary, learning how far it reached, learning how Mercer moved when he thought he had leverage.

Adrian's heart hammered. He kept his gaze on the ground, but he could feel the pale points in the dark like pressure on the back of his neck.

Predators learned the fence before they tested it.

Mercer's jaw was set hard, face still angled down, flare held like a knife between worlds. He made one last backward pull on the deputy's vest strap, then released it, leaving the body closer to the passage, closer to escape, if escape was still possible.

He made two quick clicks.

Move.

They retreated up the slope toward the upper chamber, and the pale lights followed.

Not rushing into the flare's red wash, not crossing it, but pacing them from the darkness, repositioning with every shift of their boots. Patient. Studying. Like something that had all the time in the world and knew that sooner or later human discipline failed.

And as Adrian climbed, smoke stinging his throat, the red flare hissing in Mercer's grip, he realized the predator's game wasn't only to lure them deeper.

It was to teach them that even when they ran, they were still being herded.

They made it back to the slope between chambers without running, because running was a kind of panic the mountain could read. Mercer went first, backing up with the flare held low, his arm rigid from the effort of keeping the red boundary steady. Smoke dragged behind him in thick curls, clinging to the damp air and turning their breath harsh.

Adrian kept his eyes on the rails and the grit between them. The pale points were still there, farther down now, but not gone. They hovered just beyond the reach of the red wash like cautious animals at the edge of firelight.

The moment they gained the upper chamber, Mercer angled the flare toward the timbered drop and made a short, hard motion with his hand.

Down. Stay down.

They crouched behind a braced beam where the chamber widened enough to feel like a room. The old warning on the timber, DO NOT CALL TO THEM, hung above Mercer's shoulder like an accusation. Adrian could still taste the rotten-sweet cold that had touched his cheek when one of the lights slid too close. That smell did not belong in air.

The clicking had faded to something intermittent, testing rather than frantic. A tap here. A tap there. Like a thing moving its attention around the chamber.

Mercer kept the flare burning, but he lowered it into the coffee can he'd brought for exactly this, the same battered can that had held their last flare on the porch. He did it carefully, as if even the small clank of metal might be an invitation. The can glowed red inside, the flare hissing and spitting, a contained sun.

The pale lights held position in the lower cut, visible only as faint points beyond the drop. They did not retreat further. They simply waited.

Marissa leaned close to Mercer, not speaking at first. Her eyes flicked toward the lower passage, then to the deputy's flashlight they'd found near the rail. She picked it up with two fingers and turned it over in her hand without clicking it on. The plastic casing was scuffed. The lens was cracked.

Bellamy shifted his weight. Gravel whispered. One of the pale points down below slid sideways in direct response, aligning itself with the chamber opening as if it could see through rock.

Bellamy went very still.

Mercer's gaze moved to him, then to all of them in turn, and Adrian saw the question behind Mercer's discipline: How long can we keep doing this without losing someone?

Foster's face stayed angled down, jaw clenched so hard a tendon stood out in his neck. He looked like a man holding his own instincts under water.

They could leave. They could back out of the mine, get back into daylight and air and radio signal. But leaving meant abandoning the lower chamber, abandoning whatever human breath they'd heard beyond the lights, abandoning Team Two and Delaney's people to whatever was down there with their names on its tongue.

Mercer made one click. Not their coded signal. A soft, involuntary sound of thought.

Marissa understood it anyway. She leaned closer until her words could be barely more than breath.

"We need to know what the boundary is," she said.

Mercer didn't answer immediately. His eyes stayed on the lower cut, on the pale points that held like patient bait.

Marissa continued, careful, controlled. "Not philosophically. Practically. Is it the red wavelength? The intensity? The heat? The smoke? If we understand what makes it recoil, we can move. If we don't, we're just buying seconds and hoping."

Bellamy's throat worked. He didn't like it, but he couldn't deny the logic. "That's an experiment," he said, voice low.

Foster's head lifted a fraction, just enough to show his eyes were wide and angry. "In here?"

Marissa didn't flinch. "Not to satisfy curiosity," she said. "To survive. And to get people out."

Adrian felt his stomach tighten. The word experiment had a weight in this mine. It sounded too much like what the company men had tried, what private interests had tried, what Pike had warned them about. People treating the mountain like a system to be exploited.

Mercer's jaw flexed. "We already have one data point," he said softly. "Red flare creates distance."

"One," Marissa agreed. "But it also created a lot of noise and smoke. If it is just red light, a filtered headlamp might do it without the hiss and scent. If it is the chemical reaction, we can't replace that. But we should know before the flare burns out at the worst time."

Bellamy's eyes flicked to the coffee can. The flare inside was bright, but it was not infinite. Everything in this mine had a clock, even if they'd stopped listening to ticking.

Mercer looked at Adrian briefly, then at Foster. He made a small circling motion with his hand, gathering them in close. They leaned until their shoulders nearly touched, a huddle that still refused to become a conversation loud enough to be heard below.

"We do it controlled," Mercer whispered. "Minimal sound. No names. No radio. If it surges, flare comes back up. We leave, immediately. No arguing."

Foster's lips pressed together. He didn't like it, but he nodded once. He was learning the new discipline the hard way: sometimes you had to do something dangerous on purpose so you didn't do something worse by accident.

Marissa reached into her bag and drew out a small red lens cover, the kind used for preserving night vision. Adrian remembered seeing it earlier and thinking it was irrelevant. Now it looked like a lifeline.

She held it up to Mercer. "I can put this over my headlamp. Same beam, red filtered. We see if it changes their behavior."

Mercer's eyes narrowed. "Low beam," he said.

She nodded and slipped the cover over her lamp with careful fingers. The light that spilled onto the grit turned a dull, bruise-red, much weaker than the flare and without the living hiss. It felt almost harmless.

Almost.

Marissa angled the beam toward the lower cut without raising her face. The red light slid down the slope like a cautious hand.

The pale points below did not recoil.

They held steady for two seconds, then one shifted upward slightly, as if leaning in. The clicking returned, faster, a thin wet flutter that did not sound pleased.

Marissa's shoulders stiffened. She lowered her lamp toward the ground again, cutting the red spill down.

"They're not reacting to the color alone," she murmured.

Bellamy swallowed. "Or not to that intensity."

Mercer reached into his bag with his free hand and pulled out their second flare. He held it unlit and motioned toward Marissa's lamp, then toward the coffee can.

Compare.

Adrian understood. Mercer wanted a gradient, a scale. He wanted to know whether the flare was a wall or just a suggestion.

Marissa nodded once, then did something that made Adrian's skin tighten. She edged forward a foot, closer to the drop, and angled her red-filtered beam down again, broader now. Her face stayed pointed at the ground, but her body posture shifted into a kind of forced calm that Adrian recognized from lecture halls: the posture of someone determined to remain analytical while the world tried to become myth.

The pale points in the lower cut drifted upward, slow and deliberate, toward the edge where the drop began. Not surging. Not darting. Approaching.

One of them rose to about chest height relative to the upper chamber, hovering just beneath the timber beam with the warning. It stopped there, as if it had found a boundary marker of its own.

A second point rose beside it.

The clicking came from below and from somewhere deeper too, layered, like multiple mouths making the same small sound.

Marissa held her position. Her lamp stayed red and low, but her knuckles were white where she gripped it.

Mercer's hand hovered near her shoulder, not touching. Touch would be a signal. But he was ready to pull her back if she froze.

Adrian's heart hammered. They were watching the phenomenon learn in real time. The flare had made it recoil violently. This weak red beam did not. If anything, it invited it closer, because it was not painful enough to be avoided.

Then the voice came again, not from above, not from the chamber walls, but from down the lower passage with the pale points, closer than Adrian wanted to believe.

"Marissa," it said, soft and coaxing, as if they were in a hallway and she'd dropped her keys.

Marissa jerked despite herself. The red beam wobbled a fraction.

One of the pale points shot upward a foot, fast enough that Adrian felt the air change. Not wind. That damp, dead chill again, rolling up like breath from a grave.

Mercer struck the second flare.

The ignition hiss was violent in the tight chamber, the red blast immediate and bright enough to turn the timber braces into black silhouettes. The pale points recoiled at once, snapping backward down into the cut, their formation breaking like startled birds.

The clicking turned frantic for half a second, then thinned as distance returned.

The voice cut off mid-word, severed as if someone had yanked a line.

Mercer held the new flare low and steady, then motioned sharply for Marissa to back up. She did, breathing hard through her nose, her red-filtered lamp now aimed at her own boots like a chastised gaze.

Adrian felt his muscles trembling with the delayed shock. The experiment had lasted less than a minute and had taught him something that made his stomach sink.

The flare wasn't just light. It was a specific kind of light, a harsh chemical brightness paired with heat and stink and sound, something the phenomenon treated like injury.

Marissa leaned back against the chamber wall, shoulders tight. "It's not the color," she whispered, and her voice carried the strained satisfaction of a hypothesis confirmed by terror. "It's the reaction.

Heat, combustion, something in the smoke. Something it avoids because it cannot tolerate it."

Bellamy's face was pale. "Which means," he said slowly, "we can't replicate it without flares."

"And when we run out," Foster murmured, eyes still down, "we're just meat with names."

Mercer didn't contradict him. He lowered the first flare deeper into the coffee can to preserve control, keeping the second flare burning in his hand as an active barrier. Smoke gathered under the ceiling and rolled along the timbers like a low cloud.

Adrian looked toward the lower cut. The pale points were still there, deeper now, regrouped in the darkness. Waiting again.

But something had changed.

They weren't just watching for a mistake anymore. They had been shown a weaker red light and learned it wasn't dangerous. They had been shown hesitation and learned exactly how close they could come before the flare answered.

The mountain, Adrian thought, took tuition in small observations.

Marissa's breathing steadied. She looked at Mercer, then at the lower cut, and Adrian saw the next thought forming behind her eyes, the one that made experiments turn into gambles.

"If the flares are the only thing that buys space," she said softly, "then we can use that space."

Mercer's gaze sharpened. "Say what you mean."

Marissa hesitated, then forced the words out in a whisper that still felt too loud for the mine.

"We could lure them back," she said. "Pull their attention into the lower chamber while we move the deputy out and search the side passage. We can control when the flare goes up and where. We can make them react."

Foster's head lifted a fraction, anger and fear tightening his face. "We're not bait," he whispered.

Marissa's eyes flicked to him. "We already are," she said, and there was no cruelty in it, only a bleak honesty.

Mercer stared at the flare in his hand, then at the dark below. Adrian could see the calculation in his posture, the ranger's instinct turning terrain and risk into a plan.

A dangerous experiment, Adrian thought, wasn't always about asking a question.

Sometimes it was about doing something you hated because the alternative was leaving people behind.

Mercer made one click, sharp and decisive.

Hold.

Then he pointed down, then back toward the tunnel they'd come through, then to the deputy's dropped flashlight on the ground near the rail.

A decoy. A pull. A move.

Adrian's stomach tightened as the plan took shape without words.

Behind the pale points in the lower cut, the clicking resumed, slow and patient, like something tapping its fingers against the edge of a table.

Waiting for them to decide how much they were willing to risk to get a man out of the mountain.

And how much they were willing to teach it in the process.

Mercer held the burning flare steady in his right hand and pointed with his left toward the deputy's dropped flashlight. Then he pointed down into the cut, made a small circling motion, and brought two fingers back toward his own chest.

Draw them. Move.

The plan was simple enough to be frightening. They would give the chamber something to pay attention to, something human-made that implied presence and motion, and use the seconds bought by red fire to do what they'd come to do in the first place: pull a body out and find the living before they became another line on Lenora Sutter's list.

Simple plans were what people trusted right before the mountain punished them for trust.

Marissa's eyes stayed down, but her voice came in a whisper that barely made it past her teeth. "You want it down there."

Mercer nodded once. His jaw was tight, not with fear exactly, but with the strain of staying in command while the mine tried to take the idea of command away.

Foster shifted, careful, and angled his head slightly toward the slope that led back the way they'd come. Not toward the lower cut. Toward escape.

Bellamy lifted two fingers, then pointed from the deputy's flashlight to Mercer's flare and then down, as if asking how close they intended to go.

Mercer answered without words. He held up his hand, palm out. Stop. Then he held up two fingers and moved them back and forth, small and controlled.

Two steps. No more.

Adrian watched Bellamy swallow. Even now, in a mine full of pale points that spoke names, Bellamy still tried to make the world legible by rules and measurements. This plan didn't have any he could write in a notebook. It only had the kind of rule that lived in the body: move too far, and you teach it something; hesitate too long, and you give it time to learn you anyway.

Mercer crouched near the edge of the drop. The flare hissed, painting his gloved knuckles red. He gestured for Bellamy.

Bellamy froze for a half-second, then moved, careful, as if each shift of gravel was a broadcast. He picked up the deputy's flashlight with two fingers, held it low, and inched toward Mercer.

The pale points below remained out of sight from this angle, but the clicking carried upward in thin bursts, like something tapping on stone to let them know it was still there.

Bellamy reached Mercer and paused. His thumb hovered near the flashlight's power switch.

Adrian saw the impulse in him like a twitch: the historian's reflex to verify, to test whether the tool still worked, to turn the unknown into a controlled variable.

"No," Marissa breathed, a syllable so soft it might have been just breath.

Bellamy didn't look at her. His eyes were down, but his thumb was still poised.

Mercer tilted his head a fraction, not toward Bellamy's face, but toward the flashlight. He made one click, sharp and deliberate.

Hold.

It was their signal, but it carried something else too: an order, and a warning.

Bellamy's thumb lowered, away from the switch. He swallowed again, and Adrian felt a brief, bitter gratitude. Curiosity resisted was its own kind of discipline.

Mercer took the flashlight from him and hooked a length of orange survey tape through its wrist lanyard, not tying it to anything, just creating something that could drag and flutter. Then, with a motion as controlled as placing a chess piece, he lowered the flashlight over the edge and let it slide down the slope into the lower cut.

Plastic scraped rock. Tape hissed softly. The sound was minimal, but in the mine minimal was still information.

For two seconds nothing happened.

Then the clicking below tightened, becoming denser, as if multiple points of attention had turned at once. A pale glow rose into view at the edge of the cut, hovering just below the lip. Another appeared beside it, and another, their cold brightness clustered where the flashlight had slid.

They did not illuminate the tape. They didn't need to. They oriented to it like animals scenting something dropped into their territory.

Mercer didn't wait for admiration of the effect. He jerked his head once toward Foster and Adrian, then pointed back toward the slope that led out.

Move.

Foster and Adrian shifted together toward the deputy's body, which lay farther down the lower passage, just out of sight from here. Adrian's knees protested as he lowered again, keeping his head down, feeling for balance in the grit. Foster moved like a man carrying two weights: the deputy's limp reality and the memory of voices calling names.

They descended two careful steps back into the lower passage, staying within the red spill from Mercer's flare, and found the deputy where Mercer had dragged him closer earlier. The body had settled in a way that made Adrian's stomach clench. The head was still turned away. The face still hidden. Not mercy. Procedure.

Foster hooked his hands under the deputy's shoulders and began to pull. Adrian grabbed the vest strap and the beltline, trying to lift enough to reduce drag without making the body swing. Every scrape of fabric against stone sounded too loud.

Above them, Mercer held the flare like a boundary marker at the drop, using red light to keep the pale points clustered around the decoy instead of around the retreat.

It worked, at first.

Adrian caught a glimpse of the pale points in his peripheral vision. They had gathered near the flashlight, hovering in a loose knot, pulsing faintly. The orange tape attached to the flashlight fluttered once, as if something had moved past it.

Then the voice came again, from below and to the left, farther into the chamber.

Not Mercer's name this time.

"Deputy," it called, the word shaped with a roughness that suggested the speaker didn't fully understand what it meant, only that it was how people referred to one another when authority mattered.

Foster's shoulders jerked as if the word had struck him. He did not answer. His hands tightened and he pulled harder, jaw clenched.

Adrian felt his own mind scrabble for a way to make sense of what they were doing. They were moving a dead man like contraband, trying to keep their faces and names out of the air. It was grotesque, and the mine wanted it to feel grotesque. Shame was another hook.

The pale points shifted suddenly. One peeled away from the cluster near the flashlight and drifted toward the slope they were climbing, slow but purposeful.

Marissa, still up in the upper chamber, made two quick clicks.

Move back.

Mercer didn't click back. He couldn't afford to add sound. Instead he lowered his flare closer to the lip of the cut, intensifying the red boundary where the pale point approached.

The pale point hesitated, pulsed, then slid laterally, searching for an angle around the red.

It was not retreating. It was problem-solving.

They reached the slope into the upper chamber with the deputy's body dragging between Foster and Adrian. Adrian's arms shook with the effort of lifting and pulling while crouched. He kept his eyes down, but he felt the air change again, that damp, dead chill rolling up against his cheek and ear, close enough to make his skin tighten.

A pale point had come nearer than it should have, skirting the edge of red light like something testing how much pain it could tolerate for one more foot of distance.

Mercer saw it. He lifted his second flare slightly and angled it outward, forcing the pale point back. The clicking surged briefly, aggravated.

Adrian and Foster hauled the deputy up into the upper chamber and laid him behind the braced beam, out of the direct line to the cut. Foster's hands lingered for a fraction of a second on the deputy's sleeve, the way hands did when they didn't know what else to do with grief or anger.

Mercer made one click.

Hold.

They froze, crouched, and listened without letting their bodies turn into a question.

The pale points below pulsed. The cluster near the flashlight shifted again. The orange tape fluttered more strongly now, as if something had brushed it. Adrian's mind supplied an image he didn't want: translucent membranes moving in the dark, the wet clicking fluttering as they repositioned.

Bellamy, pressed against the chamber wall, tilted his head a fraction, too close to looking. The highest pale point rose in the cut, aligning itself with the level of Bellamy's face even though Bellamy hadn't offered it fully.

Adrian understood the message with ugly clarity: it didn't need you to stare at it. It only needed to know where your face was.

Bellamy's breath hitched, just once.

The pale point darted upward half a foot, then stopped, checking the red boundary. Calculating.

Bellamy's fingers curled around nothing. Then, with a small motion that felt like betrayal, he made a single click.

Hold.

He had copied Mercer's signal.

And from below, in the dark beyond the cut, the clicking answered back.

One tap. Clean. Precise.

Then another.

Then a third, faster, as if the mine had decided to practice their language the way it practiced their names.

Marissa went rigid. Adrian felt his stomach drop.

They had taught it the signals.

Not the words, not the names, but the structure. How they communicated without speaking. How they coordinated movement. How they kept discipline.

That was the cost of curiosity, Adrian realized. Not Bellamy's small failure, not the urge to test a flashlight, not even the need to run an experiment with red lenses and flares.

The cost was that every time they learned something about it, it learned something about them in return.

Mercer's posture changed, tightening into a decision. He pointed toward the tunnel back the way they'd come, then to the deputy's body, then to the coffee can holding the first flare, which was burning lower now, hissing less, the red glow not as violent as it had been.

Time.

Mercer made two quick clicks.

Move.

They lifted the deputy again, Foster at the shoulders, Adrian at the vest and beltline, and began to retreat up the tunnel, dragging him away from the cut and whatever waited below. Marissa and Bellamy followed close, heads down, no words, no names, only breath and grit and the smell of chemical smoke.

Behind them, the pale points did not rush.

They drifted upward in the cut just enough to keep the upper chamber in sight, pulsing faintly like watchers at the edge of a fire.

And from deep below, in the Chamber of Lights, the clicking came again.

Not random now.

Measured.

Three taps, spaced like a signal.

As if the mountain, patient as it had always been, had added a new entry to its ledger.

Not a name.

A code.

Chapter 16

Revelations in the Dark

They moved in the only way they could: crouched, tight, and quiet, the deputy's dead weight dragging between them like an anchor that scraped grit and rail with every foot of progress.

Adrian took the vest strap and beltline again, lifting where he could. Foster had the shoulders, his arms locked and trembling, jaw clenched as if he could hold grief in his teeth. The deputy's boots caught on a rail joint and bumped loose stone. The sound traveled up the tunnel and came back wrong, multiplied by the mine's thin resonance.

Behind them, in the direction of the lower cut, the clicking continued.

Three taps, spaced like intent.

Adrian felt the awful inversion of it: they had built silence into a language, and now the mountain was using it as a rope.

Mercer led them backward, flare held low in his right hand, the red glare smeared thinly across damp rock. It was weaker than before, more glow than wall, smoke rolling along the ceiling timbers in a lazy layer that made the air taste metallic and sour. Marissa stayed close to Mercer's left shoulder, eyes down, one hand lifted slightly as if she could physically press the sound of her breathing into the ground. Bellamy followed behind her, white-faced, his lips parted but soundless, as if his body kept trying to speak and his mind kept slamming a door.

They reached the point where the lower passage narrowed again and the timber braces drew closer, forcing them single file. The deputy's body snagged once more. Foster adjusted, pulling at an angle, and Adrian shifted his grip.

The movement made their boots whisper.

A pale point of light rose in the tunnel behind them, just at the edge of the red spill, not entering it but keeping the boundary in sight. It did not behave like a lamp. It did not cast a beam. It hovered, steady, as if it knew exactly how far it could come and still remain unburned.

Mercer did not look at it. He did not let his chin lift. But Adrian saw Mercer's posture tighten, a man using every ounce of training to keep his face from becoming a target.

The pale point pulsed faintly, then another appeared above it.

Two watchers, stationed like sentries.

The clicking came again, not from the lights this time but from deeper below, and it was unmistakably patterned.

One tap.

Pause.

Two taps.

Pause.

Three.

Marissa stiffened. Her eyes flicked toward Mercer's flare, then to the tunnel ahead, and Adrian knew what her mind was doing: trying to decide whether this was mimicry or message.

Bellamy's breath caught. He swallowed it down too late.

The two pale points in the rear shifted instantly, sliding laterally as if aligning on the sound of his throat.

Adrian's hands went slick inside his gloves. It was learning in layers, responding not only to voices but to the small betrayals of a body under stress.

Mercer raised his left hand without turning. His fingers made a small, tight motion close to his thigh: keep moving.

They did.

They reached the upper chamber again, the one with the smeared charcoal cross and the old warning, DO NOT CALL TO THEM, and Mercer guided them behind a braced beam where they could lay the deputy down without being silhouetted against the cut. Foster and Adrian lowered the body carefully. The deputy's head bumped stone with a dull sound that felt like an accusation.

Foster's hands lingered for a fraction of a second on the man's sleeve.

Mercer made one controlled click.

Hold.

It was their signal. A command. A prayer. Adrian hated that it was also now a lure.

From below, the mine answered.

One click came back almost immediately, clean and precise, like a reply from something that had been waiting for the right prompt.

Then a second, as if correcting itself.

Then three in a row, evenly spaced.

Not random. Not an echo. Not rails settling. The timing was too deliberate.

Marissa's eyes widened, and for the first time Adrian saw something break through her fear that wasn't panic. Recognition, but the cold, analytic kind.

"It's not just copying sound," she whispered, the words barely shaped, more breath than voice. "It's copying structure."

Mercer didn't answer. He shifted his flare hand, bringing the red glow a little higher. The pale points in the cut dipped away by inches, as if the flare's heat and chemical sting were a sensation they could measure.

Bellamy's gaze stayed fixed on the ground. His voice came out as a rasped whisper, controlled with effort. "That click," he said, then stopped, and tried again with less breath. "It answered."

"Yes," Adrian whispered back, because the word felt inevitable. "It answered."

The mine clicked again.

One. Pause. One.

As if it wanted them to respond in kind.

Adrian felt his mouth go dry. In his lectures, he'd spoken about folklore as interface, rules as user manual, survival knowledge passed down because official channels had refused to hold it. But he had not, in any version of that tidy theory, pictured the interface becoming two-way.

Mercer lifted his left hand and made the signal for back, tight, close. Then he pointed toward the tunnel out, the way they'd come in, and to the coffee can where the earlier flare had been burning lower. The red glow in the can was dimming, the hiss less violent, the smoke thinner.

Time was tightening. Their one reliable boundary was finite.

Marissa's mouth tightened. She glanced toward the lower cut again, then toward the orange tape Delaney's people had left like a rash along the walls. "If it can answer," she whispered, "then it can coordinate."

Bellamy shook his head once, very small. "Or it's just—" He stopped, as if the word just had become too weak to hold anything.

The mine clicked again.

Two taps. Pause. Two taps.

Marissa's eyes flicked to Mercer, then to Adrian. She wasn't asking permission. She was asking whether they understood what this meant: a thing that used names and obligation had now learned their nonverbal discipline.

Mercer's jaw flexed. He shifted the flare closer to his body, and with his other hand he pulled a small notebook from his vest pocket.

Adrian's stomach sank. Words were dangerous, and Mercer knew it. If Mercer was reaching for paper, it meant the situation had crossed into a place where even whispers felt like bait.

Mercer tore out a page with slow care, the rip quiet but still a sound. He wrote with his pen without clicking it, the scratch of ink minimal, and then held the page low where the red light from the flare would let them see.

Change signals. No repeats.

Under that, he wrote: No answering.

Then, after a brief hesitation, as if admitting it cost him something, he added: But it will try.

Adrian nodded once. Marissa nodded too, eyes sharp. Bellamy's lips pressed together, guilt and fear living in the same tight line.

From below, the clicking shifted.

A single rapid burst now, not evenly spaced. Then silence.

Adrian realized, with an unpleasant clarity, that the thing wasn't only communicating. It was probing. It was testing how quickly they responded, whether they would match pattern with pattern the way people always did when they believed they were talking to another person.

Mercer's flare burned lower still. The red wash in the chamber softened, the shadows deepening at the edges.

And in that deepening, the pale points rose again in the cut, edging upward as if emboldened by the weakening boundary.

Marissa's throat moved with a swallow. She didn't speak. Instead, she lifted her hand and made a small, new gesture: a slow spread of fingers, then a close. Scatter. Randomize.

Adrian understood. No more neat codes. No more three-click sequences that could be learned. Humans loved patterns. Whatever was down there loved them too.

A sound came from deeper in the mine, farther away than the cut, muffled by rock.

Not clicking. Not wet flutter.

A knock.

Then another.

Three, unevenly spaced, not the clean timing of the thing below. These were clumsy. Human.

Foster went rigid, his head lifting a fraction before discipline caught him. His eyes widened, and his hands clenched.

A second series of knocks followed, faster now, like someone using the last of their strength to make the rock answer.

Adrian felt his heart hammer so hard it made him lightheaded. A human signal. An old one. Miners had used knock codes long before radios, long before flares and folklore bulletins.

Marissa's eyes locked on Mercer. Her face held a question she refused to voice: do we respond?

Mercer didn't move for a beat. He stared at the ground as if he could force his instincts into order by sheer will. Then he lifted the notebook page again, flipped it, and wrote quickly.

If it's them, they'll knock wrong. We knock back once. Only once.

He underlined it with a single hard stroke.

One knock. No pattern.

Adrian's throat tightened. One knock was still an answer, still a signal, still an offering. But it was also minimal, a compromise between abandoning the living and feeding the dark.

Mercer looked at Foster, and Adrian saw Mercer's leadership become something harder than command. It became responsibility with blood on it.

Foster nodded once, not trusting himself with anything else.

Mercer reached down and picked up a loose stone from the grit near the rails. He held it for a moment, as if weighing not its mass but its consequence. Then he leaned slightly toward the direction of the knocking, kept his face down, and tapped the stone once against the rail.

A single dull clang.

It rang through the mine, not loud but clear.

For two seconds there was nothing.

Then, from below the cut, the thing answered.

One click, perfectly timed, perfectly clean.

Not a knock. A click.

As if it were saying: I heard you.

Adrian's blood turned cold.

And then, from deeper in the mine, beyond that, the human knocking resumed, frantic now, a messy burst like someone who had heard the rail sound and taken it as hope.

Foster made a small strangled sound in his throat and choked it off before it became a name.

Mercer's flare guttered, brightening once and then dimming again as if it too had a pulse.

Marissa's eyes shone in the red light, wide with the kind of terror that came from clarity.

They had confirmation now, brutal and immediate: the mine could distinguish between channels. It could reply in its preferred language even when humans tried to switch.

Communication and response, Adrian thought, wasn't a theory anymore.

It was a battleground.

And somewhere deeper in the dark, a living person was knocking themselves raw against stone, while something else answered in clicks, patient and precise, learning exactly how hope sounded when it was trapped underground.

The human knocking came again, a frantic scatter of impacts that didn't know how to be a code, only how to be desperate. It wasn't coming from the lower cut. It was coming from farther down the main tunnel, past the branch point, as if someone had crawled into a side run and was trying to beat sound through stone the way miners once had.

Mercer didn't lift his head. He didn't look toward it like a man answering a call. He listened like a man measuring distance.

The pale points in the cut held their positions just beyond the red flare's reach, pulsing with a steady patience that felt like hunger pretending to be calm. The flare in Mercer's hand was burning shorter, its hiss uneven now, its smoke thinner, and that scared Adrian more than the brightest moment of it had. The boundary was weakening, and the lights knew it.

Marissa shifted her weight, careful, and leaned close enough that her whisper barely existed. "The knock is not their pattern," she said.

Bellamy's eyes stayed down. "The click answered anyway."

"It answered because we answered," Marissa said. Her voice hardened slightly, not with anger at Mercer, but with anger at the trap. "It doesn't need to know what the knock means. It needs to know what it does to us."

Foster made a tight sound in his nose, a breath that wanted to be a word. He swallowed it and looked at Mercer with the raw, pleading focus of a man trying to do the right thing without giving the mountain anything it could use.

Mercer reached into his vest pocket again and pulled out the small notebook page he'd been using. In the red light he wrote a single sentence, slower this time, as if he were forcing himself to choose words that wouldn't become another kind of bait.

Not voice. Not name. Find by touch.

He held the page low so the others could read it.

Adrian nodded once. It was what the rules had always said in their blunt old way: do not answer. But it was also something else, something newly modern and ugly. In a place where sound was weaponized, the most humane thing they could do was refuse to behave like humans usually did.

The knocking came again, weaker now, the impacts sliding into irregularity.

Mercer's flare guttered, flared briefly brighter, then settled lower. As the red boundary softened, one of the pale points in the cut rose a few inches, testing.

Adrian felt the mine's pressure change in his chest. Not air pressure. Attention. The sensation of being watched without eyes.

Mercer made a small, new hand motion, one they hadn't codified in the station because they hadn't known they needed it. Two fingers, a short sweep to the side, then down.

Side passage. Quiet.

Marissa's gaze flicked toward the right-hand branch at the split, the one the old map had marked as a collapsed storage chamber. Not safe, but different. And, crucially, not the path Delaney's tape had pulled people down. The knock seemed to be coming from that direction too, through stone, through timber, through whatever void still existed past the collapse.

They began to move, slow and low, taking care not to scrape boots, not to let their breathing become a signal. The deputy's body remained behind the braced beam, a grim weight of proof that Delaney's confidence had become a casualty.

As they edged away from the cut, the pale points drifted upward slightly, tracking the change in their positions like pieces adjusting on a board. They did not rush. They didn't need to. The flare was dying, and time was on their side.

At the branch point Mercer stopped, lifted his fist. Hold.

He crouched and angled his headlamp low, not at the dark ahead, but at the ground between the rails. Adrian followed his gaze and saw what Mercer was looking at.

A faint smear along the rusted track.

Not oil. Not mud. Something clear that caught the headlamp's dull spill and gave it back with a weak, pearly sheen. It clung in strands, like wet spider silk, stretched from one rail to the other as if something had been dragged across.

Marissa lowered herself beside it, careful not to touch with bare skin. She pulled a small plastic evidence bag from her pocket, the kind she'd started carrying after the first mine descent, and slid it beneath a hanging strand. With the edge of a folded map paper, she coaxed the strand down into the bag without making it snap.

The strand recoiled slightly as it fell, not like something alive in a dramatic way, but like something with tension, like connective tissue.

Bellamy watched, face pale. “That wasn’t there last time.”

“No,” Adrian said quietly. “Last time we saw the lights, not what carried them.”

Marissa sealed the bag with a quiet press of her fingers. She held it low and angled it toward her headlamp. The material inside wasn’t just clear. It had tiny flecks suspended in it, as if dust had become part of its structure. It shimmered faintly, but the shimmer didn’t spread into illumination. It was local, self-contained. A glow that didn’t light anything else.

Foster stared at the bag, then at the cut behind them. “That’s them?”

Marissa hesitated, then shook her head once. “That’s not a them,” she whispered. “That’s a what. A medium.”

Adrian felt the phrase land in his mind and connect to too many earlier pieces at once. The lights in the valley that didn’t bounce like headlamps. The way they moved against wind. The way they clustered when people shouted. The way the flare didn’t just push them back but made them recoil like a body pulling away from injury.

Not gas. Not distant headlights.

A system.

Mercer pointed, not at the strand, but along the wall near the branch, where the old timber braces met damp stone. His headlamp stayed low, but even in the low spill Adrian saw it: more of the pearly material, stretched in thin sheets between rock and wood, so subtle it could be mistaken for mineral film until you saw the way it bridged gaps.

Webbing.

And within the webbing, tiny dull points like trapped stars.

Marissa's eyes narrowed. She leaned closer, still not lifting her face toward the cut, and raised her red lens-covered headlamp briefly. A weak red wash spilled across the film.

The tiny points brightened in response.

Not recoiling. Not fading. Brightening, as if the webbing itself carried the ability to glow when stimulated.

Marissa lowered the light again quickly. "Photoreactive," she breathed. "Or electrically responsive."

Bellamy's voice came thin. "So the lights aren't free-floating."

Adrian looked back toward the lower cut, where the pale points hovered like watchers at the edge of a fire. For the first time, he understood the sick elegance of it. They weren't lanterns in air. They were not even individual objects. They were nodes. Sensory organs. Lures. A distributed thing that could place its attention in multiple positions at once.

"They're connected," Adrian whispered.

Mercer didn't reply, but his posture confirmed it. He reached down and picked up a small stone again, held it over the rail, and instead of knocking, he let it fall from an inch high.

A tiny clink. Barely sound.

The nearest sheet of webbing trembled.

Not because the mine shook. Because the vibration traveled through the rails, through the timber, through the damp stone, and something in the film responded. The tiny points within it pulsed, a faint sympathetic flicker.

Marissa's eyes widened, and her fear took on a new shape. "It's not hearing like we hear," she said. "It's feeling. Vibration. Pressure waves. It's using the mine as a body."

Bellamy swallowed hard. "Then the clicks…"

"Communication," Marissa said, then corrected herself as if the word was too human. "Coordination. It can make vibration. It can receive vibration. It doesn't need a throat."

Adrian's mind flashed to the wet fluttering sound in the lower chamber, the hint of translucent membranes. He had assumed, automatically, that the lights were separate from the thing that moved. But what if the membranes were the thing? A thin-bodied organism or colony that could slide through narrow spaces, stretch across rock, embed itself in damp timber, and produce light as a lure the way an anglerfish did, except distributed, multiplied, patient across a mountain.

A network.

It learns you, Ruth Calhoun had said. Because it doesn't just see faces. It maps patterns of movement and sound the way a spider read the tremor of its web.

The knocking came again, very faint now, as if the person making it had shifted position or was losing strength.

Mercer's flare gave a weak hiss and shortened again.

Marissa held up the evidence bag and angled it so Mercer could see. In the dim red light the strand inside looked like a piece of tendon pulled from something larger.

Mercer made one small motion with his hand: later. Not now.

Then he pointed toward the right branch, the collapsed passage, and made the gesture for tight and low. He wasn't going to leave whoever was knocking. But he wasn't going to call either. He was going to move through a place that might still be part of the web and hope touch could find what sound could not.

As they began to edge into the right-hand passage, Adrian glanced back once, not lifting his face fully, only letting his peripheral vision catch the cut.

The pale points had risen higher.

They were no longer hovering just beyond the flare's red boundary. They were positioned along the timber braces, spaced as if marking a corridor. Not drifting aimlessly. Lining up.

Herding them away from the lower cut and toward whatever waited in the darker run.

Adrian felt a cold, sudden certainty. The revelation wasn't only what the lights were made of.

It was what they were for.

They weren't an accident. They weren't a strange atmospheric event.

They were the mountain's lure, deployed through a living network that could feel vibration, mimic structure, and place its light exactly where human reflex would break.

And now it was guiding them, gently and relentlessly, toward the sound of a dying man's hope.

The right-hand passage had never felt inviting, but now it felt like the only honest choice left. The left cut led down into the Chamber of Lights, into the place the web seemed thickest and the pale points most practiced. The right cut was marked on the old mine map as a storage run that had partially collapsed, a dead end on paper.

Paper, Adrian thought, didn't account for living networks.

Mercer kept them low and tight, guiding by hand signals alone. Their headlamps stayed angled at boots and rail ties, never aimed fully into the black ahead. Marissa moved just behind him, one hand hovering near the wall without touching, as if she could sense the webbing by proximity. Bellamy brought up the rear, posture rigid with the effort of not looking where his instincts screamed to look.

The knocking came again, faint and uneven, and this time Adrian could tell it was closer. Not close enough to be safe, but close enough to be real. It wasn't the clean click language the mine had begun to mirror. It was messy, human desperation wearing down into weakness.

Mercer paused and held up a fist.

Hold.

They froze. The mine seemed to freeze with them, as if it had learned that stillness was how humans tried to disappear. In the quiet, Adrian heard something else beneath the drip and distant trickle. Not a voice, not clicking. A soft rasping breath that didn't echo like Mercer's or Marissa's.

Someone was alive. Nearby.

Mercer lowered his hand and made a new gesture, something improvised and unmistakable: two fingers to his own chest, then outward, then down. I'm here. Stay down.

He didn't knock back. He didn't answer. He didn't give the mine any more language than he had to.

They edged forward.

The right passage narrowed quickly, walls pinching in with fallen rock and warped timber. Old crates lay splintered under a drift of debris, their contents long since dissolved into damp rot. The air here was different, less of the rotten-sweet undertone from the lower cut and more of a wet mineral chill that clung to skin.

Marissa's headlamp caught a faint sheen on the rock near her knee. She stopped and pointed.

Webbing, stretched thin along a crack, almost invisible unless the beam hit it just right. Tiny embedded points shimmered like dust caught in glue.

Mercer lifted his flare hand slightly, not igniting anything new, just bringing the remaining red glow forward. The sheen dulled under it, and for a second Adrian thought it might withdraw.

It didn't. It only trembled.

Like a muscle bracing.

They kept moving.

The passage dipped and then ended in a slanted choke of collapse, a wedge of fallen stone and timber that sealed most of the run. But a narrow gap remained along the left side, just wide enough for a person to squeeze through if they were desperate and willing to lose skin for it.

The knocking came again, right on the other side of that gap.

Foster went rigid, his face still angled down. His hands flexed as if he wanted to reach through the crack and pull someone out by force alone.

Mercer held up a fist and then, slowly, extended his other hand toward the gap, palm down, fingers spread.

Easy.

He eased himself toward the opening, careful not to scrape gear against rock. Adrian watched him with a tightening throat. In daylight, Mercer had seemed like the kind of man who could read the forest like a map. In here, he was reading something else: pressure, vibration, the sense of a web underfoot.

Mercer leaned closer, keeping his face turned slightly away, and extended two fingers into the gap. Not far. Just enough to offer touch.

A hand darted out and grabbed him.

The contact was so sudden Adrian almost flinched into motion, but he held himself still. The hand that seized Mercer's fingers was human, dirty, shaking, and cold enough to make Mercer's wrist tense.

A hoarse whisper came through the gap, so faint it was more breath than sound. "Please."

Not a name. Not a hook. Just a word shaped by pain.

Mercer didn't answer. He tightened his grip on the fingers he could reach, a physical yes without speech. Then he shifted his body and began to feed his arm further in, testing how much space there was, how much leverage.

The person on the other side made a small, broken sound and crawled closer. Adrian caught a glimpse through the gap: a face half-smeared with mud and dust, eyes wide and glossy. A deputy? One of Delaney's locals? Hard to tell in the low light.

The face turned, searching instinctively for Mercer's eyes.

Mercer angled his head down even more, refusing the face-to-face contact. Adrian understood why with a sick clarity. If the web mapped patterns, then faces were landmarks. Recognition was the mine's currency.

The person's lips moved again. "Sheriff… he—"

Mercer's hand tightened, a warning transmitted through touch. Don't. No titles. No names.

The person swallowed and nodded faintly, as if they understood even in shock. Their fingers clung to Mercer's forearm like a lifeline.

Adrian saw Marissa shift behind Mercer, preparing to help, but keeping her hands to herself until Mercer signaled. Bellamy's shoulders were high and tight, eyes fixed on the grit.

Then the mine clicked.

Not from behind them, not from the lower cut, but close. Too close. The sound came from somewhere inside the collapsed rubble, as if something within the stone had tapped a hard part against timber.

Adrian felt his blood chill. The webbing wasn't only in the open passage. It was threaded through cracks, stretched behind debris, hidden in seams where rock met wood.

Marissa's gaze snapped to the wall and then to Mercer's flare. Her mouth tightened. She didn't speak, but her eyes said it clearly: it can feel this.

Mercer held still, one arm wedged through the gap, the survivor's hand locked around him. The flare's red glow was weak now, the chemical burn approaching its end. Adrian could smell the thinning smoke, could hear the hiss becoming intermittent.

A pale point of light appeared down the right passage behind them, hovering at about knee height.

Then another, higher.

They didn't cast beams. They didn't have to. They were placement and attention, like nodes lighting up in a nervous system.

Foster's breath hitched.

One of the pale points slid toward the sound.

Mercer made a quick, sharp motion with his free hand without turning his head: back. Then, immediately after, he pointed to the gap and drew a tight circle.

Pull through. Now.

Marissa moved forward, low and controlled, and crouched beside Mercer. She reached in with both hands and found the survivor's wrist, then forearm. Her grip was firm but careful, a practiced handling of injured tissue. She began to pull, inch by inch, guiding the person's shoulder through the narrow space.

The survivor stifled a cry, jaw clenching so hard Adrian could hear teeth grind.

A pale light behind them pulsed brighter, and the clicking resumed, layered now, as if multiple points in the web were signaling.

Bellamy shifted his weight, and gravel whispered.

The nearest pale point slid closer, its cold presence tightening the space.

Mercer struck his remaining flare.

Red fire burst alive again, harsher this time because the darkness had grown used to the dim. The pale points recoiled instantly, snapping backward down the right passage, their approach interrupted like an animal startled by flame.

The survivor gasped and surged forward with the pull, momentum finally overcoming pain. Their shoulder scraped rock. Fabric tore. Then they spilled through the gap and collapsed onto the grit at Marissa's knees.

Adrian saw the person clearly for a second: a local man, one of Delaney's two companions from the station porch, his knit cap gone, hair matted, face streaked with dirt. His eyes flicked up, desperate to find a familiar face.

Marissa pressed his head down with a firm hand on the back of his neck, not cruel, just urgent. She kept her voice to almost nothing. "Down."

The man nodded rapidly, trembling, and kept his face angled toward the floor as if he finally understood that looking was dangerous.

Mercer made a sweeping motion toward the main tunnel. Leave. Now. No debate.

They moved as one.

Adrian helped the man to his feet by hooking an arm under his elbow, careful not to let him stand fully upright. The man's body shook with adrenaline and cold. His boots dragged. He kept trying to turn his head, trying to orient in a way humans did automatically.

Foster stayed close on the other side, a steadying presence without words.

Behind them, the pale points hovered at a safer distance now, regrouping beyond the flare's red radius. But they didn't retreat far. They tracked, repositioning at the edges, waiting for the boundary to weaken again.

And it would. Every flare was a countdown.

As they reached the branch point, the rescued man's hand tightened convulsively on Adrian's sleeve. His lips moved, and a whisper pushed out, barely audible over the mine's breath.

"It's down there," he tried to say. "He's down there. And the other—"

Adrian didn't let him finish. Not with words. With pressure. He squeezed the man's forearm once, hard and deliberate, the same language Mercer had used through the gap. Stop. Not here.

The man swallowed and nodded, tears cutting clean tracks through the grime on his cheeks.

Then, from the direction of the lower cut, a voice drifted up, conversational and patient, as if it had all the time in the world.

"Evan?"

Mercer's posture tightened, but he did not turn his face.

He raised the flare higher, not to chase, only to hold space, and made a single motion that left no room for interpretation.

Go.

They did.

They moved toward the mine entrance, not running, but fast enough that their boots began to betray them with soft scrapes. Adrian could feel the web responding through the rails, could feel how every vibration was a message.

Behind them, the clicking followed, not frantic. Coordinated. Like a network adjusting to prey moving toward daylight.

Adrian kept his eyes down and his hands steady on the rescued man's arm.

The mine had revealed enough to terrify them for the rest of their lives.

Now it only had to decide whether it would let them leave with what they'd learned.

Chapter 17

The Lore Hunter's Choice

Daylight hit them in thin, gray sheets the moment they cleared the mine mouth, as if the mountain didn't want to grant them the clean relief of sun. Fog still clung to the laurel and young pines, and the air outside smelled of wet leaves and cold soil, so ordinary it felt like a lie.

Mercer stopped just beyond the collapsed timbers and let his arm drop, the flare finally reduced to a sullen ember in his gloved hand. Smoke unspooled from it in a last lazy ribbon. He didn't look back into the mine. He kept his face angled slightly down even out here, as if the habit had fused into him.

Adrian's hands were still on the rescued man's elbow, guiding him away from the entrance. The man's knees buckled once, then steadied. He dragged in air like he didn't trust it, like he expected the damp chill of the lower chamber to follow and settle in his lungs.

Foster set the deputy's body down gently on the ground outside, away from the opening, where the dead weight no longer scraped rock but seemed heavier under the sky. The deputy's face was still turned away, and Adrian realized with a small shock that Foster hadn't once tried to correct it. The rules had gotten inside him too.

Marissa stepped back from the mine mouth and kept her headlamp pointed at her own boots until she reached open ground. Then, slowly, she shut it off. The click of the switch was too loud for all of them, and she winced as if she'd said a name.

Bellamy stood with both hands on his knees, breathing through his mouth. He looked pale in the flat morning light. The mine had taken something from him that wasn't physical. It had taken his distance.

Mercer finally ground the dead flare into the dirt and straightened. He looked at the rescued man for the first time, keeping his eyes on the man's chest and shoulders rather than his face, as if even now he was refusing the mountain the geometry of recognition.

The man's lips trembled. He was shaking so hard his jaw chattered, but he forced words out anyway.

"It talked," he whispered.

No one told him not to. They were outside. The fear didn't care.

Mercer held up a hand, palm down, a calming gesture that wasn't a command. "Name," he said quietly. Not loud. Not a question anyone else could overhear in a mythic way. Just procedure.

The man swallowed. "Toby," he said. "Toby Hensley."

Adrian filed it away. One of Delaney's two locals. A real name to pin to a man who had almost become only a sound in the dark.

Marissa crouched a few feet in front of Toby, careful not to crowd him. She kept her voice low. "Are you hurt?"

Toby shook his head too quickly, then winced and brought a hand to his shoulder where rock had scraped him coming through the gap. "Just… stuck. We went down and it—" His eyes darted to the mine entrance, and his whole body tightened as if the opening could look back. "It found us."

Foster's voice came out rough. "Sheriff Delaney?"

Toby's throat worked. "He went after the deputy. He went after the other one. Jesse." He swallowed again. "Jesse dropped back. Jesse started calling. Sheriff told him to shut up, but he wouldn't. He thought he heard somebody from the search teams. He thought it was… them."

Adrian felt his skin tighten at the pronoun. Them. Team Two. The missing rangers. The mine didn't need names to be specific. It only needed people to supply the story they wanted to hear.

Toby hugged his arms around himself. "Then the lights came closer. Not like up on the ridge. Not floating out there. They were… right in there. Like they belonged. Like they were waiting where we stepped."

Marissa's gaze flicked briefly to Adrian's bag, as if she remembered the evidence bag with the pearly strand inside. She had it still, tucked safely away. A piece of the web, the medium, the thing that made the lights not an optical trick but a mechanism.

Mercer looked toward the trees as if measuring how far they were from the road, from radio range, from human infrastructure. "We move," he said. "Station. Now."

Foster's jaw clenched. "We're leaving them."

Mercer didn't flinch from the accusation. "We're bringing back a living witness and a dead deputy. We're getting medical. We're getting more flares and bodies. We go back in with daylight and enough support to pull people out." His voice hardened. "We don't go back in with one flare and a half-learned language."

Bellamy straightened slowly. His eyes stayed on the ground, but his voice came in a thin thread. "It answered," he said, as if he still couldn't accept that the sentence belonged in the world. "It responded. Not just mimicry. It adjusted."

Adrian glanced at him. Bellamy wasn't arguing anymore. He was trying to rebuild his worldview with shaking hands.

They carried the deputy's body between Foster and Mercer using the vest and beltline, the same careful grips they'd used underground. Toby walked between Adrian and Marissa, stumbling at first, then moving faster as if distance from the mine loosened a knot inside him. Adrian kept his voice locked behind his teeth. Every time he felt the urge to ask questions, to gather testimony, he remembered the click that had answered their knock. The mountain didn't just want bodies. It wanted information.

The walk back to the creek shelf felt longer than it had on the way in. The forest was brighter now, but brightness didn't make it feel safe. It only revealed more places the web could hide: damp hollows, root tangles, cracks in stone. Adrian caught himself scanning for sheen on bark, for the faint pearly film Marissa had found in the mine, and hated how quickly his brain had accepted the new normal.

At the shelf, Mercer allowed one short radio transmission once they were high enough for signal.

"This is Mercer," he said, voice controlled. "We have one survivor and one deceased deputy. Delaney and at least one other are still inside the mine system. Prepare medical and additional personnel. And listen carefully: no one goes in alone, and no one answers voices from the dark. Understood?"

Static, then a clipped reply. "Understood."

Adrian didn't recognize the voice. That, too, felt like danger. Fresh people meant fresh mistakes.

By the time they reached the ranger station, the fog had thinned into a cold drizzle. The porch boards creaked under boots. The building smelled faintly of old coffee and disinfectant, an attempt at cleanliness that couldn't erase the flare smoke still embedded in their clothes.

They laid the deputy on a tarp near the back office. Someone, a new ranger Adrian didn't know, covered the body without asking questions.

Toby sat on a chair by the heater; hands wrapped around a paper cup of water he hadn't yet managed to drink. His eyes kept tracking the corners of the room, as if he expected a pale point to appear above the filing cabinet. Marissa checked his shoulder scrape with a first aid kit and said very little. She seemed to understand that speech was now a resource, not a default.

Mercer stood at the conference table again, the dry-erase board behind him still bearing the rules from dawn, smeared slightly as if the building itself had sweated. Foster hovered near the window, staring out at the line of trees as if he could see through them to the mine entrance.

Bellamy sat down heavily and put his hands flat on the table. He looked at Adrian without his usual contempt, which was almost worse. “You’re going to tell me,” he said, voice low, “that this is folklore.”

Adrian didn’t answer immediately. He found that his mind kept returning to the sensation of the web trembling when Mercer dropped a stone. The way the pale points had repositioned. The way the clicks had moved from random flutter to structured response. He thought of Ruth Calhoun’s porch voice: it learns you. And of the church bulletin rules that read, suddenly, like engineering notes.

Marissa spoke first, but her tone was not triumphant. It was careful, like someone handling a specimen that might bite.

“It’s not ghosts,” she said. “Not in the way people mean it. It’s biological, or bioelectrical, or something in between. A colony. A network. It uses the mine like a resonant body. Vibration. Response. Light as lure." She looked at Mercer. "And voice as leverage."

Toby made a small, broken sound. "But it sounded like Jesse. It sounded like... like it knew him."

"It knew what worked," Adrian said quietly.

Bellamy's mouth tightened. "So we're saying a... thing lives in the mountain, makes lights, makes sounds, and learns language."

Marissa's gaze flicked to the evidence bag in her pocket. "I'm saying we took a strand of it off the rail. We can test it. But tests don't matter if we don't survive long enough to run them."

Foster's voice came out raw. "My team is still out there."

Mercer nodded once. "I know."

Silence gathered. Outside, rain ticked softly against the window.

Bellamy leaned forward. "What do you believe, Cross?" he asked, and there was something like desperation in it. Bellamy wanted Adrian to say something that made this fit into a category. History. Hallucination. Hoax. Anything with a shelf to put it on.

Adrian looked down at his hands. Dirt still rimmed his nails. He could still smell the mine's damp mineral breath, could still feel the dead chill of a pale point sliding too close.

“I believe,” Adrian said slowly, “that the old rules weren’t superstition. They were fieldcraft. People watched this thing for generations and wrote down what kept them alive.” He lifted his eyes. “And I believe we’ve spent two centuries calling it a mystery light so we didn’t have to admit the simpler truth.”

Marissa’s eyebrows tightened. “Which is?”

Adrian let the words come out without decoration. “Something in that mountain hunts. It uses story the way a predator uses camouflage. And it doesn’t care what we call it.”

Mercer’s jaw flexed. His gaze went briefly to the board, to the smeared letters: Do not answer.

Bellamy shook his head once, small. “That isn’t belief,” he muttered. “That’s surrender.”

Adrian met his eyes. “No,” he said. “It’s choosing the right story.”

Marissa watched him, and for the first time since they’d arrived in North Carolina, Adrian saw her skepticism shift. Not into belief in ghosts, not into fear-driven mythmaking, but into something harder: acceptance that the phenomenon didn’t need permission to be real.

Toby’s hands tightened on his cup. “Sheriff’s still down there,” he whispered.

Foster's face twisted, grief and rage held back by discipline that was fraying. "Then we go back."

Mercer didn't argue. He only looked at each of them in turn, as if counting what the mountain had taken and what it had left.

Adrian understood then what the choice truly was, and why it felt like belief.

They could keep pretending this was a puzzle that would reward curiosity. Or they could treat it like what it had proven itself to be: an intelligent trap that used human reflex as a trigger.

Folklore, Adrian thought, had never been about whether something was real.

It was about what you did next, once you admitted it was.

The station filled the way small buildings did when fear pulled people toward heat and walls.

Two more rangers arrived within the hour, boots thudding across the porch, rain beading on their jackets. They came in speaking too loudly until Mercer met them at the door and held up a hand, palm down, the same gesture he'd used in the mine.

The newer of the two, a woman Adrian didn't recognize, lowered her voice immediately. The other, a broad-shouldered man with a trimmed beard, didn't. Not at first.

"Where's Delaney?" he asked, as if the sheriff might step out from the back office wiping his hands on a towel.

Mercer's eyes stayed steady. "Inside," he said. "Lower cuts."

The man's gaze slid to the tarp-covered shape on the floor, then away as if looking too directly would make it contagious. "Jesus."

"Not helpful," Marissa murmured, but Adrian could hear the strain under it. She had the evidence bag tucked into the inner pocket of her jacket; every time she shifted, the plastic crinkled softly, a tiny sound that seemed too loud now.

Toby Hensley sat by the heater with his shoulders hunched and his hands wrapped around the cup like it was the only thing tethering him to the surface. He stared at nothing in particular, eyes jumping at every radio squawk and door creak. He looked up when Mercer approached him.

Mercer didn't crowd. He crouched a few feet away, eyes on Toby's chest, the posture of a man who had learned that faces were information.

"Toby," Mercer said quietly. "I need specifics. Not theory. Where did Delaney go. What did he do."

Toby swallowed. "He kept telling us not to talk," he said. His voice wobbled on the last word, shame and fear tangled together. "He… he was mad about it. He said those old rules were for tourists."

Foster made a sound in his throat, not a word, more like a bark of anger that died on his tongue.

Toby flinched anyway. "Then the deputy fell," he continued, quick now, like he had to get it out before his nerve failed. "He went toward the lights. Like they were… like they were placed. Sheriff grabbed him and pulled, and then Jesse started saying names. Just… saying them. Like reading a list."

Adrian's stomach tightened. Names as a prayer, names as a roll call, names as proof you were doing something. Exactly the kind of human habit the mine could weaponize.

Marissa's voice stayed low. "Did Delaney answer anything?"

Toby shook his head hard. "No. He told us not to. But Jesse kept saying he heard somebody. He said he heard the ranger team. He said he heard Ryan, the kid that went missing." Toby's eyes shone, wet and unfocused. "And then the voice started."

Bellamy's jaw worked. He looked like he wanted to demand it all in proper sequence, but he didn't. He had learned, at least, that the mountain didn't respect orderly testimony.

"What did it say?" Adrian asked.

Toby stared at Adrian like he didn't want to see him clearly. "It said 'Sheriff?' like that," Toby whispered. "Not yelling. Like you call out in a house when you think somebody's in the next room."

Mercer nodded once, slow. "And the clicks?"

Toby's hands tightened on the cup until his knuckles whitened. "They were everywhere. Like… like the mine had teeth."

Silence settled hard after that. Outside, rain ticked against the glass with steady indifference.

Mercer stood and went back to the conference table. He didn't use the dry-erase board this time. Instead he took a stack of printer paper from the station's supply cabinet and began writing in thick black marker, one page at a time, large enough that anyone in the room could read without leaning in close.

No names. No calling. No radio in the mine. No repeating signals. If you hear a voice, you do not answer it. If it says your name, you do not look up.

He set the pages in a line across the table like placards at a briefing. Then he added another sheet and paused, marker hovering for a beat before he wrote the last line.

If you panic, you leave.

The bearded ranger read it and frowned. "So we're going in to rescue people, but we're not allowed to talk?"

Mercer's gaze sharpened. "You want to talk, you can do it outside," he said. "Inside, talking is a lure."

"That doesn't make sense," the man said, and Adrian could hear the reflexive scorn in it, the same tone Bellamy used to use about folklore.

Mercer didn't rise to it. "Neither do half the things that kill people in these mountains," he replied. "Gravity doesn't make sense when you're sliding."

Marissa stepped closer to the table and placed her hand flat on the edge, grounding herself. "We're not dealing with a ghost story," she said. "We're dealing with something that responds. Vibration, sound, movement. The mine amplifies it. And whatever it is, it learns."

Bellamy's eyes flicked up at the word learns, then down again.

The bearded ranger looked from Marissa to Mercer. "And your proof is what, exactly?"

Marissa reached into her jacket and pulled out the small evidence bag. The pearly strand inside caught the overhead fluorescent light with a faint, sick shimmer. Not bright enough to illuminate anything, just enough to look wrong.

"This," she said.

The man leaned in, then stopped himself as if leaning was suddenly risky.

Bellamy spoke, voice thin. "It isn't atmospheric plasma."

The bearded ranger stared at him. "You're saying that like it's an insult."

"It's a correction," Bellamy said, and for once there was no argument left in his tone, only a bleak acceptance.

Mercer tapped the table twice with his fingertip, a quiet, controlled sound that drew eyes without becoming a signal pattern. "Here's what we're doing," he said. "We go back in with daylight. We take flares. More than we think we need. We do not make ourselves a choir."

Foster's hands were clenched at his sides, fingers flexing like he was trying to keep blood moving. "And Team Two?" he asked, voice rough.

Mercer held his gaze. "We find them by ground. By gear. By touch if we have to. We don't call."

"And Delaney," Foster pressed.

"We bring him out if he's alive," Mercer said. "And if he isn't, we bring out what we can. But we do not trade four more bodies for one."

Foster's face tightened as if the words were a physical blow. For a moment Adrian thought he would argue anyway, break the room's fragile discipline just from sheer human refusal.

Then Foster looked away. Not surrender. Control.

Adrian watched it happen and felt something shift in his own chest. He had come here as an observer, a collector. He had told himself he was studying a story. But the story had teeth, and it had already tasted their names.

Mercer began packing in a methodical line: flare packs, gloves, a roll of cloth tape that didn't crinkle, a small pry bar, water in soft bottles, not hard plastic. No radios. No whistles. Nothing that turned panic into noise.

Marissa moved beside him and spoke so quietly Adrian almost didn't catch it. "The webbing," she said. "If it's threaded through the mine, then every step is a broadcast."

Mercer nodded. "Which is why we keep steps slow."

"And if it's not just in the mine?" Marissa asked. "If the same medium exists in the forest, in the roots, in the ravines—"

Mercer's jaw flexed. "Then the mine isn't the only mouth."

Adrian heard Toby make a small, involuntary sound from the heater chair, as if his body remembered the damp cold of the lower chamber and couldn't stop trembling.

Bellamy, still seated, pressed his palms flat on the table. He looked at Adrian, and something in his eyes was almost pleading. "You said folklore is fieldcraft," he said quietly. "So what does it tell you to do now?"

Adrian thought of Ruth Calhoun's porch, her voice like dry leaves: do not let it see your face. Do not whistle. Do not call to them. He thought of the church bulletin rules Mercer had carried like a relic. And he thought of the mine answering their single knock with a click, perfectly timed, as if the mountain had been waiting for permission to speak back.

"It tells me not to pretend I'm smarter than the people who survived," Adrian said.

Mercer glanced at him, quick. "And?"

"And it tells me something else," Adrian added, surprising himself with how steady his voice sounded. "Folklore also says there's always a moment when you stop studying the thing and decide whether you're going to face it."

Marissa's gaze met his, sharp. "You're not going back in to collect a better story."

"No," Adrian said. The word came out flat, honest. "I'm going back in because if we leave this as rumor again, it keeps eating people who think it's just lights."

Mercer's expression didn't soften, but something like agreement settled into his posture. "Then you do exactly what I say."

Adrian nodded.

They were moving toward the door when the station radio crackled from the desk, a sudden burst of static that made everyone's shoulders jump.

A voice came through, thin and distorted. "Hello? Anyone copy?"

For a fraction of a second the room froze as if the sound had reached through the mountain and into the building.

Mercer crossed the room in two strides and shut the radio off.

The silence afterward was heavier than the noise had been.

Foster stared at the dead radio like it had tried to become a mouth. "That wasn't on our channel," he said.

Marissa's face had gone pale. "It doesn't have to be," she whispered. "If it can learn structure…"

Mercer held up a hand, cutting off the spiral before it could start. "We go now," he said. "We don't sit here and let it crawl into our heads."

They stepped out into the drizzle, and the cold air hit Adrian like a slap. The mountain was hidden behind the gray veil of rain and fog, but he could feel its presence anyway, a pressure at the edge of sight.

As they loaded into vehicles and started down the road, Adrian found his hands trembling, not from cold but from the simple, brutal understanding that confronting the unknown wasn't an act of bravery.

It was an act of discipline.

It meant refusing every comforting habit the human body reached for when frightened: the urge to call out, to explain, to name. It meant accepting that the thing beneath Brown Mountain did not need to be believed in to be real.

It only needed you to answer.

And Adrian Cross, lore hunter and professor, had never felt the weight of a choice so clearly as he did now, driving back toward the mine with a pocket full of old warnings and a mind that finally understood why those warnings had survived.

The road back toward the mining tract ran slick with rain, darkened asphalt threaded through fog and bare-limbed trees. Adrian watched the world slide by through the passenger window and tried not to think about how easily the forest swallowed angles and distances. The mountain was somewhere behind the gray curtain, unseen but felt, like pressure behind the eyes.

Mercer drove with both hands on the wheel, posture rigid. He hadn't turned the radio on. The cab held only the soft shush of tires on wet pavement and the occasional click of the wipers, a sound that made Adrian tense every time it repeated. Pattern. Rhythm. Anything repeating started to feel like a language the mountain could borrow.

Marissa sat in the back seat with her knees pulled in, head down, holding the evidence bag between both hands as if warmth might change what was inside. Bellamy rode beside her, staring fixedly at his shoes. Foster, in the second vehicle behind them with the new rangers, had been silent since the station.

The mine, Adrian thought, had not only taken people. It had taken their habits.

They reached the chain barrier and parked. Rain beaded on the windshield and crawled downward in slow, heavy trails. Mercer didn't speak. He got out, slammed the door a fraction too hard, then paused and stood still in the drizzle as if listening to the woods with his whole body.

Adrian followed, boots sinking slightly into wet leaf litter. The air smelled clean in a way that felt theatrical, as if the forest were trying to prove its innocence. Somewhere overhead, a crow called once and went quiet.

The approach on foot felt shorter than it had any right to. Familiarity compressed the distance. That frightened Adrian more than the fog had. Familiarity was how you stopped being careful.

They stopped well short of the mine entrance, tucked behind a screen of laurel where they could see the dark mouth between rotting timbers without standing directly in front of it. The opening looked smaller in daylight, less like a doorway and more like a wound that never closed.

Mercer raised a hand, palm down. Still.

Everyone sank into the silence. Adrian could hear rain tapping leaves. Water dripping from a branch. The distant rush of the creek.

No voices. No clicks.

Mercer looked over his shoulder toward the others, eyes steady, then reached into his pack and pulled out a flare. He didn't strike it. He only held it, fingers already positioned to make the motion fast.

Marissa's gaze stayed down, but her voice came out in a thin whisper close to Mercer's shoulder. "We're doing this now?"

Mercer shook his head once. "Not until we have the only advantage we can trust."

Bellamy frowned faintly. "The flares?"

Mercer's mouth tightened. He glanced toward the eastern treeline where the fog thinned slightly, the sky behind it a paler smear of gray. "Light," he said. "Real light. Dawn. The kind that makes everything else look honest."

Adrian understood then that the drive had been a test of discipline as much as logistics. Fear pushed you to act immediately. The mountain counted on urgency to make you sloppy. Mercer was refusing to let it set the schedule.

Foster arrived with the other rangers a few minutes later, boots quiet, jackets dark with rain. The bearded ranger from the station looked like he wanted to speak and stopped himself when Mercer met his eyes. The woman ranger glanced once at the mine entrance and then kept her gaze deliberately low, as if she'd already internalized the rules without needing to like them.

They waited.

Time did something strange in that pocket of forest. It stretched and tightened in alternating waves, as if the minutes were elastic. Adrian found himself thinking of all the times he'd used dawn as a metaphor in lectures, as if it were always revelation and relief. Here it felt like a negotiation. A thin window between one kind of danger and another.

As the sky lightened, the fog began to lift in reluctant strands, revealing more of the slope, more of the laurel, more of the mine entrance. The black mouth stayed black. No amount of daylight reached far enough inside to change that.

Mercer finally lifted his chin slightly, a signal that was not sound. He gathered them close, pointing and gesturing, building a plan with hands and looks.

Tight formation. No speaking. No radios. No repeating click codes. Touch only when necessary.

Then Mercer did something Adrian didn't expect. He reached into his pocket and took out a folded scrap of paper. It was the church bulletin copy he'd shown Adrian days earlier, Guidance for Evening Travel in the Brown Mountain Region, softened now by handling.

Mercer held it out toward Adrian.

Adrian hesitated. Taking it felt like accepting a role he hadn't wanted. Not witness. Not scholar. Participant.

Mercer's eyes were steady. "You said it yourself," he whispered, barely shaping the words. "Fieldcraft."

Adrian took the paper. The rules sat in his palm like something weighted.

Marissa's gaze flicked to it, then down again. Bellamy watched without comment, the historian's discomfort now braided with something closer to respect. Foster stared toward the mine as if anything not related to Team Two was an insult.

They moved.

Mercer went first, stepping out from the laurel toward the entrance. The others followed in a tight line, boots placed carefully. Adrian kept his eyes on the ground, searching automatically now for that faint pearly sheen, the suggestion of webbing where it did not belong.

The mine breathed cool air outward. Adrian felt it on his face, damp and mineral. The smell was there even in daylight: mold, old oil, and beneath it that rotten-sweet undertone that had no honest place in rock.

Mercer raised a fist.

Hold.

They stopped just outside the mouth. Mercer leaned down, scanning the ground. Tracks were still visible in the damp grit, layered over older ones. He pointed at one set, then another, communicating without words: Delaney's boot tread. The deputy's. The locals'.

Then Mercer's hand paused.

He pointed at a new mark near the edge of the entrance. Not a boot print. A smear, faint and glossy, stretched like a dragged strand along the timber.

Marissa lowered herself beside it, face angled down. She didn't touch. She only looked. Her shoulders tightened.

It's here too, Adrian thought. Not only inside. The mine wasn't the whole body. It was a nerve-rich part of it.

Mercer made a motion toward the flare in his hand and then toward the entrance. Ready.

And then, from inside the mine, very faintly, came a knock.

Not a click. Not a voice.

A single impact, dull and irregular, like a fist against wood.

Foster went rigid so fast Adrian saw it like a snap. His throat worked. His mouth opened a fraction as if a name had already formed.

Mercer's head turned a fraction, not looking at Foster's face, but reading his posture. Mercer lifted a hand, palm down, and pressed it slowly toward the ground.

Down. Control.

Another knock came, followed by a pause, then two more in quick succession.

Human, Adrian thought. Messy. Not the clean click language the mine had mirrored. This sounded like someone who had no strength left for code, only for being heard.

Foster's hands clenched. His shoulders hunched as if he could force himself smaller. He did not speak.

Mercer made a decision with his body. He stepped into the mine mouth.

The others followed, the daylight behind them narrowing to a cold gray rectangle. Adrian felt his lungs tighten as the air changed. He kept his eyes down. The rails began under his boots, old iron half-buried in grit. He listened for the involuntary betrayals: the scrape of gravel, the breath caught too loud, the small sounds of fear.

The knocking came again, closer now, from somewhere deeper along the main tunnel rather than the lower cut. Three impacts, uneven, followed by a pause so long it felt like waiting at the edge of a grave.

Mercer lifted one finger, then pointed toward the right-hand wall, toward a timber brace. He guided them to hug that side, as if avoiding a central line mattered.

Adrian's mind flashed to Marissa's words: it uses the mine like a resonant body. Rails, timbers, stone. If the webbing threaded through those materials, then footsteps were broadcasts and rails were conduits.

They moved with a deliberate slowness that made every instinct scream to hurry. Mercy wanted speed. Survival wanted precision.

The tunnel widened slightly near the branch point. Adrian recognized it even without lifting his head:

the place where orange tape had hung like flags, the place where their language had been answered back.

The air felt colder here. Not temperature alone. Something like attention.

A faint click came from below, from the direction of the lower cut.

One. Pause. One.

As if it were checking whether they still spoke that way.

Mercer did not respond. He did not even pause. He kept them moving.

Adrian realized, with a grim clarity, what Mercer was doing. He was refusing the mountain's preferred conversation. No names. No click codes. No neat patterns. He was trying to become, as much as a human could, unreadable.

The knocking came again, closer and weaker. A scuff followed it, like someone dragging a boot.

Mercer stopped and lowered himself to a crouch. He extended a gloved hand forward, palm down, then moved it slowly side to side: stay low.

Then he did something that made Adrian's stomach knot.

Mercer turned his head slightly toward Adrian and tapped two fingers against his own chest, then pointed forward.

You. With me.

Adrian's mouth went dry. He understood immediately. Adrian was smaller than Foster. Less likely to jolt with raw emotion. Less likely, maybe, to break discipline if he heard a familiar voice.

Mercer was choosing tools, not people. He was making the kind of choice that saved lives and shredded friendships.

Foster's eyes flashed, anger and fear, but he didn't make a sound. His restraint looked like suffering.

Adrian nodded once. He moved forward beside Mercer, both of them crouched, both of them keeping faces angled down.

The knocking came again, directly ahead now.

Mercer reached the point where the tunnel bent slightly, where debris narrowed the path. He extended his hand toward the darkness beyond the bend, not far, fingers spread, the same gesture he'd used at the collapse with Toby.

A hand found him.

The grip was weak but frantic, skin cold through the glove, fingers trembling as if they couldn't decide whether to cling or let go.

A whisper came, barely air. "Please."

Adrian's chest tightened. It was the same word Toby had used, the same human plea stripped down to its simplest form. Not a name. Not a lure. A request that did not require language to be answered.

Mercer didn't speak. He tightened his grip and began to pull, inch by inch, drawing the unseen person forward.

A body slid into the faint spill of their lowered lamps. A ranger jacket. Mud. Blood darkening fabric at the shoulder. A face kept down, whether by discipline or exhaustion.

Foster made a sound that was not a name but came close to breaking into one.

Mercer lifted his free hand and pressed it down again, hard.

Control. Now.

Adrian swallowed and felt something settle inside him like a stone dropping into place. This was the decision at dawn, he realized. Not whether to believe. Not whether to publish. Not whether to chase answers.

It was whether to remain human in the exact ways the mountain exploited, or to become something else long enough to get people out.

Adrian looked at the folded church bulletin in his pocket, felt the paper's edges through the fabric.

Folklore wasn't comfort, he thought. It was instruction written by survivors.

And as Mercer and Adrian pulled the injured ranger closer, as the mine's colder air seemed to tighten around them like a held breath, Adrian made his own choice, quiet and absolute.

He would stop hunting the story.

He would hunt the way out.

Chapter 18

Echoes on the Mountain

They brought him out the same way they had brought Toby Hensley out: by touch, by leverage, by refusing the mine the clean geometry of a face.

The injured ranger's hand stayed locked on Mercer's glove as if letting go would drop him back into the dark. His other arm hung wrong, shoulder soaked through with a dark patch that looked almost black under the weak spill of headlamps kept pointed at boots and rail ties.

Foster moved in close, sliding in beside Adrian without a word. His hands found the ranger's belt and vest strap, the practical grips that kept bodies from slipping. No names. No reassurances. Nothing that could be mistaken for an invitation.

The ranger's breath came in ragged pulls. He made a sound that might have been a sob or just pain and the mine answered immediately, not with a voice this time but with a single clean click from the direction of the lower cut.

Adrian felt it in his teeth, the way a vibration could become an idea.

Mercer's posture tightened. He raised a hand, palm down, and pressed it toward the ground.

Control.

The ranger's fingers clenched harder, then, with visible effort, loosened just enough to stop shaking.

They moved, slow and deliberate, away from the bend and back toward the mine mouth where dawn had turned to a thin gray day. Every step was a negotiation with rails that carried vibration too well, with timbers that groaned if you let your weight fall wrong, with a silence that was no longer empty.

Behind them, the mine clicked again.

Two taps. Pause. One.

Not a code they recognized. Not a pattern meant for them. It was closer to something testing its own instruments, like a predator flexing a new muscle.

Mercer did not respond. He did not even pause.

At the branch point, Marissa was waiting low against the wall, head angled down, hands ready. Bellamy crouched beside her, lips pressed tight, eyes fixed on the grit. The two new rangers hovered behind them with the stiff posture of people trying to learn discipline in real time.

The rescued ranger sagged as soon as he saw more bodies. Not relief exactly. Something like collapse. His knees threatened to fold.

Marissa slid in and took his wrist, then his forearm, careful around the injury. She didn't speak. She simply shifted his weight onto her shoulder in a way that said, You are not alone, without giving the mine a sentence to steal.

They started toward the entrance.

The air changed as they got closer to the mouth, damp mineral cold giving way to wet leaf and rain. Adrian felt the forest's smell hit him like a memory, too normal to trust.

Daylight, when it finally spilled across their boots, did not feel like safety. It felt like exposure.

They eased the injured ranger out onto the wet ground beyond the timbers. Foster and one of the new rangers lowered him carefully onto a tarp someone had brought for bodies, only this time the tarp held breath and pain and shaking muscle.

The ranger's head stayed down for a long moment. Then he lifted it a fraction, eyes unfocused, scanning instinctively for faces.

Mercer stepped into his line of sight and held up a hand, not a command, an anchor.

"Don't," Mercer said quietly. One word. The smallest amount of voice they could afford.

The ranger's throat worked. He swallowed, then nodded once, understanding or at least obeying.

Foster's jaw was clenched so hard Adrian could see the muscle working near his ear. He crouched, close but not looming.

"Team Two?" Foster asked, and the question came out like gravel.

The injured ranger's eyes squeezed shut. A sound escaped him, half breath, half grief.

Mercer bent closer, careful not to block the open air behind them as if even the forest could become a corridor. "Name," Mercer said, softer now.

The ranger hesitated, then forced it out. "Alvarez."

Adrian felt the name land with weight. It wasn't just a survivor. It was continuity, a thread pulled back from the prologue quiet, from the scream in the trees, from the radio static that had swallowed answers. Alvarez was real enough to bleed.

Marissa's fingers pressed briefly at Alvarez's uninjured shoulder, a silent instruction to keep his head down. "Can you walk?" she asked, keeping her voice low, controlled.

Alvarez shook his head once. His lips moved, and for a moment Adrian thought he was about to say a name, the reflexive human reaching for the comfort of calling out who was missing.

Alvarez stopped himself with visible effort. His eyes flicked toward the mine mouth, and he flinched as if something inside had turned its attention.

"It learned," Alvarez whispered. "It learns fast."

No one asked him what he meant. They already knew.

They got him back to the vehicles and the station in a quiet convoy that felt less like a rescue return and more like retreat from a front line. By the time they reached the porch, rain had thinned into a cold mist again, the kind that made every ridge look softened, harmless, like an old photograph.

Inside, the station was crowded in a way it hadn't been before.

Not with volunteers.

With people in clean jackets and dry boots.

Two men stood at the conference table with credentials clipped to their belts. Another woman leaned against the file cabinet holding a tablet as if it were a shield. Their presence changed the room's temperature.

Mercer stopped in the doorway and looked at them without bothering to hide his fatigue.

"Who are you?" he asked.

The taller man stepped forward. He had the careful calm of someone trained to sound helpful while taking control. "Special Agent Kline. State Bureau. We were notified of multiple missing persons, a fatality, and hazardous conditions on federal land."

Bellamy's shoulders tightened. He stared at the man's badge as if it were a primary source he didn't like.

Mercer's voice stayed flat. "We notified medical. We notified command. Not the Bureau."

Kline glanced at the tarp-covered deputy in the back office doorway and then away with professional speed. "It traveled," he said.

Marissa moved subtly closer to Adrian. Her hand brushed her jacket pocket where the evidence bag had been earlier, but it wasn't there now. Adrian had watched her slip it to a deeper pocket, closer to her body, before they'd left the mine road. Instinct. Protection.

The woman with the tablet spoke without looking up. "We need all recovered items logged and submitted. Clothing, gear, samples."

Mercer's gaze sharpened. "Samples," he repeated.

The woman finally looked up. "Anything removed from the site. Potential contaminants. Biological risk."

Marissa's face went still in a way Adrian recognized: the moment an academic realized the question wasn't about safety, it was about ownership.

"We're not handing you research," Marissa said, and her voice was controlled but edged. "Not until we know what we're dealing with."

Kline smiled faintly, a practiced expression meant to disarm. "Ma'am, with respect, you're dealing with an ongoing public safety incident. We will determine what the public needs to know."

Adrian felt Foster's anger flare beside him like heat off a stone. "The public needs to know not to follow the lights," Foster said.

Kline turned toward him. "The public needs to not panic," he replied, and the calmness in his tone was more unsettling than open threat. "Brown Mountain is already a tourist draw. If 'predatory luminous organism' hits the news, we'll have amateurs, ghost hunters, and people live-streaming into an active hazard zone."

Bellamy let out a short, humorless breath. "So you'll tell them it's train headlights again."

Kline didn't deny it. That was the worst part.

"We will tell them the mine is unstable," the woman with the tablet said. "We will tell them the disappearances are due to terrain, weather, and poor decision-making. Which," she added, "is not untrue."

Mercer's hands curled once, then relaxed. "And Delaney?" he asked. "And Jesse? And my missing rangers?"

Kline's expression softened by a fraction, as if he'd been waiting for the question he could answer like a human being. "We are coordinating a larger search," he said. "But the mine will be sealed. Today."

Marissa took a half-step forward. "You can't," she said. "If you seal it with people inside—"

"We don't know anyone is inside," the woman said immediately.

Alvarez, on the chair by the heater with his arm immobilized in a temporary sling, gave a small shaking laugh that sounded like it hurt. Everyone turned toward him.

He kept his eyes down. "You don't know," he whispered, "because you don't want to."

Silence thickened. Even the rain against the window seemed to lower itself.

Kline looked at Alvarez, then back at Mercer. "Ranger," he said, voice still calm, "your incident report will reflect a hazardous collapse environment and disorientation. No mention of anomalous lights beyond the known folklore phenomenon. Understood?"

Mercer held his gaze for a long moment. Adrian could see the conflict in Mercer's posture. Protect the public, protect the forest, protect his people. And also, protect the truth, because the truth was the only thing that had kept them alive.

"What happens if you lie about it?" Adrian asked quietly.

Kline's eyes moved to him. "And you are?"

"Dr. Adrian Cross," Adrian said. He didn't add his title for pride. He added it because titles were currencies in rooms like this.

Kline nodded once as if filing it away. "Dr. Cross. If we don't control the narrative, the mountain will."

Marissa's mouth tightened. "That's a convenient excuse for a cover-up."

Kline's smile vanished. "It's triage," he said. "And whether you like it or not, it's what's going to happen."

Bellamy spoke then, voice thin but steady. "There are records," he said. "Old reports. Company letters. Warnings in the mine. People have been covering this for a century."

Kline looked at him as if he were indulging a minor irritation. "Then consider this continuity," he said. "We close it. We classify it. We keep people out."

Foster's voice came out rough. "Until somebody follows a light again."

No one answered that.

Because there was no good answer that didn't involve admitting what the mountain did and how long it had been allowed to do it.

Later, when the agents had moved to the back office to make calls and fill out forms, Mercer stood by the window and watched the treeline as if expecting to see pale points hovering just beyond the rain.

Adrian came to stand near him. He didn't speak at first. Words felt too easily borrowed now.

Mercer finally said, without turning, "They'll seal it."

Adrian nodded once.

Mercer's jaw flexed. "And if we tell people it's just a collapse, they'll treat it like any other closure. A fence to climb. A sign to ignore."

Adrian thought of the church bulletin in his pocket, its old rules passed hand to hand because official channels had failed. He thought of Ruth Calhoun's porch voice: it learns you.

"Then the old way continues," Adrian said quietly. "Warnings passed in kitchens and church aisles. Not in reports."

Mercer turned his head a fraction, eyes flicking to Adrian's chest, not his face, as if even inside the station he was careful with geometry. "You going to write about it?" Mercer asked.

Adrian didn't answer immediately. He could already imagine the book deals, the interviews, the eager skepticism, the way people would try to turn it back into entertainment because entertainment was safer than truth. He could also imagine silence, official and clean, burying everything again until the mountain chose new names.

"I don't know," Adrian said honestly. "But I know what happens if nobody does."

Outside, the fog shifted, thinning for a moment. Through the gray, Brown Mountain's ridge line appeared, dark against lighter sky.

And in that brief clearing, far out across the valley where the trees thickened into distance, a small white light drifted above the slope.

It hovered.

Then it slid sideways, slow and deliberate.

As if it had all the time in the world.

As if it could wait out any agency, any report, any sealed entrance.

As if story, controlled or not, was only ever a temporary fence.

Mercer's hand rose unconsciously, palm down, pressing toward the floor.

Control.

Adrian felt his own body obey, shoulders settling, breath quieting. The discipline wasn't just for the mine anymore.

It was for whatever came next.

Because consequences were already arriving in clean jackets and official language, and the cover-up was already being written.

And the mountain, patient as it had always been, was already practicing the shape of the next invitation.

The light across the valley didn't linger long enough to be photographed.

It hovered above the treeline for a handful of seconds, then slid sideways and dimmed into the fog as if it had never been there at all. The kind of sight that, if you tried to tell it later, sounded like you'd dressed up headlights in poetry.

Inside the station, the people in clean jackets would have called it misinterpretation.

Outside, the mountain families would have called it a reminder.

Mercer kept his hand raised, palm down, as if pressing the room quieter could press the valley quieter too. Adrian felt his own muscles do what they'd learned underground: settle, minimize, refuse to become an easy target even when the threat was half a mile away and separated by glass.

Marissa stood near the back office door, her posture tight with restraint. Since the agents arrived, she'd moved like someone protecting a pocket of fragile glass. Not the evidence bag alone, though Adrian knew she still carried it on her somewhere, close to her body where it could feel her heat. She was protecting the idea of proof, because she understood what happened to proof in rooms full of authority.

Bellamy was at the conference table, hands flat, staring at the placards Mercer had written as if words could become a barricade.

No names.

No calling.

If you hear a voice, you do not answer it.

The bearded ranger, the one who'd resisted the rules at first, read them again in silence. He didn't look skeptical now. He looked newly initiated, the way people did when their education came with a cost.

Special Agent Kline came back into the main room with the woman and her tablet. They spoke in low voices, deliberate, controlled, not because they were afraid of the mountain, Adrian realized, but because they understood optics. Fear traveled. Panic traveled. Their job was to keep both contained.

Kline nodded once toward Mercer. "We have a crew en route. Barriers, signage, the works. The old entrance will be sealed. The road in will be shut with a locked gate."

Mercer's gaze didn't move to Kline's face. He kept it on the agent's chest, as if the habit had become a form of refusal. "And the people still missing?"

"We'll keep the search active," Kline said. He had the tone of a man offering a reasonable consolation. "But we are not going to keep sending bodies into an unstable mine."

Marissa's jaw tightened. "You're not sending bodies," she said quietly. "You're sealing them."

The woman with the tablet looked at her without expression. "There is no confirmation of survivors. You have one witness, one deceased, one injured. That's what we have."

Alvarez, slumped by the heater with his sling, made a sound that might have been a laugh if it didn't hurt. He kept his eyes down. “You talk like the mountain writes your numbers for you.”

Kline’s attention shifted briefly to Alvarez, then away. Adrian saw the calculation: injured ranger, traumatized, unreliable if you needed him to be.

Foster stood at the window with his arms crossed, staring into the mist. His anger had gone quiet, compressed into something that looked like control and felt like suffering. When he spoke, his voice was low and rough. “People are going to keep coming up here.”

Kline’s mouth tightened. “They won’t get in.”

“They’ll climb the gate,” Foster said. “They’ll cut a fence. They’ll follow a light to some other hole in the mountain you didn’t even know was there. Because they’ve been doing it for two hundred years.”

For a moment, no one answered. The silence sat heavy with the truth nobody in a clean jacket wanted to admit: closures were temporary. Curiosity was not.

Mercer finally spoke, measured. “You can seal the mine. You can’t seal the ridge.”

Kline’s gaze flicked to him. “That’s why we control the narrative,” he said again, as if repetition made it stronger.

Adrian watched Mercer's shoulders rise and fall with a slow breath. Control, Mercer's hand had said. Discipline. Choose what you offer.

"I want copies of the old records," Mercer said.

Kline's expression didn't change, but his tone cooled by a degree. "Those are now part of an active investigation."

Bellamy's mouth tightened. "So, they disappear again."

Kline gave him a flat look. "So, they're secured."

It was the same word, Adrian thought, that people used when they put something dangerous in a locked drawer and told themselves the danger had been handled.

Mercer didn't argue further. Adrian could see him making the same calculation he'd made in the mine: sometimes you didn't win by pushing. Sometimes you won by enduring longer than the other side expected.

When the agents stepped away again, drawn into the back office by radios and phone calls, Mercer moved to the bulletin board by the door where locals pinned notices for lost dogs and yard sales. The church guidance sheet was still in Adrian's pocket, softened from handling, its rules printed in faded ink like a relic that had survived because it had to.

Adrian took it out and held it for a moment. Guidance for Evening Travel in the Brown Mountain Region. The words looked almost quaint now, like a caution about bears or sudden weather. But he had felt those rules in his body underground. They weren't superstition. They were field notes written in the only language people had been allowed to use.

He folded it again carefully and slid it back into his pocket as Mercer approached.

"You think they'll stop it?" Adrian asked, not meaning the sealing, but everything else.

Mercer's gaze went past him, toward the window, toward the fog. "Stop?" he said. "No."

Marissa joined them, standing close enough that her voice could stay low. "They can reduce access," she said, the scientist in her offering a practical concession. "If they seal the entrance properly and patrol—"

Mercer shook his head once. "The mine isn't the whole problem," he said. "It's just the part we can point at."

Adrian thought of the glossy smear on the timber at the entrance at dawn. The web outside the mine. The sheen on stone. The way the light had moved across the valley like a slow eye.

"It's in the mountain," Adrian said.

Mercer nodded. "And the mountain's been here longer than the Bureau."

Bellamy drifted closer, reluctant, like a man approaching an altar he didn't believe in but couldn't ignore. "If they bury it," he said, "what happens to the truth?"

Marissa's gaze flicked toward the back office where the agents were. "The truth becomes rumor," she said. "Again."

Adrian felt the word rumor land wrong. Too soft. Too dismissive. Folklore, he'd told his students, wasn't the opposite of truth. It was what communities remembered after history forgets. But watching a cover-up take shape in real time made him realize how active forgetting could be. It wasn't absence. It was effort.

The station door opened, and a gust of cold damp air rolled in. A volunteer stepped inside, hat in his hands, eyes wide with the kind of fear that wanted to attach to anything. Behind him came a woman Adrian recognized from the diner, the narrow waitress with pinned white hair. She paused in the doorway and looked around as if counting who was still alive.

Her eyes found Mercer first, then Foster, then Adrian and Marissa and Bellamy.

"So, it's true," she said.

Mercer didn't ask what she meant. "Ma'am," he said quietly, "this is an active situation."

"I know what it is," she replied. She stepped farther into the room, ignoring the way the new rangers watched her. She wasn't afraid of uniforms. That was the advantage of age and mountain life: you'd seen authority come and go.

Her gaze landed on Alvarez by the heater. She went to him and crouched, not trying to meet his eyes directly, her attention on his hands, his sling, his posture. An old way of being careful without being told. She set a paper bag on the floor beside his boot.

"Soup," she said. "And cornbread. You eat it while it's hot."

Alvarez's throat worked. He nodded once, small.

The waitress stood again and faced the rest of them. "They're going to lock it up," she said, not a question.

Marissa hesitated. "Yes."

The woman's expression didn't change. "They locked it up before," she said. "Back when the mine shut down the first time. Didn't stop the lights none."

Bellamy opened his mouth, then closed it. For once, he had no historical correction that improved anything.

The woman looked at Adrian. "You the lore man."

"I am," Adrian said.

She nodded once, as if confirming what she already knew. "Then you know what happens next."

Adrian held her gaze. "People keep telling the rules."

"Exactly," she said. "And people keep breaking them." She glanced toward the window, toward the fog hiding the ridge. "But the rules still get told. In kitchens. On porches. In churches where nobody from Raleigh listens."

Mercer's jaw tightened. "We're going to post warnings."

The woman gave him a look that was almost pity. "Signs don't talk back," she said. "But the mountain does."

Foster shifted, restless. "What do you want us to do?"

The waitress's mouth tightened. "I want you to stop acting like this started yesterday," she said. "I want you to understand you're in the same story my mama was in. The same one her mama was in. You just finally went far enough in to hear it say your name."

Marissa's face went still. The scientist in her wanted to reject the framing, to insist on mechanism and containment. But Adrian could see she understood the larger point: story was how the mountain's behavior had been mapped for generations. Story was the only warning system that had kept working when official systems failed.

The woman reached into the pocket of her apron and pulled out a folded slip of paper, creased and soft from being carried too long. She offered it to Adrian.

Adrian took it carefully. It was handwritten, a copy of a copy, the ink dark in some places and faint in others. The same rules as Mercer's bulletin, but with additions in the margins, small notes that felt like someone's grandmother trying to save them.

If it comes close, do not let it see you smile.

If you hear it use your voice, bite your tongue if you have to.

If you must make sound, make it ugly.

Adrian stared at the words.

Make it ugly.

Not poetic. Not cinematic. Not the kind of instruction you made up for fun.

Mercer read over Adrian's shoulder, and his posture tightened. "Ugly sound," he murmured.

The woman nodded. “Fire hurts it,” she said. “So does things that don’t belong. That’s what my granddaddy said. Don’t sing to it. Don’t whistle. Don’t call. If you got to make noise, make it something it don’t want.”

Adrian thought of the flare’s chemical hiss and stink. The way the lights recoiled like burned flesh. The way the web trembled under vibration.

Things that don’t belong.

Bellamy’s voice came out quiet. “And you’ve been passing this around.”

“Not me alone,” she said. “Everybody that learned the hard way. Everybody that got buried and left somebody behind to remember why.”

In the back office, a phone rang. A voice answered in clipped tones. Paper shuffled. The machinery of control kept turning.

The waitress looked toward that room and then back at them. “They’re going to tell tourists it’s headlights,” she said. “Or swamp gas, or plasma, or whatever word makes folks laugh and feel smart. But you all know better now.”

Adrian folded the handwritten paper carefully, mirroring the care he’d used with Mercer’s bulletin. He didn’t put it in his pocket yet. He held it as if holding it mattered.

“What do we do with it?” he asked.

The woman's gaze was steady. "You do what mountain people always did," she said. "You tell it quiet. You tell it right. And you tell it to somebody that'll live long enough to tell it again."

Tradition endures, Adrian thought, not because it was romantic, but because it was adaptive. Because it carried instructions that didn't require permission. Because when agencies sealed entrances and edited reports, a grandmother could still lean close to a child's ear on a porch and say: when the light stops, you stop.

And somewhere out beyond the fog, across the valley, the mountain waited with all the patience in the world, practicing the next invitation in a language older than any official statement.

Adrian slid the paper into his pocket beside the church bulletin. Two versions of the same truth, carried by different hands.

Mercer's hand rose again unconsciously, palm down.

Control.

This time, Adrian didn't just obey.

He understood why the gesture had survived.

The station settled into an uneasy rhythm after the waitress left, as if the building itself had learned to hold its breath.

Rain kept ticking against the windows in a steady, unremarkable way. The agents in clean jackets moved through the back office with clipboards and phones, their voices lowered but efficient, the kind of calm that made panic feel childish. Outside, vehicles came and went. Someone delivered barricade posts. Someone else brought a roll of bright orange mesh. The machinery of response spun up fast, greased by experience.

And through it all, the mountain remained where it had always been: invisible behind fog, present in everyone's posture.

Adrian sat at the conference table with a legal pad in front of him, pen uncapped, not writing.

The waitress's handwritten slip sat in his pocket beside Mercer's faded church bulletin. Two versions of the same instructions, one printed and one inherited, both refined by people who'd lived long enough to warn someone else. He could feel the paper edges when he shifted, a physical reminder that the most useful truths in this place were small enough to fold.

Marissa stood near the filing cabinet, arms crossed. She watched the door to the back office more than she watched anyone in the room, tracking who went in, who came out, who might decide to ask for the wrong thing at the wrong moment.

Bellamy hovered at the edge of the table like a man unsure where his hands belonged. He'd stopped performing skepticism and started performing restraint, which was a stranger transformation. Every so often his eyes flicked to the placards Mercer had written and then to the station radio, as if he expected it to light up with a voice that didn't belong on any channel.

Mercer was by the window again. His hand was not raised now, but Adrian saw his fingers flexing at his side in the same palm-down impulse, the muscle memory of control.

Foster paced once, stopped, and leaned against the wall without looking at anyone. The grief in him had sharpened into a different kind of vigilance. He didn't speak, because every word felt like something that could be overheard by a mountain that had already proven it could learn structure even when it couldn't hear meaning.

A knock sounded at the front door.

Everyone froze anyway.

It was only one of the new rangers returning with a clipboard, rain on his shoulders, but the room took several seconds to remember that normal sounds could still happen without turning into a lure.

Mercer turned away from the window and made a small motion to Adrian with two fingers. Come.

He led Adrian toward the supply closet off the hall, not the back office where the agents were, but a cramped space that smelled like pine cleaner and old fabric. He closed the door until it was almost shut, leaving it cracked just enough that it wouldn't latch and make a sharp sound.

When he spoke, his voice was low and careful. "They're sealing the entrance within hours."

Adrian nodded. "Kline said today."

Mercer looked down at the floor tiles as if they were safer than faces. "They'll put up barriers. Signs. Threaten fines. It'll slow people down."

"But it won't stop them," Adrian said.

Mercer's jaw tightened. "No."

Adrian hesitated, then asked the question that had been sitting in his chest since Kline's first calm sentence. "What happens to the reports?"

Mercer's mouth twitched in something that wasn't humor. "They become paperwork. Then they become storage. Then they become 'lost.'"

Adrian thought of Bellamy's earlier comment about facts surviving bad memory. Facts didn't survive deliberate forgetting. They only survived stubbornness.

Mercer leaned closer, not conspiratorial, just intimate in the way a warning had to be. "They're going to want to talk to Toby again. They're going to want him to repeat what he heard down there. Names. Voices. Details."

Adrian felt a chill move across his skin. "And every retelling becomes a script."

Mercer nodded once.

"Then don't let them," Adrian said.

Mercer's eyes lifted briefly, sharp. "I can't stop an agent from interviewing a witness."

"No," Adrian agreed. "But you can change how the witness is handled. You can keep him from being alone. You can keep him from being pushed into repeating names like it's a litany."

Mercer's shoulders rose and fell with a controlled breath. "And you," he said, voice still low, "need to decide what you are. Scholar or problem."

Adrian heard the question under the bluntness. Would he publish? Would he turn this into a spectacle? Would he become another kind of lure, drawing people toward the ridge with language?

Adrian reached into his pocket and took out the waitress's handwritten slip. He unfolded it carefully and held it between them, angled so Mercer could read without leaning too close.

"If you must make sound," Mercer read silently, eyes tracking the line, "make it ugly."

His mouth tightened. “Flares. Chemical.”

“Things that don’t belong,” Adrian said. “That’s what she called it.”

Mercer stared at the paper, and Adrian watched something settle in him with the slow inevitability of a plan forming. “We teach that,” Mercer said. Not loudly. Not formally. But with certainty. “Not publicly. Not in press releases. We teach it to the ones who actually go out after dark. Rangers. Deputies. Volunteer teams. The people who’ll hear a voice in the trees and answer because that’s what good people do.”

“And if the Bureau shuts you down?”

Mercer’s gaze moved to the cracked door. “Then we do what they can’t stop. We tell it sideways.”

Adrian nodded, understanding. Kitchen talk. Porch talk. Training that wasn’t labeled training. The way wildfire crews passed down the stories nobody wrote into the manual because they sounded too much like superstition until the moment they saved you.

Mercer folded the paper back and handed it to Adrian. His fingers didn’t touch Adrian’s skin. Gloves. Procedure. Habit. “Keep it,” Mercer said. “You’re the one who knows how to carry words without turning them into a billboard.”

Adrian slid the slip back into his pocket, beside the church bulletin. Two layers of the same shield.

When they stepped back into the main room, Marissa's eyes flicked to them and then away. Bellamy was at the table now with his notebook open, writing fast, head down, as if he'd decided that if official records could be buried, he would make his own copy in ink that lived in a private bag.

Foster was by Alvarez again, speaking in short, quiet questions. Alvarez answered with his gaze on his own knees, his voice rough, never using names if he could avoid them, describing instead by gear and movement and places in the tunnel. The story became a map, not a roll call. It was fieldcraft even in grief.

The agents emerged from the back office and scanned the room. Kline's gaze landed on Marissa, and Adrian saw her shoulders tighten, protective.

"Dr. Calder," Kline said, tone polite. "We'll need any samples collected."

Marissa's expression remained controlled. "I didn't collect anything," she said. It was a clean lie, delivered without flourish.

Kline studied her for a beat, then nodded as if making a note in his own mind. "Then we'll need your statement."

Marissa's eyes did not flick to Adrian, but Adrian felt the unspoken exchange anyway. She'd keep the strand. She'd test it. But she would not hand it over to a system that treated containment as a substitute for understanding.

As the day dragged toward afternoon, the station began to feel less like a command post and more like a border.

Outside, men in hard hats arrived. Barricade posts went in along the old access road. Orange mesh unfurled in bright strips against wet green. The contrast was almost insulting, as if human color could mark off a living mountain.

Toby was taken to a clinic under escort. He left without looking toward the ridge. Before he went, he had gripped Mercer's forearm once, hard, his fingers shaking. A thank you, delivered in touch. A goodbye, delivered in fear.

Alvarez was driven to the hospital in Morganton with Foster riding beside him. Foster kept his voice low in the cab, asking no questions that required names. When Alvarez began to tremble at the sound of the turn signal click, Foster reached over and shut it off, then drove with his hand signals and eye checks like an old-fashioned man, refusing the comfort of automated noise.

Bellamy stayed in the station. He sat at the table and wrote until his hand cramped, then switched hands. Adrian watched him for a moment and realized Bellamy wasn't only recording facts. He was building a parallel archive, a private continuity that could outlive a locked drawer.

When evening came, the fog thinned enough to show the ridge line again. The agents left, promising calls, promising coordination, promising a controlled narrative. Their vehicles disappeared down the wet road with taillights that smeared red in the mist.

Mercer remained by the window after they were gone, watching the treeline.

Adrian joined him.

For a long moment they stood without speaking, letting the forest be a forest again: wet leaves, distant creek, the occasional bird settling into roost. Ordinary sounds that didn't feel ordinary anymore.

"Do you see it?" Mercer asked finally.

Adrian followed his gaze out across the valley.

There, faint but unmistakable, a small white light hovered above the far treeline. It didn't bounce like a headlamp. It didn't hold steady like a star. It drifted sideways with slow intention, then paused, as if listening.

Adrian felt his body respond before his mind did. Shoulders lowered. Breath quieted. Face angled down by reflex even though he was behind glass.

Mercer's hand rose, palm down, pressing gently toward the floor.

Control.

The light held for a few seconds more, then dimmed and vanished into fog like a thought abandoned.

Adrian exhaled slowly. "It's not punished by barriers," he said. "It's trained by them."

Mercer didn't answer, but his silence agreed. A closed mine meant people would gather elsewhere. A controlled story meant the curious would come looking for what was being controlled. The mountain didn't need access to one entrance. It had ridges, ravines, old cuts hidden by laurel and time.

Adrian reached into his pocket and felt the folded papers. The rules. The warnings. The ugly, practical instructions that had survived because someone had survived.

He realized then what "a new story" truly meant in this place.

It wasn't a fresh mystery for tourists. It wasn't a new chapter in a book deal. It wasn't even the Bureau's cleaned-up incident summary.

It was the beginning of the next cycle of remembering.

Adrian went back to the table, opened his legal pad, and finally began to write. Not a sensational account. Not a mythology. A set of field notes in plain language, shaped by everything they'd learned the hard way.

Do not call out.

Do not repeat patterns.

If it speaks like someone you know, do not answer.

If you must make sound, make it ugly. Heat. Chemical. Smoke.

He paused, pen hovering, then added the line he hadn't expected to write when he'd first driven down from Great Lakes State University with a skeptical anthropologist and a hostile historian.

Treat the lights as placement, not phenomenon.

Adrian glanced at Mercer, still by the window, and understood that the most dangerous thing about Brown Mountain wasn't only what lived beneath it.

It was how easily people turned survival knowledge into entertainment.

He lowered his pen and wrote one final sentence at the bottom of the page, not for publication, not for the Bureau, but for whoever would sit at this table after him when the fog was thick and a radio crackled and someone said, "Hello? Anyone copy?"

Folklore is what communities remember after history forgets. Do not let them make you forget.

Outside, somewhere beyond the valley, a light appeared again for an instant, pale as a breath, then slid away as if satisfied that it had been seen.

As if the mountain, patient and practiced, was already inviting the next person to follow.

www.ingramcontent.com/pod-product-compliance
Lightning Source LLC
LaVergne TN
LVHW050909080826
845145LV00001B/21

* 9 7 8 1 9 6 9 7 7 0 3 1 9 *